Half Moon Rising

US Marshal Charlie Harlow

Gregory Payette

8 Flags Publishing, Inc.

Also by Gregory Payette
Visit GregoryPayette.com for the complete catalog:

HENRY WALSH MYSTERIES
Dead at Third
The Last Ride
The Crystal Pelican
The Night the Music Died
Dead Men Don't Smile
Dead in the Creek
Dropped Dead
Dead Luck
A Shot in the Dark
Dead or a Lie

JOE SHELDON SERIES
Play It Cool
Play It Again
Play It Down

U.S. MARSHAL CHARLIE HARLOW
Shake the Trees
Trackdown
Half Moon Rising

JAKE HORN MYSTERIES
Murder at Morrissey Motel
Body on the Beach

CRIME FICTION/STANDALONES
Biscayne Boogie
Tell Them I'm Dead
Drag the Man Down
Half Cocked
Danny Womack's .38

Join My Readers' List

I'd like to invite you to join my reader list to receive free stories, giveaways, and VIP announcements when my new books are released.

To sign-up, visit: GregoryPayette.com

Chapter 1

THE COLD AIR CUT through Charlie's jacket as soon as he stepped out of the Suburban parked outside the Best Western in Maggie Valley, North Carolina. He looked over the mix of evergreens and bare oaks behind the hotel, toward the clouds hanging over the Smoky Mountains.

Breathing into his cold, dry hands, he was sure he caught a hint of the Jack Daniels he drank the night before.

He'd spent a good part of the evening at the Coyote Grille, but left early to sit by the firepit alone outside his Winnebago. Thanks to a friend who owned the property, he'd been living on the edge of the Swannanoa River ever since he and Jennie split up. Without any real roads to speak of to get in and out, most considered the heavily wooded area the middle of nowhere.

Charlie didn't think he'd had that much to drink. At least not until his phone rang a little after five that morning—a few hours after he'd gone to sleep—with an anxious chief deputy on the other end.

But Charlie felt all right by the time he made it to the motel, for the most part.

He sipped coffee and placed the to-go cup on the front fender of the Suburban. "So much for getting the day off," he said, fixing his Glock in his holster. He made sure the U.S. Marshals Service star on his belt was visible.

Deputy Kim Riggins had just stepped out of her Chevy Tahoe, parked next to Charlie's Suburban. "The sooner we can get out of here, the sooner I can get on with my day off."

Charlie grabbed his coffee and got in one more sip. "I told Frank I'd take care of this myself. According to intelligence, she's here alone."

"We still need to be careful," Kim said. She walked ahead of Charlie, along the front of the building, both she and Charlie watching the room numbers as they passed each door before finally stopping at room number 136.

The curtains on the room's window were pulled closed, but some light slipped out from inside, through the narrow slit where the curtains came together. Kim didn't wait for Charlie to do anything, stepping up to the door. She knocked. "Claudia Sanborn? This is the police. Open the door." She watched Charlie, his hand on his holstered Glock. Kim knocked again, a little harder this time. "Mrs. Sanborn? Please open the door. This is Deputy U.S. Marshal Kim Riggins, with the U.S. Marshals Service. We have a warrant for your arrest."

Charlie kept his gaze on the crack of the door, ready to pull his Glock as soon as it opened, if he felt he had to. He pulled at his black bulletproof vest, shifting it around to make it more comfortable. It fit better than the old ones they used to wear, but his preference was to go without, especially with an allegedly nonviolent case like Claudia Sanborn's.

Charlie stepped to the side of the large square window and leaned with his back against the building's exterior. He got a better look through the curtains, where they hadn't completely closed, and caught a glimpse of the TV across from the foot of the bed, turned on loud enough he could hear it outside. He eyed the door at the back of the small room, a sliver of light coming out from under it. "She's in the bathroom," he said. "You want me to give it a try?"

"Give *what* a try?"

He nodded at the door. "Open it."

"We can get a key," she said.

Charlie gently eased her aside, stepped back, then drove his shoulder into the steel door. It barely budged on the first try, so he did it once again, putting a little more into it. This time the door swung open with enough force it smashed against the interior wall on the other side of it.

Charlie stepped over the threshold, surveying the motel room. He picked up the remote from the unmade bed, turned off the TV, and wiped his hand on his pants when he put the remote down with a look of disgust on his face.

"Mrs. Sanborn?" he said. He heard the shower running, but before going farther into the room, he crouched down and looked under the bed. "All clear."

Kim stepped past him and stood in front of the bathroom door. She turned her ear to it, listening.

The shower stopped.

"Well?" Charlie said. "You gonna let her know we're out here?"

"I'm surprised she didn't hear the door," Kim said, lifting her hand to knock, but before her knuckles touched the wood, the door opened.

A naked woman stepped out, wrapping a towel on her head. She screamed and ran back into the bathroom, slamming the door behind her.

But Kim drove her shoulder into the door and knocked it open, her gun raised.

Charlie stood in the doorway and watched Kim grab the woman and push her against the counter. The towel fell off the woman's head, showing off her long, wet hair.

The woman gazed at Charlie through the mirror, but he did his best to look away without taking his eyes off his fellow deputy making the arrest.

"Are you cops?" the woman said.

"U.S. Marshals Service," Kim replied. "Please state your name."

"Claudia. Claudia Sanborn."

"Claudia Sanborn," Kim said, slipping the handcuffs onto the woman's wrists. "You're under arrest."

Charlie went into the bathroom and squeezed past Kim and the woman, grabbing another towel from the chrome rack by the shower. He did his best to keep his eyes to himself, handing Kim the towel and walking back out into the room.

Claudia Sanborn didn't appear surprised. She knew why they were there. "Can you at least let me get dressed?"

"Probably not a bad idea," Charlie said, his eyes meeting Kim's when she led Sanborn out past him into the room. "Especially if I'm driving her back." Charlie poked his head back in the bathroom and took a quick look around to make sure he hadn't missed something. Or someone. "Where's your stuff?"

"In the closet."

Kim looked at Charlie, as if she wanted him to give the okay. He gave a nod, and she removed the handcuffs. Kim said to her, "Make it quick."

The woman didn't even put the towel around her, giving Charlie a sly smile, stepping past him to the closet. She slid open the door and pulled out a sweater and a pair of jeans.

Charlie didn't feel right making any kind of judgment about the woman, aside from what little facts he had about her case. But he couldn't help appreciate how attractive she was from the neck up. Not that the rest of her wasn't, but he still hadn't allowed himself to look.

There was a strong smell hanging in the room. Mostly women's perfume, or maybe it was just her shampoo.

"All right," Kim said, looking at her watch while Claudia Sanborn got dressed. "Hurry up."

Charlie said to Sanborn, "Deputy Riggins was supposed to have the day off, but she came to work this morning just for you. So I hope you feel special."

The woman slipped on her tight jeans, nothing else under them, and started across the room and over to a duffel bag on the other side of the bed.

Charlie and Kim both drew their Glocks.

"Whoa," Charlie said, grabbing Mrs. Sanborn by the arm, still doing his best to ignore that she still wasn't fully dressed. "Don't do that."

"Do what?"

Don't pull anything out of that bag. Tell us what you need, and I'll—"

"I need a bra," she said, turning to him, holding her gaze on Charlie, like she was playing games with him.

Charlie picked up the opened duffel bag and tossed its contents on the bed. "Deputy?" he said. He didn't feel right, digging through the woman's things, looking for her bra.

Kim flipped the bag over and dumped all of its contents on the bed.

"What'd you do that for?" Sanborn said.

Kim tossed a few things around, found a beige-colored bra and tossed it at her. "I told you to hurry. We don't have time for games."

"Geez," Sanborn said. "Can't you be a little—"

"You have one minute," Kim said. "Or we're dragging you outside as you are. And it's cold out there."

Charlie cleared his throat and tried not to smile. He could tell Kim wasn't in the mood for much of anything, had a little edge to her he hadn't seen in a while. She wasn't supposed to be there, but the Western North Carolina U.S. Marshals office, where she and Charlie worked, had been short-staffed with a couple older deputy marshals retiring.

Even Chief Deputy Frank Carter was out on a case and had no choice but to take Ethan Holden, the youngest marshal in the office nobody seemed to care for. Mostly, the dislike for the kid was because he happened to be related to someone with some pull who got him the job the deputy didn't seem to want in the first place.

Claudia Sanborn was fully clothed now, and Kim handcuffed her again, leading her out of the hotel room and around front to the parking lot.

Charlie stayed behind, gathering what he could, including the items Kim had dumped on the bed. There wasn't much else there. Claudia Sanborn had packed light.

He walked out with the duffel bag and tried to pull the door closed, the lock mangled beyond repair. He went around to the front of the motel where Kim had already put Claudia into the back of Charlie's Suburban.

He grabbed his coffee from the front bumper and walked around back, lifted the rear hatch and tossed the bag inside.

Claudia Sanborn peered over her shoulder at him with that same sly smile, like she was playing with him. He slammed the hatch closed and walked back around the front to where Kim stood, looking at her phone.

"Are you ever going to get that partition installed?" Kim said.

Charlie shrugged. "Thinkin' about it."

"You'll regret it, something happens when you're transporting someone back there. You're not even supposed to—"

"I'm not so sure there's much we need to worry about with this one," he said, glancing through the windshield at Sanborn in the back seat. He opened the driver's side door.

"I'll follow you," Kim said, looking at her watch.

"You don't have to," he said. "I'll be fine."

"You know what Frank would say, if I left you on your own?"

"Frank knows you got the day off. He'll understand. Besides, there's construction on 321," Charlie said. "I'll probably jump off Hardin Road. Rather take the long route than sit in all that traffic."

Kim looked at her watch. "That's going to slow me down. I have to stop at the courthouse by eight thirty."

Charlie had one foot inside the Suburban. "Go ahead. We'll be all right."

Kim looked as if she had to think about it for a moment. "You know how Frank's been lately."

"Yeah, a pain in my ass," Charlie said. "More than usual."

"I'm not sure there's anything wrong with following the rules," Kim said, then turned for her Tahoe. "I'll stick behind for a few miles. You want to take the back roads, feel free."

Chapter 2

Charlie tipped his sunglasses down and looked into the rearview mirror at Claudia Sanborn in the back seat. She hadn't stopped talking since they left the Best Western.

He assumed it was mostly nerves, the way she kept going on, telling him how she did nothing wrong.

But he knew better. He'd heard it all before.

After not saying much of anything for the first thirty minutes of the ride, he glanced into the back seat. "You know, you're already in a bit of trouble, considering you snapped that monitor off your ankle. I'd be willing to put a good word in for you if you'd tell me where I might find your husband?"

He knew it was a long shot, and it wasn't likely she'd give the man up just because Charlie asked. And he knew he was running out of time before he dropped her off at the Gaston County Jail.

"I honestly don't know where he is," she said.

"Honestly?" Charlie said. He cracked a smile. "I've learned over my life that when someone starts a sentence with 'honestly' there's a pretty good chance that person's full of shit."

She let out a loud laugh, almost like a cackle. "I'm telling you the truth. And I'm not sure I care where he is," she said.

Charlie looked at her in the rearview. "How come he wasn't with you at the hotel?"

Claudia Sanborn looked at Charlie in the mirror. "He went *his* way. I went mine."

He laughed. "Am I supposed to believe that?" He paused, thinking about it. "So what made you come back this way, into town?"

"To see my sister," she said, looking to her right again, out the window. "She's sick."

Charlie looked out at the road. "What kind of sick?"

"Cancer."

"Oh, uh... I'm sorry to hear that," he said. "She gonna be all right?"

She didn't respond right away.

"Ma'am?"

"It's cancer," she said. "Not good. But I was supposed to go see her this morning."

He didn't say much else about it right then, looking ahead at the road.

A few minutes went by without either saying a word.

"You think they're going to add a lot to my sentence?" she said.

"You mean, because you escaped?" He paused, knowing the answer. "I don't know many judges who take too kindly to convicted felons who don't show up to their sentencing. Never mind one who cut the monitor off her ankle. Now, I'm not a lawyer or anything, but if I had to guess, you could be looking at another five to seven. On top of what you already had coming."

Claudia didn't respond, and Charlie noticed her turn and look toward the rear of the Suburban.

"Are you looking for something?" he said.

She turned back to him, shaking her head. "No."

Charlie wasn't sure he believed her, the way she kept turning to look out the back. He took a glance in the mirror, making sure Kim was still back there in the Tahoe, following.

Something bothered him, but he wasn't quite sure what it was.

"So, listen," Charlie said, knowing he was running out of time. "As I was saying earlier, the way it works is if you help me out, I can put in a good word with the judge. I know it'd be appreciated if you cooperate, help me bring your husband back in too. No reason you should be the only one to pay the price."

"I told you. I have no idea where he is," she said, a bit of a bite to her response.

Charlie said, "I know you're trying to protect him, but pre-trial services were both alerted the monitors had been compromised at the same exact time, two weeks ago. I find it hard to believe you both took off and ran in opposite directions?"

She sat in silence for at least a minute. "We just kept moving," she said. "But once I heard my sister's health had taken a turn, I had to come back. He said I was on my own."

"You want to at least tell me where this was? The last time you saw him?"

She took her time answering, then said, "We were at a Holiday Inn, in Georgia."

"Georgia's a big state," Charlie said. "But we're going to catch your husband, one way or the other. Only thing I'm asking is for you to help speed up the process. And I'm making you a promise you'll see the light of day a little sooner than you will if you don't help us out."

He watched her look out the back of the Suburban again, then he glanced out his side view at two work vans in the passing lane on the left, close to being in his blind spot.

One van was a faded blue, old and banged up like it'd been in a demolition derby, six or so ladders stacked on the roof. The other was newer, white with lettering on the side, which Charlie couldn't make out from the angle.

Deputy Riggins was a couple of cars back but still following.

Charlie wanted to call her, let her know something didn't feel right. But she was already running late, having to do more than she was supposed to on her day off.

Charlie said to Mrs. Sanborn, "You looking for something back there?"

It took a few moments before she answered. "We're just the small fish, you know."

Charlie waited, thinking there'd be more. "I don't think much of anything about whatever it was you've done. Small fish, big fish. I just reel 'em in, put 'em in the tank." He looked in the mirror at her and grinned, knowing he didn't know the details about her case.

"What'd you do, get involved in some kind of mortgage scheme?" He eyed the folder on the passenger seat.

She said, "It's not easy out there, you know. Sometimes you gotta do things you don't want to, just to pay your bills."

Charlie was starting to get somewhat curious. "Well, just so it's clear, I'm not really the one you have to explain anything to. When you get involved in a federal crime, such as—"

"You're the one who asked," she said.

The two were quiet after that, for another good mile or so. All Charlie wanted to do was finish the job, grab something to eat—maybe a greasy sausage sandwich—soak up whatever alcohol he had left in him. He thought about the report in the folder, and wondered if he should've read it this time. The thing was, he never cared much for the details or, frankly, felt he needed them. Tell him who and where, and he was good to go. But the fact the husband was still out there meant Charlie had more to do.

"So, just so I understand... You and your husband got involved in some kind of scheme where you ripped off old people. Is that right?" He lifted his U.S. Marshal baseball cap and scratched his head. "But from what I understand, you've told the agents at the FBI you don't know who you were working for? And they believed you?" Charlie laughed.

"We only worked with these people, who... They called themselves runners," she said. "Nothing was done on the computer. It was all paper. Old school. These runners would show up... We never knew their names, but they'd show up, drop off an envelope, pick up the money... They rarely spoke. And if they did, it was barely English."

Charlie was curious now. "And you claim to've had no contact, ever, with whoever was running this scheme?"

"I didn't. No."

"But what about your husband?" Charlie looked back at her, but she was gazing out the side window now, as if she wasn't going to answer.

He had a hard time believing anything she'd said. She was a talker, and he imagined whatever story she was telling him was the same one she gave to the bureau.

"So, how do you get involved in something like this when you don't even know anyone's name?"

"I told you. We dealt with the runners. Nobody used names."

Charlie peered in the rearview out at the highway behind him, making sure Deputy Riggins was still back there. The two vans he'd noticed earlier had fallen back somewhat, along with a dozen or so vehicles bunched up together, with the way traffic had picked up.

He started thinking about Frank's call at five thirty that morning, before the sun had even come up. Turns out it was just a handful of hours after Charlie had leaned his head back on the Adirondack with a glass of whiskey in his hand and fell asleep under the stars, in the cold, the firepit burning at his feet.

Charlie's phone rang, and he picked it up as soon as he saw it was Kim. "You heading back?"

"Are you going to be all right?" she said. "You're driving like an old man, and if I don't get to the courthouse in time..."

"We'll be fine," he said. "The exit for Hardin is coming up. You got somewhere to be, might as well stay on the highway. I'm taking the scenic route."

Kim took a few moments to respond. "You sure?"

"Don't worry. Me and Mrs. Sanborn are just having a nice conversation."

Kim said, "Can you do me a favor. Maybe keep it quiet?"

"You mean, don't tell Frank?" Charlie smiled, thinking he'd rubbed off on Deputy Riggins, when Frank had hoped it would've been the other way around.

Kim Riggins was the one who normally followed the rules, did everything by the book. Charlie, on the other hand, took a different approach.

Do what you gotta do.

He watched Kim pull into the left lane behind him and start to pass. He gave her a quick wave as she drove by.

Charlie waited for another vehicle to pass him, then cut into the left lane himself, the sign on the left showing the Hardin Road exit a half mile ahead.

Claudia Sanborn said, "Do you have a dog?"

Charlie gave her a quick glance over his shoulder. "No. Why?"

"It stinks in here." She took an exaggerated sniff. "Like a wet dog."

Charlie hadn't realized the smell or even noticed it, although he'd recently taken in a dog that showed up wandering one night when he was outside his Winnebago. He thought she was a coyote at first, ready to fire his Glock into the air to scare it off. But once she came out of the dark shadows, he saw the black and white fur, ribs showing like the poor thing hadn't eaten in weeks

He'd grabbed some burger left over in the fridge and left it out for her, took a good hour or so before she'd come close to it. It wasn't until the next night she showed up again, starting to realize she could trust Charlie. At least enough to get her something to eat.

Charlie sniffed, but didn't smell much of anything inside the Suburban.

"Might've been a dog I had back there, drove to the shelter. Wasn't mine. Just a guest for a few nights."

He, in fact, missed the dog quite a bit, and had somewhat regretted taking her to the animal shelter, thinking he was doing the right thing at the time. But he wasn't quite sure.

He also assumed her rightful owner would be out looking for her, if such a person existed. He knew it wouldn't have been right had he tried to keep her, as much as he wished he had.

Claudia Sanborn sniffed again. "Maybe you oughta clean this thing out, before you have people in it."

Charlie said, "I'm not too worried about pleasing the people I put back there." He put on his turn signal and started for the exit.

Chapter 3

CHARLIE HAD BEEN ON Hardin Road for a good mile when the white van that was behind them on the highway came up out of nowhere and crossed the solid yellow line, blowing past them. He tried to get a look at who was inside, but the windows were tinted.

The van turned the corner ahead and Charlie slowed, glancing at the sign for Hardin Community Baptist Church up ahead. He looked behind him and didn't see any other vehicles, but as soon as he turned the corner he saw the van stopped in the middle of the road, the hood open.

Charlie didn't like it. He thought about calling Kim, but she'd likely gotten too far down the highway by that point. He slowed more, almost to a stop, and slowly approached the van, putting the passenger window down as he cut into the left lane and pulled up next to it.

He couldn't see inside the van, or anyone outside of it. "Hello?" he said.

Charlie looked ahead at the entrance to the church parking lot, where a dark sedan, too far away to get the make or model was parked facing the road, like it was about to pull out from the church, but had yet to move.

Looking in the rearview mirror, he noticed a pickup truck through the trees, stopped on the road just before the corner.

Claudia Sanborn hadn't said a word.

Charlie yelled, "Anybody out there?" He blew his horn a couple of times, looked in the rearview and saw the pickup truck still hadn't moved. Looking ahead, the car was still parked at the entrance to the church.

He grabbed his Glock and knew the best thing he could do was get out of there, call the local cops and let them see what the story was. But before he pulled away, he caught a glimpse in the side view of a man in a ski mask coming around from behind the van, gun raised and pointed at the Suburban.

Charlie yelled, "Get down!" He slammed his foot on the gas. The Suburban took off, heading west on Hardin, but they hadn't even made it fifty yards when the vehicle at the church entrance pulled out in front of them.

Charlie hit the brakes. Gunshots rang out from somewhere behind them. The rear window shattered and he ducked down, yelling for Claudia Sanborn. "Stay down!"

He poked his head up and saw two men go past the van, running at them. He hit the gas, slapped the vehicle in reverse, tires squealing, and raised the Glock at the opening in the rear.

Claudia Sanborn was on the floor behind the front passenger seat, arms covering her head.

Charlie fired six shots out the window.

One of the two men dropped, falling face-first to the asphalt. The other ran for cover, somewhere behind the van.

He tried to control the Suburban going in reverse, but he was going too fast. With one hand on the wheel, looking over his shoulder, he sideswiped the van, then hit the brakes and cut the wheel.

The Suburban spun around, facing east on Hardin.

But the pickup truck had come around the corner and stopped, no other vehicles coming off the highway.

Charlie assumed someone must've blocked the exit.

Shots fired from somewhere around the pickup, and Charlie immediately lost control of the Suburban. His tires had been shot out by whoever was in the truck. "Stay down," he repeated, his voice somehow calm. He couldn't control the Suburban or stop it from veering off the road, but continued. He was headed straight for the pickup, pedal to the floor.

"What are you doing?" Sanborn yelled, her head poking up from behind the front passenger seat.

The pickup's driver-side door opened. The man inside jumped out and ran from it, gun raised, firing shots at the Suburban fishtailing out of control.

Charlie held the wheel with both hands, the Glock on the seat between his legs.

More shots were fired at his vehicle, one after another. Two more windows shattered, and Charlie did all he could to control the oversized vehicle, rocking and swerving like a ship in a storm. "Hold on!" he yelled, braced himself, and finally crashed head-on with the pickup truck.

The airbag deployed and smashed him in the face with such force he felt his neck snap back, knocking his head against the headrest. The airbag deflated instantly, and he used both hands to clear it out of his way.

It took Charlie a second to get his head on straight.

He touched his face and saw the blood on his fingertips. "Are you all right?" he said, looking over the back seat.

Claudia Sanborn was calm, but her voice cracked, getting up off the floor. "I'm... I'm all right."

"Stay down," he said, almost in a whisper. He looked around. It was quiet. Too quiet.

And when Charlie turned the key in the ignition, the engine wouldn't start. But he kept trying the key, turned forward, holding the ignition in the starter position.

It took what felt like a minute, but the engine finally turned over. He revved the engine and slapped the shifter into reverse, slamming his foot on the gas. But the Suburban went nowhere, tires squealing and fluttering at the same time, the smell of burning rubber filling the vehicle inside. He tried a lower gear, shifting down, pedal to the floor, but it was as if the two vehicles were locked together.

Charlie looked around, but saw no one. He wished he had.

"Don't get up," he said to Claudia Sanborn, his voice hushed now, gaze moving in all directions around the area. With the Glock on the floor in front of him, he'd started to reach down for it. But he froze when out of the corner of his eye saw the barrel of a rifle come in through the passenger-side window, the muzzle so close he could smell the pungent stench of burnt gunpowder.

The man on the other end, wearing a black ski mask covering his entire head, said, "Don't move, cowboy."

Charlie eyed the Glock on the floor, thinking about it, but decided to do as the man said. He remained still, raising his hands in front of him. "Not a smart move," he said, looking past the gun and into the man's eyes through the slits in the mask.

Charlie shifted in the seat and used his boot to move the gun on the floor closer. It was somewhat within reach, but he had no idea how to actually reach for it without being shot at.

Someone else stood outside the back passenger door and tried to open it from outside. But Charlie had hit the lock on the driver-side door.

Whoever was out there tugged at the handle, and the man with the rifle leaned in through the window a little farther, the muzzle so close to Charlie's face it made him cross-eyed looking at it.

"Keep your hands where I can see them," the man said, reaching in, holding the rifle steady with one hand without taking his eyes off Charlie.

The locks clicked, and the rear passenger-side door swung open.

Claudia had been quiet, but screamed when the other man, also with his face covered, reached for her and pulled her from the vehicle.

"You're making a grave mistake," Charlie said, sweat dripping down his face now. He tried to control his heart pounding in his chest, his breathing heavy, but his adrenalin was getting the best of him.

He eyed the Glock on the floor, then looked at the empty back seat.

Claudia Sanborn was walking away, being pulled by the man who had her by the arm. She didn't appear to put up much of a fight.

Charlie's gaze shifted to the rifle, then the man holding it. He was tempted to just close his eyes, take what he was sure he had coming.

But giving up wasn't what Charlie was up for.

"You don't have to shoot me," he pleaded. "I can't see your faces." He was admittedly scared. It wasn't that he was afraid of dying. Not as much as he was afraid of what came next. Heaven? Darkness? He glanced in his rearview, trying to see what they were doing with Claudia. He said to the man with the gun, "What's your plan here?"

The man didn't respond or move an inch, keeping the gun steady on Charlie like he was waiting for the go-ahead to pull the trigger.

From somewhere outside, in the distance, a man yelled, "Let's go!"

The man turned away for a split second to look at wherever the voice had come from.

But that was all Charlie needed. He reached to the floor and had the Glock in his hand, finger on the trigger, and before the man's eyes shifted back, Charlie knocked the barrel from his face and fired two shots.

The man fell back but grabbed the inside edge of the door with one hand. As he fell from the window, his finger tightened on the trigger, and he fired twelve rounds wildly into the interior, piercing the roof with holes before he fell to the ground outside.

Thin beams of sunlight shone through the padding and steel above Charlie's head like lasers.

Charlie tried to open the driver-side door but it wouldn't budge. He leaned and drove his shoulder into it, and the door made a loud pop, creaking open enough for Charlie to squeeze out of it. Pain shot through his knee and up his leg when he stepped out and put his boot on the pavement. He limped, taking his first few steps, doing his best to ignore it.

The other man who had Claudia Sanborn had already pulled his mask off and dropped it on the ground. Charlie could almost make out the man's face, but he was more focused on Claudia looking back at him.

Even though the man had her arm in his grasp, it wasn't like she was being dragged against her will. She almost looked to smile at Charlie, but by that point they were too far ahead for him to be sure.

Charlie started to run, but the pain was too much. He moved as fast as he could, continuing after them. He watched the two slip into the back seat of the dark sedan in the road in front of the church. Raising his Glock, he was ready to fire. But before he got off a shot, the passenger-side window went down on the vehicle, and out came a rifle, firing at least ten rounds in Charlie's direction.

He dove for cover behind the white van. Staying low, he spotted the bloodied body of the first man he'd shot.

Charlie stuck his head out from around the back of the van, but the vehicle with Claudia Sanborn inside it was already heading west on Hardin Road in the opposite direction from the highway. He raised the Glock, but by the time he had the vehicle in his sights, it was too far away. It'd turned the corner, no brake lights, tires screeching, and practically on two wheels before it was out of sight.

Charlie went back over to the Suburban, smoke coming up from under the hood, the front end smashed like an accordion. He got a strong whiff of fuel as he crouched down over the body of the man he'd shot and reached into the man's pocket. He pulled out some cash, tossed it on the ground, then reached in the other pocket and took out a phone. There was no wallet. No ID. Charlie tried to unlock the phone with no luck, at first, but then pulled the ski mask off the dead man's face and held the phone in front of it. He even tried to get the man's eyelids raised, but facial recognition didn't work.

It didn't help that Charlie had shot him in the face.

He dropped the phone on the man's chest and started to walk away. But before he'd taken two steps, he heard the phone ring.

Charlie reached down and picked it up. "Hello?"

"Henry?"

"Is that his name?" Charlie said. "I'm sorry, but Henry can't come to the phone right now." He listened, the phone to his ear. "Hello?"

But there was no response. The caller had hung up.

Charlie tapped the number to call back, and after a couple of rings, it stopped ringing. Charlie waited for voicemail, but all that came on was an automated message saying there was no voicemail set up.

He dropped the phone on the man's chest.

The odor of gas had gotten stronger, and with the heat and smoke coming from the engine, he thought the best thing he could do was get as far away as possible.

He went around to the back of the Suburban to grab a rifle he kept hidden underneath the floorboard. But when he tried to open the cargo hatch, it wouldn't budge. There was too much damage.

Charlie looked ahead where flames had started coming out from under the hood. He then saw a stream of liquid seeping from under the vehicle. And when he crouched down and put his finger to it, he knew right away it was gas.

The flames started to rise from under the hood, and Charlie didn't have to think twice before he started to run. Even with the pain shooting up his leg from what felt like a cracked kneecap, he moved as fast as he could.

He made it to the other side of the white van when the Suburban exploded, the hood being blasted straight up into the air before crashing down no more than a couple of yards from where Charlie was standing. He kept moving away, and almost fell when a second explosion shook the ground. He stumbled and fell on the dirt along the side of the road. He looked back at the flames and black smoke shooting thirty feet in the air from what was left of his Suburban.

Chapter 4

By the time Deputy Riggins showed up, the heavily wooded Hardin Road was busy with two fire trucks, three rescue vehicles, ten law enforcement vehicles from both the Dallas Police Department and the Lincoln County Sheriff's Office, and at least twenty law enforcement officers from both departments. State police were also on the scene.

A *WZAZ News* truck parked near the church where the pastor had come out of to pray for the two men Charlie shot.

"This isn't good," Kim said, shaking her head as she looked around at the mess of a scene.

Charlie hadn't said much since Kim arrived, his eyes fixed on the lone firefighter blasting water at the smoldering pile of steel that was once his Suburban.

Kim said, "I should've stayed with you."

"I'm the one, told you to go ahead," Charlie said. "Who ever expected—"

"I'm not sure Frank's going to care who told who to do what. We didn't follow procedure, and..." She stopped, and she and Charlie both turned to look east.

Chief Deputy Frank Carter's blue F-150 drove along Hardin Road. He stopped, his window down, and spoke to one of the officers blocking the road, then drove onto the dirt along the woods to get around the roadblock.

He parked under the shade of the trees at the edge of the road and stepped out, coming right for Charlie, with his head down, as if he wasn't in the mood for speaking with any other law enforcement officials. But he managed to stop and take a quick glance at the covered body by the white van, then over at the other covered body, or what was left of it, next to the smoldering Suburban.

Charlie shifted his stance and rubbed the back of his neck. "This's gonna be fun," he said to Kim, but under his breath.

"Oh, come on, now, Charlie," Frank said.

Charlie raised his head, acting as if he hadn't noticed Frank show up. "Hey, Frank. When did you get here?" He grinned, but Frank didn't appear to be in the mood for Charlie's antics.

Frank said, "Can you make it just one goddamn day without getting in some kind of trouble?"

"It wasn't his fault," Kim said, doing her best to stick up for Charlie, as she often did, even against her own best judgment.

"It wasn't *anybody's* fault," Charlie said.

Frank looked at the two of them, but then fixed his gaze on Charlie. "You mind explaining to me exactly what happened here?" He looked back at the body by the van and gave a nod to one of the deputies from the sheriff's office who was watching him and Charlie.

"Aren't you going to ask if I'm all right?" Charlie said.

Frank looked him up and down. "You look fine to me," he said, then turned to Kim. "You all right?"

She swallowed hard, nodding. "I wasn't involved, sir."

"Sir?" Frank took a deep breath and exhaled, running his hand over his white, buzz-cut head of hair. "Only time you call me sir is when you've done something wrong. So why don't you tell me what you mean by you 'weren't involved.'"

Charlie said, "Don't blame her. You had her double booked on two assignments. On top of it all, this was supposed to be her day off."

Frank waited.

"Charlie took the back roads," she said. "There was a lot of traffic on 321, some construction, and—"

"You weren't following him?" Frank said. "Don't you know better than that?" The way he said it was like a disappointed father, his tone more empathetic with Kim than it would ever be with Charlie.

"This was a low-risk case. The suspect didn't appear to pose any serious risks," Kim said, looking around at the scene. "But we obviously didn't understand the situation."

"It's never up to either of you or any other deputy to make that kind of call," Frank said. "This isn't the old days, riding horseback, shooting our way to justice." He held his gaze on Charlie. "We have rules for a reason. Procedures, made by people smarter than either of us." Frank cleared his throat and ran both hands up and down his face.

"There was nothing Kim would've been able to do, Frank. I'm glad she wasn't around. These men were heavily armed. I gotta say, I'm lucky to be alive." He nodded at the body of the man who had the rifle pointed inside the Suburban. "I'm not one for praying, but I gotta say I'd started to."

Frank took a deep breath and let out a sigh, still shaking his head as if in disbelief. "Any chance you could identify any of 'em? I mean, the ones that aren't dead?"

"They wore ski masks," Charlie said. "And the thing I can't help thinking is she seemed to maybe know they were out there, following us. It certainly seemed at first she'd been abducted. But, I don't know. Something wasn't right. She didn't put up much of a fight."

Kim said, "What did you expect her to do?"

Frank cocked his head, face pinched like he'd bitten into a lemon. "You trying to say this wasn't an abduction?"

"I don't know," Charlie said. "Maybe I'm wrong. But, she seemed fairly calm though it all. Didn't even really scream or make a peep, outside of when we were crashing around." He reached down to rub his knee, feeling the pain now but not even sure at what point he hurt it. He straightened up and looked around at the scene. He still couldn't believe the Suburban had gone up in flames the way it did, although it wouldn't have made much of a difference, all the damage it'd been through already.

Charlie went on, telling Frank and Kim whatever Mrs. Sanborn had talked about on the ride. At least the parts he'd listened to.

Frank said, "Didn't it raise any kind of red flag? I mean, the way you said she was looking out the rear window like she was looking for something?"

"Well, yeah. I suppose it did. I had my eye out. Did everything by the book. I mean, well, not everything. But, come on, Frank. You're saying it all like I should've known we were gonna be ambushed? This was clearly something planned. Somebody had to've been watching that motel."

Frank crossed his arms. "You didn't read the report, Charlie. Did you."

It wasn't exactly a question. Because Frank knew the answer.

Charlie swallowed hard. "I looked it over. As far as I understood, the Sanborns are nothing more than a couple of small-time con artists."

"That's all you've got?" Frank said. "Small time? You know they were involved in the theft of nearly ten million dollars in the past two years? And there are others involved, so, of course, the hope was Mrs. Sanborn would be able to lead law enforcement to the bigger prize."

Charlie didn't respond. He hadn't much of the report beyond the top sheet inside the folder. "She told me she and her husband don't know any of the names of the people she worked for."

Frank narrowed his eyes. "And you believed her?"

"Well, no. That's not what I'm saying."

"Then what *are* you saying?" Frank said.

Charlie didn't know what to say. The most he could do was admit he hadn't done his homework. Not the way he used to, when he was fresh and young and thought the small details made a difference, when they rarely did. He tried to make light of the situation. "I thought maybe you'd at least be happy I'm alive?"

Frank scoffed, "I'll be happy when we find Mrs. Sanborn. But clearly, what happened here wasn't exactly amateur hour. These men knew what they were here to do."

Charlie didn't like what'd happened. He felt responsible, of course, and knew he wouldn't be able to rest until he found Claudia Sanborn, making sure whoever was responsible would pay the price.

Of course, if it were up to Frank, it would have to be done by the book. But as far as Charlie saw it, there was more than one way to get a job done. When he made a mistake, and someone made him look like a fool, he promised himself he'd stop at nothing to make sure that person paid the price.

One of the deputies from Gaston County called out for Charlie, then walked over to him. Charlie introduced him to Kim and Frank as Deputy Mike Gormley.

Deputy Gormley said, "Both vehicles are reported stolen. We also found six AR-15s in the back of the van, empty crates of hundred-round ammo, on top of a dozen cartons of Newport cigarettes."

Frank turned to Charlie. "These guys show up with automatic weapons, and somehow you manage to kill two of 'em and end up with barely a scratch?" He huffed out a laugh, almost as if he felt maybe he should stop being so hard on Charlie. Frank said, "At some point, your luck's going to run out, Charlie. I know you tend to think you're like a cat with nine lives. But if I had to guess, you've gotta be gettin' down to your last two or three."

Frank turned from Charlie and Kim and headed for his blue Ford F-150. He didn't look around much, walking like he had sore feet, or maybe his bad back was flaring up. He opened the truck's driver-side door and looked at the two. His voice raised, he said, "Deputy Riggins, please see to it Charlie makes it back to the office in one piece. As you know, we're short-staffed." He put his foot up on the truck's side rail and pulled himself up inside the vehicle behind the wheel, slamming the door closed. Hanging his arm out the window, he started the engine, pointing at Charlie's Suburban being pulled by a chain onto a flatbed. He yelled to Charlie, "There's gonna come a point, the U.S. government's gonna make you pay, you keep destroying them the way you do."

Charlie kept a straight face and said, "It's not as bad as it looks."

Frank rolled his eyes and turned the truck around, dirt and leaves kicking up behind it as he drove off-road and around the scene until he was past the roadblock, before he cut back onto the pavement and headed toward 321.

Chapter 5

Sorry about this mess," Charlie said, leaning back in the passenger seat of Kim's Tahoe, the brim of his baseball cap down low over his eyes. He needed a nap, and wished maybe he could get one in before they were back at the office. He yawned, rubbing his face. "I can't imagine this is how you'd planned to spend your day off."

"I was just going to clean the house," Kim said. "I can't even have anyone come in, the way it looks right now."

"I'm sure it's fine," he said. "You ever gonna come by my place?" he said. "I bet you'd like it out there. It's quiet."

Kim glanced at him without an answer.

Charlie's phone rang, and he looked at the screen, seeing it was Jennie calling. He said to Kim, "You mind?"

Jennie had already called him a couple of times, but he hadn't answered.

"Not at all," Kim said.

Charlie answered, "Hey, Jennie."

"I've been calling you," she said.

"I know. I work. Remember?" He didn't mean to come across snappy with her or anything, but lately he couldn't help himself. Jennie called him nearly every day, sometimes more than once. And the whole thing made him uncomfortable. Or maybe just a little bit confused, trying to understand what might've been going through her head. He also hadn't really gotten over things. It wasn't *his* idea to get divorced.

Best thing he thought he could do was move on, but for some reason Jennie didn't seem to want to let him.

She said, "I was just wondering if you'd be able to come by later tonight, when you get off work?"

He looked at the clock on the dashboard. "I don't know, Jennie. I might not be getting off at all today, if I'm being honest. I've already had a bad start to my morning. And I'm not sure it's going to get any better."

"Is everything all right?" she said.

He looked at the bandage on the back of his hand, a deep cut he wasn't even sure at which point he got it. At least it wasn't a gunshot wound. "Yeah, things are all right," he said. "The usual."

There was a pause between them.

He said, "Maybe I can call you later, let you know?"

"Yeah, okay," she said.

Charlie thought for a moment. "What about you? Is everything good with you? You sound—"

"Yes, everything's fine. Good. I'm good. I just... I wanted to talk to you about something."

"Uh-oh," he said, the sound of it like he was in trouble.

Jennie let out a quiet laugh that didn't give off any sense of joy, her voice almost hushed. "No, it's nothing. Not a big deal. If you can't come by tonight... just call me later, when you have a chance. I know you're a busy man, Charlie."

He'd picked up some odd vibes from Jennie. She'd been acting differently all along, ever since she found out about Lindsey.

Considering the fact Jennie and Charlie were no longer married, he didn't think she'd take it the way she did. Of course, it was all right she'd been on dates herself, Charlie stopping by the house one evening, seeing some strange man eating off the same plates Charlie and Jennie received as gifts when they first got married.

"I'll call you when I can," he said, and left it at that, hanging up without another word. He tried to get comfortable in the passenger seat, slouching a little more, staring to his right out the window.

"Is everything okay?" Kim said.

He had to think about it. "Sure."

Kim gave him a look like she didn't believe him. "What is it with you two?"

He lazily rolled his head against the headrest to his left to look at her. "What is *what*?"

She paused, like she was hesitant to say. "I know it's none of my business. But you talk to her more now than when you were married. Usually, when people get divorced, the last thing they want to do is talk to each other."

Charlie nodded. "I still remember my dad, came home one night... Me and my sister were in bed. He told Mom he was leaving, turned around, and walked out. Left all his things, not that there was much for him to take. Only thing Mom said on his way out the door was don't come back. He never did." Charlie grinned, as if it was some kind of enjoyable childhood memory for him.

"You don't talk to him?"

Charlie straightened up in the seat. "He came around one summer, five years after he left. It was a couple weeks after my tenth birthday, took me and my sister camping. I remember Mom wasn't too happy with the fact he'd showed up, acting like it was just another day. But me and Anna begged for her to let us go with him. We had an all-right time, but I remember he cut the trip short, took us back after a couple nights, and that was the last we saw of him."

Kim's eyebrows were raised like she was surprised where the conversation had turned. It was rare for Charlie to open up about much of anything. Especially his past. "I had no idea," she said. "I'm sorry."

"There's nothing to be sorry about," he said. "It's in the past. It is what it is. And here I am. Midlife. Divorced. I guess I'm just glad Jennie and I never had kids." He thought about it for a moment. "Or maybe that woulda given us an excuse to stay together."

Kim turned the wheel and took the exit for I-240 west, her mouth open like she was about to say something.

But Charlie's phone rang, and he waited before grabbing it from the center console where he'd left it. When he picked it up he let out a sigh, glancing at Kim with a straight-lipped grin as he put it to his ear. "Hey," he said. "I was just thinking of you."

"I guess it's not Frank?" Kim said, under her breath.

Charlie gave her a look, a side-eye, the phone to his ear.

It was Lindsey on the other end.

"You said you were going to call me," she said. "I left you a message."

"I'm sorry about that." He hadn't even listened to it. "It's been a long day already."

"Is everything all right?"

"Yeah, good."

That wasn't exactly the truth.

Lindsey said, "I was lonely last night. Why'd you leave so early?"

Charlie had to think about it before he answered, afraid he'd say the wrong thing. "I'm sorry about that. Like I told you, I just needed to get some rest." He noticed a smirk on Kim's face as she, of course, had to have heard every word. He said to Lindsey, "Listen, I'm in the middle of something right now. Do you mind if I call you a little later?"

"Charlie," she said. "I thought everything was good between us. But, the way you've been acting lately..."

"Everything *is* good between us. I promise. But, you know how it is. I told you, being hooked up with the U.S. Marshals comes with its downsides."

"Hooked up?" she said. "Is that what this is?"

Charlie almost laughed at how it'd come out, or more about that she'd called him on it. But he kept it inside, knowing it wouldn't go over so well if he had. "No, that's not what I... I didn't mean to call it that." He closed his eyes and ran his hand down his face. "Can I just call you a little later?"

"Will I see you?"

Charlie said, "Yeah, I think so. But it'll be tonight. I don't know what time. Maybe late, but hopefully before you close. 'Cause I think I'm going to need a drink."

"Okay," Lindsey said. "Then I guess I'll talk to you later. Bye, Charlie."

And with that, Lindsey hung up, and Charlie stared at the phone's screen for a good handful of seconds.

Kim said to him, "You really are caught in the middle of two women, huh?"

"Not really. It's over with me and Jennie. We both know it. Lindsey has no idea Jennie's still calling me all the time. She thinks we had a normal divorce, split up what little we had, and went our separate ways. I mean, she knows Jennie got the house, but..."

"I like Lindsey," Kim said, giving Charlie a quick glance. "I like Jennie too. But, well... I think you and Lindsey are good together. I don't know how serious it is between you two, but... I just hope you don't screw it up, end up an old man alone." She gave him another quick look out of the corner of her eye, looking ahead just as they passed the sign for UNC Asheville.

"I don't know," he said. "Is being alone really that bad? Especially when you're old. Who needs it, at that point? I say I get to that point, shoot me. Like an old dog."

Kim cracked a grin, knowing Charlie said a lot of things he didn't mean. "Well, I'm not sure I'd like it."

Charlie said, "Being alone? Now? Or when you're old?"

As soon as the words left his mouth, he wished he could've sucked them right back in.

The thing was, Kim and Charlie had known each other for a long time. At least five years, maybe more. They didn't work side by side back then the way they had the past three years, and had only recently started to open up more with each other. Up until that point, even with all the time they'd spent together each day, they'd never really got deep into any kind of personal discussions.

Charlie didn't even know for sure if Kim was dating anyone. She'd mention something here or there about going out with this one or that one, but never with any detail. He did wonder, though, if she'd ever gotten serious with any of them. Sometimes it'd cross his mind to ask, but it wasn't like she'd answer if he did.

Chapter 6

FRANK SHOWED UP IN the conference room at the Western District of North Carolina headquarters, sipping from a blue-and-gold U.S. Marshals Service coffee mug. He placed a few eight-by-ten photos in the middle of the long maple-topped conference room table between Charlie and Kim, sitting across from each other. Frank had a manila folder tucked under his arm he placed in front of his chair at the end of the table. "You'll see in these photos the two men you met today. Both likely in the van, on the way to the morgue."

Charlie took his baseball cap and brushed his hand over the US Marshals emblem stitched on the front, as if dusting it off, then placed it on the table. He picked up the top two photos and looked at the first one. "Which one's this?"

"Joseph Caruso," he said.

Charlie looked at the other photo and recognized the face right away. "This Henry?"

Frank said, "Henry Avella. Both ex-cons. Avella did ten years in Raiford, down in Florida, for attempted murder. Only been out six months."

Charlie placed both photos face up, studying each, his arms folded and resting on the table.

Kim had picked up the other photos and flipped through them. She held up one to Charlie and Frank, showing a black-and-white picture of an older man, dressed in a white suit with sleeves too long for his arms. He stood outside what appeared in the photo to be the entrance to a restaurant, with Frankie's on the sign over his head.

"This him?" Kim said.

Frank nodded. "It's believed Denny Caprio was running the entire operation the Sanborns were involved in. Now, neither of the two had admitted to knowing him, but the bureau was preparing a deal, to get them both to talk, before they both disappeared."

Charlie was still looking at the other two photos. "And these two, they're somehow related to Caprio?"

"The belief is they worked for him," Frank said. "Apparently they're also related to him. Cousins."

Kim said, "Is there a warrant yet?"

"No, not yet," Frank said. "I don't know if what happened this morning will move things along or not. There's not much evidence yet to tie him to it, but I also haven't spoken to Stan. Maybe one of you can talk to him, when you get a chance. He didn't return my calls."

"Caprio is Stan Cooper's case?" Kim said.

Frank nodded. "There may be more to him—to Caprio—than whatever scheme the Sanborns were involved in. There's a lot we don't know."

Charlie pulled out his phone and started tapping away with his thumbs. He sent FBI Agent Stan Cooper a message without telling anyone else what he was doing:

Call me when you get a minute.

He placed his phone on the table.

Charlie said, "So, are we supposed to believe these clowns took Claudia Sanborn to keep from ratting out Caprio?"

"At this stage," Frank said, "it's our best guess."

Charlie said, "But what do *you* think?"

Frank waited before responding, part of him looking annoyed at Charlie pressing him, the other part like he understood

Charlie wasn't going to let this one rest and, of course, would take it personally, as he had most of his cases.

Frank said, "There are others out there, like the Sanborns, working for Caprio. We're going to need to find who they are."

"We don't know?" Kim said.

"The bureau claims Caprio partners up with middle-aged suburban couples with local connections, looking to make more money so they can keep up with the Joneses. There is one couple Stan said they had an eye on, but the husband disappeared. They ended up getting the wife on some kind of lesser crime. She's in Virginia Correctional for Women."

"Goochland?" Kim said.

Frank nodded. "She never admitted to knowing Caprio either."

Charlie said, "Same gig as the Sanborns? Praying on senior citizens?"

"Not exactly," Frank said. "Something to do with getting people out of bad investments. Time-shares, I believe."

Charlie was quiet, pulling at his chin. "They ever bring him up on anything?"

"Caprio?" Frank shook his head. "Nope. And then when they finally felt they had something, Caprio went underground."

"Underground?" Kim said.

"The businesses disappeared, as did Caprio."

Charlie said, "And what about this woman behind bars in Virginia? Nobody could break her? Get her to talk?"

"The assumption," Frank said, "is that there's likely a deal set in place. The sentences are almost always going to be short, within the judicial limits. Caprio promises to take care of his people if they go down for him. We assume this was the case with Claudia Sanborn."

Charlie said, "Sentence is typically going to be five years or less. No kids, maybe nobody else out there to worry about... It goes by faster than you'd think. Especially if there's a big payoff once they're out."

Frank rolled both sleeves and pushed them past his elbows, leaning on the table with his hands spread wide. "With all that said, I still don't know if the right approach here is to hunt for Caprio or not."

The three were quiet, Charlie and Kim still seated, Frank looking from one to the other from the end of the long table as if waiting for one of the two to talk.

Charlie said, "Can we talk about the fact these people showed up out of nowhere this morning?"

"You mean, at the motel?" Frank said.

"The hotel. The highway... It doesn't make much sense. If they knew she was hiding out, why would they wait for us to show up?"

Kim said, "I was thinking about that myself, and can only come up with two scenarios. One possibility is they didn't know she was there. The other is they were watching out for her, to protect her."

"One of those two would have to mean they'd kill her right there, in the back of my car," Charlie said. "I see no reason they'd take her like that if they were looking for her in the first place."

Frank said, "And it would have to be quite a coincidence they just happen to show up at the same time you did, if the first scenario were true."

"Unless they followed one of us?" Kim said.

Charlie looked from Kim to Frank. "Out of all the law enforcement officials around, they'd have to know something from the inside to know Kim and I were the ones on the case. Shit, would they even expect anyone from the Marshals Service to be the one looking for her?"

Frank pushed his sleeves up a little higher on his arms. "If perhaps they somehow knew she was going to be in the area, maybe they were caught off guard or ill-prepared when you two showed up."

"She was in town to see her dying sister," Charlie said. "At least, that's what she told me."

Frank raised both eyebrows. "She told you that?"

Charlie nodded. "Well, I'll go back to the fact they didn't kill her right there; makes me believe there's a chance they're all on the same side."

"What if she has something they want?" Kim said. "And didn't want to kill her until she told them whatever they needed to know?"

Frank and Charlie both nodded, like maybe things were starting to make more sense.

"What about the husband?" Charlie said. "Scott Sanborn. Any updates on his whereabouts?"

Frank gave Kim a nod. "You mind checking up on that when you get a chance? Intelligence still hasn't gotten back to me. Maybe you can call your friend in DC, see if you can get this moving along. There's a good chance the husband's out there, maybe even nearby. Could certainly help us. Maybe he decides to talk, now that his wife could be in danger." He turned to Charlie. "She say anything about him?"

"Just that she hadn't talked to him since they broke out of those ankle monitors, each went in separate directions. At least that's what she told me."

Kim reached for the folder and shuffled through the papers inside. "So, there's nothing on the husband? No leads at all?"

"Not really," Frank said. "There's an assumption he's still here in North Carolina. No record of any flights, trains, buses... Hasn't touched his credit cards or been to the bank since they emptied out whatever they had shortly before their arrest. All other assets have been frozen, so I'd have to guess he's either got nothing, or some cash."

Kim said, "Mrs. Sanborn had a few hundred dollars in her duffel bag."

"That's it?" Frank said.

"Maybe the husband kept it all," Kim said.

"Or it's hidden somewhere. Which takes us back to whoever it was that grabbed her. Good chance they want something she has."

"What if he's dead?" Kim said.

Charlie looked at her, then nodded. "There's that."

Frank said, "Anything's possible. Including Caprio being involved in getting her out of there this morning."

There was more silence in the room, the rest of the office empty other than one deputy marshal making photocopies on the other side of the glass wall.

Frank said, "So, for now, let's try to focus on Scott Sanborn. I'd love to say we try to track down Caprio, but we haven't exactly gotten the go-ahead. FBI requested we continue to hold on standby. But that was two weeks ago. Haven't heard a word since, and I don't know if this opens the door for us or—"

"Doesn't what just happened give us some leeway?" Charlie said.

Frank waited, thinking. "We've got warrants for the Sanborns. And now, of course, we'd like to think Mrs. Sanborn's alive."

"We don't want to call it a rescue mission?" Charlie said.

"You can call it what you'd like," Frank said. "But we don't need to bring any more attention our way by calling it that. She's a fugitive, and she escaped. I think that's the best way to frame it right now. For your sake and for mine."

Charlie nodded, like he understood, and had a slight grin on his face, appreciating the fact Frank always had his back.

Frank picked up the papers on the table and tucked them neatly together, slipping them back inside the folder. "I'm not sure how much we can do right now. Not until we have more from intelligence."

"I'll make a call as soon as we're done here," Kim said.

Charlie said, "We should probably get a move on, start heading out to find her."

Frank laughed, shaking his head. "What are you going to do? Go drive around in your Suburban, hoping you see her at the local diner?" He rubbed his hands together. "Oh, wait. You destroyed your Suburban." He held up his index finger and left the room, but came right back in and tossed a set of keys on the table, in front of Charlie. "I got you a Town Car."

Charlie picked up the set of keys and looked them over. "I'm supposed to drive a Town Car? What am I, a ninety-year-old woman?"

Frank said, "Would you rather ride a bike? It's all we've got available."

"But I need four-wheel drive. How am I supposed to make it to the Winnebago in a Town Car? You've been out there, Frank. There's not even a road."

Frank said, "You'll make it work."

Charlie studied the keys, and placed them next to his phone. He saw he had a text message come in. He picked up the phone and looked at the screen.

Agent Stan Cooper with the FBI had replied:

Okay.

Frank looked out through the glass into the rest of the office, then pulled a chair out from the table. He sat and leaned forward, arms folded in front of him. "Now, listen. Both of you." His voice was hushed. "We need to be cognizant of the fact somebody out there knew where you were heading this morning. I'd like to think we shouldn't have to worry. But let's all just be real careful for now. Maybe keep things to ourselves, at least until we have more answers."

Charlie said, "So you do think someone might've followed us this morning?"

"All I'm saying is I want us to be careful, until we have more answers," Frank said.

Charlie sat quiet, looking from Kim to Frank, then glancing at his phone when it started to buzz. "It's Stan," he said, then stood from his chair and answered. "Mr. Cooper."

"Good to hear you're not dead," Stan said.

Charlie smiled and left the room without another word to Frank or Kim. "Only on the inside," he replied to Stan.

Frank yelled out from the conference room. "Where you going, Charlie? We're not done here."

Charlie turned to Frank and gave him a nod with his chin, but didn't respond, the phone to his ear. He continued into the kitchen and said to Stan, "So, what do you know?"

"Besides the fact you lost a convicted felon and a potential witness in a case we've been working on for thirteen months?" Stan said.

Charlie didn't respond at first. He wanted to think Stan was kidding, but he knew that wasn't Stan's thing. "Give me a break, will you?"

"Sorry," Stan said. "But you're the last person I'd ever expect to—"

"Stan, I'm going to hang up the goddamn phone, you don't shut up about it. I know what I've done. And I'm going to rectify the situation."

Stan was quiet on the other end.

Charlie said, "So, what can you tell me about this guy Denny Caprio? I understand he's the one you were hoping Sanborn would bury?"

"I wish I could say that was a fact, but we don't have a lot of answers," Stan said. "Nobody's been able to find him. Not for lack of trying."

"Then why hasn't it landed on our desks over here?" Charlie said. "That's what we get paid to do: hunt down the bad guys."

"It's just not quite official yet. We don't even have enough for an arrest warrant. But we all know the man's track record. We've just never been able to take him down. I wish we did, when we had the chance."

"Before he disappeared?" Charlie said.

"Long before. The man's a snake. I'm telling you, I wish we had called in the Marshals Service. But you know how it goes."

"Yeah, too much red tape," Charlie said. "That's why I'm surprised you follow the rules the way you do. I don't know how you ever get anything done."

Stan cleared his throat on the other end, but didn't quite respond.

"We need to find Claudia Sanborn," Charlie said. "Any chance you can help me?"

Stan said, "I'm going to be in your area in the next couple of hours. I'm on 40 right now."

"You eat?" Charlie said, pouring himself a coffee. "I'm starved. Maybe we could meet up, get lunch?"

Stan said, "Name the place."

"You remember the Coyote Grille, don't you?" Charlie said.

"In Weaverville? The place you and Frank like to hang out, right? Got that pretty bartender you were always staring at?"

"I don't know what you're talking about," Charlie said, thinking about Lindsey. "I watch all the bartenders. They pour my drinks."

Chapter 7

It was barely past noon when Charlie made his way into the Coyote Grille. Even though it was open, and Lindsey, the owner of the place, ran a decent kitchen, it wasn't the kind of place that filled up much earlier in the day. After three or four o'clock, the first wave of customers usually came, mostly the local, blue-collar crowd looking to drink away a hard day of work.

There were only a couple of people at the bar when Charlie sat down right in the middle of it, to the left of the beer taps. One man was seated in a stool at the far end, facing Charlie from where the bar turned into the wall. To Charlie's left were two women seated six stools away, leaning into each other giggling, half-empty martini glasses with pieces of fruit inside, in front of them.

Charlie removed his hat, placed it on the bar, and fixed his hair.

The door on the other side of the bar swung open, and Lindsey walked out carrying two plates. "Hey," she said, smiling. Her eyes appeared to light up when she saw him. "Give me a minute." She moved past Charlie, then the two women, and out the far end of the bar into the dining area at the back of the place.

There were six tables, a couple of dartboards, and a jukebox. Only one of the tables was occupied, by a man and a woman sitting on the same side together, snuggled up like schoolkids. Charlie watched, and the two barely noticed Lindsey when she put their food down in front of them.

Charlie had little doubt the two were having an affair.

A song he hadn't heard before played on the jukebox, and wasn't pleasing to his ears in any way. He thought maybe it was what had been called modern country. Or maybe it was "pop" country, which didn't make much sense to Charlie. How can it be both?

Either way, whatever was playing wasn't music he liked.

For Charlie, he hadn't heard a musician born in the past twenty years he'd wanted to hear more than once. There were some who weren't half-bad, but he'd gotten to the age he'd stopped looking for anything new. If someone were to get a look at his small collection of CDs—something he still preferred over listening to music on his phone—they'd find Johnny Cash, Tom T Hall, John Prine... Even Bruce Springsteen, a musician he'd rank up there with any other songwriter.

Charlie couldn't remember the last time he'd picked up his own guitar. It was the one thing he'd left with Jennie when he moved out, and had been meaning to dig it out of the attic, or wherever she'd put it. But being what Charlie himself considered an average player on the six-string, he always had a deep appreciation for musicians like Eric Clapton or Stevie Ray Vaughn, and the way they could play.

Eyes on the TV on the wall behind the bar, Charlie saw the news was on, with the sound off. He never understood the idea of going to a place to have a drink, to forget about life for a while, and have to be exposed to all the bad things going on in the world. But he'd never mentioned it to Lindsey, knowing it wasn't his place to tell her how to run her bar.

He had just started to look away when the footage they showed was of the highway exit to Hardin Road, the camera then cutting to Charlie, with Kim and Frank standing there, doing nothing.

Charlie remembered the news van, but hadn't even noticed the cameras at the time, with all the commotion going on.

He shifted in his seat, glancing around the bar to see if anyone else was watching, or would realize it was him up there on the screen. He certainly hoped Lindsey wouldn't see it for no other reason than he wasn't in the mood for explaining what had gone down.

It was still hard for him to swallow the way it had all gone down. He could see it happening to a rookie, perhaps... a deputy marshal without the years Charlie had under his belt. Or maybe a local cop.

But Charlie?

He lost a fugitive. And if she was dead, Charlie knew her blood would be on his hands.

But he was also aware enough to know he couldn't let it eat at him. He couldn't dwell on it.

He wouldn't.

The news had covered another couple of stories by the time Lindsey was back behind the bar. In fact, it had gone to a commercial, and Charlie couldn't figure out why there were people dancing on the screen, until he realized it was another one of those pharmaceutical ads making it look like taking pills for some kind of disease was fun.

Lindsey stood in front of Charlie, and he turned from the TV, a look on his face like his mind had gone somewhere else.

"Hey," she said, leaning across from him with her elbows on the bar. She reached for Charlie's hand and gave it a squeeze.

Hers was warm and wet.

"How's everything?" he said, smiling. "You good?"

Lindsey leaned closer. At first, he thought she was about to give him a kiss. But the smile eased from her face as she reached out and touched the bruise above his eye.

Charlie winced and leaned against the back of the stool, away from Lindsey's reach. "Hey, take it easy," he said, and felt the painful lump himself.

Lindsey said, "What happened?"

He thought about it. "Long morning."

"You didn't get in a fight, did you?"

"Work stuff," he said.

Lindsey straightened up, arms folded, eyes slightly narrowed, like she knew he wasn't going to be straight with her.

He never wanted to go into details with her about his work anyway, the way he always had with Jennie. Of course, that turned out to be a mistake, turning Jennie into a woman too scared to go to sleep until Charlie was home safe next to her, to where it eventually got to a point she could no longer handle living with a deputy U.S. marshal.

Lindsey turned and pushed open the swinging door to the kitchen. "I made a stew," she said, her voice trailing off with the door swinging closed behind her.

Charlie looked through the small round window on the door, and could see the back of her head until she was out of sight.

He looked behind him at the door to the outside, expecting Stan to show up at any minute. He then turned back when Lindsey came out of the kitchen.

She had a bowl between both hands, placing it down in front of Charlie. "Brunswick stew. Made it this morning." She reached under the bar and came up with a napkin and a spoon she tucked under the side of the bowl.

Charlie didn't say much of anything or even reach for the spoon.

The smile dropped from Lindsey's face. "I thought you liked my Brunswick stew?"

Charlie looked up at her, nodding. "I do. It's just..." He leaned forward and took a deep smell, savoring the stew's hearty aroma. It made his mouth water. "It smells delicious," he said. "But I'm, uh, I'm meeting a friend. Stan Cooper. You know Stan, right?"

"The FBI agent? Uh-huh." She appeared to be somewhat offended Charlie didn't touch the stew right away.

He looked at the dining area, where the two people back there were practically on top of each other, hadn't even touched their food. Charlie kept his voice low. "Can't you tell them to go get a room?"

Lindsey grinned, looking over in their direction. "No harm done," she said. "It's not like there's anyone else over there."

"Well, I was thinking Stan and I'd be able to have ourselves some privacy. Eat some lunch." He smiled. "I'd, of course, recommend he eat the stew."

Lindsey just rolled her eyes, had a look like she felt foolish for being excited about her soup. She reached for Charlie's bowl and took it back into the kitchen.

Charlie raised his voice as the door swung closed behind her. "Keep it on the heat; he should be here any minute."

He actually felt bad he didn't at least taste it.

There was a time, when Charlie had first started going to the Coyote Grille, when all they had was burgers, dogs, pickled eggs, and Slim Jims. Didn't even have a way to make french fries or anything. But that was before Lindsey took over the place and started serving up more food.

Charlie looked straight ahead at the bottles of liquor on the shelves behind the bar. It crossed his mind to have a drink, take the edge off. But he knew Stan wasn't the type to drink during working hours, and would likely frown upon it if he'd walked in right when Charlie was throwing back a shot of Jack.

Lindsey stepped out from the kitchen, this time empty-handed. She gave Charlie a nice smile but went right past him, heading for the man down the other end of the bar. Grabbing the man's empty mug, she filled it from the tap almost in front of Charlie without saying a word to him, then brought it back to the other end of the bar.

She stayed there talking to the man for a little while, her foot rested on top of the stainless cooler tucked under the bar.

Charlie wondered sometimes if she did it on purpose, knowing how he might get, maybe hoping he'd get jealous. But it wasn't like he'd ever acted like some crazy fool or came across that way. Not much bothered him, and understood Lindsey talking to her patrons was part of the job.

But it didn't mean he didn't watch out for her, even though he knew if any woman could take care of herself, it was Lindsey.

He sat there, watching her, thinking about how attractive she was. She was in her mid-forties, but it was hard to tell. Most people would guess she was thirtysomething.

Truth is, there was only one or two times Charlie couldn't stop himself from getting involved in her business. He thought about the time it was late, almost closing, and a patron who'd hung around for one too many drinks had happened to cross the line.

At least that's the way Charlie saw it.

For one reason or another, he had a hard time letting things go that night. So he took it upon himself to teach the man a lesson.

The lesson didn't last more than a handful of seconds.

He went ahead and helped the man off the floor, gave him a napkin to wipe the blood from his mouth, and helped him out the door. Charlie even told the man he'd pay his tab, as he did, but then suggested maybe it'd be best he didn't come back to the Coyote Grille.

As far as Charlie knew, he never did.

Lindsey went back over to where Charlie was seated. "How come you won't ever tell me about your work?"

He once again touched the bruise up over his eye. The skin on his face still burned and his jaw hurt. Both from the airbag, he assumed. "It's nothing I really want to talk about right now. I screwed up. Maybe worse than I ever had. You don't need to know much more than that."

Lindsey just stared at him, then brushed a strand of hair from her face. "I'm sorry, I was just asking, making sure you're all right."

"I appreciate that," Charlie said, then turned and looked behind him at the door when he heard it open. But it wasn't Stan.

An older gentleman he'd seen there once or twice before walked in and gave Charlie a nod. The man continued past him to the far end of the bar and sat next to the other man who was already seated.

Lindsey said, "Be right back," then grabbed an empty mug and filled it with Miller Lite from the tap, carrying it to the old man.

Charlie was starting to wonder about Stan, then pulled his phone from his pocket when it started to buzz.

It was Stan calling, and Charlie answered right away. "Not like you to be late for lunch."

Stan said, "Did you talk to Frank?"

Charlie could hear it in his voice, something was wrong. "No. Should I have?"

Stan was quiet for a moment on the other end.

He said, "I'm heading back east."

"East? To Charlotte?"

"Not exactly." He paused again. "Kings Mountain. A body was just pulled from Moss Lake. A couple of kayakers out there ran into it."

Charlie wondered who would go kayaking, as cold as it was outside. "Kings Mountain side?"

Stan said, "About a mile north of Oak Grove Road. I'll have more information once I get there. I'm still forty minutes away."

Charlie said, "This have anything to do with me?"

"It may," Stan said. "Nothing's confirmed yet, but I'll tell you what I know. Apparently, a pastor from a small church over there picked up a wallet on the side of the road, not far from where the body was discovered. The identification inside said it belongs to Vincent Avella."

"*Avella?*" Charlie knew the name right away.

"It appears the wallet belongs to the victim. We haven't confirmed yet, but—"

"Hang on one second." Charlie stood from the stool, holding the phone by his side and waved for Lindsey. She stepped over to him, and he rested one arm on the bar, leaning closer to her, keeping his voice low. "I'll have to catch up with you a little later. Something's come up." He straightened up off the bar, then headed for the door.

"Are you coming back?" she said.

Charlie had the door open and nodded Lindsey's way as he raised the phone to his ear. He stepped outside and closed the door behind him. "Sorry about that, Stan." He cleared his throat, and said, "I'm going to assume you already know one of the men from this morning? One of them... His name was Henry Avella?"

"Yes," Stan said. "It appears the victim at the lake is his brother."

Charlie's mind raced, as did his heart, standing on the top step on the deck.

The Coyote Grille was on the second level of a commercial building, with a couple of offices and retail establishments below, on the ground level. The deck outside the bar overlooking the parking lot had tables on it during the warmer months.

Charlie hurried down the steps, the air feeling cold, compared to when he first got there. He said to Stan, "Can you give me specifics on the location?"

Stan said, "I don't have a precise location yet, other than it's somewhere off New Camp Creek Church Road. There's a picnic area, stone's throw from the water. But I don't think it makes any sense, if you're planning to drive out here. By the time you're—"

"I'd just like to know if it's one of the men from this morning," Charlie said.

"Did you not hear the part about the man being dead?" Stan said.

Charlie appreciated Stan's dry wit, especially coming from someone as reserved and buttoned-up as Stan. He said, "I'm just saying, I got a look at the one who grabbed Mrs. Sanborn. Don't you want me to come out, see if it's him?"

"It was my understanding, from the report, the men were all wearing ski masks, covering their faces. Is that not the case?"

"I got a look at one of them, apparently couldn't wait another minute to take it off," Charlie said.

"That's interesting," Stan said. "I guess it wouldn't be a bad idea, then. It's up to you, if you want to come out. I clearly haven't been given all the details."

Charlie pulled a set of keys from his pocket, the blue tag with the license plate number for the Town Car written on the tag, in pencil. "I thought that was the reason for our getting together, no?"

He unlocked the driver-side door and right away didn't like the smell inside when he slid in behind the wheel, almost sour, like old leather seats or an old pair of shoes. The car wasn't new, but it wasn't that old either. Maybe it just needed a good cleaning, although he'd hoped the vehicle was temporary. Going from a tank, like the Suburban he'd been driving, to what he felt was an old lady's car would be a tough adjustment.

But he'd trashed enough vehicles belonging to the U.S. government, whether his fault or not, he had a feeling the days of him being able to choose whatever he wanted to drive would eventually come to an end.

Stan said, "How long's it going to take you to get out here? Hour and a half, I'd bet. Might be too late if—"

"I can be there in an hour," Charlie said, turning the key in the ignition. "Just do me a favor: call me if you end up leaving before I get there."

Chapter 8

CHARLIE WAS ALREADY ON I-40 and halfway to Kings Mountain by the time he finally picked up the phone to call Frank. This was after three or four texts and two phone calls Charlie had received from him, but ignored.

Frank answered on the first ring. "Where've you been?"

The truth was, Charlie didn't answer Frank's calls because he knew he should wait until he was close enough to Moss Lake. And by that point, even if Frank told him he didn't want him going out there, he'd be close enough it would make little sense to turn around.

"Sorry, Frank," Charlie said. "My phone must've been on silent. I didn't even know you called until now."

"Why do you continue to treat me like I'm a fool?" Frank said.

Charlie cleared his throat, glancing in the rearview at a car that'd been behind him since he left Coyote Grille, or soon after. But the car had been far enough back he didn't think much of it. "Well, I'm calling you now."

There was a long pause, then Frank said, "You talk to Stan?"

"Yeah, I'm on my way to meet him at Moss Lake."

"Moss Lake? You're driving all the way out there, without checking in with me first? What about Kim? Did you talk to her?"

"Not yet," Charlie said. "But she left a message. I thought I'd call you first, since you're the boss."

The line went quiet, but Charlie could hear Frank's breathing.

"Why do I get the feeling you're keeping something from me?" Frank said.

"I don't know. But I assure you, that's not the case," Charlie said. "I'm just driving. Made a few calls on the way."

"Well, if you'd stop ignoring us, you'd know Kim had apparently dug into something. You'd think she'd be the one taking a leisurely ride out to the lake, considering it's supposed to be her day off."

"You make it sound like I'm going on some kind of fishing trip."

Frank paused on the other end. "I can think of better things for you to be doing than being in your car. I see no need for you to be out there."

"I'd like to talk to Stan, face-to-face," Charlie said. "You know how it is with him. I don't get right in there, he either won't call me back, or we'll never get what we need." Charlie again glanced at the car in the rearview. "So, you gonna tell me what Kim came up with?"

"Well, like I told you already, our priority right now needs to be tracking down Scott Sanborn. Apparently Deputy Riggins was the only one who listened."

"She find him?"

"She's got a lead. I'd like you to check with her."

"I thought the priority was finding Claudia Sanborn, no?"

"Are you telling me that's what you're doing?" Frank said.

"If it's the same man I saw this morning, it's certainly something we should be taking seriously."

Frank said. "I just feel we've got a better shot at finding the husband. Maybe I'm wrong, but if we can track him down and get us some answers..."

"Why do you think I'm driving out to the lake? You don't think it's going to provide us with some answers? Especially if it turns out this man was whacked by one of his own men, by chance."

"Why would you suspect that?" Frank said.

"I already told you, the idiot ripped his mask off for some reason at the scene. And if whoever else was there thinks I got a look at him..."

Frank said, "So you think whoever he was working with might've killed him?"

"I wouldn't be surprised," Charlie said.

Frank paused on the other end. "I guess it makes sense. But no need to jump to conclusions yet. Not until we hear more."

"Well, again, that's why I thought it made sense I head out to the lake. I'm not going to sit around waiting for a report from the bureau, set us back three weeks."

Frank didn't respond.

Charlie said, "So what about Kim? What are these so-called leads?"

"Well, there's nothing confirmed yet, but she spoke to a friend in DC, and from what she was told, there's a good chance Scott Sanborn may've been having an affair with a woman he may still be hanging around with."

"Are you kidding?" Charlie said. "You got a name?"

"Yeah, uh, hang on." The phone sounded muffled for a moment. "The name's Kristen Salvatore."

"Salvatore? What else do we know?"

"Why don't you talk to Kim yourself," Frank said. "I don't have time to play operator. She'll give you the details. She wanted to go talk to her—the alleged girlfriend—but I told her to wait."

"For what?"

"I just, well... I don't trust anything about this right now. I feel we need to be extra vigilante, so I'd prefer the two of you stick together. I know you like to go off on your own, as you're doing right now, but—"

"When have you ever known me not to be vigilante?"

Frank huffed out a laugh. "Do I really need to answer that? Listen, Charlie. There are some things going on with this case that don't add up. It's more than just some white-collar fraud scheme."

"I realize that," Charlie said. "I assume it's got something to do with those automatics in the back of the van?"

"Potentially. But I don't have anything yet. Serial numbers had all been removed, so nothing can be traced. Hopefully forensics can get us something, but I'm not sure we can count on it any time soon."

By the time Charlie hung up with Frank and turned the wheel for exit 86, North Carolina 226, headed toward Shelby, the same vehicle was still following. It had gotten close enough now he could make out it was a black sedan, but couldn't quite get the make of it.

He tried to tell himself it was nothing, but kept his eyes in the rearview without taking them completely off the road ahead. But after he drove another mile, the vehicle had fallen far enough back Charlie started to assume he was just being paranoid, deciding he had nothing to worry about.

He picked up his phone and dialed Kim, placing the phone on speaker and resting it on his thigh.

Kim answered, "Charlie? Where are you? I've been calling you."

"Sorry," he said. "On my way to Moss Lake, to meet Stan. I assume you heard, there's a dead guy out there might've been one of the men at the scene this morning?"

"Only know what Frank knows, which isn't much," Kim said. "Did he tell you what I found?"

"He told me Mr. Sanborn was having an affair?"

"It looks that way. I just pulled into the parking lot of the girlfriend's apartment building."

"You're there now? I thought Frank wanted you to wait."

"I am waiting. I haven't gotten out of the car yet. But I can see right in her window, up on the second floor. It looks like there's someone home, and maybe a second person."

"What if it's Sanborn?" Charlie said. "Maybe you should call Frank, have him come out. I'm too far away, or—"

"If I get into any kind of trouble, I will. But, like I said, I'm just watching. But I can't imagine he'd be foolish, come around here."

Charlie saw brake lights up ahead and wondered why what little traffic there was on the highway appeared to be slowing down. It took him a moment to realize—at least he was *fairly* certain—there was some kind of speed trap up ahead.

"Hey, let me call you back," he said. "Just do me a favor and don't do anything I wouldn't do."

"That's not leaving me a lot of options," she said.

Charlie looked at his phone, but Kim had already hung up. He'd eased off the gas and dropped the Town Car down to around sixty-five. There was no time for him to have to deal with a local cop, having to explain who he was, or why he was speeding. He'd run into enough local cops over the years to know there were plenty out there who needed to be convinced the badge belonged to a real deputy U.S. marshal.

Charlie, doing the speed limit now, looked up in the mirror and saw the dark sedan was close to him. Charlie tapped his brakes to see if the car would back off.

But it didn't. The vehicle appeared to be speeding up. And before Charlie was able to do anything, his head slammed forward and whipped back, the car behind him crashing into the rear of the Town Car.

It was the last thing Charlie had expected, and his first reaction was to slam his foot on the pedal and get away from whoever it was. But the car had already pulled up to his left and smashed into the Town Car's driver's side. It knocked Charlie off the road, and he skidded into the grass on the other side of the breakdown lane.

Gripping the wheel with both hands, Charlie tried to control the Town Car bouncing up and down on the uneven ground. He yanked the wheel hard left and drove back onto the pavement. At that point he was riding alongside the other vehicle, but the windows were tinted dark enough he couldn't get a look at anyone inside.

The two cars were speeding now, side by side, racing along the highway.

Charlie had his Glock in his hand and raised it, ready to fire at the other vehicle. But before he had a chance, shots were fired at him. Bullets hit the side of his car and shattered the rear passenger window.

Slamming on his brakes, Charlie skidded and cut the wheel so hard the Town Car went up on two wheels. He had to drop his Glock to maintain control, but he spun completely around before he came to a screeching halt.

The oncoming traffic came to a sudden stop, with tires squealing and horns blasting all around him.

Charlie slammed his foot on the pedal and spun the car around in the right direction and immediately saw the vehicle, blue lights flashing and coming toward him.

It appeared to be a local cop, clearly driving the wrong way.

What the hell is he doing? Charlie thought. He looked around for the vehicle that had crashed into him, but it had already taken off. It was speeding south, heading straight for the oncoming police car.

Charlie hit the gas and raced after the sedan, already far behind. But as he got close enough, he saw it was an older Chrysler 300, the front end and sides smashed.

It wasn't good, the way the two vehicles were driving straight for each other.

Charlie was too far behind, and could only watch as the cop appeared to change course at the last second.

The cop took a sharp turn out of the way, drove off the highway at high speed, and smashed head-on into the concrete construction barrier at the edge of the road.

The car crashed so hard the tail-end of the police vehicle lifted a good ten feet off the ground, crashing down with a loud thud, dust and dirt flying up around it.

The dark Chrysler kept going, swerving in and out of traffic.

Charlie had to make a choice, knowing the cop was likely in rough shape, assuming the officer was even still alive.

Charlie raced off the highway and stopped behind the officer's car. He had to use his shoulder to get his own door open, the way it'd been crashed into, then rushed for the driver's side of the cop's car, where a deputy with the Rutherford County Sheriff's Office turned to him with an empty stare, clearly dazed and bloodied.

Charlie reached in and moved the deflated airbag out of the man's way. "You all right?" he said.

The deputy didn't answer.

Charlie removed his own badge from his belt and held it up near the man's bloodied face, just so the man could see it. "Deputy Charlie Harlow, U.S. Marshals Service." He grabbed his phone and dialed for help, raising it to his ear. He rested his free hand on the deputy's shoulder. "Hang in there, kid. You're gonna be fine."

Chapter 9

By the time Charlie made it out to Moss Lake, the sun had already gone down, the temperature dropping another ten degrees.

FBI Agent Stan Cooper was in the parking lot with three Kings Mountain police officers, plus two others—a man and a woman—dressed in plain clothes. There were no other vehicles beside those belonging to law enforcement.

Stan looked at Charlie as he stepped out of the Town Car, but shifted his gaze to the damage on the driver's side. He said to Charlie, "You all right?"

"I think so."

"How about the deputy? Heard he's just a kid."

Charlie eyed the other law enforcement officials looking their way, then turned back to Stan. "He'll be all right. Hard way to learn a lesson." Charlie touched his own forehead with his finger. "Got a good crack right here, likely gonna be a reminder not to try and be the hero. Still don't know why he thought playing chicken on the highway, no matter what was going on, would make any sense."

"Sounds like something you would do," Stan said, his expression serious."

Charlie didn't respond, looking in the direction of the lake where two forensics technicians wearing light-blue protective coveralls with masks and gloves trudged along a path worn through tall, yellowed grass. He followed them with his gaze as they stepped into the parking lot and continued to a van, until they stood outside the opened sliding door on the side and removed their masks and gloves.

"As I told you on the call," Stan said, "we're still waiting for official confirmation on the victim's identity."

"I wish I'd gotten here sooner," Charlie said.

"Well, we should know soon enough. It appears he's who we think he is."

"Vincent Avella?" Charlie said.

"Based on the ID in that wallet, it is. Face wasn't exactly what it looked like in the photo, banged up a bit. But I'll be surprised if it turns out to be someone else." Stan looked down, pulling at his chin. "If it *is* him, and he's who was at the scene this morning..."

"Raises a lot of questions," Charlie said, as if completing Stan's thought.

Stan said, "Then, here you are, on your way out here and somebody, somehow, tracks you down. As if trying to stop you."

"Doesn't make a whole lot of sense," Charlie said. "They wanted me dead, whoever it was. Hard for me to say for sure, but seemed to be the same weapon the men were firing, over on Hardin Road."

Stan paused. "I'd say you might want to be careful."

"You sound like Frank," Charlie said.

"You don't agree?"

"Of course I do. But I'm not going to go running scared. Somebody's trying to send me a message."

"You really think that's all it is? Trying to send a message?" Stan had his eyebrows raised, watching Charlie.

Charlie said, "I told you. I don't know what to think. We're still all wondering how those men ended up behind me this morning in the first place. Starting to make me think this is more about me than anything else."

Stan was quiet, watching Charlie. "Who was wondering?"

"Me and Kim. Frank, too, I suppose. It's just... the way it happened, kind of feels like there's a possibility someone was watching one of us—me or Kim—before we got to that hotel." Charlie looked at his watch and removed his hat, running his hand through his hair, then neatly pushing his bangs to the side, off his forehead. "I'm having a hard time believing it's still the same day. Been a twelve-hour stretch, almost to the minute, and I've been shot at on both ends of it."

Stan appeared to understand where Charlie was coming from. He opened his mouth, like he was about to say something, but didn't.

Charlie said, "So what about Denny Caprio? What else can you tell me about him?"

Stan cleared his throat and took a moment to answer. "We don't know if he's got anything to do with this or not."

Charlie said, "But from what I understand, he's your best lead. Is that right?"

Stan paused. "He may be our only lead."

"So you can't tell me anything else about him? Or where he might be?"

Stan held his gaze on Charlie. "We don't have enough information to be able to turn any of this over to the Marshals Service, if that's what you're asking?"

Charlie laughed, shaking his head. As long as he'd known Stan, it had never been easy getting Stan to let go of anything he felt the bureau could handle themselves. Both the FBI and the Marshals Service stood on equal footing, both law entities of the U.S. government, serving similar, but different, purposes.

All Charlie wanted to do was capture the bad guys, no matter what it took or what rules he might have to break. Stan, on the other hand, did everything by the book. If he didn't feel it was time for the U.S. Marshals Service to step in, then he made Charlie work a little harder to get what he wanted.

"As far as I understand," Charlie said, "Denny Caprio has been running these business schemes for a long time, and making it almost impossible for the FBI or anyone else to pin any of it on him. Is that right?"

"We feel he uses others, such as the Sanborns. And for one reason or another—money, I'd guess—nobody's ever talked. It doesn't matter; they end up behind bars themselves, or what kind of legal trouble they face. Denny Caprio's name has never once been mentioned."

"How many people are we talking about?" Charlie said.

"Who've been charged with crimes we believe Caprio is behind?" He appeared to have to think about it. "At least eight, in the past five years."

"Are you serious?"

Stan had a look on his face that suggested embarrassment. "And now that we've finally gotten close enough to potentially having a stronger case, he's disappeared without a trace."

"Then, can you explain to me why you won't let us in?"

Stan said, "The Marshals Service? You know how these things work, Charlie."

"I know how *you* work. It's not always the FBI holding back. All you have to do is say the word, unleash the dogs."

Stan nodded, like he understood, looking off in the distance at the lake, beyond the tall grass between the asphalt where they stood, and the water glistening under the moonlight on the other side. He turned to Charlie. "You get a good look at the vehicle?"

"It was a Chrysler 300. Dark blue. Tinted windows. Wish I got a better look at the man shooting at me."

"So there were two of them?"

"As far as I could tell," Charlie said. "The window only went halfway down, and by the time I realized what was going on, I was more focused on trying to stay alive."

Stan was quiet for a moment, looking at Charlie like he had something to say but took his time, at first. "I imagine you have plenty going on. I know how busy you all are over there. But I assume there's little doubt in your head, what just happened is directly tied to this morning, and the death of Vincent Avella?"

"There's a long line of people out there who'd love to put a bullet in my head." Charlie removed his cap, and scratched his head, looking around the parking lot where the others had begun to disperse. "I was thinking there's likely a good chance someone's afraid either Claudia Sanborn told me something she shouldn't have on the ride from her motel, or there's concern I saw something else this morning that'd lead us closer to whoever's behind it."

"And the man you saw does turn out to match the identity of the victim, then it could be they were just covering both ends," Stan said.

"Right now," Charlie said, "that seems to make the most sense."

A white-haired deputy Charlie recognized and thought may have, at one time, been a sheriff in another county, yelled over. He said, "Stan, let's touch base in the morning so we know how you plan to handle this, and if there's anything you'll want us to do."

Stan gave the officer a thumbs-up.

Charlie said, "You have no idea where he is?"

"Who?"

"Caprio."

Stan said, "That's why I'd said, at least until now, there'd been some hesitation to share the case with the Marshals Service. We just haven't had enough evidence or, frankly, any answers at all." Stan rubbed the back of his neck, turning his head as if trying to unravel a knot. "I don't need to tell you how these things work. But I think, at this point, we can consider Caprio a suspect, especially considering what just happened to you. I don't think anyone needs to wait around for us to fill out the paperwork, tell you what to do."

"Does that mean I have your blessing to pursue him?"

Stan let out a gasp and made a face, almost like he was going to roll his eyes. "Has there ever been a time you've waited for someone to give you their blessing before you go after someone?"

Charlie grinned. "I guess the thing I'd like to be sure of... I haven't come across any kind of evidence Caprio's some kind of killer. That's the only thing making me somewhat hesitant."

"Like I said, we've had a real hard time pulling it all together. Caprio is smart. Covers his tracks and has other people do his dirty work. But out of those I'd said we felt worked under him, or for him, but were never willing to admit to anything or give up his name, there are also victims related to, or connected to, those we were able to prosecute, who have either entirely disappeared or, in some cases, were met with suspicious deaths. Such as this one tonight."

Charlie said, "So, loosely connected to Caprio, but enough you feel he's had his hand in most of them?"

"This isn't just some white-collar criminal looking to pad his pockets with more cash," Stan said. "We just haven't been able to pin a single thing on him. Almost had him on tax evasion at one time, but even then, somehow, the son of a bitch got off. That was the closest we'd ever come to bringing him in. And probably the last time we knew where he was."

"So, what are the chances he's even around here?" Charlie said. "He could be anywhere at this point, no? Why would he hide out in North Carolina?"

"I can't answer that," he said. "But, even if he is the one behind everything that happened here today, I can't imagine he's anywhere in the area unless he's looking for something."

"Something, or some*one*," Charlie said.

Chapter 10

IT WAS CLOSE TO ten by the time Charlie drove into the parking lot of the apartment where Scott Sanborn's alleged girlfriend, Kristen Salvatore, was apparently living. Kim had waited the entire time for Charlie, as she'd promised she would, and put down her window when Charlie approached. "Nobody's left the building," she said.

Charlie turned to look over the three-story building. "How many units?"

"Eight. She's on the second floor." She pushed open the door and stepped out. "I should've just gone in there. If she was alone, I would have."

"Does Frank know you've been out here the whole time?"

"I told him I was leaving," Kim said. "He wanted more information before we went knocking on her door."

"He's getting a little too careful. Must be an age thing," Charlie said.

The two made their way to the building, and Kim said, "After what happened to you earlier, I don't think he wants either one of us doing anything alone from here on out."

Charlie showed a small grin, but didn't respond.

Kim raised her phone and showed Charlie the screen. "This is Kristen Salvatore."

Charlie was surprised at the woman he was looking at on Kim's phone. Dark hair, pretty, and very young. "She looks like a kid," he said. "And they're sure she's Sanborn's mistress?"

"Intelligence didn't have the word mistress. But Sanborn clearly had some kind of relationship with her. Whether or not it was ongoing or romantic, we're going to have to find out for ourselves."

The entrance to the building was locked, with a keypad to the left and a unit number next to each of the eight buttons. Kim reached past Charlie and pushed the button for unit 201.

They waited, both looking in through the glass door toward a small lobby, with an elevator door straight ahead and a set of stairs to the right. There was a single tall plant in the corner.

Charlie said, "Stan seems pretty certain Denny Caprio is behind all of this. We'll talk to Frank in the morning, see what he wants to do. The priority, of course, is making sure Claudia Sanborn is found, hopefully alive. So, I don't know if it matters whether it's the husband or Caprio, or someone who will lead us to either."

"The lights were still on up there," Kim said. "I don't think she's asleep."

"Did you see any movement?" Charlie said, turning to look around the parking lot. There were only a dozen or so spaces, all but two of them occupied.

"Not since I saw two people in the window when I first arrived. The television's been on." She reached for the button of unit 201 and pressed it again.

Charlie was studying the door now, wondering if it would be easy enough to break it open without causing too much damage. They had no warrant, and cracking open a door to talk to a woman they weren't sure had any continued involvement with Scott Sanborn, or where he might be, could be considered crossing the line. Not to Charlie, of course. But, legally, he knew it wasn't something Kim was going to go for.

But before he had to act, a woman's voice came over the speaker. "Who is it?"

Kim said, "Is this Kristen Salvatore?"

"Who's this?"

"My name is Deputy Kim Riggins, with the United States Marshals Service. I'm here with another deputy, and we'd like to ask you some questions."

There was silence.

"Are you there?" Kim said, leaning closer to the speaker. She gave Charlie a quick glance.

But the voice came back on. "What is this about?"

"If you'd let us in, we'll explain," Kim said.

Charlie was back to looking at the glass door, feeling around the lock in case the woman refused to let them in, which he was beginning to think might be the case.

There was more silence, until a moment went by and the woman said, "What if I can't talk right now?"

"It would be best for all of us if you would," Kim said.

"Am I in some kind of trouble?"

Charlie stepped closer to the speaker. "Ms. Salvatore, if you'd please just let us come up. We won't take much of your time. We need to ask you some questions about Scott Sanborn. If there's a chance, we believe, he's in there with you right now, we'll find our way into your apartment one way or the other, whether you let us in or not."

Kim looked at him and rolled her eyes.

There was a click on the steel-framed door and a loud buzz that came from it. Charlie reached for the handle and opened the door, holding it open for Kim.

She went in ahead of him. "I didn't think we should mention his name just yet." It was as if Kim didn't appreciate Charlie's approach, even though it worked.

"What good would it do keeping her in the dark?" he said.

The two turned up the stairs and onto the second floor. There were three doors, the first one on the left with the number 201 opened just as they stepped in front of it.

The woman from the photo on Kim's phone stood looking out at them, holding the door in a way, she was at first hesitant to let them in.

Kim showed her badge. "Kristen Salvatore?"

Salvatore looked from Charlie to Kim. "I don't know anything."

Charlie knew the fact she was offering up some kind of defense before she needed to was a definite red flag. "We haven't even asked you a question," he said, trying to look past her into the apartment. "Are you here alone?"

Kristen Salvatore peered back into her apartment before she shook her head. "No."

"Can you ask whoever it is you're with to come out here?"

"He's my, um…" She lowered her voice, as if she was afraid to say it. "He's my boyfriend," then turned from the door. "Jay? The, uh…" She wrinkled her nose and looked Charlie over. "Did you say you're the police?"

"U.S. Marshals Service."

She repeated herself again, yelling into her apartment. "Jay? Can you come out here?"

A male turned the corner from inside, as if he'd been right there waiting, listening, and walked up behind Kristen.

The two looked like a couple of kids, the young man shirtless, his body more like a boy's than a man's, with his thin frame, muscles packed tight on his bones.

Charlie couldn't help but feel a little bit old.

Kim showed her badge and asked the kid his name.

"Jay. Jason."

"Jason what?"

"Dexter."

Jason Dexter was clearly nervous, as most people are when law enforcement shows up at the door. But Charlie had already gotten a whiff of marijuana coming from inside the apartment, and said to the kid, "We're not here for your weed." He cracked a slight grin, but the kid's nerves didn't appear to settle.

Kim said, "Do you mind if we come inside?"

Kristen Salvatore seemed to hesitate at first, giving her boyfriend a quick look of approval he didn't seem to want to give her.

"You're not in any kind of trouble," Charlie said. "At least I don't think you are. We need you to answer some questions."

Kristen swallowed hard, then finally opened the door all the way and backed away from it. "I'm telling you the truth. I don't know anything."

Jay Dexter said, "We were just trying to relax a little. I had a long day at work, that's all."

Charlie and Kim stepped inside, and Charlie said to the boyfriend, "That stuff'll make you paranoid, but I told you that's not why we're here." He looked over the half-naked boy. "Can you please go put a shirt on?"

Jay acted as if he'd snapped out of a trance and hurried ahead of them down the hall, turning into a room where the light went on and glowed into the hallway. He came right back out, pulling a T-shirt down over his head.

The T-shirt had Johnny Cash on the front.

"You like Johnny Cash?" Charlie said, looking at the shirt.

"Yeah, I guess so."

Charlie had a feeling the kid barely knew who Johnny Cash was, probably had never even listened to him, the way he'd answered.

Kristen continued ahead of them and into where it opened to the rest of the apartment, with a tiny kitchen area and a TV on in the adjacent room. There were two closed doors on either side.

Charlie said, "What's behind those two doors?"

There was also a sliding glass door before a balcony, curtains pushed open.

Kristen looked at Charlie like she didn't understand the question. "What's behind the doors?" She went over and opened one of the two, nothing but darkness behind it. "It's just a bedroom." She reached inside and flicked on the light so Charlie could get a look. "I use it as an office."

Other than a small desk with a laptop computer on top, there was nothing else in there. When Charlie looked away, she turned off the light and closed the door.

Kim had already opened the other door. "Bathroom," she said, glancing over at Charlie.

"I promise you, he's not here," Kristen said.

Her boyfriend said, "Who's not here?" He appeared as confused as anyone, his mouth hanging open like a dope.

"Scott," Kristen said, turning to her boyfriend.

Jay frowned. "What the hell would he be doing here?"

Kim said to him, "You know Mr. Sanborn?"

"Yeah, I know who he is. He knows better than show his face around here. I can promise you that."

The kid suddenly showed some bravado.

Kim looked from Kristen to Jay and shifted her gaze to the couch on one side of the room, right after the door to the bedroom. The TV was on the wall on the other side, across the narrow room. "Why don't the two of you sit down."

Jason sat right away, but Kristen straightened out the mess on the coffee table where they had a couple of glasses with nothing in them and an empty serving dish with crumbs on it, but nothing else. She carried them into the kitchen, put it all in the sink, then asked Kim and Charlie if she could get them anything. She didn't seem to have any of the nervousness Jason did.

Charlie and Kim both declined, with Charlie taking a seat on a wooden chair he dragged from the kitchen table, turning it backward. He had his arms folded and resting on top of the chair's backrest. "So, where should we begin?"

Kim leaned against the counter dividing the kitchen and the room they were in. "Is it okay if I ask you first..." Her gaze went to Jason, then back to Kristen. "What was your relationship with Scott Sanborn?"

Kristen glanced at the kid again, as if looking for approval and likely hesitant to go into details about whatever there was between Kristen and Scott Sanborn. "We were friends," she said, her swallow so deep it was impossible for her to hide.

"If you'd prefer we discuss this in private," Kim said, "perhaps your friend can go wait outside?"

Kristen swallowed again. "He knows all about it," she said. "We messed around a few times. That's all."

"Messed around?" Charlie said. "So, you had a romantic relationship with Scott Sanborn?"

She paused, as if thinking about it. "It was nothing."

Jason was leaning forward on the front edge of the couch cushion, elbows on his knees.

Charlie said, "But this wasn't long ago. Is that correct?"

"It's been a few months." She gave Jason a look, but he had his eyes on his own hands. "Jay and I had broken up. But it was a mistake, the whole thing..."

"What about you?" Charlie said, eyes on Jason. "You knew him?"

"He was a customer at the restaurant where we work."

"That's what you do?" Charlie said. "You both work in a restaurant?"

The two nodded.

Charlie gave Kim a quick glance, then said to Kristen, "What do you do there?"

"I tend bar and wait tables. Scott used to come in all the time with his wife until I guess something happened between them. He started coming in alone, and—"

"How old are you?" Kim said.

"Twenty-four."

Kim's eyebrows raised. "Are you aware Mr. Sanborn is twenty years older than you?"

"I'm not stupid," Kristen snapped, as if being defensive about her math knowledge."

"He's a piece of shit," Jason said, his glare on Kristen now.

She looked at him but didn't say anything or disagree.

"So, you had a romantic relationship with him," Charlie said. "How long did this go on?"

"I don't know," she said. "A couple of months?"

"Then what happened?" Charlie said. "One of you break it off?"

She swallowed hard again and coughed, putting her closed fist to her lips to cover her mouth. She waited, like she wasn't sure how to answer.

Jason was watching her.

Kristen said, "I don't know what happened. After he was arrested... I haven't heard from him again."

"Not once?" Kim said, her gaze fixed on Kristen. "I need you to tell me the truth. Have you heard from him since he was arrested?"

Kristen looked to her right at Jason, then at Charlie and Kim. "He called me. Two days ago."

Jason put his face in his hands, shaking his head. "You said you were done with him!" He stood, fists clenched, and hovered over Kristen. "You promised me it was over!"

Charlie didn't like it, seeing the way the kid was clearly upset and a bit angry. "All right, let's all take it easy." He took Jason by the arm and eased him back onto the couch.

"He wanted to see me," Kristen said. "I told him no. I knew it wasn't right, but…"

"What else did he say?" Kim said. "Did he tell you where he was?"

Kristen's eyes were red, but it was hard to tell if it was from the tears or the weed they'd obviously been smoking. "He just said he was going away for a while." She paused, sniffled her nose, and wiped it with her hand. "He asked if I'd go with him."

"Are you fucking serious?" Jason said, his arms crossed now. "You promised me you wouldn't lie no more about him."

Charlie looked at Kim, then turned back to Kristen. "Where could he have gone? Think good and hard about it. I'd hate to see you in trouble for—"

"You told me I wasn't in trouble," Kristen said, a sense of fear in her voice. "I told you I didn't do anything wrong. I swear, I don't know where he is."

"We just need whatever you can tell us," Charlie said, his eyes on the two phones on the coffee table. "Which one of these is yours?"

"The phones?" Kristen said, reaching for the one closest to her, of course. "Why?"

"Can you show me the number, where he called from?"

Kristen's eyes were wide now, frozen, with her stare on Charlie. "Can you do that?"

"Do what?"

"Look at my cell phone? I mean, without a warrant, or…?"

Charlie took a deep breath, and a grumble or almost a growl came from somewhere inside when he exhaled. "Don't make this more difficult on yourself than it needs to be," he said.

Kim and Charlie were both standing on the other side of the coffee table, across from Kristen and Jason.

Kim said, "If you have nothing to hide, then you have nothing to worry about."

"But it's my phone. I don't want you looking at my…"

"Listen," Charlie said. "I'm sure you don't care in the least, but Mr. Sanborn's wife's life is in danger. And if we don't find him, who knows what's going to happen. You don't want to be responsible if something happens to her, do you?"

Kristen's eyebrows were raised now, gaze fixed on Charlie. "No, sir. She's a nice lady."

"All we're asking is for you to show us the number he called you from. That's all."

Kristen swallowed hard, tapped the screen of her phone and started flipping her thumb over the glass. She stopped and turned the phone to Charlie. She held it tight, and didn't appear to want to let go.

Charlie leaned in, and Kim had her phone out, taking a picture of Kristen's screen.

"Right there," Charlie said, pointing. "The call you got at two in the morning?"

Kristen turned the phone to look at it. "Yeah."

"Can I get one more look?" Charlie said.

Kristen seemed hesitant, but after a brief moment, turned it to him again.

"My eyes aren't great," he said. "I really oughta get glasses, but..." He grinned. "I'm not quite ready to admit I'm at that point in my life." He held out his hand. "You mind? I promise, I'll give it right back."

Kristen looked at Jason, who was leaning back on the couch now, barely paying attention to her, a frown on his face, child-like. She finally handed her phone to Charlie.

The first thing he did before the screen locked was tap the number she claimed came from Scott Sanborn. He put it up to his ear and listened as it rang.

Kristen jumped from the couch. "What are you doing? You can't do that!"

But Charlie moved away from her, walking out of the room and down the hall, then out the front door. He started for the stairs from her apartment, but stopped when the phone stopped ringing.

Someone had answered, but wasn't saying a word.

Charlie didn't, either, and there was nothing but silence on the line.

After a couple of moments, a man said, "Kristen?"

"This Scott?" Charlie said.

"Who the hell's this?"

Before Charlie could answer, Kristen came up behind Charlie and shoved him from behind, screaming at the phone, "Scott! Don't say anything! He's a cop! A marshal!"

Charlie turned and tried to hold her back, but she'd started to get aggressive the way she was swinging her arms, trying to get to her phone.

Kim came up behind Kristen and tried to restrain her, or at least calm her down. "I need you to calm down. I don't want to have to arrest you."

Charlie spoke into the phone, "Sanborn? You there? I need you to listen to me real good. Maybe you don't care, but your wife is in danger, and—"

"That's not my problem," Sanborn said. "Let me guess. Are you the marshal who let them take her?"

Charlie started to speak, but wasn't exactly sure what to say. What came out of Sanborn wasn't much of a surprise, but it somewhat solidified what Charlie had been thinking all along. "Mr. Sanborn, listen to me..." But he felt the silence on the other end. Looking at the phone, he saw that Sanborn had ended the call. He handed the phone to Kristen Salvatore. "Where is he?"

A tear came down her cheek. "I'm sorry. I... I don't know. That's the truth."

"He didn't tell you where he was going?" Kim said, looking straight into Kristen's eyes.

Kristen turned to look when her boyfriend walked out of the apartment, a duffel bag over his shoulder. "Jay? What are you doing?"

"I'm leaving."

He continued down the stairs.

But before he got far, Charlie said, "You know better than to drive high, right?"

Jay froze at the bottom step, turning to look up at Charlie. "I'm all right."

Charlie said, "No. You're not. I don't blame you, you don't go back in that apartment. But don't let me see you behind that wheel." Charlie took out his wallet, reached in and took out his business card. He handed it to Kristen. "You want to keep yourself out of any trouble, you call me, you hear anything from Mr. Sanborn." He turned and headed down the stairs, past Jay Dexter, and down to the parking lot. He stood by the Town Car, and leaned against it, waiting for Kim.

Chapter 11

THE COYOTE GRILLE WAS still open when Charlie showed up and took a seat at the bar. Lindsey was cleaning up, chairs all turned upside down on top of the tables in the dining room area. There was no music playing, the place almost too quiet.

He sat in the stool, straight ahead from the door, and looked to his right at a man and woman down the far end of the bar. He recognized them both—a couple of regulars who stayed late and never seemed to want to go home. The two had that worn look to them, like the cigarettes and booze hadn't been too kind to them over the years.

Neither was saying much, the man watching the TV, the woman scrolling through her phone rested flat on the bar, her other hand under her chin, holding up her head.

"I didn't know if you'd be back," Lindsey said, placing a glass down in front of Charlie. She poured him a shot of Jack Daniels, then looked him over. "How're you doing?"

Charlie took the glass but held it there without taking a drink at first. "Been a tough day," he said, and looked up at the clock on the wall behind Lindsey. "I just wanted to come by, say hey." He forced a grin. "I was going to head home in a bit. I need a good night's sleep as much as anything."

Lindsey held her gaze on him for a moment, then turned to grab the broom leaning by the register behind her. She started sweeping the floor on the other side of the bar, acting as if she didn't know what she should say, or maybe just didn't like that it sounded as if Charlie had no plans to stick around.

Charlie recognized she didn't like what he'd said, and did his best to backtrack. "Hey, you want to come back with me, you can. But I gotta get up early, that's all. And I gotta sleep. I'm so damn tired. Tomorrow's going to be a long day."

Lindsey gave him a quick glance, like she was half listening.

"It's up to you," Charlie said.

"You make it sound so inviting," Lindsey said. "You don't have to do me any favors."

"What? No, it's not like that at all. I'm just saying..."

The man down the other end of the bar called for Lindsey, and she gave Charlie the same weak grin he'd given her a moment earlier. Without a word, she placed the broom against the back wall and headed down toward the man and woman.

Charlie watched Lindsey take both their glasses and came down to the tap a few feet from where he was seated.

She started to fill each glass with beer.

"I'm sorry," he said.

"Nothing to be sorry about," Lindsey said. "I get it." She didn't make any kind of eye contact with him, filling each glass with the cheap beer.

"So what do you say?" he said.

She didn't answer, instead taking the two beers down to her last two customers for the night. She grabbed from the cash and coins scattered on the bar in front of the couple and counted out exactly what they owed, then took it back to the register, her back to Charlie.

Lindsey leaned over the sink underneath the bar and washed her hands, then grabbed a clean cloth and wiped them dry, walking over to Charlie. "How come you don't ever tell me about your business? You think I can't handle it? Like your ex?"

Charlie finally raised his glass and took a drink. The first one always had a slight burn, but it'd slowly dissipate before the second one. "Do I have to talk about work?" he said.

"If it wasn't on your mind all the time, I wouldn't say so. But I know you're always thinking about whatever it is you have going on, and I wish you'd talk to me about it. That's all."

He took another sip and sat, nodding, but wasn't exactly sure what to say to Lindsey. He knew she was right. But it didn't mean he felt he should share things with her that, as she's said, already ruined one relationship, the only one he'd known for most of his adult life.

"It's not exciting stuff," he said. "I've told you that before."

Lindsey started sweeping again. "I just wish you'd talk to me more. I think you should know by now I'm not scared of what you tell me, if that's what you're afraid of."

"It's not that," he said, keeping his voice hushed enough the people down the other end wouldn't hear their conversation. "But it's not like I'm sitting in some office pushing pencils."

As soon as the words left his mouth he knew he sounded like an out-of-touch old man.

"I'm just saying, the reality is..." Charlie was going to throw out a statistic about divorce rates being higher in law enforcement. It'd been said enough times, even if the true statistics proved otherwise.

Lindsey was still, as if resting with the broom she held with both hands, watching him. "Forget I said anything. And I'm not asking you to explain it to me. It's not my place to..." She looked at Charlie. "I was hoping you'd want to spend the night, that's all. But I understand, you've got your priorities. And that's good. It's why I..." She leaned the broom against the wall, then wiped a strand of hair from her forehead with the back of her hand. "I'm tired too. Maybe another night."

She turned from Charlie, and he watched her go through the swinging door into the kitchen.

He liked Lindsey. He liked her a lot. More than he ever thought he would, when they first met. It had gone beyond her good looks, when part of him wished it hadn't. Not when he still had Jennie acting the way she'd been, like she'd fallen for him all over again after their divorce.

It was more than he could handle, on top of everything else.

But he knew in his heart it was long over with him and Jennie. He'd accepted the fact she didn't want to be married to someone as unstable as Charlie, a man who put his work as a deputy U.S. marshal above anything else. Lindsey claimed she understood that's how it was. But did she?

He had his doubts.

The door swung closed, and Charlie raised his glass to his lips and finished whatever was left in the glass. He leaned back in the stool and glanced at the couple down the other end of the bar, the woman staring his way like she'd been watching him, but turned away as soon as their eyes connected.

The door swung open, and Charlie pushed his glass forward on the bar. "I think I'll have one more." He grinned, folding his arms. "I actually feel better already."

Lindsey had a questioning look on her face, watching him as she turned and reached for the bottle of Jack. She poured him a healthy drink, filling half the glass, and used the metal scoop and dropped a couple of ice cubes inside.

Charlie remembered his father telling him, long before Charlie was old enough to drink, that real men drank Jack Daniels. He also said no man should ever drink it with ice. Sure enough, Charlie grew up to enjoy Old Number 7 quite a bit, but never felt it had anything to do with manhood. Of course, he added the ice to it from day one, if for no other reason than his father had told him not to.

Lindsey grabbed a white towel and ran hot water onto it, in the sink under the bar. She squeezed it out and came around to the other side, wiping the bar down from the end where nobody was sitting, and worked her way over to Charlie. She stopped when she got to him and leaned, one hand on her hip, giving him a nod with her chin. "You finish that, I'm not going to let you drive."

"You don't think I can handle a couple of drinks?"

"Don't make me call the cops," she said, giving him a sly smile as she continued past him, wiping down the rest of the bar. She stopped before she got to the couple at the other end, both looking like they were half-asleep and ready for bed. "Either of you want a coffee, before I throw you out of here?"

Neither accepted the offer, but stood up from their stools. The man went and got their coats from the coatrack on the wall, helped the woman with hers, then slipped his on.

"You need a ride home?" Lindsey said.

The man, walking with a limp now as he made his way to the door, shook his head, waving her off. "I could make the ride with my eyes closed. We're only half a mile away."

Lindsey smiled with a nod, like she understood. Overall, she tried not to worry about every person walking out of the place, or at least tried to tell herself not to. But she also couldn't help herself. She'd been in the business long enough to know few people left a bar in the same condition they were when they'd first strolled in. People having drinks was how she made a living, and she could only do so much.

There'd been plenty of times she refused to let someone drive. She wouldn't think twice about taking keys or paying to get a customer home who'd had too much to drink. Lindsey had shut off plenty of patrons over the years, knowing when the point had come it'd been enough, and her foot had to be put down or trouble would soon follow.

She locked the door behind the couple after they left and went around the bar to flick the switch for the sign outside.

Charlie sat, quiet and thinking. He drank half the glass of Jack by the time he made up his mind to stay upstairs at Lindsey's, considering he hadn't done so lately for one reason or another, and he didn't want her to get the wrong idea.

Work would be there waiting for him in the morning, one way or another.

"I was thinking," Lindsey said, removing the metal drawer of cash from the register and placing it on the bar not far from Charlie. She took out a stack of twenties and started straightening them out, turning each one to make them all facing the same way. "You still feel bad about not keeping that dog?"

"Did I say I felt bad?"

Lindsey said, "Are you going to try to tell me you didn't like having her around?"

"It was only a few days," he said, sipping his whiskey. He looked at her over the rim and watched her count the money. He waited until she was done, then threw back the rest of the Jack. "It crossed my mind, take a ride by the shelter, see how things turned out for her."

"I wouldn't be surprised she's still there," Lindsey said. "They don't normally adopt them out right away. And the older ones... She wasn't a puppy, was she?"

"When I brought her in, they thought maybe three, four years old." Charlie was well aware most people showed up at shelters hoping to take home a puppy. The older ones took more time, sometimes waiting weeks for their new person. "Even if I go by there... what kind of dog wants to live in a Winnebago?"

Lindsey said, "What kind of dog wants to be in a cage in some shelter? Locked up in three feet of space?" She wrapped a rubber band around the stack of twenties and reached into the drawer for more bills, repeating the same process she'd done with the twenties.

Charlie continued, as if he'd clearly thought through the idea of keeping the dog himself. "You know how it is with me," he said. "Sometimes I don't even make it home." He gave Lindsey a quick nod with his chin. "Look at tonight. I wouldn't be able to change my mind like I had to stay here. And it's not like I could take her to work with me."

She stopped what she was doing and smiled, gazing at Charlie with a look that made him unsure if she was being serious. "Maybe she'd turn out to be a good partner?"

Charlie laughed, shaking his head. "I don't know," he said, leaning back in the stool. He rested his hand on his stomach. "Any chance you have any of that soup left? I haven't eaten all day."

Chapter 12

CHARLIE FUMBLED FOR THE phone on the side of Lindsey's bed when it buzzed on top of the nightstand. He wasn't exactly sure where he was or what day it was until he looked at the phone's screen. Sitting up on the edge of the bed, he cleared his throat and answered, "Chief?"

Frank said, "You done with your beauty rest?"

"Not really." He yawned. "Is there something wrong with that?" He pulled the phone from his ear to look at the time on the screen. "It's five twenty."

"Yeah, I know what time it is. We gotta get into the office. We may have some information on that vehicle from yesterday. Local police may have located it."

"Whereabouts?"

"In the mountains," Frank said.

Charlie grabbed his jeans off the floor and was up on his feet now, the phone between his shoulder and ear. He pulled on his pants and felt a chill, the air in the apartment cold, almost as if the heat wasn't turned on. He looked around for his shirt and jacket but couldn't see them in the darkness. Looking out the window, he saw the sky starting to brighten, but he wasn't sure. He slipped on his watch, the sun still twenty or so minutes from rising.

"Shouldn't I just go now?"

Frank paused. "If you can get over here... Kim's on her way over there now."

"To the office?"

"Can you head over there now?"

"Give me ten minutes."

Charlie hung up and thought about Frank calling Kim first. It wasn't always that way, but maybe it didn't matter or make much of a difference either way. But it was little things like that which sometimes made Charlie think. Frank had taken it easy on him after the incident with Claudia Sanborn, even though it was as big of a mistake as he'd ever made. It didn't matter that there was nothing he could've done about it; not following protocol was inexcusable, as Frank would say. Especially when something had gone so wrong.

But there might've been more to it, Charlie thought, like Frank always saying it was the last straw, but it never really was. Or maybe he was losing faith in Charlie, holding something back, knowing IA (internal affairs) would complete their investigation and make some kind of determination, leaving it out of Frank's hands entirely.

It wasn't the first time Charlie was under investigation. Usually it was for firing his weapon, which isn't all that uncommon. Shoot and kill a fugitive, no matter what the circumstances, brought on an automatic investigation.

The thing was, Frank knew Charlie was a damn good marshal. One of the best. But Charlie made his own rules, and that rubbed the higher-ups the wrong way. It had even been said, by more than one person, that Charlie's the kind of deputy who gave the United States Marshals Service a bad name. He'd earned a reputation for his shoot-first-ask-questions-later approach to justice. He had to be reminded far too often it wasn't supposed to be the Wild West, even though Charlie felt the other side didn't seem to care if it was or not.

The murderers and criminals he brought to justice didn't follow any kind of rules.

Why should he?

That kind of thinking is what usually got Charlie in trouble.

He would argue, of course, if a man—or woman—had already proven to be willing to pull the trigger, then he'd be a fool to wait around to see what was going to happen next. As far as he saw it, if someone happened to be on the other end of Charlie firing his Glock, then he sure as hell deserved what was coming next, if that's what it had to come to.

. . . .

Frank and Kim were already in the conference room in the office when Charlie showed up. They both turned and looked at him through the glass walls surrounding it.

Charlie could smell the coffee in the kitchen. "Let me grab a coffee. Be right in." He went and poured himself a cup, sipped it and wished he'd stopped for better java on the way, even though they didn't have much time.

He went into the conference room where Kim and Frank stood at the map, looking it over. Frank turned to him. "Did you get some sleep?"

Charlie wasn't actually sure if he had.

Kim said, "You don't look it. Is everything good?"

Charlie sipped from the cup. "Too early to know for sure." He yawned, stretching his other arm, and took a seat at the end of the table. He leaned back and looked up at the map. "Where we heading?"

"Boone," Frank said, looking at his watch. "Ought to get going soon, so let's get right down to it."

Charlie yawned again, even though he tried to cover it up by attempting to keep his mouth closed. But he couldn't fight it.

Frank said, "Maybe you oughta think about getting some kind of more stable living situation, huh? How long do you plan on living out there in that trailer? It starts affecting your work, then—"

"Who says it affects my work?" Charlie said. He didn't bother to tell Frank a Winnebago isn't a trailer—as he had a dozen of times before—or that he didn't actually sleep there the night before. "You'd think you'd be a little more sympathetic to the day I had yesterday," he said.

Frank said, "You'll get my sympathy after we catch these sons of bitches. You know that officer they drove off the road is in critical condition?"

Charlie's eyes opened wide. "Are you serious? I thought he was all right? He looked all right, when I left him. Even the paramedics said he appeared to be okay."

"Had some kind of internal bleeding. Punctured lung."

"So let's go get 'em," Charlie said, looking at the map, and Frank turned toward the table, handing Charlie two printouts of photos. "These are the two men located at a bar last night, ten miles outside of Boone, a place called Pug's."

"Pug's?" Charlie said. "A bar?"

"A bar. Restaurant. Either way, cops up there say it's a younger crowd. Turns out these two guys get into a scuffle after one of 'em said something to some guy's girlfriend. This guy, a big guy—you'll see—follows them outside, and the three end up fighting it out."

"Two on one?" Charlie said, shaking his head. "Doesn't anyone know how to fight fair anymore?"

"It gets worse," Frank said.

"One of the two pulls an automatic out of the trunk, turns it on the man. The man on the wrong end wisely chose to go back inside. But turns out someone was out there, got the whole thing on video." Frank pointed at the laptop on the table. "Take a look."

Charlie watched the shaky video with the narrow frame from someone's phone, on the laptop's screen.

Frank pointed to the car on the screen as one of the two men opened the trunk and pulled out the rifle. "That the car?"

Charlie had his gaze on the laptop. "Yeah, I'm pretty sure that's it. Wish I could see the driver's side; I'd know for sure if it's damaged."

"Oh, you'll see it," Frank said, nodding at the screen again.

Charlie watched as the two men got in the vehicle and took off. Whoever had the phone, shooting the video, kept it rolling until the car was out of the lot and the darkness outside made it impossible to capture anything else on video. He picked up the blurry photos from the table and turned them to Frank. "This them?"

"Those are images blown up from the footage. Video was posted all over social media right after it went down."

"Any names?"

"Not yet. Deputies from the Watauga Sheriff's Office are moving in on a location from a tip they received. Vehicle was spotted by someone who said their neighbor's out of town, and a car was parked in the driveway all night. Turns out, they believe it's the same one from the bar." Frank looked at his watch. "I'm expecting a call any moment from Sheriff LaPlante, let us know where things stand. But you should get out there." He opened a folder from the table, looked it over, then handed it to Kim.

"Aren't you coming?" Kim said to Frank.

Frank said, "Got a call with the deputy director."

"What about?" Kim said.

"Well, there's some talk inside someone within the FBI." He turned to Charlie. "We're not talking about Stan here, but somebody—I don't have details—somebody might've buried some information about Denny Caprio."

"A dirty agent? Inside the FBI?"

"There've been some recent developments, that's all. But this case is turning out to be much more than a couple wrapped up in a white-collar crime."

"What are we talking?" Charlie said.

"Well, you saw those weapons yesterday, in the back of that van? And then you've got these two men at the bar, one of them pulling an automatic from the trunk..." Frank looked from Charlie to Kim. "That's why, as I've told you enough times already, we gotta be real careful on this one. This appears to me more than tracking down some white-collar paper pushers from the suburbs."

Kim said, "Did you talk to Stan? About the potentially dirty agent?"

"Not yet," Frank said. "I don't even know what he knows."

"You don't think they're looking at Stan, do you?" Charlie said.

"Stan?" Frank laughed. "What kind of question is that? You might be a more straight-laced agent. But either way, this is information that needs to stay between us for now, until we know more."

Charlie said, "You mean don't mention it to Stan?"

"That's what I said. It stays between us. I didn't mention it to Sheriff LaPlante up there in Boone either. He's aware this is federal at this stage, and only doing what he can to help with whatever we need."

Frank picked up his phone from the table when it buzzed. "Hang on," he said, then answered, "Chief Deputy Carter." Frank listened for a moment, then turned to the map. "Well, okay. You got names?" His expression showed disappointment. "All right. I'll let them know. Keep me in the loop, at least while they're en route." He hung up the phone, shaking his head. "They lost 'em."

Charlie looked at Kim, her gaze coming back at him.

Kim said, "Who was that?"

"Sheriff LaPlante," Frank said.

Charlie said, "They lost *who*? The two men?"

"They found the vehicle which, of course, had been stolen. There was an AK-47 in the trunk."

"What the hell happened?" Charlie said.

"You mean how'd they lose them? Well…" He paused. "It sounds like shots were fired from inside the house. So they were being careful. By the time they finally got inside, the place was empty."

Charlie said to Kim, "Can you drive?"

"Is there another option?" Kim said.

Frank looked out through the glass into the rest of the office with three desks out in the open and three cubicles—one, Charlie's and the other one, Kim's. "This changes things." He was quiet for a moment, hands on his hips now. "Deputy Holden will be down in court this morning, but you're going to need some help."

"We'll be all right," Charlie said. He gave Frank a look like he didn't like the suggestion.

Deputy Ethan Holden was as raw as they'd come. He'd been a deputy U.S. marshal for barely two years, on account of his political connections. Charlie didn't care much for Holden. He didn't have to deal with him often. Frank never came right out and said it, but Charlie knew he wasn't fond of the kid, either, and made sure the deputy's days were spent in the courtroom.

Charlie and Kim turned for the door.

"Oh, by the way," Frank said. "Charlie, you didn't file your report yet. I know how much you like your paperwork, but—"

"If I have time when I get back, I will," Charlie said. "I don't have much of it lately."

"Like the rest of us," Frank said. "But this is directly related to what we're doing here. The more we can share in the database, the better. I know I don't have to remind you we don't work in a silo here, as much as I know you wish we did."

"I get it, Frank. But right now, we gotta get up to Boone. Who knows how far these two've gotten away. And they're our closest leads that aren't dead yet. And, believe it or not, I'd kind of like to know who's trying to kill me."

Frank ran his hand over the top of his buzzed head of hair. "That car firing at you last night, you think it was an AK-47?"

"I didn't get a close enough look. I was busy avoiding the bullets coming my way. But, if I had to guess…"

All three started heading out of the conference room.

Frank said, "Is that Town Car a mess?"

"You could say that," Charlie said. "I'm going to need something else."

"Well, I don't know how soon that's going to happen. You barely had it twenty-four hours. I'm not even sure the papers on it were filed before you cracked it up."

"Cracked it up?" Charlie said. "Is that what you call it when someone tries to run you off the road, firing shots at you?"

Frank said, "We'll get it cleaned up for you, make it just like new."

"I don't want it, whether it's new or not. I won't even be able to get it up that hill to the Winnebago."

Frank said, "Well, maybe you oughta look at living somewhere else, besides deep in the woods away from civilization."

"Would you rather me come live with you?"

Frank laughed. "I'm not even sure the wife wants *me* living there."

"Well, I can't afford much, the way the prices are around here. I'm lucky my buddy set me up, or I'd be sleeping in Pack Square."

"Well, maybe the way you two've been acting since your divorce, you'll end up back at your old place with Jennie," Frank said.

Charlie didn't know if he was joking or not, even though Frank smiled when he said what he'd said. But Frank, and everyone else, knew Jennie had been calling Charlie more than she had when they were married. She'd ask Charlie to go down to the house—the one that used to be his—to fix something or because she heard a noise in the attic. She'd even stopped by the office once or twice, almost acting as if nothing had changed, dropping off a piece of mail or some muffins she made.

Charlie wasn't the only one she'd confused.

But he also hadn't let on about his relationship with Lindsey. Maybe Frank and Kim both knew something was going on—they'd both been in Coyote Grille enough to have a drink with Charlie—but his new relationship was something Charlie kept to himself.

Charlie said, "All I'm asking for is something with four-wheel drive to replace the Suburban. You get used to driving around a tank like that, it's hard to go back, be so low to the ground, driving a granny car, looking like I run some kind of chauffeur service."

Chapter 13

KIM TURNED DOWN SAMPSON Road in Boone and right away had to stop when a Boone police officer stepped out in front, hand up, signaling for her to stop.

Charlie looked ahead at the blue lights flashing, at least a dozen vehicles parked on either side of the road for as far as he could see.

Kim held up her badge for the officer. "Deputy Kim Riggins, U.S. Marshals Service. We're here to assist the search."

Charlie held his badge up but didn't say who he was or anything else.

The police officer, who looked like a kid to Charlie, pointed toward all the cars. "We've got a half-dozen officers from Boone PD in the woods right now. Eight or nine deputies from the sheriff's office. Sheriff brought the dogs, but both men are still at Large. Lot of acreage out there."

"Thank you," Charlie said, and Kim hit the gas and drove straight ahead until they got to the house where Charlie spotted the vehicle parked on the grass, tucked on the side of the house under the gray, leafless trees.

The woods were thick and deep, and from what Charlie could see as he stepped out of the vehicle was that they appeared to go on forever. He could see the rugged peaks of the Blue Ridge Mountains in the distance, stretching across the horizon, white clouds hovering above them.

Charlie stopped at the car and without a doubt knew the black Chrysler 300 was the same one that'd run him off the road and took out the officer who still hadn't left the hospital. The windows were tinted dark, the residue from the fingerprinting on the door handles. The passenger window was down, and Charlie poked his head inside without touching anything. He was never a fan of cologne, but that's exactly what the smell was inside the vehicle, as if one of the men had taken a bath with some cheap stuff and got it all over everything.

"Deputy?" a voice said.

Charlie turned to a towering man he recognized as Sheriff Kenneth LaPlante, walking over to him and Kim.

"Sheriff," he said, reaching out to shake the man's hand. "You remember Deputy Riggins," Charlie said.

The sheriff shook Kim's hand. "Of course I do." He turned to the woods, using a pair of binoculars, panning back and forth before lowering them. "These woods go on for miles. I appreciate you coming out here, but at this rate, we're going to need more bodies if we expect to find these men."

A helicopter could be heard off in the distance, and Charlie looked up but couldn't see much of the sky from where they stood, closer to the edge of the woods behind the house.

Charlie said, "Well, as you know, these men are involved in something big."

"Illegal arms dealing?" the sheriff said.

Charlie was surprised the sheriff knew about it already. "We got involved after a woman and her husband were allowed to go home and await sentencing. They cut their ankle monitors and both took off in opposite directions."

"We've been on alert for the woman," the sheriff said. "But I'm not exactly clear what her involvement is."

"Well," Charlie said, "it turns out they were working for this man, name's Denny Caprio. The FBI's been after him, but sometimes they don't share as much as they should with us. I'd never even heard the name until earlier."

He left out the part about the belief there may be a federal agent, with the FBI, who possibly destroyed evidence to cover up Caprio's wrongdoings.

Kim said, "These two men we're looking for had gone after Charlie on the highway, tried to take him out. It's believed they work for Caprio."

The sheriff turned as two deputies came out of the woods.

"Sheriff," one of them called, wiping the sweat from his brow with his sleeve. Both deputies appeared to be somewhat out of breath. "We need more manpower," the one said. "There's just too much ground to cover in these woods."

The sheriff didn't look happy, shaking his head as he turned from Kim and Charlie and over to the two deputies. He started yelling at them both for coming out of the woods, as if they'd given up. "You get your asses back out there and don't come out until you find something. You understand?"

Charlie cracked a slight smile. "They might not be wrong," he said, eyes on the woods but talking to Kim. "The two suspects likely won't be coming back this way. Best thing we can do is drive out, north of here. We'd be guessing, of course." He pulled out his phone and looked at the map of the area. "They'd headed west, they could walk or run all the way to Blowing Rock in under three hours, crossing a handful of roads. That's assuming they don't steal another vehicle. Or they might've gone east, but it looks like a few homes along the way, back roads... a few dead-ends..." He looked at the sheriff. "Any chance you got your men knocking on any doors?"

Sheriff LaPlante said, "We alerted all the neighbors in the area, told them to stay inside."

Charlie said, "No, what I mean is..." He thought for a moment. "Wouldn't you agree there's a chance these two didn't keep going on to those woods? Maybe took refuge in any one of these homes around here? I know how deep those woods can be. But if I'm running from the cops, good chance I'm going to go find someplace else to hide, wait it out, the way they did right here in this house."

The sheriff had a look on his face like he perhaps didn't appreciate Charlie asking questions, but had to have also realized where Charlie was coming from. "Between my office and the Boone Police Department, we've got the surrounding neighborhoods covered. We got some of the roads blocked, knowing it's likely these men've got phones and most likely already called someone, come pick 'em up. Nearest major road, assuming they continued north, is the parkway. Otherwise, it's a lot of dirt roads and dead-ends, no more than two or three homes on each."

"With all due respect, Sheriff, Deputy Riggins and I drove in here from 321; only law enforcement we passed was the deputy standing in the road, three quarters a mile from here."

"What's your point, Charlie?"

"I'm saying, you don't have enough deputies or vehicles to cover all this ground. No fault of yours by any means, but everyone you've got in there, on top of the dogs, I'm just not sure it's the best approach."

Sheriff LaPlante stared back at Charlie and held his gaze, a look on his face like he was close to saying something, but maybe thought it was best to bite his tongue.

Charlie could sense the sheriff's uneasiness. "I don't think I have to tell you; I'm not here to step on your toes. But we want these men as much as you do. Probably more, considering I seem to have a target on my back."

"Yeah?" said the sheriff, looking from Charlie to Kim.

"Charlie's lucky to be alive," Kim said.

Charlie said, "I've been shot at quite a bit the past forty-eight hours." He took a few steps toward the edge of the woods, slowly scanning the area. "All I'm saying is chances are slim your deputies'll come out of those woods with either of these men in custody."

"You don't know that," the sheriff said.

"No, I don't. But there's just too much ground to cover. Which is why I feel we might want to spend some time knocking on some doors, maybe take a look around the—"

"You're suggesting we go knock on every door in this town, hoping we get lucky?"

"Not every door in town," Charlie said, looking through the woods and at what looked like a house in the distance. Without the leaves on the deciduous trees, it was certainly easier to get a deeper look into the woods.. He turned to Kim. "You think it's a bad idea? We go knock on some doors?"

She waited a moment before she answered. "I can't say I agree anyone's wasting time walking through those woods. You never know. But I'd also be willing to go knock on doors." She turned to Sheriff LaPlante. "How many homes would you say are within two, three miles of here?"

LaPlante looked at Kim for a moment, eyes narrowed, before he answered. "Well, let's see. There are maybe seven side roads—neighborhoods, if you want to call them that—with three, four houses. A lot of land, you know? I could get an exact count, if—"

"No, I don't think that's necessary," Charlie said. He looked over at the two officers who'd just come out of the woods. "Maybe they can help us? Between the four of us—five, if this is something you'd be up for—we can knock on every door within a two- or three-mile radius. Take us maybe an hour or two, we make sure we get a good look at each one."

Chapter 14

CHARLIE STILL HAD A good feeling the two men were holed up in one of the homes north of Sampson Road, and with Kim, who had already knocked on the doors of seven homes. There was no evidence of either suspect. They had requested permission from each person who came to the door to look around outside for any signs of the men they were looking for. Of course, there was always a chance one might lie, not by their own choice—perhaps with a gun to their heads—making it so they couldn't be straight with Charlie and Kim.

They'd checked in with the sheriff already, and the other officers going through the homes in the southern part of where the men were initially spotted. But at that point, they all had come up empty.

Charlie still couldn't help but think he was right, that the men were hiding somewhere in one of the homes. But the more doors they knocked on, the more he'd started to have his doubts.

Kim pulled the Tahoe up in front of a yellow farmhouse, the roof on the home worn and grayed with a dip in the middle like one good rain would cause it to cave in. There was an old red pickup truck in the driveway that looked like it hadn't been driven in years.

Charlie wondered if the place was even lived in.

The two stepped out of the Tahoe and along a pathway of bricks sunken into the soil and covered with leaves.

Looking in the window of the truck as he walked by, Charlie saw a newspaper on the front seat. He tried the passenger door handle, and sure enough, it was unlocked. He opened the door and grabbed the newspaper, checking the date. Holding it, he showed Kim. "It's today's paper." He folded it over and tucked it under his arm, carrying it to the front door, placing it down on an old wood chair outside on the porch.

A dog barked in the distance, but it was quiet around the house. The faint smell of burning wood filled the air, perhaps from somewhere in the distance. There didn't appear to be any smoke coming from the chimney running up the side of the house.

Charlie shot a quick glance over his shoulder at Kim, then turned back to the door and knocked. "Hello? Anybody home?" There didn't appear to be any lights or sound inside, or much of anything going on around the property. He put his hand on his holstered Glock.

Kim stepped away from the steps. "I'm going to go look around back."

Charlie had an uncomfortable feeling he couldn't shake.

He knocked again and looked in through the pane of glass on the door, and could see down a hallway with a kitchen at the end of it. There were no lights on, and a closed door to the right. A single coat—a barn jacket—hung on a peg on the wall just inside the door. The floor was covered in worn hardwoods.

He waited a few moments, then turned and strolled along the front of the house, glancing in each window, trying to get a better look inside. He got to the end of the house and peeked through the last window, looking inside at a dining room table covered in newspapers and magazines. There were hundreds of them, not only stacked on the table but also on the chairs surrounding it. There were boxes piled along the wall, and a china cabinet with glass so covered in dirt or dust, he could hardly see what was inside.

Charlie knocked on the window as he gazed inside at two wingback chairs. He looked through a doorway on the other side of the room and could see what looked like the other end of the kitchen, but he wasn't sure. It was too dark in there, as if the windows on the back of the house were covered with closed blinds or curtains.

He continued into the backyard, where Kim was down the far end, her face close to one of the windows, looking inside. She said, "What are the chances nobody actually lives here?"

Charlie stepped around a wheelbarrow filled to the top with water. As cold as it felt outside, it was above freezing. "I'd say that was the case, if it weren't for that newspaper someone had to've picked up this morning." He looked up at the second floor of the house, cedar shingles on the back grayed and curled and split, some missing. But there were plenty of old homes in the area in need of repair, including some of the ones they'd already stopped at. But the ones they visited were all clearly lived in. This was the first one that appeared to be abandoned, where nobody came to the door.

Kim made a quick move and pulled her gun from the holster on her hip, getting away from the window, her back against the exterior of the house. "There's somebody in there."

Charlie pulled his Glock and got away from the windows. "They see you?"

"Yeah. He looked right at me."

"*He?*"

"Pretty sure," she said, ducking low and moving under the window now out of sight and toward the far end of the house.

Charlie looked up at the exterior door on the back of the house a few feet from where he stood. He signaled for Kim to go around front, and she disappeared around the corner. He stood outside the rear door and straightened up to try to get a look inside. But the small panes of glass at the top were covered from the inside.

Charlie pounded on the door. "Open the door!" He had his Glock raised now, standing to the side, out of the way.

Nobody came to the door, and he pounded on it again. "U.S. Marshals Service." Just as he was about to try the doorknob, he heard gunshots. Numerous rounds were then fired, echoing through the trees surrounding the home. Charlie didn't wait. Leading with his shoulder, he crashed into the door and knocked it inward and smashing it off its hinges. "Police!" he yelled, Glock raised, looking back and forth as he moved swiftly through the house. He heard more shots, three or four he knew came from a handgun.

Another dozen rounds followed.

He made it to the open front door as two men jumped into the truck that was parked out front, both holding what Charlie recognized as AK-47s. The one in the passenger side aimed and fired at Kim's Tahoe, unloading on it, filling the sides with holes, taking out the windows and blowing out the tires.

Charlie ducked back inside, raising his Glock to take aim. He had no idea where Kim was, or if she was even alive.

The truck had already started down the driveway, the back end fishtailing, rocks and stones and dust kicking up from under the tires.

Charlie ran out with his Glock raised and took a shot, but the man in the truck's passenger seat hung out the window and sprayed bullets into the front of the house.

Charlie ran back inside and took cover.

The windows were all blown out, glass exploding on Charlie as he crawled on the floor under each one. But then he came up firing, shooting ten rounds at the truck driving away.

But Charlie stopped, knowing he had four left in the magazine and one in the chamber.

With the truck almost out of sight, he ran for the door and fired his weapon again, shattering the rear window on the truck. But he turned with the Glock pointed at a wood pile when he saw someone out of the corner of his eye.

It was Kim, climbing over the wood and running down the driveway after the truck. Charlie ran past her, stopped and took aim with his gun held in front of him with both hands.

He fired one shot, and the truck started to swerve, sideswiping a tall pine tree and taking a chunk of bark with it. But the truck continued straight ahead without stopping, making it out to the road.

Kim fired one last shot but stopped once the truck was out of view, well beyond the trees and out, headed for the road. She leaned over, hands on her knees, shaking her head. "Shit." She appeared to be trying to catch her breath.

"Shit is right," Charlie said. "But I'm pretty sure I got 'im. At least I think I did. You see the way he almost lost control?" He looked through the trees and caught a glimpse of the truck in the distance driving past the property. "Or maybe I didn't."

Kim had her two-way out and spoke into it: "This is Deputy U.S. Marshal Kim Riggins. Sheriff LaPlante, do you read?"

She and Charlie stood in the middle of the dirt driveway, both breathing heavy, walking back up to the yellow house.

"This is Sheriff LaPlante. Go 'head."

Kim said, "Suspects are driving a black Ford F-150 pickup."

"You found them?" he said, a sound of excitement in his voice.

"We did. But again, they escaped. We exchanged fire. Deputy Harlow may've hit the driver. But we don't know for sure. They're armed and dangerous, as I'm sure I don't need to tell you. But the way they stopped firing, there's a chance they're out of ammunition."

"Where are you?" the sheriff said.

"We're on Virgil's Lane. They were heading north, toward, I believe, George Hayes Road."

"Why didn't you go after them?" the sheriff said.

Kim paused, holding the mic near her chin. "No, sir," Kim said. "My vehicle's inoperable. They shot out my tires."

A helicopter sounded to be heading their way.

"We'll get the roads blocked,"

Charlie headed for the house, hearing the sheriff say road blocks would be set. But Charlie knew it'd be too late, and continued first to the Tahoe, where he circled it to look over the damage. But even if the vehicle would start, it had two tires flat and one spare. They were stranded.

Charlie went inside the house, now filled with the cold from the outside with the windows now gone, glass all over the wood floors. But he went ahead and closed the door behind him, as if it'd make a difference. There was a smell in the air Charlie hadn't noticed when he first crashed through. It was a muted, smoky aroma. He looked at the fireplace filled with charred wood inside it, but not burning.

When he crouched down in front of it he'd stepped in a puddle of water, then touched the black logs and felt that they were still warm, but soaking wet. The fire had clearly been extinguished with water. And the only thing he could guess was the two men didn't want it to look like anyone was home. So perhaps they put out the only source of heat keeping the place warm.

"Hello?" he said, afraid of what might've happened to whoever was there when the two men arrived. "Anyone here?"

He made his way into the kitchen at the back where he'd first crashed through. He tried to push the door closed, knowing it wasn't going to stay like that, the way it'd splintered from when he busted it open.

He poked his head into the back corner room, the one with the table covered with newspapers, and boxes filled with even more newspapers and magazines. He continued back to the room in front where he spotted an old console TV with rabbit ears on top. The plug had been pulled from the wall.

His boots crunched on the glass, and he stopped at the bottom of the stairs, looking up. He could feel it in his stomach, and knew it wasn't good. He yelled, "Anybody up there?"

He heard a bang on the floor, and rushed up the stairs with his Glock in his hand, just in case.

Charlie looked back down the stairs at the front door when it opened and Kim walked in, looking up at him.

"Anyone here?" she said.

Charlie didn't answer, walking past a bathroom toward a closed door at the end of the hall. He pushed the door open, looked around, and at first saw nothing. But he opened a door he assumed to be a closet.

Right there, on the floor, was an older man and a woman, each white haired and frail, both of their eyes red and filled with fear, gazing up at Charlie.

He yelled out for Kim. "Up here!" then turned to the elderly couple. "Don't worry, I'm not going to hurt you."

Duct tape was wrapped around their wrists and ankles, then the two were tied together, back to back, with a thick rope wrapped around each of them several times. Their mouths were also covered over with duct tape.

He showed his badge. "I'm Charlie Harlow, with the U.S. Marshals Service. You're safe now."

The first thing Charlie did was remove the tape from their mouths, and the two gasped for air and started coughing, almost choking. The woman was crying.

Kim was behind him and he turned to her. "Get them a couple glasses of water." He pulled his knife and cut away the tape and untied the rope, helping them both get to their feet.

Chapter 15

Sheriff LaPlante stepped out of his vehicle with a look of embarrassment on his face, shaking his head. "The pickup was located, left at the Cracker Barrel just off 321, on Blowing Rock Road."

"They were in Cracker Barrel?" Charlie said, walking over to the sheriff. "Nobody inside meets the description of these men?"

Sheriff LaPlante said, "I don't think they'd have the balls to go inside, get themselves breakfast."

Charlie paused, squinting. "Are you telling me you don't know if they were in there? I mean, didn't your deputies go inside?"

"Of course they did," LaPlante said. "All I'm saying is they didn't walk in expecting to find them. One thing I can tell you is there was a lot of blood in that truck, on the driver's side, glass from the windows all over the seats."

Charlie turned to Kim, knowing at least he hadn't missed. "Couldn't have gotten very far, if they're on foot and injured," he said.

Sheriff LaPlante said, "They're out looking, and I assure you we won't stop until we find 'em."

Charlie knew local law enforcement wasn't equipped or trained to handle a manhunt the way the Marshals Service was. No other agency was. It just wasn't in their blood, and took a different approach. Most of the sheriff's deputies spent a good part of their days on traffic violations or giving out speeding tickets to out-of-state travelers.

Two more cars from the sheriff's office pulled up the driveway and stopped close to where the sheriff was standing.

Charlie wanted to turn and ask the sheriff why the two officers were even there. The two wanted men certainly weren't, and if it wasn't for the fact Charlie and Kim were still waiting for Frank to show up, they'd been out there themselves, searching.

Kim was on the phone with USMS intelligence, trying to get more information on the two men's identities.

The older couple inside the house had done their best to describe the two, and Charlie passed on the information, hoping they could somehow make a match in the database, and end up with less of a wild-goose chase than they already had on their hands.

He went past the paramedics and turned when an old Chevy pickup truck pulled in the driveway. Charlie had asked the sheriff to make a few calls, get someone out to fix up the house as best they could, to at least keep the couple from freezing inside their own home, the way the windows were all blown out.

He stopped and waited for the truck to drive closer, and approached the young man who stepped out.

"Thanks for coming right out," Charlie said, and reached over to shake the man's hand. Charlie handed him his business card. "Now, as you can see, we've got quite a mess here. I know you probably can't replace the windows right away, but here's my card. I'll cover whatever it'll cost to get these windows boarded up, so these poor people don't freeze to death. The back door needs to be repaired; fill any holes you see in the side of the house. There are a lot of 'em."

The young man looked over Charlie's business card, then raised his gaze. "You're a U.S. marshal?"

Charlie said, "*Deputy* U.S. marshal."

"I heard there were a lot of shots fired over here today?"

Charlie looked at the house. "Yeah, you could say that."

"They okay?"

"The couple that lives here?" Charlie nodded. "Been a traumatic day. I just want to make sure they're taken care of, all right? I know how this stuff works, and I'd rather them not have to deal with it right now. You call me, once you know what it's all going to cost. I'll give you my credit card. You can take a card, huh?"

"I can run it right through my phone, as long as I get a signal. It can be spotty out in these parts."

"Okay, well, whatever works. Just let me know. If you can't swing whatever it'll cost for materials..."

"I'll be all right. Don't they have insurance?"

"I don't know," Charlie said. "But again, these people don't deserve to have to deal with any of that right now. I just want to make sure they're comfortable. They've been through enough."

The man already had a measuring tape in his hand, went right up to the windows, and started working.

Charlie continued into the house, where the couple were seated together on the couch with blankets covering them, sitting in front of the fireplace Charlie had started for them.

They both still appeared to be in shock and had refused to go to the hospital to be examined further, even though the paramedics had suggested it.

Charlie stood to the side of the fire, being sure not to block what little heat came from it. "Now, you sure you don't want to go to a hotel? We'll cover the cost, nothing you'd have to worry about. Might be nice for the two of you?"

The woman looked at the man with sadness in her eyes, as if she wanted him to answer yes.

But he just shook his head. "I appreciate the offer, but you have to understand this is our home. We don't have no plans to ever leave. Especially not like this. I suppose I need to get up anyway, cover up those windows."

Charlie said, "I've already got someone here to take care of that for you. He's outside now, measuring. He's gonna cover over the openings with plywood for now, until he can get you some windows.

"We can't afford no new windows," the man said, his gaze fixed on Charlie.

"What I'm saying is you don't have to worry about a thing," Charlie said. "You did nothing wrong, and I wouldn't want you to have to worry about any of it. You've been through enough."

The woman began to cry, and the man, her husband, wrapped his arm around her and pulled her tight against him, lifting the blanket and making sure it was up over her shoulders.

Charlie looked at the mess. "You got a broom?"

The man started to get up, but Charlie put his hand up to stop him. "That's all right; just tell me where it is. Stay right there with your wife."

The man pointed into the kitchen. "There's a closet in there, to the right of the fridge. Should be a broom in there. But you don't have to—"

"I'm just going to get this glass up off the floor. That's all." He smiled, and headed into the kitchen where the back door was cracked open. He could feel the cold air coming through, but nothing like what was coming in the front of the house through the windows.

He grabbed a chair from under the table and pushed the door closed, leaning the chair with the top of the backrest tucked under the knob to keep the door from opening again.

• • • • • • • • • •

Frank drove up the driveway in his blue Ford F-150, going around the other vehicles and stopping close to the house. As soon as he parked, Charlie walked over to him and looked into the truck. "The three of us gotta squeeze into the front of this thing?"

"Unless you want to walk?" Frank said.

Kim's Tahoe had already been taken away on the flatbed.

Frank approached Charlie and pulled out his phone, looking down at the screen before he turned it to Charlie and Kim. "You recognize this man?"

Charlie and Kim both stared at the photo for no more than a couple of seconds, both nodding.

"That's him," Kim said. "The one with the automatic."

Charlie said, "The couple who lives here's still inside. They can confirm the identity."

"Well, we might've just gotten lucky. Intelligence was able to match one of the two from the video obtained at the bar last night. Turns out this man's an associate of Denny Caprio's."

Charlie said, "What kind of associate?"

"Worked with Caprio over twenty years ago, in New York. Name's Whitlock. Jack Whitlock. Did ten years in Upstate New York for trafficking drugs and firearms. Come to find out Caprio was never charged, but he was involved."

"Should we be surprised?" Charlie said.

The sheriff went over and reached out to shake Frank's hand. "Just let me know what we can do to help. I'm sure you know the truck they used was found parked outside a Cracker Barrel, twenty minutes from here?"

Frank nodded. "Somebody either picked them up, or they stole another vehicle. I can't imagine they'd still be on foot."

"You feel they'd have a reason to stick around the area?" the sheriff said.

"Are you asking if you should still have your deputies out there looking for them? Because I'd say the answer is yes, until we know for sure they've left."

Sheriff LaPlante said, "Whatever you want us to do, just say the word, Frank. We don't see any reason to hold up over here any longer." He turned to the house. "I'm glad they left those two in there alive."

"Me too," Charlie said, hands on his hips, watching the man nail the plywood over where the windows were.

Frank's phone buzzed and he stepped away to answer it, going over to his truck. All Charlie could hear was "Uh-huh," every handful of seconds, Frank nodding with the phone to his ear.

After a couple of minutes, Frank was back over with the others. "You're not going to believe this, but the FBI's taken a federal agent working out of Miami into custody. He's being arraigned right now, charged with corruption and falsifying records of activities related to illegal arms trafficking."

"Let me guess," Charlie said. "Denny Caprio?"

Frank grinned. "You bet. The agent received over a hundred and fifty thousand dollars in cash, and has now claimed the money came from Caprio. He's also admitted to having knowledge of several homicides Caprio's involved in, including Vincent Avella, out by Moss Lake."

Charlie didn't respond, his eyes narrowed like he was thinking, looking around the house. "Where do we begin? Unless we locate these two men, we're back to square one."

"The driver's injured," Kim said, and Charlie looked at her like he wasn't sure he wanted it mentioned."

"Injured?" Frank said.

"I got a shot off," Charlie said. "Pretty certain I hit him, but the son of a bitch kept going. But I'd have to guess he's going to need some medical attention sooner than later."

Frank said, "But you don't sound like you're sure you hit him or not?"

Charlie thought for a moment. "Nintety-nine percent sure."

A helicopter could once again be heard in the distance.

A call for the sheriff came over the two-way on his belt. He slipped an earpiece on and pushed the button on the mic clipped to his vest. "Sheriff LaPlante, go ahead." He listened, eyes slightly widening as he turned with a glance at Frank, Charlie, and Kim. He held a finger up, as if asking them to wait. "Banner Elk? You sure? All right, yeah, just sit tight. I'll let you know." The sheriff removed the earpiece. "A nurse from Dr. George Harris's office, out in Banner Elk, called the Avery County Sheriff's office. The doctor just treated a man with a gunshot wound to the head, sewed up his ear at gunpoint. There were two other men and a woman outside waiting in the car."

Chapter 16

Deputies from the Avery County Sheriff's Office were parked outside the medical facility where a man in a white lab coat sat outside the office with a paramedic, a bandage on his forehead and his right eye partially closed and swollen.

Charlie recognized Sheriff Mike O'Leary and went straight over to him. "Sheriff," he said, shaking his hand.

Frank and Kim went over to where Frank said, "Mind if we talk to the doctor?"

Sheriff O'Leary stepped out of the way. "Of course, Frank."

Frank went over to the doctor and pulled out his phone, holding the screen out so the man could see it. "Is this the patient you treated?"

The doctor said, "No. But he was one of the two men here with the man I treated." He pointed to his eye. "He's the one who hit me." Frank turned to Charlie. "Jack Whitlock."

Frank opened the folder he had in his hand and pulled out a photo of Denny Caprio. "What about this guy? Was he one of the three?"

The doctor said, "Yeah, he was here. He seemed to be in charge. Did all the talking. The other one, whatever you said his name was..."

"Jack Whitlock," Frank said.

"Yeah, him. He was like, I don't know... He didn't look well, like he might've been ill."

Charlie moved closer to the doctor and leaned with his hands on his knees, looking over the bruises and dried blood on the doctor's face, and said, "They knocked you around?"

"What does it look like?" the doctor snapped, holding an ice pack in his hand, but didn't have it over his swollen eye.

Charlie knew the doctor was just upset about what had happened, and might've already answered the same questions by someone from the sheriff's office. He stepped away, looking out at the road where every few moments a car would drive by, slowing down to see what all the commotion was about.

Kim said to the doctor, "Can you tell us if you heard anything these men were saying, the might have—"

"It wasn't just men," he said. "There was a woman with them. I didn't see her. My receptionist did. I guess she was the one behind the wheel, waiting outside."

"Did you see what kind of car it was?" Kim said.

The doctor snapped, "Why don't you ask the sheriff? How many times are you people going to ask me the same questions?"

"We're sorry," Frank said. "These are dangerous men, and we need to find them. We just want to make sure we have whatever you can tell us. Whatever it is..."

The doctor let out a sigh, squeezing his eyes closed like he wanted it to all go away. He placed the ice pack on his swollen eye. "I'm sorry. It's just... It's the last thing you'd ever expect, you know? I take care of people. And here I am, get a gun shoved in my face, punched in the eye for no reason at all..."

"These are bad men," Frank said. "We need to stop them before they hurt someone else. Or worse."

A tall woman wearing white pants and a purple scrub top stepped outside and lit up a cigarette.

The doctor removed the ice pack from his eye and said to the woman, "Did you cancel the rest of the day's appointments?"

The woman nodded and took a deep drag from her cigarette between her long fingers, cheeks puffed out before she exhaled and blew a stream of smoke into the overhang outside the entrance.

Frank introduced himself to the woman as Chief Deputy Frank Carter of the United States Marshals Service. He acted calm and as polite as could be, then turned and stood next to her, shoulders almost touching. He opened the folder and took out a large photo of Claudia Sanborn. "Is this the woman who was behind the wheel of that car?"

The woman looked at the photo. "I don't know. Maybe. I saw her get out of the passenger side and walk around, getting in the driver's side when the other two helped the patient."

"Patient?" the doctor said, almost with a laugh, but clearly mad about the situation. "That son of a bitch..."

The woman said to Frank, "I'd say that looks like her. She had short hair though."

Frank turned to Charlie and Kim. "She must've cut her hair."

"Apparently after the fact," Charlie said. "She had long hair when we picked her up at the hotel."

Frank looked from the doctor to the receptionist smoking her cigarette.

Charlie said to the woman, "Do you know what kind of car they were driving?"

The woman paused, smoke floating up near her face, waving it away with her hand. "It looked like a Ford Taurus or maybe a Chevy. An Impala."

"Any chance you saw the plate?" Charlie said.

"I thought I woulda been smart enough to look, but I wasn't thinking straight," she said. "I just wanted to do what they asked. Not get shot, you know?"

"Yeah, I know," Charlie said. "Was there anything you heard? Anything they said, that would indicate where they might've been going? Or what they were doing?"

"I don't know. There was a lot of yelling between them," the woman said.

"Between them? Like they were fighting?"

"They were arguing about something when they came through the door, the one in charge"—she eyed Frank—"the one in that photo you showed me. He was talking to the other man like something had gone wrong. Besides the injury."

Charlie gave Frank a quick glance, then said to the woman, "But you can't think of anything specific they said, you might've heard? Anything at all?"

"I'm sorry," the woman said. "I can't even think straight. I'm still shaking."

Charlie paused, like he was giving the woman some time. "What about the nurse? She inside?"

"Stacy," the woman said.

The doctor said, "She's still a bit shaken. We all are."

The woman with the cigarette said, "I just wish I'd had my forty-five."

Everyone looked at her without a word.

Kim said, "There weren't any patients in the building at the time. Is that correct?"

The woman held her cigarette in front of her. "Thankfully not," she said. "The last patient had just walked out of here a few minutes before these nutjobs showed up." She sucked another drag from the cigarette, her lips puckered like she couldn't quite get enough out of it.

"I'm sorry about what happened here," Frank said. "But whatever else you can tell us would be helpful. As you know, these men are dangerous, and we'd like to stop them before they hurt someone else."

The doctor raised the ice pack to his eye and held it there, quiet for a couple of moments before he shrugged. "I don't know what else they said. They just wanted me to help the man. But when they first showed up, I told them to leave or I'd call the cops. They didn't like that." He pointed to his swollen eye.

"Was it bad?" Charlie said. "The man's injuries?"

The doctor stood up from the rear of the rescue vehicle. "Not as bad as it looked. A piece of his ear was missing, so I did what I could to stitch it up."

Charlie never wanted to kill anyone. That was never his goal when he fired his weapon. But he did what he had to do, and in this case almost wished he'd gotten a better shot, and thought to himself the next time he saw the man, he wasn't going to miss. He said to the doctor, "So, you sure you heard nothing else? Nothing about where they were going? Or what they were doing here?"

The doctor looked at Charlie out of one eye, the other covered with the ice. He paused for a moment. "I don't know. I might've heard something, when the two were talking, maybe mentioned Roan Mountain, but I'm not certain. Honestly, I wasn't too worried about anything other than getting their friend stitched up and out of here, before they killed me."

Charlie turned to Kim and Frank. "Roan Mountain? Tennessee?"

Frank rubbed the back of his neck. "I'd call the eastern district office up there, but I believe Roan Mountain's just north of us. Closest marshals up there's gotta be two hours away."

"This is my case," Charlie said. "We don't need to involve any of the Tennessee offices just yet."

Frank held his gaze on Charlie. "No matter what you think, we're going to need some help, Charlie. So far, you're oh-for-two against this crew. And we have no idea what they're up to."

Kim said, "Or why they're sticking around in the first place."

Charlie said, "They've gotta be looking for someone else. My guess is Sanborn."

"The husband?" Kim said.

"Scott Sanborn. Wouldn't surprise me he's got something that's theirs. Who knows. Maybe he ripped them off. Could be the reason he took off on Mrs. Sanborn, kept something he felt belonged to him that doesn't."

"But who's to say Sanborn's still in the area?" Frank said.

"I don't know. Maybe he's got something hidden. Or the girlfriend?" Charlie turned to Kim. "We probably let her off too easy. It couldn't have been any more obvious she was lying to us the whole time."

"We could talk to the boyfriend again," Kim said.

Frank had a confused look on his face. "The boyfriend? Sanborn?"

Charlie said, "No. I thought I told you already. She had some little stoner boy over there, two of 'em sittin' on the couch getting high. Kid stormed off once it was clear his girlfriend was still in touch with Sanborn."

"And what was this girl's name again?" Frank said.

"Kristen Salvatore," Charlie said. "A kid. At least compared to Sanborn." He paused, thinking. "Wouldn't hurt we pay her another visit. Put a little scare into her if she doesn't want to talk."

Frank said, "We could even bring her in if we have to. Did you let her know what it means to be harboring a fugitive?"

"Maybe we weren't clear enough about it," Charlie said.

Kim turned for the building. "I'm going to go inside and talk to the nurse; see if she might've heard anything else?"

Charlie said, "I think we need to head up to Roan Mountain right now."

Frank said, "And just drive around the woods?" He watched Kim go through the open door into the office, then turned to Charlie. "If I didn't have to play taxi driver for you two, one of us could head up there to Roan Mountain, the other maybe go talk to Sanborn's girlfriend again. I don't know about the three of us driving around in the front seat of my truck."

Charlie said, "I'm still not sure why you're driving that thing. You're the one who should be driving around in the Town Car."

"Are you saying that because I'm old?"

"I'm saying, you'd look good in the Town Car. Maybe once they fix it up..."

"I don't think so," Frank said, looking down at his phone. "Who's the sheriff up there?"

"Roan Mountain?" Charlie said.

Frank nodded. "I know it's Carter County, but..." He walked over to Sheriff O'Leary. "Mike, you have any idea who the sheriff is up Carter County?"

"Lee Walker. You know him?"

"I don't think so," Frank said. "But we're going to head up there, have a look around."

The sheriff looked from Frank to Charlie. "You ever been there before?"

"Not in a while," Charlie said.

Frank nodded, but didn't say much else.

The sheriff said, "Well, being situated in the Appalachian region, of course you've got the mountains. A lot of steep terrain. Lots of trees, of course. If you think they're up they're, trying to hide, it's a good place to do so." He followed Frank and Charlie to Frank's truck. "This all you got? Just the one vehicle?" He gazed around the parking lot at his own department's vehicles being all that were there, besides the doctor's Mercedes, a Toyota, and a small Ford parked around the side of the building.

Frank said, "Well, we're down two vehicles, thanks to these men we're looking for."

"Men and a woman," Charlie said. "Just to make sure we're all on the same page."

Frank gave him the same look he always did when Charlie corrected him, then turned back to Sheriff O'Leary. "Any chance you spoke with him? Sheriff Walker?"

"Not directly. No. We put out an APB, maybe twenty minutes ago. But no, I hadn't talked to any other law enforcement agency outside my county, as of yet."

Chapter 17

IT WAS NEARLY DARK by the time Frank turned off Highway 19 and pulled into the parking lot of Reed's Mart, a local grocery store in Roan Mountain.

Four law enforcement officials stood at the back of the lot by two Carter County sheriff's vehicles watching Frank's Ford pickup truck drive toward them across the lot.

One of the four, tall and thin and appearing young, walked over to the truck, undoing the zipper on his jacket as he approached, tucking the hem of it back as if he wanted to show off his badge and the gun holstered on his hip, maybe in case he had the wrong truck.

Frank, Charlie, and Kim all climbed down and met him halfway.

The sheriff reached out to shake each of their hands. "Sheriff Walker. Pleasure meeting you."

Charlie looked past him at the uniformed woman with two uniformed men he assumed were the sheriff's deputies. "Just the four of you?"

The sheriff looked over at his deputies, then turned back to Charlie. "You don't think we're enough?" He smiled. "We can get more deputies out here, you think we need more, but they're my best deputies, and I assure you we can more than handle the situation.

Charlie gave Frank a look and wondered if the sheriff misunderstood exactly what the situation was. He said to the sheriff, "These men are armed and dangerous. They're carrying automatic weapons. Of course, we're hoping to avoid any kind of a gunfight. But that means we're going to need enough bodies to make sure that doesn't happen."

Frank must've felt the way Charlie was coming across could potentially rub the sheriff the wrong way.

Charlie looked the sheriff over and right away didn't like the way the young official carried himself, showing off his gun the way he did, chest out, chin held high.

Frank said, "We were thinking it might be wise, put up some roadblocks, at least along the main road, and—"

The sheriff said, "I thought you'd asked me to help you find two men?"

"Two men and a woman," Charlie said.

"Well, I'm just not sure it's wise I have one of my deputies here break off, go stand in the road while we all—"

"No offense," Charlie said. "But that's why I just asked if you had anyone else to help. You understand what I'm saying?"

"Listen," Frank said. "We're all on the same team here, all right?" He cleared his throat and got in between the two men. He said to Sheriff Walker, "If you have some other deputies out on patrol, I can show you where I believe we'll want to block the roads, assuming we know where they've gone."

"You haven't told me where that might be," the sheriff said. "And, no offense, Chief Deputy Carter, but I know these roads around here as well as anybody. If you'd like, perhaps I can share my thoughts on where we should or, in some cases, should not block the roads."

"Of course," Frank said. "And I didn't mean to say I knew these roads as well as you do. We'd be grateful for whatever assistance you can provide." He smiled, but Charlie could see it in Frank's expression he was having the same thoughts about this cocky sheriff as Charlie was.

Kim spoke up and said, "We received a call on the way up here, there's property in Roan Mountain, owned by someone with a potential association to one of the suspects, Jack Whitlock."

The sheriff pulled at his chin. "Whitlock? The call we received was regarding a fugitive, name's Denny Caprio. Is this not who we're looking for?"

"It is," Frank said, "But there are three men, and one woman. Denny Caprio's apparently the man in charge, at least, as far as we know. Jack Whitlock is another, and we believe the woman is Claudia Sanborn, although that has not yet been confirmed."

"You said there were three males?" the sheriff said.

"We don't have the identity of the third one yet," Frank said.

The sheriff looked from Kim to Frank. "And what exactly is it these men are doing here in my county?"

"We're not sure yet," Frank said. "The truth is, this case began a couple of days ago, when we were informed a woman, who'd committed wire fraud, embezzlement, and forgery, disappeared prior to her sentencing trial. We got word she'd been holed up in a hotel, east of our office, and both Deputy Riggins and Harlow went to pick her up. The expectation was it'd be a quick drive out, pick her up and let her wait it out behind bars."

Charlie said, "Make a long story short..." He grinned at Frank. "She was working for a man, at least allegedly, who had one of his buddies in the FBI helping him sell illegal firearms."

"Someone from the FBI?" Sheriff Walker said. "Are you serious?"

"Although we don't have all the evidence just yet," Charlie said, "there's a real possibility this agent had something to do with the fact these men showed up at the same hotel we'd gone to. It only makes sense; they knew our every move."

Frank said, "Both Deputy Harlow and Riggins were shot at multiple times by these men, or someone associated with them. So, the hope is they don't know we're here right now. It'd be nice if we can track 'em down, throw them a nice surprise party."

Kim said to Charlie and Frank, "You left out the murders."

Frank turned to the sheriff. "As you know, these men are armed and dangerous. But we're likely going to be able to get them on three different murders so far."

Kim said, "We have intelligence telling us there's a good chance they've come up here to hide out for a while. And that's what we have to assume."

Frank said, "There's a chance they have a location somewhere they've been using all along. But we don't know. We have very little information."

Kim had her phone out. "The property is located north of Buck Mountain Road, but there's no recorded address. We have a general location, but..."

"Well," the sheriff said, "that's not exactly uncommon around these parts. Lots of folks own land, or have had land in their families for decades. Some live off the grid in cabins or mobile homes. But you're right. That's quite a general location." He turned to Frank. "We have a helicopter we can—"

"No. We don't want them to even know we're out here," Frank said. "Not yet."

"Well, I'm just offering," the sheriff said. "Just in case. There's a lot of land out there. Most of it you can't get to on foot. And there are some roads, if you can even call them that, don't even have names. As I said, a lot of people around here live in trailers, some with no real address or anything."

Frank had a sly grin on his face. "Deputy Harlow knows what that's like."

Charlie wasn't going to try to explain to Frank, as he already had dozens of times, living in a fairly decent Winnebago on a river wasn't half as bad as what Frank often made it out to be. But he wasn't going to waste his breath.

"Listen," Charlie said. "Obviously, you're familiar with the area?"

The sheriff reached for Kim's phone. "May I see that?" He took it from her hand before she could answer and looked at the screen, moving his finger all around it, then bringing it closer to his face, staring at it. "I'm not sure how familiar you are with Roan Mountain, but..." He handed back the phone. "What you're looking at there, could be ten or twenty acres, maybe more. And that's not something I'd suggest we cover on foot, of course." He looked up into the sky. "And, with sun already down, I'm not sure it's wise of me, send my deputies out there, in the middle of the night, when—"

"Middle of the night?" Charlie said, raising his gaze to the evening sky. "We still got a couple hours until darkness. And we think we can wait around till daylight. We have no idea they're even up here. But come morning, there's a good chance they're long gone."

"He may be right," Frank said, turning to Charlie. "Maybe it's just something we'd be better off waiting out."

"Wait," Charlie said, gazing at Frank. "You're being serious? Then why'd we even drive up here?" He looked over at the old grocery store, the parking lot's asphalt cracked all over, the building itself looking like it'd had better days, the way half the bricks along the edges were missing or broken. "For the scenery?" He looked at Kim. "You hear what they're saying? We can't wait, Kim. We're going to miss them again. And who's to say we'll have another chance."

Kim appeared hesitant to say what she wanted to. "The fact is," she said, "we don't know where they could be. We have a road with hundreds of acres of forest around it. To think we can just start walking around, with no real direction..."

Charlie held out his closed fist and extended his forefinger. "One. We have a witness who heard them mention this place." He extended his second, middle finger. "And, two... We have intelligence telling us one of the men we're after has a relative up here."

"A *distant* relative," Frank said. "You heard what they said on the call; they're barely related."

"Don't play games with me, Frank. You know it makes too much sense."

Frank said, "Don't make this another one of your personal vendettas, Charlie. It's not about you."

"Oh, are you the one who was shot at multiple times? And nearly killed?" Charlie pulled at his chin, sarcasm all over his face. "Wait, no. That was me."

Kim raised her hand. "Me too," she said, almost as if she was just playing along.

But it was true. Someone had gone after Charlie, and the two of them—he and Kim—were lucky to be alive.

The sheriff said, "Listen. You can follow us out there. We'll show you where the property can be. We may even be able to drive in through the back roads." He pointed with his thumb over his shoulder. "My deputies are the last ones who'd refuse to go out there, just because it's dark. But they're my responsibility. I'd rather not put them in harm's way when it may not be necessary."

"I also prefer to keep myself out of harm's way," Charlie said. "But most of the time I don't get that luxury. That means I can't just hit the brakes, because I'm afraid I may not make it to the finish line."

Sheriff Walker held his gaze on Charlie, pausing for a moment before he turned to Frank. "Whatever you feel you need from us, just say the word."

Charlie said, "We'd like you to at least get us a little closer to where we think they may be."

"I think what Sheriff Walker's saying," Frank said, "is between the amount of land out there we'd have to cover, and the darkness that's just about set in…"

"I understand what he's saying, Frank. I don't need it explained to me. But as I said, what kind of fools would we be to turn our backs now?" Charlie looked at the ground, shaking his head. "Something's telling me there's something here. We're too close."

Frank rolled his eyes, almost smiling at Charlie. "You know how much I love when you follow your gut." He turned to the sheriff. "If you can take us out there to get a look around, we'd appreciate it. I know it's almost dark. We won't hold you and your deputies up for long, but I think Charlie's right. We drove all the way up here, it'd be foolish to turn around now without at least taking a ride out there."

Chapter 18

THE LIGHT GLOWED FROM inside an isolated mobile home fifty or so yards off Buck Mountain Road. Frank, Charlie, and Kim followed Sheriff Walker's SUV, the other two deputies behind Frank's pickup.

There were no other cars on the road as they continued east, the half-moon rising ahead of them. The sheriff turned left onto Blevins Road, covered in asphalt for the first quarter mile until it became dirt, and narrowed.

Other than the slight glow from the moon and their headlights from the vehicles, they were surrounded by trees and total darkness. There wasn't a single home within sight.

"Now you understand why we were a little hesitant," Frank said, his eyes on the road, wearing the glasses he hardly wore but needed.

Charlie said, "You really think we should've waited for daylight? Maybe hope they'd send us an invitation for breakfast?"

Kim, seated in the middle, had one hand on the dashboard in front of her, as if bracing herself, staring ahead. "I think I have to side with Frank and the sheriff," she said. "We're not going to find anybody out here at this time. We missed our window."

Charlie held his gaze on her for a moment until she looked at him, then he turned away, staring out the window to the right.

The red brake lights from the sheriff's vehicle ahead of them brightened, causing a red glow inside the truck's cab. Sheriff

Walker stepped out of his vehicle, and through the beam from the truck's headlights, headed over to Frank's side of the truck.

Frank rolled down his window.

Sheriff Walker pointed straight ahead, then moved his hand slowly from east to west. "This road ends another half mile ahead. We can keep driving, but based on the property details you showed me, the land starts here, and continues for the next mile, beyond where this road'll end. The thing is, this land right here... most of it is owned by Ned Jackson. He's a developer in the area, been buying up any available piece of land for the past twenty years."

Charlie leaned forward to see past Kim and Frank to get a good look at the sheriff outside Frank's window. "If what you're saying is that this man, Mr. Jackson, owns this property, then this must not be what we're looking for."

The sheriff leaned with one arm on the edge of the driver-side window. "No. What I'm saying is"—he reached his hand inside the open window—"can I see that land area you showed me?"

Kim handed the sheriff her phone, the light from the screen glowing as he reached for it and looked it over before handing it right back.

"All right," he said. "I'm thinking most of that property there is landlocked. That would explain why there's no specific address, and no driveway or any real way to get back there." He stepped away from Frank's truck and started toward the darkness of the woods. "Follow me," he said, and went back over to his vehicle and drove forward.

Frank shifted into drive and continued after the sheriff. He adjusted the mirror to change the reflection of the headlights coming from the sheriff's vehicle behind them.

Charlie let out a sigh, gazing out into the woods as they moved along faster now than they had before they stopped.

The dirt kicked up like smoke from behind the sheriff's vehicle. And the faster he moved, the thicker the cloud of dirt and dust became, with the headlights from the truck barely cutting through it.

Charlie was looking outside the truck through the window and noticed a tiny light far off, somewhere, deep in the woods. "Wait!" he said. "Stop!"

But Frank kept going. "What is it?" Frank said, adjusting the rearview mirror again to look out behind them.

"I saw something," Charlie said, now turned in the seat, looking over his shoulder into the woods but had lost whatever it was. "Why didn't you stop?"

"You want me to just slam on my brakes? Damn deputy behind me's all the way up my rear end." He kept his eyes fixed on the road. "What'd you see?"

"I don't know," Charlie said. "A light."

"A light?" Frank said. "That's it?"

Charlie turned again to look into the forest, but there was nothing but darkness.

They continued following Sheriff Walker until once again the red lights glowed in front of them when he came to a stop. There was a chain across the road, or what was left of it. The road ended, and turned to woods.

Charlie jumped from the truck and met the sheriff and his deputy stepping out of the vehicle.

Frank and Kim came up behind them, with the other two deputies following.

"What's back that way?" Charlie said, turning to look down the road, in the direction they'd just come from. "Anybody live back there that you know of?"

The sheriff looked in the same direction as Charlie. "Like I said a little bit ago, all this property abutting the road, from back there where it turned to dirt, is owned by the same man I'd mentioned. We're talking five miles back from here, so..."

"It was less than a mile back," Charlie said. "I saw a light in the woods."

The sheriff paused, giving Frank and Kim a skeptical glance. "Either of you see it?"

Charlie didn't like it, as if the sheriff was questioning whether or not he actually saw something.

"It doesn't matter if they saw it or not," he said. "I know I saw something. You don't think we should at least go back, see what it was?"

The sheriff pointed to where the road had ended. "Back there you'll see some clearing, where someone'll sometimes take a vehicle back there. You know, usually it's kids or..."

"How far's it go?" Frank said.

The sheriff looked in the same direction again. "Maybe another fifty yards or so. I'm not sure I'd suggest any of us drive back there. Terrain gets a bit rough. And this time of night..."

"Can we walk it?" Charlie said.

The sheriff and his deputies all looked at him like he was crazy.

Sheriff Walker said, "I'm not sure what you think you're going to find."

"Well, you said there's property that way that's landlocked, right? But that doesn't mean someone can't get back there."

"Not legally," the sheriff said. "But of course, there's always a chance another property owner, maybe on the other side, might've had some kind of agreement, but..."

Frank made a face, looking annoyed. "Wait, what do you mean on the other side?"

"You can't get back there," the sheriff said.

Kim had her phone out, looking at the screen. "What you're saying is whatever this land is, nobody can actually get to it?"

"They can get to it. But, like I said, you're gonna have to do it on foot. Or with some kind of all-terrain vehicle."

"You have ATVs available?" Charlie said.

The sheriff said, "Are you asking me to bring them out here now? At this time of night?"

There was a noise from off in the distance, like some kind of pop or a bang. Not loud like a gunshot… but it was something.

The group all stayed quiet, turning in the same direction at the same time, back in the direction of where Charlie thought he saw a light.

"So it wasn't just me that heard that?" Charlie took a few steps toward the sound, staring into the darkness of the woods around them. He kept going.

"Charlie?" Frank said. "What are you doing?"

But Charlie didn't stop. He kept walking.

Sheriff Walker said, "It could've been anything."

Charlie kept going, thinking for a moment he should grab a flashlight out of Frank's truck, but he also knew carrying a light would be like putting a target on his back, if that was something he even had to worry about at that point. The headlights from the vehicles had all been turned off, but they weren't off when they were driving. He had thought about it at the time, but knew it didn't make sense driving down a dark dirt road without lights.

"Charlie," Frank said, his voice loud enough Charlie knew he was following behind.

Charlie paused, then stopped and said, "Am I losing my mind here?"

Frank didn't respond at first. "How so?"

"I'm going to walk in there."

"In the woods?" Frank said, nodding. "Yeah, you're losing your mind. If you really think there's something out there, then we need to gear up. Vests on, guns ready. I'm not taking any kind of chances with—"

"I just gotta see what that light is," Charlie said, and started walking again. He didn't look back at Frank, and continued into the woods. The moon had risen high enough now it gave some light through the leafless trees, and his eyes had adjusted enough he could almost see in front of him. The sticks snapped under his boots with each step he took, using his hands to push the branches out of his way, continuing ahead and glancing back just once, seeing Frank through the darkness, more of a silhouette, standing at the edge of the woods.

"Charlie," Frank said, his voice in a loud whisper. "Wait up, will you?"

It was up ahead, maybe a couple hundred yards, where Charlie spotted the light from the road. He put his hand on his holstered Glock and did what he could with each step to avoid the sticks and branches on the ground, but without much luck.

Charlie saw Kim and Frank following, but could only assume the sheriff and his deputies had stayed behind. It didn't make sense to him, the way it almost seemed the sheriff was afraid of the dark. Or maybe he knew better, and Charlie was the fool.

The light grew as Charlie got closer, his pace getting faster with each step. He heard a sound from up ahead, the same one he'd heard, and again, like a door of some sort closing, but not a vehicle. Something lighter. Or smaller.

He made it another thirty yards before he stopped when he saw what looked to be a trailer with a sliver of light coming from inside. It was apparent the area had been cleared at one point, but was now overgrown.

Frank, in a hushed voice, said, "Will you hold up a minute?"

Charlie continued at a good pace until he was close enough to the trailer, he could see the sliver of light coming through windows that looked to be almost completely covered from the inside.

He heard voices and moved closer. Two ATVs were parked on the other side, away from where the area had been at one time cleared, but closer to where the woods grew dense again. Continuing all the way around to the other side of the trailer, Charlie stopped and looked at the door with makeshift steps made of boulders stacked in front of it. The moon reflected off the two small windows to the right of the door.

Charlie headed around to the back where a propane tank was set on the ground, attached to a hose feeding into the back of the trailer. There was a strong urine odor around him, as if someone had just taken a piss.

Checking out the two parked ATVs, he felt the engines on each. One was warm, the other cold.

The trailer was up on blocks and needed a truck to get it out there, but there was no vehicle anywhere in sight. At least not that he could see. It was too dark to say for sure, but he couldn't imagine how the trailer had gotten there in the first place.

It was too dark to see what kind of condition the trailer was in, but he guessed it'd been there awhile. Years, perhaps.

Charlie watched Frank and Kim looking over the area.

Frank waved him over. "We have no idea if this is them."

Charlie pulled his Glock from the holster. "Only one way to find out."

Frank grabbed Charlie by the arm. "No way. We need to do this the right way."

"What's that?" Charlie said, pulling his arm away from Frank's grasp. "You want to knock? See if we'll get invited in for tea?"

Frank let out a sigh, shaking his head. "We're not doing this your way, Charlie. I can't allow—"

"We don't have another choice."

Frank turned and looked into the thick wooded area around them. "We should at least wait for Sheriff Walker."

Charlie kept his voice low. "Don't kid yourself, Frank. I don't know why, but they're not coming down here."

Kim kept her voice hushed, and said, "What if we just wait? We go take cover, watch the place until someone comes out? They won't get far."

Neither Frank nor Charlie responded, but Frank had a look on his face like he liked Kim's suggestion, but knew Charlie well enough to know waiting wasn't Charlie's thing. And once he had his mind set, there was no changing it.

Charlie turned his good ear. "You hear that?" A woman laughed and he recognized it right away. That cackle. "It's her," he said, pulling his Glock. "Claudia Sanborn. I remember the laugh."

Frank just stared back at him, but didn't respond.

But Charlie turned from them without saying another word and went back around to the other side of the trailer. He first tried the doorknob, but it was locked. The laughing and noise inside had stopped, as if they'd heard something.

It was almost as if Charlie made noise on purpose, daring them to think they could be ready for what was about to happen.

His Glock lowered, he stepped up the top step and drove his shoulder into the door. It flew open with ease and dangled, hanging on one hinge.

It was dimly lit inside, and as soon as he stepped in, saw a man with a bandage on his ear seated across a round table from Claudia Sanborn. There were bottles of beer in front of them, along with a lamp that barely lit up the interior.

"Let's see your hands," Charlie said, Glock pointed at the two. He reached for a set of cuffs with the other. "Where are the others?"

The two sat, wide eyed, hands raised, staring back at Charlie without saying a word.

But before either answered, a shot was fired from somewhere outside the trailer. Charlie turned and saw a flash of light come from the woods, hearing another gunshot.

He could hear Frank and Kim yelling, then more shots went off like it was a gunfight out there.

He wanted to turn back to the two at the table, but his body wouldn't let him. He took a step and fell into the hanging door, trying to hold himself up before he finally stumbled with his next step and fell out the open door, first onto the boulder steps, then onto the cold ground beneath, with a thump.

At first, there was little pain. It was as if he'd convinced his body to ignore it. But face down on the ground, sticks and stones and dirt pressing into his cheek, he felt the aching pain bore through him like someone had driven into him with a drill.

He heard yelling. More shots. An engine screamed from somewhere nearby.

Frank was kneeling next to him, turning Charlie over. "No, no, no. Shit. No." Frank had never sounded the way he had before, acting like a scared old man on the edge of tears.

Charlie had his eyes open but couldn't keep them that way. He let them close. It felt better.

Frank turned and yelled, "Go get those sons of bitches!"

Footsteps crunched on the ground, moving fast past Charlie until the sound silenced and it was quiet.

He opened his eyes enough to see beams of light bouncing off the trees. He coughed and felt pain shoot through his ribs and back. Trying to raise his head, he wanted to sit up. But Frank eased him back down.

"Just relax," Frank said, looking down at him. "Just keep breathing, buddy. You're going to be all right."

Charlie wanted to smile. He'd never heard Frank call him "buddy" or anything else like it before. Frank wasn't one for using profanity directed toward someone else, but Charlie remembered the only time Frank called him anything, he'd said he was an asshole, then apologized a moment later.

Footsteps moved fast past Charlie, and when he looked up he saw the sheriff and his deputies running past him.

Frank yelled, "Hold your fire! My deputy's in there!" He turned back to Charlie. "Stay with me. All right?"

Charlie started to talk but Frank told him not to.

"Save your energy," he said.

Charlie looked through the trailer's open door.

Claudia Sanborn was handcuffed and standing next to a uniformed law enforcement official. Charlie assumed he was one of the sheriff's deputies, but he wasn't sure. He couldn't see well, like it was blurry, watching the man talking to Sanborn. Charlie couldn't make out what he was saying.

The uniformed official led Claudia Sanborn out the door of the trailer and down the steps. He asked Frank if Charlie was going to be okay, but there was no response.

Charlie didn't even know if anyone else was there. He wondered about the man with the bandage on his ear and thought he might've gotten a shot off before he was hit himself. But he didn't know.

Frank removed his jacket and then the sweatshirt he had on underneath, using it to cover Charlie, putting pressure on Charlie's side. "Hang tight," Frank said, then yelled out, "Make sure they know where we are!"

Charlie didn't know what or who he was referring to. Paramedics, he hoped. He was aware enough to know he needed them. He thought about how cold it had gotten and licked his lips. His mouth was dry.

A moment later, he was warm. Hot, in fact.

He pictured Jennie with her hand on his forehead. Whenever Charlie would even hint he wasn't feeling well, which wasn't often, Jennie would reach for his forehead. But he'd push her hand away. "I'm fine," he'd say.

He closed his eyes to rest them, opened them again and saw nobody. There was no sound. Was he alone?

"Frank?" he said, his voice strained to a point he wasn't sure any sound came out. He saw blue lights in the distance, then lights coming through the trees. He wanted to know what was happening but couldn't get another word out. He closed his eyes.

The sirens were louder now.

Charlie felt the warmth of Frank's hand on his shoulder, but then it was gone and felt as if the cold seeped through his skin. He watched Frank with his back to him.

Frank had a flashlight in his hand, waving his arms. He yelled out, "Can't you people move any faster?" He stepped back over to Charlie, kneeled next to him, and put his hand on his shoulder. "Hang tight, Charlie. They're almost here."

Chapter 19

CHARLIE WAITED FOR HIS eyes to adjust and looked up at Frank and Kim standing on one side of him, to his left. He followed the needle in his arm, to the IV hanging over him, then raised his hand to his chest, touching the electrode pads stuck to his shaved skin. He cleared his throat. "Am I dead?" His voice was raspy, his throat sore.

He had a cannula in his nose, delivering oxygen.

Frank smiled, and Charlie followed his gaze to Jennie standing on the other side of the bed. His eyelids were heavy, and he closed them for a moment.

Jennie put her hand on his arm. "Oh, Charlie," she said, her eyes red and glazed over with tears.

He held his gaze on her, but couldn't seem to get his head on straight, as one would expect. He lay there in the bed, quiet for a couple of moments, trying to clear the cobwebs, then raised his head from the pillow enough to get a look at his right side, under his arm. A bandage covered most of the area, from his armpit and over his ribs, to halfway down the side of his abdomen, a few inches up from his hip. "Did I have surgery?"

Jennie nodded, but appeared too upset to speak.

Charlie turned to Frank and Kim on the other side, clearing his throat. "Did... did you get them?"

Frank and Kim both exchanged a glance, and Kim shook her head. She said, "One of them escaped on the ATV. The other on foot, but it was too dark. I lost him in the woods."

Charlie took a breath, like it was hard to talk. "Caprio?"

"We believe so," Frank said. "And Whitlock. Claudia Sanborn is in custody, and she's somewhat cooperating. There was a third man—the one you'd shot in the truck—who tried to get away, but..."

"Frank shot him," Kim said, almost as if she was proud of him.

Charlie was pleased, forcing a smile but it almost hurt. He knew he'd made a mistake and looked at Frank. "Do you want me to admit you were right?" He tried to use whatever strength he had to push himself where he could sit up.

But Jennie reached out for him, as if holding him down. "I don't think they want you to move. You need to rest."

He turned to her, almost as if he'd forgotten she was standing there, nodded, then eased his head back down into the pillow.

Frank said, "I guess I'm just happy you're alive. I don't know for sure how, but once again you got lucky. I gotta guess those nine lives we were talking about have been knocked down to one or two at this point." He smiled and put his hand on Charlie's shoulder.

Kim said, "You lost so much blood. The doctor said he was surprised how much you had in you."

Charlie took a moment, clearing his throat. "Where am I?"

"Johnson City Medical," Frank said. "You remember being in the helicopter?"

"I don't remember much of anything."

Frank said, "Well, the doctor said you went into hemorrhagic shock, from the severe loss of blood. We made the call to fly you out here. The truth is, you wouldn't have made the drive, especially not to the local ER."

Kim said, "One of the deputies said they care for both animals and people in the same place."

"Is that true?" Jennie said.

Kim laughed. "I hope not."

The doctor showed up in the room, still dressed in his scrubs. He glanced at Jennie, then stood next to her and looked at Charlie. "How are you feeling, Deputy?"

Charlie shrugged, but it hurt his side when he did. "I guess I'm not dead?"

The doctor laughed and turned to Jennie. "Are you Mrs. Harlow?"

Jennie appeared surprised by the question. "I am, but..."

"My ex-wife," Charlie said. "If we'd stayed married I might've been in the same situation I am now, but she would've been the one firing the gun."

The doctor laughed. "I just want to make sure someone is capable of understanding the outcome, and what you were up against in there."

"I'm capable," Charlie said.

"Well, I mean someone who didn't just get rolled out of surgery," the doctor said.

"I think you can talk freely," Charlie said. "One of us will remember."

He laughed again, then went to the end of the bed and grabbed the clipboard. Looking it over, he flipped the sheet and put it back. "Your vitals are all surprisingly good. The amount of blood loss for someone who's actually up and talking right now... I don't like to use the word *lucky*, but if anyone else came in the same state as you, they likely wouldn't have walked out of here."

Charlie looked down at his feet. He could feel them, wiggled his toes, making sure everything seemed to be working the way it should. "I'm not paralyzed or anything, am I?"

"No, no. Not at all. You were shot twice, both in the same area on the right side, which turned out to be a good thing." He looked down at Charlie's bandage and felt around the covered area. "Somehow, it missed your major organs. I could go over the list of what they could've hit, but the muscle built up around your side here stopped the bullet from penetrating more than it had. The buildup of muscle also caused more bleeding, the way the bullets were lodged inside your body. But, with all that said... you're going to be as good as new. Except for a couple of small scars." He looked from Frank to Kim, then back at Charlie. "This isn't the first time you've been shot?"

Frank said, "Nah, Charlie's like a magnet when bullets are flying."

"It's only been two other times," Charlie said.

Jennie held her gaze on Charlie. "Three."

Charlie looked down, having to think for a moment. "Oh, right. But they were at the same time." He raised his gaze to the doctor. "Can I go home now?"

The doctor shook his head, looking surprised Charlie would even ask the question. "Do you know how much blood you lost? You received a transfusion of two units of packed red blood cells. Around five hundred milliliters."

Charlie just stared at the doctor, of course, not really being able to do the math on exactly what that meant. "Tomorrow?"

"I'd like you to stay for at least a couple of days. We'll reevaluate you later today, and I can make a better determination. Your body needs rest."

Charlie turned to Frank and Kim, shaking his head. "I can't just sit here. I want him, Frank. I want him."

"I don't know the specifics or whatever it is you're involved in. Clearly, you have the kind of job, well..." The doctor cleared his throat. "You're a strong man, Charlie. It's what saved your life. But you're also human. If you try to get back out there, especially if it's something strenuous, which is clearly the case in your line of work, you're going to end up right back in here. It's not uncommon for an injury like this. The chance of infection increases significantly if you don't give yourself time to heal."

Jennie reached out and put her hand on Charlie's chest. "Don't worry. He's not going anywhere."

Charlie looked at her. It was all confusing enough. But the way Jennie was acting, like everything was normal, and they hadn't just been through a divorce that tore him apart as much as the bullets had the night before...

"Thanks, Doc," Charlie said, giving him a grin, his head still back on the pillow but nodding as best he could. "I get it. Whatever you say."

The doctor had a look on his face like he didn't believe Charlie. He gave Jennie and Frank and Kim all a look, like he wasn't fooling around, hoping they'd get the message more than he felt Charlie had. "He's going to need to rest." He said to Charlie, "I'll be back later to check on you."

The doctor had just left the room when Lindsey showed up, carrying a large bunch of flowers in a glass vase, her face practically covered by all the bright colors when she stopped at Charlie's side.

Everyone stood quiet, watching her, including Charlie, whose gaze went back and forth between Jennie and Lindsey.

Lindsey stopped frozen when she saw Jennie standing there looking at her.

"Oh, uh..." She put on a smile and turned to Charlie. "I brought you some flowers."

The thing was, Lindsey knew who Jennie was. She and Charlie had been in the Coyote Grille together a handful of times, back when they were still married, with Lindsey behind the bar.

But the look on Jennie's face showed she wasn't quite sure who this woman was. "How beautiful," she said, looking over the flowers with a smile anyone with two eyes could see wasn't exactly sincere.

Lindsey looked at Charlie as if she wanted to lean over and kiss him, but likely knew better. "Are you okay?"

Charlie looked at her and could see her mixed emotions and maybe some confusion in her expression. "I'm doing all right," he said. "Thank you." He raised his hand, the catheter from the IV tube still taped to the back of it, the thin tube hanging off the bed. "You can put them over there, on the window, if you want."

He wasn't sure what else to say, and the fact Jennie and Lindsey were right there standing next to each other, practically shoulder to shoulder, was more uncomfortable for him than the tubes and wires he was attached to.

Lindsey was clearly unsure of what to say, and strolled over to the windowsill.

Jennie stared at her. But it wasn't likely in a way she'd meant any sort of malevolence. "Oh, now I know who you are," she said. "You work at that bar..." She turned to Charlie. "What is it called?"

"Coyote Grille."

"Oh, that's right," Jennie said, almost as if she knew before she even asked. "It's so nice you came by to see Charlie."

Frank went over and took the flowers from Lindsey, trying to find a place to put them down. It was as if he'd noticed the tension in the room. "Let me take that for you, hon."

Even though Charlie still hadn't come clean with him about Lindsey, or anyone else, for that matter, Frank was far from dumb. He was one of the most perceptive people around. Not to mention, he'd been to Coyote Grille enough with Charlie.

Kim was the one who knew what was going on, but only because of the phone calls she'd heard between Charlie and Lindsey, and the way he'd talk to Jennie and have to answer her questions, dancing around, telling her where he'd stayed the night before.

Lindsey stood at the foot of Charlie's bed, Frank back on one side with Kim, Jennie on the other. "Maybe I should go?" she said, eyes on Charlie, waiting for his answer.

He raised his hand and moved his finger from Jennie to Lindsey. "Jennie, Lindsey. Lindsey, Jennie." He took a deep breath and winced, grabbing for his side, hoping somehow there would be no more questions about who was whom or Jennie asking why Lindsey—the bartender from Coyote Grille, as far as Jennie knew—was there to visit Charlie.

He knew, of course, it was now clear to Lindsey that Jennie knew nothing about the two of them. After all, it wasn't like it was any of Jennie's business in the first place. She's the one who wanted the divorce. But Lindsey would ask, if not right there in the hospital room, then at some point later, why he was afraid to tell his ex-wife about a girl he'd gotten more serious with over the past few months.

It was uncomfortably quiet in the room for a couple of moments, Lindsey glancing at Frank and Kim, as if she was hoping someone else would talk. After being still, she finally squeezed past Jennie and stood beside Charlie in the bed.

She had tears in her eyes. "I didn't know if you were alive or not," Lindsey said, her voice cracking. She cleared her throat, wiping her cheek with her hand. "I'm sorry." She looked at Jennie, then back at Charlie. "I think I'm going to go." Touching Charlie's arm, she turned and hurried out the door.

"Lindsey," Charlie said, calling for her, but his voice was so weak and quiet, she likely didn't hear him.

Jennie looked at him as if she should have her arms crossed, tapping her foot.

"What?" Charlie said, giving her a quick glance, then turned his head on the pillow to look over at Frank and Kim on the other side of the bed. "You two gonna just stand there, not saying nothing?"

Kim smiled—more of a grin—and turned, walking over to the window. She stood with her back to the others looking out into the morning sun rising up beyond the parking lot.

Frank said, "Sheriff Walker sends his regards."

"His regards?" Charlie said. He huffed out a laugh and grabbed his side with another wince.

"Should I get the doctor?" Jennie said.

"Yeah, you mind going out there, see if they can give me something?" He knew there was a button next to him he could've used, but needed Jennie to step out of the room for a moment.

He turned back to Frank as soon as she did. "I hope the sheriff up there's glad he kept his deputies safe, seeing apparently they must be afraid of the goddamn dark."

"Oh, come on, Charlie," Frank said. "I know the man feels he made a mistake, not following us down there."

"A mistake?" Charlie said. "Is that what you'd call it? You gotta wonder how someone like him becomes sheriff. Hard to believe it's on account of his good looks. But I didn't see many other qualities that'd gotten him elected."

"Well, I'm not sure if they'd come down, it would've made much of a difference either way," Frank said. "You're the one with the thick head, gotta do things your way."

Kim was sniffing the flowers Lindsey brought, then turned from the window. "Frank," she said. "Give the man a break. You can lay into him later, once he's up on his feet."

Charlie cracked a small grin.

"You're right," Frank said. "I'm sorry." He wagged his finger at Charlie. "But once you're up and at 'em, I'm going to kick your ass for this shit. You know how hard it is to replace a half-decent deputy these days?"

Chapter 20

Charlie had been restless all night, trying to get comfortable in the hospital bed, with all the noise and announcements and constant beeping. How was he supposed to get the rest the doctor had ordered?

By the time Jennie showed up in his room, he was pretty sure he'd already convinced the doctor to sign his release, and was still in his hospital gown and seated in the chair in the corner, looking at his phone. He looked up. "Hey."

She held a duffel bag and placed it on the bed, then stepped over to him, across the rays of light coming through the window from the sun.

Charlie was surprised when she leaned over and kissed him on his forehead. "You're not lying to me, are you?"

He stared at her for a moment, no idea what she meant. Of course, he had a few things in mind it could've been...

"About the doctor," she said, making it clear. "You sure he said you could go home already? You've barely been here twenty-four hours. When I was standing right here in this room, he said you needed to stay here at least a few days. I'm just wondering why he'd change his mind."

Charlie had a crooked grin on his face. "Maybe a weaker man would somehow get better lying around all day. But there's no way I'd be able to go through another night like this."

"So he *didn't* say you could go?"

"He needed a little convincing. But the good doctor came in this morning, told me how good everything looked. They removed all the tubes and wires, so...." He shrugged, and felt a twinge of pain in his side, but nothing like it'd been through the night. "Feeling better already."

Jennie had a look on her face like she still didn't believe it. "You've been through a lot. I just hope you're going to rest, the way you're supposed to. You think Frank and Kim can't handle things without you?"

Charlie just looked at her without a response, then started to push himself up from the padded chair. But he stopped, gave himself a moment, then realized he'd need to work up some strength just to get up out of the chair.

Jennie reached out to help him, but he pushed her hand away.

"I'm all right," he said, and tried again. He leaned forward to get some momentum and gripped the armrests to push himself up, the skin on the back of his legs peeling away from the chair's faux leather like gum on hot asphalt.

He fixed his gown, making sure all parts were properly covered, and slowly made his way over to the closet when he opened the double doors. He stood looking down at his bloodstained boots. There was nothing else in there. He liked the shirt he was wearing, but knew the bloodstains and likely holes in the side weren't something that'd ever look quite right. "Those my clothes?" he said, looking at the duffel bag on the bed.

She said, "Frank drove me over to the Winnebago. I don't know how you live out there like that. Or how someone without a truck is supposed to get up there."

"They can't," he said. "But I like it that way."

"Place could use a good cleaning too," she said.

"I didn't tell you to go in and inspect it." He was somewhat hunched when he got over to the bed and opened the duffel bag. "But thank you for getting these. I appreciate it." He gave her a quick glance. "Now, if you'll excuse me." He waited for her to get out so he could get dressed.

"You act like I've never seen you naked." She turned to the window, her back to him. "Go ahead. I won't look."

He took out a pair of jeans and the button-down shirt she'd gotten him, and the first thing he did was try to pull on the jeans. But it wasn't quite as simple as he'd hoped. There was still a lot of pain—plenty of it—even if he'd told the doctor there wasn't much at all.

"Shit," he said, and sat on the edge of the bed. He hated to have to ask her, but he had little choice. He held out his jeans. "You mind giving me a hand?"

Jennie turned from the window, like she was holding back a smile looking at him, robe open, nothing but his boxers underneath.

"Eyes up here," he said, pointing to his face.

She kneeled in front of him and helped him slip his feet through each pant leg, then helped him stand so she could pull them up.

He could smell her, the way she stood so close, the sweet smell of her hair rubbing against his chin.

"All right," he said. "Thank you." He zipped them up himself, fastening the button.

She stared at his chest. "It's been a long time since I've seen these scars."

He looked down at what used to be two holes scarred over from back a few years. Even back then, it was a different doctor who told him how lucky he was to be alive.

Maybe Frank was right about him being like a cat, but that one day his luck and those nine lives, or whatever was left, would run out.

Jennie cleared her throat and turned from him, walking back over to the window. She stood with her back to him again, looking outside into the sunny, blue sky.

"You all right?" he said, sensing something was wrong.

She took a moment before she turned to him, nodding. "Is there something between you and that bartender?"

Charlie finished buttoning his shirt, looked at the socks in the duffel bag but wasn't going to bother trying to put them on. "You know where my hat is?" he said, as if hoping he could go ahead and change the conversation and somehow Jennie wouldn't notice.

"No, I don't know where your hat is." She paused, as if thinking about it. "You mean your USMS hat?"

Charlie nodded. "Yeah. I hope someone grabbed it, and I didn't leave it in the woods."

"Can't you just get another one?"

"Are you kidding? You know how long I've had that hat?"

Jennie went over to the wardrobe, opened the doors, and took out Charlie's boots, looked them over, a disgusted look on her face. They were filthy. "Is this blood?" she said.

"I think so." He pointed at the floor in front of him. "Just put 'em here. I'll put them on."

Jennie grabbed the plastic bag hanging on the hook inside the wardrobe. She opened it and pulled out his wallet. She already had his key. "You want this?"

Charlie slipped one foot into his boot without bending down, then slipped the other one in, ignoring the pain he felt. He left them untied and straightened up, feeling as if he was almost out of breath and lightheaded. He sat back down on the edge of the bed.

"You all right?" Jennie said, handing him his wallet.

He gave a nod, but didn't say anything. He didn't feel well.

Sitting in the chair was all right at first, but getting up, moving around even just a little seemed to suck up what little energy he had.

Jennie said, "You're not going to answer me?"

"About what?"

"Your friend? From the bar?"

Charlie reached for the table next to the bed and grabbed a cup of water to fix his bone-dry throat. He took a sip. "She's just a friend, Jennie. Kim had called her, told her what happened, and—"

"Why would she call her? I don't get it," she said. "I mean, I know it's none of my business." She tried to put on a smile, but Charlie could see there was some sort of pain inside, the way she had it on her face. "If you and her are together, then I'm—"

"Would you please just give me a break?" He let out a sigh. "Would you mind going to get the nurse? They're not going to let me walk out of here on my own two feet."

Jennie didn't say a word, walking past Charlie and into the hall.

Charlie reached for his phone, on the same table next to his bed. He'd sent a handful of texts to Lindsey since she'd left the hospital, but she hadn't even replied back. He was going to text her again, but thought he'd wait until he was back at his own place and had some privacy, then he'd call her. Maybe even ask her to stop by, once Jennie had left.

At first, he was expecting he'd be going home to the Winnebago. But the fact was even when Jennie told him Frank drove her out there, it hadn't exactly entered his mind that her car, a Nissan Altima she'd recently purchased, would never come close to making it up the hills and through that rough terrain along the Swannanoa River.

He turned to the doorway when he heard the wheelchair, a nurse behind it pushing the chair into the room, Jennie coming in after her.

Jennie said to the nurse, "You sure the doctor said it's all right for him to go home?"

The nurse seemed a bit hesitant to answer, a look on her face like she didn't have any more information than Jennie. "Admittedly, I was somewhat surprised to hear he'd be released.

But Dr. Arnold's one of the best, and I'm sure your husband will keep his promise he'll rest, as instructed, and—"

"Ex-husband," Jennie said, a look on her face as if she needed to cover up some feelings inside of her. Charlie couldn't quite make out what was going through her head. She smiled at the nurse. "Don't worry, I'll strap him to the bed."

Charlie said, "She never said anything like that when we were married."

The nurse looked like she wasn't sure if she should laugh, her face turning a shade of dark red as she adjusted the wheelchair and turned it toward Charlie, taking his arm to help him. She said to Jennie, "It sounds like you, or someone else, will be with him for these next few days?"

Jennie grabbed the duffel bag from the bed and hung it over her shoulder. "Yes, he's coming home with me. And I already took the time off work. So he'll have no chance to escape."

The nurse eased Charlie into the wheelchair, and looked as if she wasn't sure what to say, or maybe didn't want to be involved in the conversation.

He looked up at Jennie, over his shoulder. "What do you mean I'm going home with you? I've got to get back to my place. Like I told you: in my own bed."

The nurse wheeled him out of the room and into the hall.

He tried to look back at Jennie, but couldn't get his head to turn that far around. "I'm serious, Jennie. We can't... Maybe we can meet Frank, have him drive me up to the river?"

"You'll still be sleeping in *your* bed," she said. "It's the same one."

He had to think about what she meant. "You mean, because I said I want to sleep in my own bed? Well, you know which one I meant. Not *that* one. It's not mine anymore. Remember? Everything you got in the settlement? None of it's mine anymore."

He knew it was a conversation they probably didn't need to be having right there as he rode down the hallway, in front of a stranger. But it didn't matter anyway. He knew Jennie, the way she'd make up her mind about something.

And people have said *he* was the stubborn one.

But they'd never met Jennie.

"What about my clothes?" he said, trying to come up with a way he could get back to his Winnebago. "I need more clothes. You think I'm just going to sleep in these jeans?"

He liked living on the river in the Winnebago that he'd gotten used to calling home, even though, technically, along with the land along the Swannanoa, belonged to an old friend of his. He just wanted to rest in his own place, and be able to do his own thing without Jennie, or anyone else, telling him what he should or shouldn't be doing.

As much as at one time he missed Jennie more than he'd ever imagined he would, especially for the first few months after he'd moved out, and even more so after the divorce had been final, he'd gotten to a point he knew he could live without her.

The thing was, he grew to like Lindsey, the more time he spent with her. And another problem he thought of, if he was to go back to Jennie's, to a house that at one time in the recent past was *his* house, he could see it messing things up with Lindsey.

And he knew, for a fact, it was likely obvious to Lindsey, when she saw Jennie in Charlie's room at the hospital, that Jennie knew nothing about Lindsey. Meaning, Charlie hadn't said a word about her to Jennie. And he knew it was the most likely reason for Lindsey still not responding to any of his texts.

Chapter 21

JENNIE AND CHARLIE DIDN'T speak much on the ride from the hospital. His arguing with her, saying whatever he could to convince her to somehow get him to the Winnebago, to maybe call Frank to get him there, turned out to be a losing proposition. And when he finally realized the choice was never going to be his, as was often the case when dealing with Jennie, he leaned his head against the passenger-side window.

He hadn't expected to fall asleep, but when Jennie squeezed his arm, and he opened his eyes after the hour-long drive, he had no idea where he was.

By the time he realized he was at his old house—Jennie's house, now—he tried to sit up straight but had a kink in his neck that hurt almost as much as the pain coming through his side.

He coughed and felt a sharp, heavy burn shoot through his ribs.

The passenger door opened, and he caught himself, as if he was going to fall out. The cool air from outside sent a chill through him, the warmth of Jennie's touch almost hot when she grabbed his hand.

"Come on," she said, his duffel bag hung over her shoulder.

He felt for a moment as if unable to speak, a thick fog in his head he hadn't quite noticed when they were leaving the hospital. It took him a moment to move, slow to get his foot out as if every move he made, anywhere on his body, would shoot pain through his side.

"Are you all right?" Jennie said.

Charlie held the armrest on the door with one hand, pulling himself up with the leather strap over his head with the other. "I'm all right." It wasn't as easy as he'd expected it to be.

He felt like an old man, but was finally on his feet, somewhat unsteady as he took a moment to gain a little more balance before he took a step. "Jesus," he said, knowing right then he was probably better off with Jennie there to help him.

She took him by the arm and held him steady. "You think the doctor was lying when he said it'd take some time?"

Charlie didn't answer, instead looking at the steps ahead leading to the front door.

They walked along the pathway, fallen red and brown leaves from the oaks surrounding the yard covering the lawn he used to cut whenever he had a day off, which seemed to be rare the last couple of years of their marriage.

It crossed his mind, for a moment, to say sorry to Jennie. Or maybe just thank her, for sticking with him as long as she had. But he knew there was no need to get all sappy, and that it was likely the drugs or whatever else he'd had inside him messing with his head.

• • • • • • • • • •

Charlie woke up in darkness. He was so warm his T-shirt was soaked through with sweat. Tangled up in the sheets with the pillow missing, his first thought was of his father, seeing him clear as day, handcuffed in the back of the cruiser, Charlie and his sister watching from the window of their mobile home.

It felt so real at first, as if he'd gone back and watched the same scene he'd dreamed about dozens of times before, the sheriff taking Charlie and his sister aside to explain to them why they were taking the man away.

The dream was so vivid—it always was—the way the sheriff kneeled down and spoke to him in a kind voice, something his father had never done.

The same man would stop by their mobile home every few days, so much so that Charlie and his sister got to wondering if there was something between him and their mother.

But eventually, the visits stopped. But that feeling Charlie had for the man was the one that led him to wanting to be a sheriff one day himself.

It took Charlie another moment to bring it all together in his mind, tell himself it was a dream. He lay there in the darkness, thinking it all felt too real—it always did—but still wondering if it was how it all actually happened. He always did, whenever he had that dream.

He was young at the time, and had convinced himself over the years the dream was mostly his mind just filling in some details with whatever it wanted to. He knew his father was arrested—more than once—but the way it happened, the way he'd dreamed about it... He had no idea if any of it was ever real.

Of course, even before his mother died, it wasn't like he'd ever ask about it or bring it up. The way she wanted it, after his father had disappeared, was that the man never existed in the first place. There was no mention of his name. No pictures, other than the one Charlie had found after she was gone, and now kept in an old coffee can with some coins and keys.

Even with his sister, at least the one or two times they'd speak each year, he wouldn't ask questions about him, beyond the one time their father showed up and took them on a camping trip but soon realized being a father wasn't something he was meant to be. Then he disappeared from their lives once and for all.

His head was flat on the mattress, but he didn't have the strength to look on the floor, where he assumed his pillow had gone. He turned, looking over at the other side of the bed. For a moment, he thought maybe Jennie would be there. He didn't remember getting in bed, or even falling asleep. At least, not at first. He knew he'd eaten something when they got home from the hospital. He remembered trying to sit at the table, having chicken broth, then not being hungry, making it to the couch where Jennie sat with him.

The rest was unclear.

But she wasn't there next to him, and he grabbed the pillow and stuck it under his head, then noticed the clock on the side table. It was 3:28. It took him a moment to assure himself it was morning and not the afternoon.

Where had all the time gone?

He wanted to take his shirt off. Even the sheets were wet from his sweat, but it seemed like a lot of work, and it hurt just to move, shifting at first to his left side, then trying his back. There was a lot of pain.

The pillow he had smelled like Jennie, and he felt a sense of comfort he hadn't had in a long time. He turned onto his back and tried to ignore the pain. He felt more awake than he had since he first got there, like the sweat had knocked out the fog he hadn't been able to clear before he fell asleep.

He was becoming restless, and pushed himself up, through the pain, and sat on the edge of the bed, rubbing his face. He sat there in the darkness and felt a lightheadedness that kept him from trying to stand. He reached out, feeling for the lamp he was sure was next to him but could barely see anything at all. And in the process of moving his hand, he knocked something off the side table. Glass smashed on the hardwood floor with a splash of liquid hitting his feet along with pieces of glass.

A light came on outside the door with a glow coming under it, until the door swung open and Jennie rushed in, wearing shorts and a T-shirt, hair going in all directions and a look of panic on her face.

The light from the hall filled the room, and when Charlie looked down he saw a puddle of water with broken glass everywhere.

"Are you okay?" she said. Her first thought, of course, was one of concern for Charlie's well-being.

He said, "Sorry about that. I—"

"You scared the hell out of me," she said.

Charlie could see lights in the hall coming from the television but barely heard sound from it. "Were you sleeping on the couch?"

Jennie didn't answer, stepping over to him in her bare feet, walking on her toes. It appeared as if she was about to crouch down and reach for the broken glass. But Charlie threw his arm out to prevent her from getting closer to it. "What are you doing?" he said. "You want a piece of glass in your foot?"

She looked at him, like she was surprised at what he did, then stretched her hand past his arm, trying to avoid the glass, and turned on the lamp. She then reached for the pillow that had slipped down between the bed and the side table.

"Oh," he said. "Thanks." He reached for it, thinking she was going to hand it to him, but she stuck it under her arm.

"It's wet," she said.

He watched Jennie, the yellow light from the lamp reflecting off her face. Her eyes looked as if she was still half-asleep, not fully with it herself just yet. Backing away from the bed and the broken glass in the puddle of water, she tried to balance on her toes until she was around the foot of the bed. She went to the closet and opened the door, sticking one foot inside, then the other, and turned to Charlie with slippers on both feet.

Charlie wanted to get up, but wasn't sure how to pull it off. He needed something he could use to push himself up, besides the mattress.

"Stay there," Jennie said. "I'll take care of it."

The slippers on her feet were the pair he'd bought her for Christmas right before he moved out for good. She didn't seem to be as excited about them at the time, when he first gave them to her. But they appeared to be well worn now, and he was surprised to see she still had them at all.

"Let me get a broom," she said, then stood still by the doorway, her gaze fixed on him, as if she forgot what she was about to do until she turned and disappeared into the hall.

Charlie was still tempted to step down from the bed and try to pick up some of the pieces of glass, but wasn't sure, with the pain he was feeling, he'd be able to bend over, or even get back into the bed once he left it.

Part of him was starting to understand what had happened to him, as if until then he hadn't taken it seriously. Or it hadn't fully sunk in how serious it was.

Jennie came back in with a broom and dustpan with a plastic trash can she placed away from the glass. She said, "Why don't you lie down, get some rest."

"I think I'm wide awake," he said. He wanted to smile, but didn't. "You don't have to wait on me while I'm here, you know."

She put the dust pan down and started to sweep the glass toward it, acting at first as if she hadn't heard him. "I know," she said, her gaze down like she was afraid to look at him for some reason. She'd gotten the glass into a pile, along with some of the water, then crouched down and swept it into the dustpan.

Charlie said, "You want me to get the mop?"

Jennie finished what she was doing with the glass, emptied it into the trash bin, then put her hand on Charlie's naked knee. "I want you to rest. So you get better. That's all."

He cracked a crooked smile. "You mean, so you can get me out of here?" He waited for her response, but wasn't even sure why he'd said it, like they were playing some kind of game with each other.

Jennie crouched down again and swept up what little glass was left, dumped it into the trash, and picked up the can and the broom and dustpan. She again acted as if she hadn't heard what he'd said. But she stopped at the door and turned, staring back at him for a moment. "The truth is, there are some days I wish we could've made it work."

She left the bedroom before Charlie had a chance to respond, even though he wasn't sure what he was supposed to say.

Chapter 22

CHARLIE WAS ON JENNIE'S couch when he looked out the picture window and saw Frank's blue truck pull in the driveway and park behind Jennie's car. Frank and Kim got out and started for the door.

Charlie raised the remote and turned off the TV, pushing himself up from the couch to get to the door. He felt stiff and sore in a way he never had before. His back hurt, but he felt it was more from the bed, or being on the couch all morning: something he rarely found time to do.

He hunched over a bit when he walked so the pain wasn't quite as bad, although when he straightened up with each step, he noticed—or at least hoped—maybe he was starting to feel a little better.

He hadn't taken the pills for pain the doctor had given him. Same with not taking any of the over-the-counter meds they'd recommended he use, to control the pain. It just wasn't his thing, and Charlie couldn't remember the last time he took any kind of medicine. Not even an aspirin.

The house was quiet, and the dead bolt popped when he turned it before he opened the door.

"Morning," he said, holding the door open. "Come on in." He backed from the door, doing his best to look strong and healthy, even though he hadn't showered or even looked in the mirror in a couple of days. He touched the top of his head as if to fix his hair, but then decided not to bother.

"How you feeling?" Frank said, stepping inside after Kim.

"Well..." Charlie took a breath and had to think about it for a moment. "I've felt better, but I think I'm coming along." He gestured for them to come into the room, then picked up the pillow Jennie had left on the couch and moved it out of the way so they could sit down.

Kim said, "You look better, I think?"

"You think?" Charlie said, grinning.

"You know what I mean," she said. "I don't think I've ever even seen you in shorts and a T-shirt."

Charlie looked down at his clothes, wishing he'd gotten cleaned up a bit before they showed up. "Well, I can't imagine I'll be like this much longer." He turned to Frank. "Any chance I can get a new vehicle soon? I'd like to get back to my place. Maybe tonight. But I can't have Jennie drive me in the Nissan. It won't make it up there."

Frank appeared to be thinking about it. "I'll see what I can do." He looked around the house and into the kitchen. "Jennie's not here?" He sniffed. "Something smells good."

"She's in the shower," Charlie said. "I think she put something in the oven. Muffins, maybe?" He could smell the sweetness but hadn't paid much attention until Frank had asked. He wondered if he'd dozed off on the couch and maybe didn't realize it, when Jennie was moving around in the kitchen.

Even though he stayed in bed, he hadn't gone back to sleep after waking up in the middle of the night, knocking over the glass. He had a feeling Jennie hadn't slept either.

"What did she do, take a few days off?" Kim said.

Charlie said, "I don't know if she's going back to work tomorrow or not. I told her to, and that I'd be out of her hair by tonight." He turned again to Frank. "I just need a way to get to my own place. And I can't do it without four-wheel drive."

Kim said. "I'm pretty certain the doctor said you're not supposed to drive for a while."

Charlie acted like he didn't know or remember, even though he did. "I'm sure it's fine." He again gestured for the couch and two large chairs on either side of it, all in a square setup, the TV on the wall directly across from the furniture. "You going to sit?"

Frank and Kim both seemed hesitant for some reason, and Charlie noticed.

"We could sit at the table in the kitchen?" he said. "I think Jennie made a pot of coffee. I haven't touched it, but I think it's fresh, if you want some?" He put his hand on his stomach. "I'm not sure I'm ready for it just yet." He started for the kitchen.

Frank followed, and said, "So, Claudia Sanford has decided to talk. And we've got a lot of the details we didn't have. Enough for the bureau to build a bigger case against Caprio. Might be moving him into the top fifty most wanted."

The sunlight came in through the tall casement windows on the back wall and reflected off the hardwood floor.

Charlie reached into the cabinet for a couple of mugs, then grabbed his side after stretching more than he should have.

"You want me to get that?" Kim said, stepping over to where Charlie was and taking the mugs from his hand. "You probably shouldn't even be on your feet." She pointed toward the table, where Frank had already sat down. "Go sit. I can pour coffee."

Charlie waited, then gave in and placed both mugs on the counter in front of where Kim was standing. He went over to the table and pulled a chair out, slowly setting himself into it. There was more pain, but he did his best not to show it.

Kim grabbed the pot of coffee and carried it with the two mugs over to the table, placing one in front of Frank, the other for her, then filled the mugs with coffee. She said to Charlie, "You're not having any?"

He shook his head and put his hand on his stomach. "If I start getting a headache without having caffeine, maybe I'll have to." He pointed at the fridge. "Milk's in there, if you need it." He pointed to one of the cabinets. "Sugar's up there."

Kim opened the refrigerator and grabbed the carton of milk, poured a little into her mug but didn't offer any to Frank, since he only drank his black.

Charlie shifted in the chair, trying to get comfortable. "So, what did my friend Claudia Sanborn have to say?"

Frank said, "Well, first of all, she tried to say she had nothing to do with what was happening."

Charlie tried to fold his arms, but just the thought of it sent pain through his side. "You believe her?"

"She's in the bureau's custody," Frank said. "I haven't spoken to her directly just yet. Not since her arrest."

"Oh." Charlie looked at Kim. "I'd guess she's lying."

Frank said, "According to Claudia, Caprio is looking for her husband."

"She say what for?" Charlie said.

"She said Caprio believes he, the husband, has something that belongs to him."

"Money?"

"That's the belief. But she claims she doesn't know the details."

"Are we supposed to believe that?"

Frank didn't respond.

Charlie said, "What about her relationship with Caprio? Considering she apparently chose him over her husband..."

"According to the report," Frank said, "she didn't come right out and say they were involved outside of business, but of course, there's reason to believe there's something more between them."

The three were quiet for a couple of moments.

Kim said, "So Caprio's hanging around. He's not leaving the area until he gets whatever it is he's after."

"Don't you think it's got to do with the firearms?" Charlie said. "She didn't admit to anything about that?"

"Apparently, this Jack Whitlock... He's the man behind the illegal sales, running that side of it. It's not clear if he's working under Caprio or they're both on equal footing. But according to the agent who's being charged for his involvement, Caprio is the one with the money."

"Like, the investor," Kim said.

Frank said to Charlie, "Claudia Sanborn believes it was Whitlock who shot you. She said Caprio barely knows how to use a gun. I'm not sure that's something anyone's going to believe, but..." Frank paused, as if to let Charlie get prepared for what was next. "We're not going to be able to bring either of these two down alone. That's for sure."

"I'm ready when you are," Charlie said.

Frank grinned and picked up his mug, sipping as he looked over the rim at Charlie. He lowered it slowly, taking his time. "This is beyond the three of us," he said. "I'm not even sure our district, or the marshals as a whole, will be running the show on this one, Charlie. I know that's not what you want to hear, but—"

"Bullshit!" Charlie said, slamming his fist down on the table. Coffee splashed from the two mugs. "These men tried to kill me. Twice. You think I'm just going to sit back and let someone else take them down?"

Frank got up and grabbed a napkin off the counter, wiped up the little bit of spilled coffee from under his mug, and did the same for Kim. "It's not going to be our choice," he said. "That's all I'm telling you. So you can get all pissed off, throw a hissy fit, and slam the table... Shit, you can tip it over, you want to be a tough guy. But none of it'll make a difference. We're talking about a major operation here. Besides the fact we're talking major federal crimes here, don't forget the FBI's got a compromised agent who went rogue, working hand in hand to get Caprio and Whitlock the information they needed to obtain illegal weapons. They want these two as much as you do."

"So, what, then?" Charlie said, calm now. "They're not going to want our help?"

Frank waited, as if he had to think about it. "All I'm saying is we're not running the show. That means, even if you think you're going to be back in action soon—which I highly doubt, by the looks of you—you're going to have to stay in line. None of this Lone Ranger shit's going to fly. It's bad enough, you refuse to listen to *me* half the time." Frank took another sip of his coffee and stood from the table. "Don't worry, Charlie. We're going to get 'em. But you're going to have to sit tight."

"More red tape," Charlie said. "That's all it is."

Frank said, "You can call it whatever you'd like. I call it *reality*."

Jennie walked in from down the hall, dressed nice in a skirt and satin blouse, hair fixed up in a way Charlie hadn't seen in a while. "Oh, hey, Frank. Kim. Is everything going well, considering?"

They both nodded.

Kim stood from the table. "You look nice, Jennie."

"You're leaving?" Charlie said, almost speaking over Kim's compliment.

Jennie ignored him and thanked Kim, then turned to him. "Remember? I told you I have to go by the school to pick some things up."

"Oh. Did you?" he said, a confused look on his face. "Everything's still a bit foggy."

Jennie poured herself a cup of coffee, then leaned against the counter. She said to Frank, "You're not here to see if you can get him out of here yet, are you?"

"No, ma'am," Frank said. "We were just telling him, there's no need to hurry back until he's ready." He pointed over his shoulder with his thumb, in the direction of the front door. "We're heading out right now. My truck's blocking you in."

"Everyone's leaving me already?" Charlie said, pushing himself up out of the chair, feeling the pain. But he didn't want Frank or Kim to see him with any kind of struggle, doing something as normal and basic as getting up out of a damn chair. Even still, he couldn't contain the grunt he made when he finally got up on his feet, realizing as soon as he made it all three looked his way.

"You all right?" Frank said, watching Charlie move from the kitchen, clearly trying to conceal the pain.

"Yeah, I'm good," he said. Jennie had her gaze on him and he smiled. "I'm just going to go sit on the couch for a bit, relax."

All three followed him out of the kitchen.

"We're going to head out anyhow," Frank said. "We'll touch base a little later, let you know where things stand with the investigation. I know you're anxious to hear, but like I said, you're going to have to be patient."

"He's not going anywhere until I say he's ready," Jennie said, a half smile on her face, like she knew the chances of Charlie waiting for her to say when he could go were slim.

Kim gave Charlie an awkward hug with one arm. "Take care of yourself, Charlie. Get better." She said to Jennie, "Let me know if you need any help with him. I know he's a handful."

The two laughed.

Charlie made his way to the door to hold it open for Frank and Kim. He said, "I'm serious about needing a vehicle, Frank. That Town Car's not going to get me home. You know that. Even after it's fixed, I won't—"

"Oh, it's already been repaired," he said. "Looks brand new. New tires. Windows... She's a beauty."

"Come on, Frank. Please don't make me drive that thing."

Frank put his hand on Charlie's shoulder. "Maybe you oughta think about moving somewhere you don't need a truck to get to." He looked around inside the house. "We'll see you later, Jennie." He turned for the door, then said to Charlie, "I'll see what I can do. We still gotta get Kim another vehicle too. And believe me, the last thing I wanna be doing is playing taxi driver for either of you." He turned and went down the steps.

Charlie stood at the door, holding the knob, watching Frank and Kim get in the truck. He closed the door and looked at Jennie coming over to him.

She said, "I'll only be a little while. Maybe half an hour. You want me to pick up something to eat?"

Charlie felt tired from just standing there. But he also felt the whole situation was strange, the way he and Jennie were acting—maybe more so, Jennie—as if they'd gone back a few years before things fell apart between them, like everything was normal.

"I still might want to get back to my place at some point today," he said. "This is your home now, Jennie. I don't need to be in your way."

She put her hand flat on the side of his face, looking into his eyes. "You're not in my way at all, Charlie Harlow." She reached up and kissed him on the cheek, opened the door, and walked out without another word.

Charlie went to the couch and sat down, then eased his head onto the pillow that was already there, whatever energy he had earlier slipping away. He heard his phone buzz somewhere nearby, but wasn't quite sure where he'd left it. He reached into the cushions, and saw it'd slipped way down. By the time he pulled it up, he saw he'd missed a call and there'd been a message.

It was Lindsey. But Jennie still hadn't left the driveway, as far as he could tell, and thought he'd wait a little bit before replying back.

Chapter 23

It was late afternoon, and Charlie had convinced himself he was getting better. Bored and restless, he couldn't even get himself to sit on the couch. He'd already spent more time in front of the TV than he had in, he didn't know how many years.

Jennie was in the kitchen making something to eat for the two of them when his phone buzzed. He got up and started to go outside to answer, thinking maybe it was Lindsey calling him back.

But when he saw it was Stan calling, he answered right away.

"Agent Cooper," Charlie said, the phone to his ear.

"Hey, Charlie. How you doing? I'm sorry I hadn't called you sooner. I—"

"Oh, it's no big deal. I got your text. Appreciate it. And don't worry. I'm doing all right. Hoping to get back in the saddle any day now."

"That's good to hear," he said. "Frank said it was a bit touch and go, when you were out there in those woods."

Charlie paused to think about it. "Yeah, well. I don't know. Mighta looked worse than it really was." Even as the words left Charlie's mouth, he knew it wasn't true, and it was likely a matter of hours, or more like minutes, he might've choked out his last breath if the sheriff hadn't gotten a helicopter to get him out of there. and up to a hospital more prepared to handle what he'd been through.

"Frank said he filled you in? On Denny Caprio? And the other man, Whitlock?"

"Jack Whitlock," Stan said. "Might be more worrisome than Caprio, from what we know."

"That's what it sounded like," Charlie said, thinking for a moment. "But let me ask you something, Stan. Frank made it sound like the FBI's not too keen on us being involved? Is that true?"

"Well, we're in the middle of an investigation, Charlie. It's early in the process, so..."

"I don't think these are his exact words," Charlie said, "but Frank said y'all are holding this one with a tight grip."

"I don't know if I'd say it's a tight grip. But the truth is, with Agent Martin being involved—"

"He's the crooked agent?" Charlie said.

"Yes. But as I was saying, we just need to be careful; make sure we're taking the right steps. We don't need the wrong information getting out there into the media. I'm sure you know what I mean?"

"But I'm sure you know how much I want to get these bastards. You know we can help."

"I know that. But you're talking as if the FBI has never tracked down a wanted man," he said. "We're not incapable."

"Come on, Stan. That's not what I meant. But you gotta admit, you're the ones with the big brains. We're the braun. And I'm sure we both agree, the longer it takes to bring these men in..."

"We're just going to have to hang tight," Stan said. "And from what I understand, you're in no condition to be out in the field anyway."

Charlie rubbed his side, the pain lessening with each passing hour. "I'm a fast healer," he said. "You get injured, the body takes care of itself."

Stan laughed. "Is that what you tell yourself?"

Charlie smiled, looked across the room and through the doorway into the kitchen at the back of the house, where Jennie had her back to him, the strap from her apron around her waist.

Whatever she was making in there smelled good, and he was looking forward to a decent meal.

Jennie gave him a look over her shoulder, as if she knew he was watching her, and Charlie walked away and with his voice low, and said to Stan, "How far are you from Hendersonville?"

"I'm not close. I'm in Charlotte. Why?"

"Nothing," Charlie said, thinking if Stan was close enough he'd hope to get together, maybe even get a ride up to the Coyote Grille. Lindsey drove a pickup, and she could get him back to the Winnebago. But there was no way he'd have her come out to pick him up in front of Jennie. And Frank wouldn't ever want to get in the middle of Charlie and Jennie, so asking him again was out of the question.

Stan said, "Didn't Frank tell you we'd be out there tomorrow?"

Charlie's head wasn't completely clear, but he would've remembered if Frank had. "Oh, yeah. Right. Uh-huh."

"He didn't tell you, did he," Stan said. "I guess maybe I shouldn't have said anything?"

"No, it's all right. Frank just thinks he's my mother sometimes. He knows once I get out there, he won't be able to get rid of me." He paused. "But what I don't understand is if you're going out there to meet with Frank, then why did you leave the impression we were supposed to stand back?"

"I'm sorry," Stan said. "It's not that we're asking the USMS to stand back. We just want to make sure we have full control of the situation. Of course, you've got your reputation, Charlie, and—"

"Oh, now I get it," Charlie said. "This isn't about the USMS as much as it's about me? Is that it?"

"Come on, Charlie. You're overthinking this. We'd be foolish to expect you're just going to sit back and wait, as if anyone would actually expect you to listen to any of us."

"But you said something about my reputation."

"There's just some talk: the way things went down out in those woods up in Carter County, maybe it could've been handled a little differently."

Charlie was silent, gritting his teeth, part of him wanting to tell Stan where to stick it, the other part trying to remain calm, show he can be a good boy like Stan and these straight-laced FBI agents with their ironed slacks and buttoned-up shirts.

"All right," Charlie said. "I don't know what you heard, but..."

"I'm sorry," Stan said. "I don't mean to make it sound the way I did. I'm sure you did what you felt was right."

"What I felt was right?" Charlie said. "I don't know what you heard. But keep in mind, we got one of them for you—Claudia Sanborn—and she's already talking. I guess that doesn't count?"

"Of course," Stan said. "Listen, Charlie. Don't get me wrong. We appreciate it."

Charlie was getting ready to throw the phone across the room, feeling helpless, sitting there stuck in the house like a damn prisoner. "Appreciate it? You say that like we're working for you, not *with* you."

There was a long pause on the other end. "Come on, now, Charlie."

The line went quiet for a couple of moments.

"What about the husband?" Charlie said. "Scott Sanborn. Don't you need to bring him in?"

"Well, yeah. Of course we do. But I'm talking about... The fact is, Charlie, we don't want any more dead bodies."

"What's that supposed to mean?"

Stan paused again, like he needed to be careful with his words. "There were two people in that trailer, right? And only one of them came out alive."

"You saying that's my fault? I didn't shoot anybody."

"Charlie, I'm trying to be straight with you."

"Sounds more to me you're trying to keep us at arm's length in this investigation, either because you want the credit yourself, or you don't like the way we do business."

"It's not that, Charlie." Stan went quiet again on the other end. "The truth is, this case goes beyond Caprio and Whitlock. It may even extend beyond our borders. We want them both alive."

Charlie took a deep breath and sat back on the couch, the way his legs felt a bit weak from standing after only a handful of minutes. When he took a breath, he felt the pain from deep inside. But he knew it was getting better.

"So, you want us involved, but we'd better bring knives to a gunfight? Is that what you're saying?"

"We're just saying, it can't be *dead or alive*. We need witnesses who know more than Claudia Sanborn. We want Denny Caprio and Jack Whitlock alive. All right? So, it's nothing personal against you or the Marshals Service. We just need to do this right, which is why we—my superiors, the director—are demanding we don't just hand this off and turn our backs. All right?"

Charlie glanced in at Jennie setting up the food on the table. He said to Stan, "Have you had this conversation with Frank?"

"Like I said, we're driving out there in the morning. If Frank hasn't mentioned it to you, then—"

"I'll see you there in the morning," Charlie said, then hung up on Stan without another word.

He understood where Agent Cooper was coming from, but Charlie couldn't help shake his irritation with the way Stan went about it. It felt dismissive, as if he hadn't collaborated with the FBI and numerous federal agencies on countless cases. He'd led operations with over thirty county sheriffs' offices across the Southeast, as well as worked closely with dozens of local police departments. In his career, Charlie had apprehended hundreds of fugitives and dismantled criminal operations, from small-time grifters to international trafficking networks.

But now he felt disrespected by a man he respected.

"Are you hungry?" Jennie said, stepping out of the kitchen as she untied her red apron and draped it over the back of one of the chairs.

Charlie was seething, upset about what he couldn't help but think was some kind of slight toward him, even if Stan had tried to deny it.

"Are you all right?" she said.

Charlie didn't answer right away, seated on the edge of the couch, hands clasped together, elbows on his knees. "Yeah, everything's fine. But I need to get home."

Jennie held her gaze on him, eyebrows raised, her mouth starting to move, but she didn't respond at first until she finally nodded. She pushed out a smile. "Is it my cooking?"

Charlie laughed, then rubbed his hands up and down his face and stood from the couch, shaking his head. "You know I love your cooking." He could smell whatever it was she'd prepared, and it made him hungrier than he already was. "I'm starving."

She hadn't moved, watching him as he stepped past her.

Charlie looked over the spread she'd put out on the table.

Jennie said, "I wasn't sure you had much of an appetite, or what you wanted. So I made a little of everything."

Charlie turned to look at her, his eyelids heavy. "You didn't have to do all this." He looked at the table, a bowl of what looked like pasta, a plate of baked chicken he knew was her special recipe she used to make just about every Sunday. There was a plate of bread, and he reached out for a piece.

"I picked it up from the new bakery, downtown," Jennie said.

He felt her hand on his back, but didn't turn or do anything as she just left it there. "If you're feeling better," she said, "and you really want to go home, I can get you there. I know you said my car wouldn't make it, but..."

He waited a moment before he turned, then reached out and gave her a hug. "Thanks for taking care of me."

They held each other for a moment. But when she squeezed him a little tighter, he jumped back and grabbed his side in pain, wincing.

"Oh my gosh, Charlie. I'm so sorry. Did I hurt you?" She held her hands on her flushed cheeks, a nervous look on her face.

"No, no. It's fine. Just a little tender," he said, reaching out for her hand. "I just don't want to be in your way, cramp your style. You know? But I guess if you don't mind..." He cleared his throat. "It's probably not the best place to be out in the woods alone. But I would at least like to get to the office in the morning. Maybe I'll just sleep here tonight, if you can give me a ride up there? Frank can maybe drive me out to the river."

Chapter 24

JENNIE PULLED UP TO the front of the courthouse in Asheville—the offices of the U.S. Marshals Service Western North Carolina District—and put the car in park, the engine still running.

She turned to Charlie, taking off his seat belt, and said, "Are you sure you should be doing this?"

Charlie reached into the back seat and grabbed his duffel bag, pushing open the passenger door. "I'm good," he said, stepping outside. "Besides, Frank's expecting me."

Of course, the part about Frank wasn't exactly the truth. Far from it, in fact.

What Frank had said, being very clear, was it'd be best if Charlie didn't show up until the doctor clears him. His exact words were that he didn't need some invalid hanging around the office.

What that meant to Charlie is he'd have to walk in that meeting Frank was having with Stan Cooper and maybe another agent or two from the FBI, possibly even the agency directors on the phone, and show he was far from an invalid, and wasn't going to wait for some doctor to tell him he was allowed to work or not.

Based on the conversation he had with Stan, he got the feeling the preference was for Charlie to not be involved at all, and it may not have been about his health.

He closed the passenger door and stood outside Jennie's car for a moment, thinking things through, then made his way over to the driver's side where the window was already down. He held the strap of the duffel bag with one hand, the other resting on top of the door, looking in at Jennie. "I can't tell you how much I appreciate everything you've done for me the past couple of days."

The area outside the courthouse was getting busy, people heading for the entrance, horns blowing out on the street, as some tried to cross in front of oncoming vehicles like it was a kind of game.

Charlie stood outside the driver-side door and gazed up at the blue sky. He thought about the alternative to getting back to work, and that perhaps it'd be smart for him to spend a few days resting by the river in the Adirondack chair his friend made... feet up on a cut stump.

Jennie looked up at him from inside the car. "I just want you to be okay. And I hope you know you're welcome to stay at the house as long as you need to." She grinned. "Or want to."

"I appreciate the offer," Charlie said, giving her a quick look. The whole thing felt weird to him, the way Jennie showed up at the hospital, took care of him like it was the old days.

His glance went to the glass-doored entrance, where the deputies opened the doors and the line that'd formed outside started to move.

Jennie seemed to get a bit choked up. "I understand that you've gotten used to how things are now, with me and you being apart." She put on a smile, lips tight together. "You always liked your own space."

He wasn't sure she was right or not, whether he'd gotten used to it. He hadn't, really. And what human didn't like his or her own space?

Jennie had slipped on her big round sunglasses and covered her eyes, so it was hard to tell if she was crying. Charlie thought she might've been, and thought about giving her a kiss, more to show his affection for her than anything else. But thought better of it and backed away from the window. "I'll give you a call," he said, fixing the duffel bag's strap on his shoulder.

He stepped around the front of her car and knew she was watching him, but kept going to the side door where he knocked with the back of his knuckles to get the attention of one of the deputies working the metal detectors.

· · · · ● ·· ● · ● · ·

The youngest deputy in all of North Carolina, Ethan Holden, was on the elevator on the ground floor of the building when the door slid open for Charlie.

"Charlie?" Holden said, eyebrows raised. "What are you doing here? Frank said you'll be out at least another week."

"I'm doing well," Charlie said. "Thanks for asking."

Ethan Holden cleared his throat. "Oh, right, uh... So, how you feeling?"

Charlie didn't answer, feeling he'd just told him he was all right. "Are you heading to court?" he said, holding the door, waiting for Ethan to step off the elevator.

Ethan moved past him. "Nope." He stopped, turning. "I'm actually going out with Kim." The big smirk on his face made Charlie want to knock it off. Ethan said, "Aren't you the one who told me we're all replaceable?"

If Charlie was up for it, he might've tackled Holden from behind as he started to walk away. "Where is she now?" he said. "Deputy Riggins."

"On her way down," Ethan said. "So you might not wanna hold up that elevator like you're doing."

Charlie let go of the door and it closed behind him. He stepped over to Holden. "Where you going?"

Deputy Holden said, "Just got a call about a dead girl, has something to do with—"

"A girl?"

"Found dead in her apartment."

"You know who it is?" Charlie said.

"I forget the name, but we were in a meeting up there with FBI agents, Cooper and Smith. Kim's the one who got the call. I think she knows who she is. Said she'd been over to the victim's apartment. She had something to do with, uh, maybe was the girlfriend of..." Holden scratched his head. "I don't know all the names yet."

"Scott Sanborn?" Charlie said, worried to even think it was who he was afraid it'd been.

"Yeah, I think that's who."

"Who *what*?"

"Sanborn. It was his girlfriend. The one found dead."

Charlie held his gaze for a moment, feeling the shock from the news, then reached for his side when he felt a sharp pain shoot through it like someone had landed him with a right hook to the body. It was odd, the way it felt like the pain had traveled, the pain almost stronger now. He did his best to ignore it.

He looked up and saw the elevator had gone all the way up to the sixth floor. The Marshals office was on the third.

He wasn't about to stand there, wasting time, and started for the stairs. He took out his phone and started to dial Kim as soon as he pushed open the door and headed up. And after about five or six steps, he started to realize attempting the climb might not've been a good idea.

He felt weak, almost immediately, but kept his phone to his ear waiting for Kim to answer.

"Charlie?" she said, picking up on the second ring.

Each step he made was heavy, his boots feeling like they were a hundred pounds.

"I was just about to call you," she said. "I just received some bad news."

"Is it Kristen Salvatore?" he said, losing strength with each step he took.

"How'd you know?"

"Because I'm on my way up to the office. I saw Ethan in the lobby."

"You're here?" she said.

"On the stairs."

The line went quiet.

Kim said, "Agents Cooper and Smith are here, with me and Frank."

"Having a little meeting without me, huh?" Charlie said.

"You're supposed to be in bed," Kim said, lowering her voice. "Frank's not going to like this."

"Like *what*?" Charlie put more of his weight onto the railing he held with his hand as he took each step.

But before Kim responded, he pushed open the door to the third floor and stepped into the hall a few doors down from his office.

Kim was already waiting for him, and reached out her hand as if she was going to help him walk.

He pushed her arm away. "I'm okay. I'm fine."

She said, "How did you get here? Jennie?"

Charlie didn't answer. "Are you going to tell me what happened? To Salvatore?"

Kim paused, like she was having trouble just thinking about it. "The boyfriend found her dead. He called the cops."

"Where?"

"In her apartment."

Charlie put his hand up and squeezed his temple. He had a headache that'd just shown up as soon as he got off the stairs, breathing heavily before he was halfway there. He felt weak and lightheaded, and wished he could sit down but didn't want to. "We should have protected her," he said.

Kim didn't respond.

The door to their office opened, and Frank poked his head out. "Charlie? What the hell are you doing here?"

"You really expect me to stay in bed? Get out of the way, so the FBI can push us around, make sure you do it their way?"

"I'm not even sure what you're talking about, Charlie," Frank said, holding open the door for both deputies to walk in ahead of him.

Kim said, "I should probably get over there."

Frank said to Charlie, "Agent Cooper and Smith are here right now, trying to give us whatever information they're willing to share." He lowered his voice. "I'm not sure they know much."

Charlie said, "Wouldn't be surprised they're holding something back. Stan made it clear they don't like the way I do my job."

Frank stopped, almost to the conference room, but stopped in the middle of the office. He turned to Charlie, standing close enough Charlie could smell the coffee on his breath. He said, "The way they explained it, I understand where they're coming from. Just like we found out the hard way this is bigger than Claudia and Scott Sanborn ripping people off to put a few bills in their pockets, there's a lot more to this entire gunrunning operation. It's bigger than Caprio and Whitlock."

Charlie stared back at Frank without a word, like he understood.

They continued to the conference room where Stan Cooper and the other agent from the FBI, Ryan Smith, were seated at the table.

Stan, like the others, was surprised to see Charlie walk in, giving him a nod. "Nice to see you up and around, Charlie."

"I'm not sure I believe you think it is," Charlie said.

Stan smiled, but it dropped from his face when he saw Charlie was being serious. "Oh, come on, Charlie. Give me a break. For such a tough man, you can be a little sensitive. You can't always take everything so personally. I'd like to think you know what I was trying to say, no?"

Kim pointed with her thumb over her shoulder toward the front of the office, "Deputy Holden is outside waiting for me. I should probably—"

"I'm going with you," Charlie said, turning to Frank in case he'd need his approval. In fact, he knew he would.

"I don't know if that's such a good idea," Frank said. "I can see it in the way you walk. You don't look right, Charlie."

Charlie tried to stand straight, chest out. "Kristen Salvatore is dead. And I feel somewhat personally responsible for what happened. We should have done something to protect her. Especially once we knew they were after Scott Sanborn."

The room was silent.

"Nobody here is to blame," Frank said.

"We knew he was in contact with her," Charlie said. "The chance Caprio or Whitlock knew the same... Should have been obvious."

"You were lying in a hospital bed, fighting for your life. If anyone should take the blame here, it'll be me. I'm the one who makes the calls. I'm the one who should have suggested we keep a better eye on her."

Stan raised his hand. "Uh, we could have also done something. We'd already spoken to her. But she claimed she didn't know him very well. I guess the mistake we made was believing her."

Charlie said, "Who's driving? Holden?" He turned to Frank. "Are you going to be okay I go with them?"

Frank appeared hesitant at first. "Just be careful. All right? I'll fill you in on everything else here when you get back."

Charlie said to Stan. "You're not going over there?"

Stan said, "We've got a couple agents at the scene already. But we'll see you over there shortly."

184

Chapter 25

Charlie and Kim were with Deputy Ethan Holden and walked up the stairs to the apartment where they last saw Kristen Salvatore alive, the police presence heavy.

Charlie had to stop at the top of the stairs to catch his breath.

"Are you okay, Charlie?" Kim said, putting her hand on his back.

"Yeah, I'm good," he said.

Deputy Holden was ahead of them and went straight into the apartment through the open door.

"I thought he was just the driver," Charlie said, walking ahead of Kim and into the apartment.

"I think he was hoping you weren't coming back," Kim said. "So he could finally step up and do something worthwhile."

They walked into the room where the couch was stained, the body already removed. There were detectives and forensic analysts on the scene, crouched over the couch. One woman had picked up something with tweezers but Charlie couldn't see what it was from where he stood.

Kim looked around, then started into one of the other rooms. "I'll go see who's spoken with the boyfriend."

Charlie went out to the balcony and looked out at the parking lot. He stood, thinking. Of course, they were going to need some kind of proof to say the murder of Kristen Salvatore occurred at the hands of Caprio and Whitlock. But Charlie had little doubt himself.

Kim showed up outside to where he was standing. "Deputy Holden is in there asking questions."

"What? Asking who?" Charlie said, slipping past her and back into the apartment. He went into the kitchen where Ethan was talking to one of the officers.

"Excuse me," Charlie said, grabbing Holden by the arm. "Can I talk to you for a moment?" He gave the officer a nod and led Ethan down the hall and outside the apartment.

"What's the problem?" Holden said, as Charlie still hadn't let go of his arm.

"I don't know what you're doing. But this isn't your case. I appreciate the drive over here, but I don't want you getting involved any more than I say you will." Charlie pointed to himself. "I'll ask the questions. You understand?"

"See?" Ethan said. "This is your problem. You won't let anybody do anything to help you. Then you end up getting in trouble, like you always do."

Kim walked out and saw the two. "Hey, what's going on here?"

Deputy Holden said, "Charlie's treating me like a kid."

Charlie looked him in the eye, then turned to Kim. "We don't need him coming in here, knows nothing about the case, talking to officers like he knows something."

"I was just trying to help," Holden said.

"You want to help?" Charlie said, keeping his voice hushed so the cops all around didn't hear him. "Go keep the car warm."

Deputy Holden shook his head. "Frank told me to help Kim. That's what I'm doing."

Charlie thought about it, then eased up, and stepped back. "All right," he said. "But don't be asking questions when you don't know anything about this case. That's all I'm saying. I know you want to help. I get it. But just... You know that officer in there you were talking to?"

Holden said, "We've met a couple of times."

"All right, then. Again, I'm sorry. I just... We need to be careful. We also don't need the local cops mucking up any of this for us until we have a better answer who we're looking for."

"Frank always tells me it's not our job to investigate crimes."

Charlie let out what almost sounded like a low growl. "Listen. We have two wanted men we need to find, regardless of what's determined here today. But I've been at this long enough, my assumptions are usually pretty good."

Kim said, "Anybody say where Jason Dexter is?"

"Who's Jason Dexter?" Deputy Holden said.

Charlie didn't even want to answer him, but maybe he was being too hard on the kid as it was. "He's the victim's boyfriend."

"I thought it was Scott Sanborn?"

"Apparently she's got more than one."

Kim looked around. "We might as well go see if we can find him. He's probably going to know more than anybody here right now."

Ethan Holden said, "I mentioned Denny Caprio and Jack Whitlock to the officer I was speaking with. He'd never heard of either one of 'em."

Charlie let out a sigh. "Yeah, they have no idea." He said to Kim, "Do we even know where the boyfriend lives?"

She said, "With his mother, about five miles from here. The police questioned him already, but he doesn't know much of anything. I still think we might be able to get something out of him."

They started heading for the stairs, with Charlie in front, but he stopped and turned to Kim. "Was there a phone?"

Kim just looked at him like she wasn't quite sure what he was asking.

"I mean, Kristen Salvatore's phone. Where is it?"

Kim said, "As far as I know, it hasn't yet been located. Who-ever did this to her must've taken it."

"Meaning, there's a chance they'll use it to get to Sanborn."

· • • • • • • • • • ·

Charlie pushed open the passenger door and turned to Ethan Holden behind the wheel. "Do me a favor, and wait right here."

"Are you serious?" Ethan said, shaking his head. "You're the one who's not supposed to be here."

Charlie struggled a bit to pull himself up and out of the car, grunting as he got to his feet in the driveway at Jason Dexter's mother's house. He straightened up outside in the street, then turned, ducking his head to look inside the car at Ethan. "Look. Don't take it personally. We certainly don't need a posse going up to the mother's door. All right? And, well, someone's gotta stay with the car." He slammed the door closed without waiting for Ethan to respond, then headed for the house.

Kim had already gotten out of the back and hurried to walk alongside Charlie, looking him up and down as they continued for the front door. "You sure you're okay?" she said, looking him over. "It looks like you're walking funny."

"Funny?" He gave her a side-eye look.

"You know what I'm saying," she said. "You look like you're in pain. With every step."

"I might be," he said.

Deputy Riggins said, "Are you sure you should even be on your feet?"

Charlie didn't respond at first, then said, "It actually hurts. Maybe more than it did this morning when Jennie dropped me off. But I'll... I'll be fine. Just gotta walk it off, get things to loosen up a little."

"I'm not sure that's how it works."

"Whatever you say, Dr. Riggins." He stepped ahead of her and up onto the concrete landing where he knocked on the blue wooden exterior door.

Charlie and Kim waited, but nobody came to answer the door at first. Charlie turned his good ear and leaned in close to the door, trying to listen inside. It was quiet on the other side. Looking at the single-car garage, he said, "You want to see if there's a vehicle in there?"

Kim went over to the garage. There were no windows on the garage door, but she went around to the side and then came back around to the front right away. "There's a vehicle in there. An older Volvo."

"You know what kind of car Jay Dexter drives?" Charlie said, but right away remembered they saw it parked outside Kristen Salvatore's apartment. "Wasn't it one of those old Saturns?"

Kim said, "It was. Brown, er, more rust colored. Don't see many on the road these days." She stood behind Charlie at the bottom step.

But before either said another word, the locks on the door clicked and opened. A middle-aged woman, who looked a bit ragged, stood in the doorway. She appeared to have maybe just woken up by the way her hair was going in all directions, eyelids barely open. "Yes?"

Charlie had his badge out and showed it to her. "Mrs. Dexter? I'm Deputy Charlie Harlow, with the United States Marshals Service. This is Deputy Kim Riggins." He saw the nervous look on her face right away as she shifted her gaze past them and toward the older Ford LTD with Ethan Holden behind the wheel looking out at them.

"That there's Deputy Holden," he said. "Don't mind him."

She brought her gaze back to Charlie. "Does this have to do with Kristen?"

"Yes, ma'am. We'd actually like to talk to your son, Jason, if he's here?"

"He didn't do it," the mother said. "I know he didn't. He was home. Or at work."

"Home *or* work?" Charlie said. "Mrs. Dexter, we're not here to investigate the crime," he said. "I'm sure you've already spoken with the police. Or perhaps an agent or two from the FBI?"

She said, "A lot of people have shown up at my door. I answered what questions I could. But they just wanted to talk to Jason."

"A lot of people, besides the police?"

She looked to be thinking about her answer. "I don't know, to tell you the truth. Like I said, there were quite a few."

"Ma'am," Kim said. "Is your son home right now?"

"No, he's not. He's at the restaurant. I swear, he had nothing to do with it. As far as I know... I mean, he told me he'd broken up with her."

"I'm not sure your son is a suspect right now," Charlie said. "But as I mentioned, that's not really our job to find out."

"What is it you do?" she said. "You said you're a marshal? Is that, you mean, like the ones who fly on planes?"

Charlie'd heard that question before, dozens of times. The U.S. Marshals Service was the oldest U.S. federal law enforcement agency, dating back to 1789. But for whatever reason, people seemed to have no problem knowing who air marshals were, even though they sat on less than 1 percent of flights, and it was rare they'd be mentioned in the news at any point. Certainly less so than the U.S. Marshals Service.

Charlie said, "United States Marshals Service. Federal air marshals have nothing to do with what happens here on the ground." He grinned, acting like he took offense to the confusion. Even though he rarely did.

Jason's mother said, "You know, a man showed up here looking for Jason. I thought maybe he was with the police, but he left so fast... I'm not sure who he was."

Charlie gave Kim a quick glance, then pulled out his phone and showed the woman a photo of Denny Caprio. "Any chance this is who was looking for him?"

She studied the photo, squinting a bit, looking at it. "I'm not sure," she said. Her gaze went from Charlie to Kim. "He had a baseball hat and sunglasses, so it's hard to say."

Charlie flipped through the images on his phone, then stopped on the only one he had of Jack Whitlock. He turned the screen to the woman. "This one?"

She studied the photo without a word for a moment. "I don't think so." She raised her gaze to Charlie. "Who is he?"

"This man's name is Jack Whitlock." He held back telling her there was a chance Whitlock or Denny Caprio were likely responsible for Kristen Salvatore's death, but felt no need to say something he himself had no proof of. "This man who was here... He didn't show you any identification?"

The mother shook her head.

"Does your son still work at that restaurant?"

"Yes, he does," she said. "Been there five years now. He talks about leaving, maybe doing something else, but..."

"Job's a job," Charlie said. "And that's the same restaurant, where he worked with Kristen Salvatore, right?"

"At the Old Canteen," she said. "I told him he didn't have to go in, that they'd understand. But I imagine everyone is pretty upset over there right now."

Charlie already knew the name of the restaurant and where it was. He took out his business card and handed it to her. "Anyone else shows up here without a badge, or someone you don't know, asking questions, you make sure you get their names and see some kind of identification. They don't want to share either, or something doesn't seem right, go ahead and call me right away."

She took the card and swallowed hard, nodding. "Should I call Jason? Tell him you're going over there?"

Charlie hesitated, wondering if it'd spook the kid, or maybe make him run off before they showed up. "Just make sure he knows he's not in any kind of trouble with us. We just want to talk to him, and make sure he's all right."

"Why wouldn't he be all right?" she said. "You think what happened to Kristen might—"

"Don't worry, ma'am," Kim said. "We'll make sure he's safe."

Chapter 26

THE INSIDE OF THE Old Canteen was somewhat dark with dark brown wooden walls, lots of dark wood in fact, from the chairs to the wood planked floor. It had a comfortable look, maybe somewhat upscale in its day, with the white tablecloths and candles in glass bowls, burning in the middle of each table. Even though the place appeared to also be a bit old-school, Charlie liked it.

It was still before lunch, and there was nobody seated at any of the tables. The doors had apparently just opened.

The dining area was wide open and big, with waiters and waitresses in black pants and white buttoned shirts, the men wearing bow ties, various servers setting up tables, moving around the dining area with their heads down. It was as if none of them wanted to look over at Charlie and Kim standing by the door.

There was music playing low, some kind of instrumental Frank Sinatra tune Charlie was familiar with but couldn't think of the name. He looked over at the long bar, at least twenty or so stools. The bartender behind it dressed like the others with the white buttoned shirt, a bow tie around his neck but hanging loose, undone. The young man kept his head down, the way the others did, getting things ready.

Charlie and Kim made their way over to him and stood there for a moment as if, also like the others, the bartender wasn't quite ready for a customer.

The man finally had to look, and put on a clearly forced smile."Morning," the man said, then looked at his watch. His eyes were glossy, with a redness to them, and Charlie wondered if he'd been crying.

"I'm Deputy Charlie Harlow, with the U.S. Marshals Service." He pointed with his thumb at Kim. "This is Deputy Kim Riggins."

The bartender said, "Oh, hello. Can I help you with something? The police were just here, asking questions, so…"

"I understand that," Charlie said. "What's your name, son?"

"Brian. Brian Cooper."

There was an odor coming from the bar, like stale beer or maybe worse. He looked down the left side of the bar to what looked like a raw bar setup, with a square steel tub filled with ice, a clear plastic cover a few feet over the top of it.

"Brian," Charlie said, "Was anybody else in to talk to you today, besides the police?"

"Just the one who talked to me. Didn't have on a uniform or anything, but said he was a detective. There were a couple of cops outside, but they never came in."

Something didn't seem right to Charlie. "Did he show you his badge?"

"Yeah. I think so."

Charlie looked at a swinging door the handful of waitstaff had been walking in and out of, buzzing around the restaurant, clearly preparing for the day. He saw the kitchen on the other side when the door swung open again. "Any chance Jason Dexter is back there?"

"Jason? I don't think so. Not after what happened."

"I need to talk to him," Charlie said. "And you're sure he's not here? Maybe in the kitchen?"

"I... I can go check, see if he came in earlier, but I doubt it. The detective asked for him, too, so last I checked he wasn't here. I can't imagine he'd be foolish enough, try to work like the rest of us. We all gotta work, pay our bills. You know? But he loved Kristen. I can't imagine..."

Charlie knew what it must've been like for Jason, and everyone else. He preferred at that point to assume Jason didn't do it, but it wasn't up to him to decide. But being a fairly decent judge of character, Charlie just couldn't see it.

He glanced into one corner of a restaurant where two women, clearly part of the waitstaff, were hugging each other, crying. He looked at Kim and nodded in the direction of the two women. "You want to go see if they'd like to talk?"

"Yeah, of course." Kim stepped between the covered tables and across the dining room.

The bartender said, "You want me to go see if Jason's here? I don't think he is. I mean, his girlfriend's dead." He took a deep breath and sighed. "I'm not sure how any of us are doing this right now."

"I understand," Charlie said. "Sounds like she was a friend of yours?"

"Yes." His voice had cracked, and he turned from Charlie as if he wanted to hide what looked like tears coming down his face. He pulled a cocktail napkin from the container on the bar and wiped his eyes, then blew his nose.

Charlie gave the man a moment. "I'm sorry."

"It's just so hard to believe. It doesn't seem real. You know? Like, she's going to come walking through that door any moment."

Charlie paused, waiting, then leaned on the bar. "You mind if I ask you a few questions?"

"I guess so. But, like I said, I already answered the detective's questions. I just hope you people don't think he did it. Jason would never... I know he and Kristen were having a little trouble, from what I heard, but—"

"The truth is, I'm not here to determine who's responsible," Charlie said. "We leave that up to the police. But we'd like to track down the men we believe may've been responsible."

"You know who did it?"

"Not with any certainty just yet, but..." He straightened up and looked around the restaurant. "There's a man I believe was a customer here and perhaps may've been somewhat friendly with Kristen. Name's Scott Sanborn."

"Mr. Sanborn? Yeah, I—"

"He used to come in here?" Charlie said.

"You think he did it?"

"Well, it's all just speculation right now. But if you can tell me anything about him..."

"I never liked him. None of us did. He thought he was something special, acting like he was all rich and stuff. He'd throw around cash, buy everybody drinks..." He leaned in closer and looked at Charlie from across the bar. "Are you the marshal who was at Kristen's apartment? Jason told me about what happened."

Charlie didn't respond or feel the need to go into any details. "When was the last time you saw him here?"

"Scott Sanborn? I... I don't know. I know he'd been arrested, which wasn't a surprise. We all knew something wasn't right about him. He would talk about this business he was in, something that had to do with helping old people, but it didn't sound to me like he was helping them at all. He wasn't very smart, you ask me." He paused, slowly shaking his head. "I just don't get what Kristen saw in him."

Charlie pulled out his phone and turned the screen with the photo of Denny Caprio on it. "You know this man?"

There was no hesitation. "Yes, he's been in here. In fact, he came in here, maybe a few days ago, asked about Scott Sanborn and if he'd been in here. Of course, I told him to talk to Kristen." The bartender's expression changed, and his face dropped. "Oh no," he said, as if realizing what he might have done.

Charlie flicked the photo on the screen to Jack Whitlock. "What about this man?"

He nodded emphatically. "He was in here last night." He looked to the end of the bar to Charlie's right. "He sat there, that last stool at the corner, right up until about closing time. Didn't say much of anything. Even when I tried to talk to him, he just stared back at me. Most people that come in alone, I can usually get them to talk." Brian shook his head. "Not this guy. He had an odd look to him."

"What kind of look?" Charlie said.

"I don't know. A creepy one, I guess. He actually looked kind of sick. I mean, like he wasn't well. He just stared straight ahead, looking around every once in a while, like he was waiting for something. But he kept to himself."

"And when did he leave?"

"I'm not sure. Late, I think. I looked to where he was sitting, and then he was gone."

"Kristen was here?"

Brian swallowed hard, wiping his eyes. "She didn't say anything to me, so I'm not exactly sure what time she left. But I know she didn't stay until close. I don't know; she left around midnight or so?"

"Same time this man disappeared from the bar?" Charlie said.

"I think so."

"But you had no idea who this man was?" Charlie said. "Did you mention anything about this man to the detective who was here?"

"I wish I had, but..." He looked Charlie in the eye. "I hadn't thought about it until you asked. The detective wasn't here for very long. Just asked a few questions about Jason."

"He didn't ask about either of the men I mentioned?"

"No."

Charlie let out a sigh. He didn't know which detective had shown up asking questions, but knew it had to have been a local cop. Everything up till that point, from Sanborn's scheme under Denny Caprio, to the illegal gunrunning Whitlock and Caprio were involved in, was at a federal level. The local cops knew little, if anything, beyond Kristen Salvatore's death.

In fact, it seemed to Charlie the FBI had other reasons for keeping things quiet.

Charlie held up his phone again, showing Jack Whitlock's image to the bartender one more time. "I just want you to be certain... Are you sure this was the man who was here last night?"

"Yes, I'm sure that's him." He swallowed hard. "Did he... did he kill Kristen?"

Charlie tucked his phone in his pocket. "I don't know. But"—he pulled out his business card and left it on the bar—"listen, I don't think you're going to see him again, at this point, but if you do happen to see this man, or the other one I showed you a picture of, or even Scott Sanborn, then I need you to call me right away." Looking at the kitchen door, he said, "Now, would you do me a favor. Go back there and see if Jason made it in today? If he did, you can tell him it's the deputy from the other night."

The bartender opened the door on a small dishwasher tucked underneath the bar, a cloud of steam rising up into his face. "Okay, let me go see if he's back there." He rolled out the plastic rack filled with glasses, but left it there, walking around to the other side of the bar. He continued through the swinging door and disappeared into the kitchen.

Charlie looked over at Kim, who had already left the two waitresses still apparently crying, and continued across the empty restaurant toward him.

Before she could say a word, Charlie said, "Jack Whitlock was here last night, right here at this bar."

Kim's eyes opened wide. "The bartender saw him?"

Charlie nodded and took out his phone. "I gotta let Frank know."

She said to Charlie, "Those two girls seem to think Kristen left late last night, to go meet Scott Sanborn."

Charlie figured that'd be the case. "You think he'd be stupid enough to show up at her apartment? Because, the fact she was there..." He listened to the ringing and gestured with his finger for Kim to hold on a moment when Frank answered.

Frank said, "Where the hell are you?"

"Why the anger?" Charlie said. "You gotta be careful. That ticker of yours is getting old."

"You want to know why I'm mad? Because I don't like the idea, you're out running around like you're in charge." Frank sighed into the phone and finally took his voice down a notch. "Listen, you jackass. Two days ago you were lying in a hospital bed, barely alive. And I'll tell you something: I'm not going to be responsible for your—"

"Frank, will you just listen to me for a moment, and try to calm down a bit? I appreciate the concern, but..." Charlie gave Kim a quick glance and continued, "the bartender here at the Old Canteen, the restaurant where Kristen Salvatore worked with her boyfriend..."

"The boyfriend? Sanborn?" Frank said.

"No, the other boyfriend. The kid—I told you about him—the kid who works here in the kitchen. The one who was at her apartment the other night."

"Yeah, I know who he is. In fact, Stan was asking about him."

Charlie said, "If you'd let me talk, let me explain what I found out."

"I'm waiting," Frank said.

"The bartender here," Charlie said. "I showed him a photo of Jack Whitlock. And you know what he told me? Whitlock was right here, at this restaurant."

The line went quiet.

Charlie said, "And then Kristen Salvatore was here, working. But she left a little before midnight. The bartender didn't see Whitlock leave and couldn't say for sure what time he disappeared, but seems to be pretty sure he—Whitlock—left around the same time."

"As the girl?" Frank said.

"It looks that way."

"Jesus," Frank said. "I mean, it's already assumed it's Whitlock or Caprio, but..." He paused on the other end.

Charlie said, "Is Stan still there?"

"Where?"

"At the office?"

Frank said, "I'm not at the office. He said he was heading out your way."

"Oh, all right," Charlie said. "Can you give him a call, just let him know what we've found?"

"Why can't you call him?"

"I can. But I thought you should know. And now that you know, I was just hoping you'd share it with the bureau; make it official communication."

The line went silent again for a moment.

Frank said, "Stan told me, you didn't seem to like the idea they prefer Caprio and Whitlock alive. Is that why you don't want to call him? You can't appreciate a simple request?"

"Come on, Frank. You really think it's fair, I've got this reputation? Like I've never taken anybody in without shooting them?"

"You say it like nobody has a reason for thinking that," Frank said. "But the way Stan explained it to me, there are bigger fish to fry. It's not about you, Charlie. Maybe you should think about not taking things so personally all the time."

Charlie didn't even respond to it. He understood where Frank was coming from but didn't feel the need to have to discuss it, even though he still hadn't gotten over the way Stan had come across, like Charlie was some gunslinger from the Old West.

"Frank said, "I'll call Stan. But, I also want you to keep in mind it's not our job to solve the crime. I'm not sure how many times I have to remind you of that."

Charlie said, "So if I happen to come across a detail that points us to a killer, I should just ignore it?"

Frank sighed on the other end. "I think you know what I'm saying." He paused, as if annoyed with the way the conversation had gone. "Can you at least tell me you're doing all right? I told you, I don't have the time, or the money, to go and replace a deputy right now."

"Thanks for looking at it that way," Charlie said. He knew that was Frank's way of checking up on him, without coming across as being too empathetic. "I appreciate your concern." He was about to hang up the phone but heard Frank say his name.

"Yeah?" Charlie said, putting the phone back to his ear.

Frank said. "Where's Deputy Holden?"

"He's out in the car, waiting for us, like a good little boy. I'll tell him you were asking for him."

"One of these days we gotta take the training wheels off the kid," Frank said. "Lord knows, the way you go about things, we're going to need him to step up one of these days."

"Well, I'm still here. So, for now, if we can't have him working the courts, next best thing is him waiting behind the wheel. I'll touch base later." Charlie hung up before Frank could say anything else and tucked his phone in his pocket. He looked at the swinging door.

The bartender walked over to Charlie. "Nobody knows where Jason is. But he was here this morning. Someone said he went outside to have a smoke and heard him talking on his phone. But I guess he never came back."

"Did you try calling him?" Charlie said.

Brian had his phone in his hand, nodding. "I just did. He didn't answer."

Chapter 27

CHARLIE AND KIM STEPPED out of the car Ethan had parked in front of Jason Dexter's mother's house. The door had opened, and Jason's mother was already standing there, crying.

She had a phone in her hand. "He just called me," she said, her voice shaking. "He told me he loved me, and he was sorry."

"Sorry about what?" Charlie said, standing at the bottom step, looking up at the kid's mother. His first thought was Jason Dexter might've confessed to killing his girlfriend, but Charlie wasn't willing to believe that was the case.

The mother said, "He said he knows who hurt her, and was going to take care of it himself."

"What?" Charlie said. "What else did he say?" He pointed at the phone in her hand. "Call him back! Get him on the phone. I gotta talk to him."

She was crying and visibly shaking. "I already tried calling him back. It went right to his voicemail."

Kim and Charlie just stood there, looking at Ethan behind the wheel of his car, then back at the mother.

Kim said, "What else did he tell you? Did he say where he was? Or where he was going?"

Charlie said, "If there's a chance this kid's going after Caprio... or Whitlock..." He kept his voice hushed, almost whispering to Kim. "This isn't good."

"How would he know it was either of them?" Kim said. "This makes no sense."

Charlie had his hands on his hips, then pulled out his phone when it started to buzz. "It's Frank," he said, then took a few steps away from the stairs to the house and closer to the end of the driveway.

"Frank?" he said. "We just got to Jason Dexter's house, and—"

"That's why I'm calling. There's a hostage situation at an inn... a bed-and-breakfast, up in Marshall. The owner called the local police, said a man's got one of their guests at gunpoint. There's a rust-colored Saturn in the lot."

Charlie turned to Kim. "We gotta go."

Jason Dexter's mother was watching Charlie on the phone. "What is it? Is it Jason?"

Charlie said to Frank, "Text me the name of the inn. I'll call you from the road." He hung up and turned to the mother. "Just sit tight, all right? We'll come back soon as we can, let you know what's going on." He didn't think he should tell her what Frank had said. At least not at first.

But she hurried down the stairs and grabbed Charlie's arm—causing him a bit of pain— before he could get away, tears running down her cheeks. She screamed, "Please, he's my son! He's a good kid! You have to tell me what's happening!"

Charlie thought about it for a moment. "It sounds like there's a good chance he's got someone held at gunpoint, some-where up in Marshall." He felt his phone buzz and looked at the screen, yelling to Ethan outside the car now, and he read him the text from Frank. "Let's go! Gotta move! Thirty-eight Little Pine Road in Marshall."

Kim was already hurrying for the car.

But the mother kept following, even as Charlie pulled his arm from her grasp. "Please! You have to take me with you. I can talk to him."

Kim stood with the car door open, waiting. "Can we bring her? Maybe she can help."

Charlie nodded and took the woman by the arm. "You'll need to stay in the car, until we know what's going on up there."

"My keys. They're inside the house," she said. "The door's open."

"Either you get in the car," Charlie said, "or we're leaving you here. We don't get up there now..." He opened the back door and led her into the back seat with Kim, then closed it, and got into the passenger seat. He had somehow ignored whatever pain he was in until that point. But as soon as he ducked into the passenger seat and slammed the door closed, he felt the pain grip him from somewhere inside. It was as if it'd moved through the rest of his body.

He watched the phone Ethan had attached to the dashboard, the GPS running. According to the digital display, they had twenty-seven minutes to go.

"You gonna hurry?" he said. "Or you need me to get behind that wheel? Let's go! We don't have a second to spare."

Ethan didn't even respond, hit the pedal hard with his foot and spun the tires. He whipped the tail end of his car into the street and hit the brakes, slamming the shift into drive and giving it the gas. The engine roared, thrusting them ahead with their heads whipping back.

Charlie braced himself and was about to put his seat belt on. But as soon as the belt crossed over his wounds, he stopped, noticing his shirt felt wet on his side. He put his hand there and felt it, then looked at his fingers and saw the blood. He lifted his shirt...

The small bandage had become soaked with blood.

He felt he hadn't done much to cause it but thought about the doctor telling him to rest once he left the hospital.

Ethan had turned from the driver's seat to look. "Charlie? You're bleeding," he said, as if Charlie didn't know. "Are you all right?"

"Yeah, I'm all right," Charlie said, pointing ahead. "Just keep your eyes on the road and get us there in one piece."

· · · · ● · ● · ● · · ·

Deputy Ethan Holden slowed when they drove through downtown in Marshall, the streets lined with historical buildings and shops. There were people out on the sidewalks, some with dogs.

Two men watched from a bench in front of a barbershop, likely glancing at the United States Marshals emblem on the side of the vehicle.

"You've gotta hurry," Charlie said, knowing there wasn't anywhere Ethan could go, the way the cars were driving so damn slow in front of them and on both sides of the road.

They continued out of downtown, traveling on Main Street along the French Broad River and turned north toward Route 70.

Jason's mother had her phone out in the back seat, her hand shaking as she held it to her ear. "He's still not answering," she said. It was the fifth or so time she'd said it, but Charlie didn't bother saying he likely wouldn't answer. But then she said, "Jason? What are you doing?"

Charlie turned in her seat to watch her. "Tell him not to do anything stupid," he said.

"Whatever you're doing," she said. "You have to stop it. Please, Jason. Don't do anything foolish." She was crying now, once again, but appeared to be doing all she could to hold it together.

"Tell him we're about five minutes away," Charlie said. "To please wait for us."

She said into the phone, "We're five minutes away. I'm with the police. I mean, the marshals. United States Marshals."

Charlie turned to look ahead. He reached for the GPS. "We're actually two minutes away. Keep him talking."

"Honey," the mother said. "Please, listen to me. You don't want to do this. The marshals are going to help you." She was quiet.

Charlie said to her, "Keep him talking."

Chapter 28

Deputy Ethan Holden turned the wheel down Little Pine Road, and after a half mile, they all looked ahead at the parking lot where at least six sheriff's cars were parked, a dozen or so deputies standing outside. There was a fire truck, and out on the road was a van with WZLX on the side of it, with "News You Can Count On" painted above the image of three news people Charlie recognized from TV.

The bed-and-breakfast was an old historical home, painted green, with shutters and a porch on the front so huge it could hold two parked cars. There were at least a dozen rocking chairs and a couple of wide swinging bench seats hung from the ceiling.

The deputies were spread out, some around the side of the building, a few staying in the parking lot by their vehicles, and three on the porch with the front door wide open.

Charlie pushed open the passenger door before the vehicle had fully stopped. "Keep her back here," he said, referring to Jason's mother, then jumped out and hurried for the porch. But he slowed after a dozen or so steps, feeling somewhat weak and lightheaded for a moment. His breathing felt heavy.

Kim ran from the car after him. "Are you all right?" she said, looking him over. "You're white as a ghost."

"Yeah, I'm all right," he said, and they both looked at the blood that had come through his shirt.

Kim tightened her Kevlar vest but noticed Charlie wasn't wearing one. "You can't go up there without a vest, Charlie. I won't let you."

He hadn't expected to need it, but knew he couldn't afford to make another mistake. "I don't have one."

Kim said, "Wait for me. Let me see what Ethan has." She ran back toward the car to where the mother was standing outside now, Ethan next to her.

Charlie watched Kim say something to Ethan, who nodded, then hurried to the trunk, popping it open, and handing Kim a vest.

She grabbed it from him and ran to Charlie. "Here," she said, handing it to him.

The thing was, Charlie wasn't prepared for any of it. He didn't even have his Glock on him, thinking how ill-prepared he'd been for what could turn out to be a dangerous situation.

Not wearing the vest was one thing. Going in without his gun was another.

Charlie slipped his arms through the vest, tightening the Velcro straps on the front and adjusted it, trying to get it comfortable. But just the subtle movements he made to get the thing on sent pain through his side. He glanced back toward Jason's mother, standing by the car. "She still got Jason on the phone?"

Kim nodded. "I think so."

The two continued toward the house and stopped at the bottom of the stairs.

Being that Madison was the next county over from Buncombe, where Charlie and Kim were based, they knew most of the deputies there, and spotted the sheriff, Sheriff Rodney Brown, at the door of the bed and breakfast, holding it wide open.

The sheriff glanced back at Kim and Charlie, coming up the steps and onto the porch. "He's got him at gunpoint in there, but thankfully hasn't pulled the trigger. I got men out back, have their sights on 'im, ready to take 'im down."

Charlie shook his head. "Tell them to stand down. I want to talk to him."

Sheriff Brown said, "I don't know if that's a good idea, Charlie. He's armed, of course, so…"

Charlie walked right past him before the sheriff finished and went into the house. He heard Kim say his name, as if questioning what he was doing, but kept going. He walked past a reception desk with an old-fashioned black phone on it, glancing back at Kim and the sheriff in the doorway, watching him.

There was classical music playing from somewhere in the building, but it was otherwise eerily quiet.

He looked through another doorway and into what looked like some kind of living room, and right away saw Scott Sanborn seated in one of a handful of wingback chairs. He was gripping the armrests and looked to be crying. Whimpering, really.

Sanborn wasn't looking at Charlie, instead staring straight ahead from where he sat. He pleaded, "You don't have to do this. I'm sorry. Please. I swear, I didn't hurt her. I never would."

There was a china cup on a saucer next to him on a side table, with a half-eaten muffin on a matching china plate, next to it. A crumpled napkin was on the floor under the table.

Charlie couldn't see Jason Dexter but heard him talking.

He said, "Please, Mom. He deserves what he's got coming." Then it went quiet. "Mom? Are you there?"

Charlie heard nothing else, still moving closer to the doorway, taking each step as if doing his best to keep the old floors under his feet from creaking.

"Jason? It's Deputy Charlie Harlow, with the U.S. Marshals. We met the other night, at Kristen's house?"

There was a long pause, no sounds in the building other than the classical music and Sanborn's whimpering.

After a few moments, Charlie said Jason's name again, then reached toward his belt, expecting his Glock to be there. But it wasn't. "I'm not armed," he said. "I just want to talk."

"He killed Kristen," Jason said. "He deserves the same fate."

Charlie had his back against the wall, staying covered on the other side of the doorway. "What makes you so sure he killed her?" He glanced toward the front entrance, where Kim and the sheriff stood watching him from the porch, the door propped open.

Jason said, "She told me he wanted her to meet him here. And he was mad, when she said she wouldn't."

"She told you that?" Charlie said.

"That's right. This fool didn't think she loved me. But she did. And he didn't like it, so he killed her."

"It's not true!" Sanborn cried, looking toward Charlie. "Please, help me! I didn't kill her!"

Charlie stepped away from the wall and looked into the room through the doorway without stepping inside. He still wasn't sure where Jason was standing, but had a pretty good idea, the way Sanborn's gaze was fixed straight ahead of Charlie.

"What's the story?" Charlie said, looking at Sanborn now.

"What story? I didn't kill her! What else do you want me to say?"

"I think you need to explain to Jason what else she might've said to you."

"She wouldn't come meet me. You think I'd kill her because of that? I told her I was leaving; I just wanted to see her one more time."

"You killed her!" Jason yelled, his voice cracking and loud but somewhat muffled coming from the other side of the wall. "She wanted nothing to do with you, and you couldn't take it!"

"I... did... not... kill... her," Sanborn said, his teeth gritted, his voice hushed now.

"Jason," Charlie said. "Let's just suppose you're right, and he did kill her..."

"I didn't!" Sanborn yelled, staring at Charlie still taking cover behind the wall but looking through the doorway toward him.

Charlie held his finger up in front of his lips in a shushing gesture. "What I'm saying, Jason, is you've done a good job here today. You got this son of a bitch, and now we can take him into custody, see to it we get to the truth, make sure he pays the price, if your assumption is correct. In fact, I'll personally see to it he never sees the light of day again."

"I can take care of it myself," Jason said, his voice cracking again. It was hard to say for sure, but he seemed to be crying. "We were going to get married, you know. Did you know that? She promised me she was done with this... with this old fool. He's twice her age anyway, like she wants some old man, pissing himself in a few years."

"You've gotta believe me," Sanborn said, looking toward Charlie. "Please, tell him I didn't do it. I'll admit to everything else. Whatever you want... Just, please. Don't let him do this."

Charlie glanced in at Sanborn. "Maybe it'd be best you just keep your mouth shut for now, all right?"

Sanborn nodded, swallowing hard. He cried like a little boy. "I can tell you who's behind everything. I have names. This man... He's killed people. He probably killed Kristen, looking for me."

"Be honest," Charlie said. "We kind of got all we need at this point." He looked in at Sanborn. "We know all about Caprio. And Whitlock. The guns..."

Sanborn's eyes were wide open. "Please. I can tell you everything. I know where the money is. Nobody else does."

That caught Charlie's attention. "Is that why they're looking for you?"

Sanborn paused, as if having a moment of hesitation before he finally nodded. "Please, tell him..." He turned from Charlie and looked straight ahead. "Jason, I didn't kill Kristen. You gotta believe me."

Charlie was thinking, trying to get a look in at Jason. There was a mirror on the far wall from where he stood, from inside the room, but he saw nothing but windows in the reflection, with a view of some trees outside. He watched Sanborn, a nervous wreck, and the way his foot bounced up and down like a jackhammer now, practically shaking the man's entire body.

Charlie said, "Jason? What kind of gun you got yourself in there?"

There was a pause. "What kind of gun? I... I don't know. I think the man said it was a forty-five? Or, maybe a... I don't know. What's it matter?"

"Okay," Charlie said. "I want you to listen to me for a second here, Jason. All right?" Charlie's heart was racing in a way it normally never did. He'd been in plenty of similar situations like it before, and never felt an ounce of adrenalin or his blood pressure going up. In fact, he'd normally felt a sense of calm. But something wasn't right. Even with the cooler air coming from outside, he was sweating more than normal. He felt his face and how clammy and warm it was. Even his hands were damp.

There was a weakness coming over him, and he tried to control what felt to him, his own heavy breathing. But he couldn't.

Charlie felt the wet under his arm, on his side, and then he looked at his hand. He was still bleeding.

"Shit," he said, under his breath. He was afraid it was only a matter of time he wasn't going to be able to hold up. He said, "Jason, are you still on the phone with your mom?"

"No," he said. "My phone's dead."

"All right," Charlie said. "Then how about I get her? She's right outside, in the parking lot, waiting for you to come out."

There was no response.

"Jason," Charlie said. "You want to talk to her?"

"No!" Jason snapped. "I don't want her to see me like this. Why is she here?"

Charlie took his phone out of his pocket. "Then, how about I give you my phone, and you can talk to her? I know she wants to talk to you, Jason. Would that be all right?"

It took a few moments for the young man to speak. "I'm going to pull the trigger now. I'm sorry. I've made up my mind."

"Wait!" Charlie said. "You pull that trigger, and I'm telling you, for your own good, there are deputies outside could shoot a fly off a horse's ass from half a mile away. You pull that trigger, they're going to fire their weapons. You don't believe me, you look right outside that window in there, you'll see them."

"I don't see anyone," Jason said, as if he didn't believe what Charlie said.

Charlie waved for Kim out on the porch watching him and pointed to his phone. "Call me. Put his mother on the phone. I'm going to give it to Jason."

Kim hurried away from the front entrance and down the steps from the porch.

Another twenty seconds went by, and Charlie's phone rang with Kim's number showing on his screen. He answered, "Let me get him." He put the phone in one hand out through the doorway into the room on the other side of the wall, and put the other hand out with it, where Jason could see them both. "Take the phone. It's your mom. I just want you to see I'm not armed. I kind of wish I was, if I'm being honest. But I'm not. I just want you to talk to her, make sure you know how much it'll hurt her, you do what you said you're going to do."

Charlie waited, but Jason still hadn't taken the phone. "If I step through this doorway, can you promise me you're not going to shoot me?"

Jason didn't respond at first, then said, "Why do you have blood all over your hands?"

"Well, the truth is, the man we believe killed Kristen took a shot at me. Got me pretty good."

"You're bleeding?" Jason said.

Charlie didn't respond, the place quiet now. Even the classical music had stopped playing. "Go ahead, take the phone," he said. "Talk to your mom. She doesn't want to see you spend the rest of your life in prison for something that doesn't have to happen."

Charlie was still, waiting for the fish to nibble. And as soon as he felt Jason try to grab the phone, he jumped through the doorway and grabbed Jason's wrist. The phone dropped, and Charlie tried to pull the kid down to the ground.

But before Charlie could grab the gun, Jason fired a shot.

Scott Sanborn cried out with a scream.

"Hold your fire!" Charlie yelled, inside the room now with his hand on Jason's neck, twisting the kid like a pretzel until they both finally crashed hard to the floor.

The gun—what turned out to be a small .38—had fallen from Jason's grasp and sat there on the Oriental rug covering the old hardwood floor.

Jason didn't put up much of a fight at that point, with Charlie holding him, his head pinned against the floor.

Kim and the sheriff were inside now and standing over the two, guns drawn.

Charlie said, "Somebody take him, please." His breathing was heavy and labored. He looked over at Sanborn, on the floor in front of the chair he'd been seated in, holding his leg. He had blood coming through his fingers.

"He shot me!" Sanborn cried. "He shot me! I need a rescue!"

"Someone get the man a Band-Aid," Charlie said, the sheriff and two deputies taking Jason from Charlie and getting him in handcuffs.

Kim was standing over Scott Sanborn, making a call for paramedics.

"It hurts so much," Sanborn cried.

Charlie felt as dizzy and lightheaded as he ever had, not even seeing clear at that point, wishing he could get in bed and close his eyes. He crawled on the floor to the wall and sat up, leaning his back against the wall with his legs straight out. He closed his eyes.

Kim had the handcuffs on Sanborn, even though he had blood coming from one of his legs. "Charlie?" she said. "Are you okay?"

Charlie opened his eyes, nodding. "Yeah. But something tells me the doctor wasn't kidding when he told me to rest a few days." He grinned and closed his eyes again. "Truth is, I could use a drink." He took his U.S.M.S. baseball cap off his head and rested it on his lap.

Chapter 29

THE SIGN FOR COYOTE Grille was illuminated over the parking lot when Deputy Ethan Holden turned in, off the road. There were just a handful of cars and a few people inside one of the shops on the lower level below the bar.

The sun had already set as Kim stepped out of the front passenger seat and opened the back door for Charlie, reaching in to help him to his feet.

"I'm all right," he said, using his own strength, as weak as it was, to pull himself up on his feet.

The wooden steps going up to the deck outside Coyote Grille weren't as much of a struggle for Charlie as he thought they'd be. It was more the overwhelming feeling of needing to rest that bothered him, more than the pain. In fact, whatever the paramedics did to his wounds outside the bed-and-breakfast made him feel a heck of a lot better than they had at any point since he left the hospital.

He reached the top step and thought he smelled marijuana burning, but didn't think much about it.

Lindsey was behind the bar when Charlie and Kim walked in, and came right around to their side to help ease him into a stool. "Thanks so much for taking him here," Lindsey said to Kim. She looked Charlie over and straightened his USMS baseball cap for him, like he was some helpless child who'd been lost and taken back to his momma.

Charlie looked at her and saw she had tears in her eyes, but didn't know why. Could've been she was simply sad to look at him in his condition; so weak and tired. Or maybe she was just happy he was there with her.

"All right, let's not make a big deal out of this," he said. "I'm fine." He gazed at the shelves of booze on the wall behind the bar. "Could use some Jack. A double. The doctor recommends it."

Kim took his duffel bag off her shoulder and handed it to Lindsey. "The paramedics said he just needs to get some rest. Of course, they wanted to take him to the ER, to be sure. To nobody's surprise, he refused."

Johnny Cash's "Like the 309" was playing on the CD juke-box, which happened to be the final song Cash recorded before he died. Charlie wanted to smile. He'd recently been thinking more about playing his guitar more than he had, which was almost never. He'd pick it up once in a while, strum a couple of chords with the dust-coated strings, barely in tune, then put it back in the corner.

"Where is everyone?" he said, straightening out in the stool, his arms folded in front of him on the bar. He turned and watched Lindsey walk around to the other side.

"It's Tuesday," she said. "I was thinking of closing early."

Charlie looked down to his right at the far end of the bar, where two mugs sat with less than half a beer in them. There was a jacket on the back of one of the stools.

Otherwise, the place was cleaned up and empty.

"Is anyone going to tell me what happened?" Lindsey said, looking from Kim to Charlie. "I thought you were still in bed resting this whole time?"

"He was supposed to be," Kim said, standing next to him now. She leaned on the bar.

Charlie gave Kim a smile when she looked at him, and said, "Well, it worked out, I'd say. No?"

Kim didn't answer, but she knew he was right.

The one thing he took away from it all was when Jason Dexter's mother watched her son get put into the back of the sheriff's vehicle in handcuffs, then turned to Charlie and told him he was a hero.

"I didn't do much of anything," he told her.

Kim started for the door. "All right, I'm going to get going now." She looked across the bar at Lindsey. "He's not supposed to come back to work, so whatever you can do to get him to rest..." She pulled the handcuffs off her belt. "You need these, let me know."

They both smiled and Charlie sat, staring straight ahead from his seat at the back of the bar. He looked up at the TV, but didn't pay enough attention to what was on. "Thank you, Kim," he said, without looking at her. "I owe you one."

"You don't owe me anything," she said. "Just get better." She turned to Lindsey and said, "He's all yours. Good luck," then opened the door, the cool from the outside hitting Charlie's back.

"I'll see you in the morning," he said, glancing over his shoulder at Kim leaving.

She had already left and closed the door.

Lindsey said to Charlie, "Are you going to tell me what the hell happened today?"

Charlie thought about it all for a moment. "Can I tell you later?" He looked her in the eye and gave her a smile that showed his obvious affection for her. "It's nice to see you."

"You don't look so good," she said.

"Thanks," he said, looking her over. "Can't say the same about you. I forgot how good you look."

Lindsey smiled and rolled her eyes. "What kind of drugs do they have you on?"

Charlie was, of course, trying to be nice. They hadn't spoken over the past twenty-four hours, other than trading a couple of voicemails, and he'd missed her more than he thought he would.

"Let me get you some tea," she said.

Charlie, slouched over on the bar, barely keeping his head up, raised a finger. "Actually, why don't you make it a double Jack Daniels."

She slipped through the swinging door as if ignoring him and disappeared into the kitchen.

Charlie turned to look at the door when it opened behind him, and two local men he'd seen before walked through.

They both stopped when they saw him, appearing surprised and maybe looking a bit nervous with their red eyes half shut with a sleepy look Charlie recognized right away.

"Boys," he said, giving them both a nod.

"Deputy," they both said at the same time, then continued to the far end of the bar and sat where the two mugs of beer were waiting.

Charlie got a whiff when they went by and knew their odor came from the skunk-like smell of marijuana like the one he'd smelled outside.

That same smell was more prevalent than it'd ever been, the way it'd been legalized in many states. But even where it hadn't been allowed, nobody ever tried to hide it anymore. It was different from when he was a kid, when you'd go deep into the woods to smoke a joint, always keep a bottle of Visine in your jacket to clear the red from your eyes, maybe spray some kind of cheap cologne on your clothes to cover up the smell.

He didn't have much of an opinion on whether or not it was right, but the fact a man could freely drink a bottle of booze and do more damage to himself than if he'd sit back and smoke a joint always had Charlie scratching his head. And it made little sense to stop anyone from doing what they were going to do anyway, legal or not.

Lindsey came through the door from the kitchen with a mug in her hand, steam coming up off the top around the teaspoon handle. There was no tea bag visible.

She placed it in front of Charlie. "Drink this, and I'll give you that shot of Jack."

Charlie leaned over it and smelled it, feeling the heat rise to his nose. It smelled earthy, which is a word he wouldn't use outside of thinking it in his head. He'd describe it more like wet leaves with a mint odor to it. Maybe some lemon.

"What is it?" he said.

"Something I make up when I'm not feeling well. It always does the trick."

He looked at her. "You won't tell me what's in it?"

"You don't trust me?" she said, smiling. "It's got echinacea, which is known for its immune-boosting properties. It's supposed to support your body's natural defenses."

He turned the tea with the spoon. "I guess I could use some of that. I should've come to see you first," he said, but as soon as the words left his mouth he wished he hadn't. The two were already acting as if he hadn't stayed at Jennie's after he was released from the hospital. He wanted to ask Lindsey right there why she didn't answer his texts at first, but thought better of it, and knew it'd be best if he went with small talk about the tea.

He lifted the mug. "What else is in it?" He looked at her over the rim, taking a sip.

The taste of it wasn't great. But it wasn't that bad either... about as he'd expected with the leaflike flavor, mint and lemon.

"It's a concoction my grandmother used to make, used whenever someone got sick, or had some kind of injury." She smiled. "Of course, none of us ever got shot." But then she pulled at her chin. "Actually, that's not exactly true."

"Which part?" Charlie said, easing the mug back to the bar.

"My cousin, Billy. He shot himself in the foot, playing with my uncle's gun."

"Did he live?"

"Yeah," she said, smiling. "But I don't think the tea would've helped." She nudged the mug in Charlie's direction. "Go on, drink it up. I promise it'll make you feel better."

"Why won't you tell me what else is in it?" he said.

"You don't trust me?" she said, then leaned on the bar, taking the teaspoon and turning the tea. "It's got ginger. Turmeric. Peppermint. Oh, and lemon balm."

"Lemon bomb?" he said.

"No. Balm. B-A-L-M. It's an herb, called Melissa officinalis. You've had it before. I've put it in our salads."

Lindsey strolled down the bar to the other end where the two men were seated. They'd both finished their beers, and she said something to them Charlie couldn't hear, then they both looked Charlie's way and stood up from their stools.

They put cash on the bar and headed for the door, not making eye contact with Charlie.

Lindsey came out from behind the bar and locked the door behind them as soon as they left.

"What was that all about?" Charlie said.

"I told them they reeked of weed, and if they stuck around they'd get in trouble with the marshal."

"Why'd you tell them that?" he said.

She went back to the other side of the bar and flicked the switch.

The glowing light from the sign outside went out. "I told you I was closing early." She shrugged. "Just having a little fun. I won't serve them when they're like that, so no sense in them hanging around."

Charlie laughed a little, then reached for his side.

"I assume since you have your duffel bag, you're staying the night?" she said.

"Well, I don't even have a vehicle, so unless you want to give me a ride out to the Winnebago..."

She leaned on the bar and looked into the mug of tea Charlie had barely touched. "I wish you were in better condition, but I couldn't be any happier to have you here." She straightened up. "You want me to take you upstairs? You can get in bed, watch TV while I clean up down here."

"I'm all right" he said, shaking his head. "I was still hoping for that shot of Jack?"

She pushed the tea right under him on the bar. "Drink the rest of this and head upstairs. I'll bring you the bottle."

Chapter 30

CHARLIE WOKE UP IN bed unsure at first where he was. He had his shirt off, but his jeans still on, the sheets bunched up in the middle next to him. Lindsey was asleep on the other side. A sliver of light came through the blinds, but Charlie wasn't sure yet if it was the sun coming up or the lamp over the parking lot.

He had no idea what time it was, picked up his phone from the table next to the bed and checked the time.

It was 5:42.

The sun still had time before it was up.

Charlie didn't even remember falling asleep, or when Lindsey came up from the bar downstairs. He touched his side, feeling the bandaged area, and was surprised it didn't hurt the way it had. Of course, the pain was still there. But it was slight.

He sat up on the edge of the bed and felt the damp sheet where he'd slept. He touched his pillow, and it felt wet. He had a feeling he'd sweated out a fever he was almost certain he had when he conked out.

He looked from the bed into the kitchen area and saw a bottle of Jack Daniels on the counter, with two glasses beside it. He didn't remember drinking any of it, and was pretty sure he hadn't.

Lindsey's loft above the bar was convenient for both of them, right up the exterior stairs. It was all one big area, with only the bathroom separate. The kitchen was a single counter with an old brown refrigerator on one side, the matching small oven on the other. There was a stacked washer and dryer squeezed in between the stove and the wall to the right of it.

He sat there, trying to put together the night, right before he went to bed. He remembered going outside into the cold and walking up the wooden steps to the apartment, while Lindsey closed down the bar. He'd been up there with the TV on, but barely remembered watching it. He was too tired to take off his pants, thought he must've put his head on the pillow and was out within seconds.

He looked over his shoulder.

Lindsey appeared to be sleeping, from what he could see in the darkness, but she opened her eyes, squinting. "Hey," she said, reaching her hand for him. "Are you feeling any better?"

He thought about it. "I think I might be." He eyed the bottle of Jack and the two glasses. "Guess I'll take a rain check on that drink?"

"I had a feeling you'd be asleep when I got up here. You were practically ready to pass out at the bar. I tried to get off your pants, but I didn't want to hurt you." She smiled. "Or give you the wrong idea."

Charlie laughed as he stood up. "You mind I take a shower?"

"Don't you need to cover your wound before you do?"

"I'm supposed to," he said, touching the area again, pushing at it with a little more pressure now, as if to make sure the pain was really going away. "Do you have any tape? And a plastic bag?"

Lindsey sat up but didn't answer, as if she was in her own thoughts for a moment.

Charlie watched her, waiting.

"Listen," she said. "I have to... I just want you to know I'm sorry for leaving the hospital the way I did. I guess I wasn't expecting to see Jennie there. I don't know why she wouldn't have been. I know she still loves you. But I guess..." She paused.

"I would've taken care of you, too, you know. I just wanted you to know, I wasn't upset with you or anything like that. I acted like a fool. I guess I'm jealous of you and her."

Charlie reached out and put his hand on hers. "There's nothing between us. But I don't even know what we have anymore. I guess we're just friends. I appreciate that she took care of me the way she did. I know some people split up, it's nothing but daggers. But...

"You don't have to explain anything," Lindsey said, squeezing his hand. She let go and sat on the edge of the bed with her back to him for a moment, with nothing on but a T-shirt.

Charlie watched her take a pair of jeans hung over the back of a chair and slip them on, thinking how beautiful she was.

"I have some tape downstairs," she said. "I'll go get it."

Charlie was examining the bandage. "You don't have to. It'll be fine."

"But if you're going to shower, you can't get it wet."

Charlie went over to the kitchen area. His throat was so dry it felt like it was stuck closed. He filled a glass from the tap and threw his head back, drinking water in big gulps. He filled the glass again and looked around. "You know where my bag is?"

Lindsey grabbed the duffel bag from under the same chair where her pants had been hanging and put it on the bed. "Don't forget; you have clothes in my dresser too."

Charlie went over and looked in the bag and thought about his Glock. He wasn't sure what'd happened to it, assuming Frank or Kim had picked it up. He couldn't remember the last time he'd gone anywhere without his gun.

Lindsey said, "You want something to eat? I can make you a nice breakfast. I assume you're hungry?"

"I am," he said. "But you don't have to go through all the trouble."

"It's no trouble at all," she said. "We gotta eat, don't we?" She smiled at him, then walked into the bathroom and closed the door behind her.

Charlie picked up his phone while he had a moment to himself and called Frank. He knew it might've been too early, but Frank was usually up before dawn. He dialed and put the phone to his ear.

It rang three times before Frank answered, taking a few moments before he spoke.

"Yeah?"

"You sleeping?" Charlie said.

"Yeah, I'm sleeping. Why wouldn't I be?" He cleared his throat. "Everything all right?"

"Honestly?" Charlie said. "I feel good. Really good. I'm surprised how good, actually."

"Are you serious?" Frank said. "We were worried about you. Kim said you looked bad when she dropped you off."

"I'm sure I did. But I'm good now. I'd like to head into the office, but I still don't have a vehicle. I was hoping maybe you could—"

"I don't care how good you say you feel. You're not coming to work today, Charlie. I'm sorry. I'm putting my foot down this time. You should've never been in that situation you put yourself in yesterday. Until you get a clean bill of health from the doctor…"

"Wait. You want a note from my doctor?"

"I want a professional to tell you you're good enough to go back to work. Whether you'd like to believe it or not, your health is my responsibility, Charlie. I'm the one who'll get the blame if you drop dead on the job because you didn't have enough smarts to stay away."

"Frank, I'm—"

"It's an order. There'll be no discussion. You take another day to relax, get the rest you need. We can talk about it tomorrow, see how things are going."

"Why can't you just take my word for it?" Charlie said. "I'm telling you. I feel good, Frank. Like new."

Frank laughed. "Take your word?" He laughed again.

Charlie really was surprised by the way he felt. It was better than he'd expected, and he wasn't even sure why. He thought about the tea. "Lindsey made me this tea. It didn't taste good, but I swear... it's like it was some kind of witch potion."

Lindsey heard what he said and yelled out from the bathroom, "It's not a witch potion!"

Charlie stepped away from the bathroom door and to the far side of the apartment, keeping his voice hushed. He didn't have anything to hide from Lindsey, but didn't need her listening to his call with Frank either.

Frank said, "I don't care what kind of magic pills you took or whatever it is you drank. What I'm telling you, right now... if I have to suspend you just to keep you away until you're ready, I will."

"I'm not sure you can do that," Charlie said.

"You wanna try me?" Frank said.

Charlie sat down in a small wooden chair, some kind of antique by the window that was hard and uncomfortable. He spread open the blinds and looked through the bare trees at the sun starting to rise and fill the cool blue sky with a tint of orange. He kept his voice low and said, "So what's the story with the kid? Jason Dexter?"

Frank said, "He was being held overnight. I don't even know what the charges are just yet."

"I hope they're lenient with him," Charlie said. "I would've done the same thing he did."

Frank didn't respond.

Charlie said, "Anyone get anything out of Sanborn? I wish I'd had a chance to shake him down myself before Kim dragged me out of there."

"Well, she had good reason. It's my understanding you could barely stand on your own two feet."

"That's a bit of an exaggeration," Charlie said.

Frank said, "I know Sanborn had to be attended to, considering he took a bullet to the foot."

"It was a thirty-eight," he said. "I bet it barely broke the man's skin."

Frank paused. "He spent a good part of the night in the ER, then the locals took him to the county detention center."

"Buncombe?" Charlie said.

"Uh-huh. The bureau's going to be interviewing him. I know Stan is driving out, heading over there this morning. We'll get our chance to talk to Sanborn later today, I hope."

"I'd like to be there for that," Charlie said.

Frank said, "Could that head of yours be any thicker? You're not working today. End of discussion. Do you understand?"

"I say you sound like my mother, but the difference is she would've told me to suck it up and get back to work."

Frank laughed. "All right. Are you still at Lindsey's?"

"Uh-huh." Charlie waited, listening.

"I'll tell you what. I'll take a ride over. We can grab some breakfast, talk a little bit. If I think you look as good as you're trying to convince me you are, then maybe—and that's a big maybe—I'll let you join us for the interview with Sanborn. But that's it. And if I get the feeling you're bullshitting me, and you're no better than you were when I last saw you, which wouldn't be much of a surprise, I'll..."

"All right," Charlie said, getting up from the chair with the phone to his ear. He looked at the bathroom door as it opened, and Lindsey walked out with a towel, wiping her face.

She tossed it into the stacked washing machine in the kitchen, then headed to the refrigerator and opened the door to look inside.

Charlie wasn't about to tell Frank he couldn't meet, but Lindsey appeared to be getting ready to make something to eat.

"Give me an hour," Frank said. "Maybe a little less."

"Frank," Charlie said, before Frank hung up. "Any chance you have my Glock?"

"I'm surprised it took you this long to ask about it."

"Do you have it?"

"Yeah," Frank said. "I have it. Foolish of you to go over there unarmed yesterday. I thought maybe you would've at least carried a spare with you, no?"

"Well, don't forget I have no way of getting to my place to get them. Not without a vehicle that can handle the terrain, as we've already discussed."

"Oh, about that," Frank said. "Yeah, well, you know they've been cracking down on our government-owned vehicles being driven for personal use..."

"Are you telling me I'm not getting another vehicle?"

"The Town Car's been repaired," Frank said. "But, replacing it... I'm just not sure. Between you and Kim, we're down two nearly brand new vehicles. Why do you think I went and bought my own truck? I knew this day was going to come when they start cutting back, cracking down on things someone in accounting seems to believe is a problem."

"It sounds ridiculous," Charlie said. "They know how many times we get woken up in the middle of the night to go hunt down a fugitive straight outta bed?"

"I'm just telling you what I'm hearing. I'll see what I can do," Frank said.

"And I'm not kidding about that Town Car," Charlie said. "It won't make it up to the river."

Frank was quiet on the other end. "Let me get going here. I'll see you in an hour."

Charlie looked at the screen and saw Frank had hung up.

"Is everything all right?" Lindsey said, her back to Charlie. She had a box of eggs on the counter in front of her and a box of pancake mix. The pan was already on the stove.

"Frank's coming to pick me up," Charlie said, feeling bad about it the moment the words left his mouth.

Lindsey turned to face him, her mouth opening and closing but words didn't come out at first.

"I'm sorry," Charlie said, looking at the ingredients she'd put up on the counter. "I can still eat, but he's coming soon. A little under an hour." He pointed with his thumb toward the bathroom. "Do you mind if I shower now?"

Lindsey started putting the food back into the refrigerator. "Go ahead," she said, frustration in her voice.

Charlie went around the narrow island and over to her. "I know I haven't told you much of anything about this case. But it's important. I can't let these men get away with what they've done."

"You say it like you work alone," Lindsey said. "Why is it up to *you*?"

"It's not up to me," he said. "But these are the men who shot me, grabbed a woman right out of the back of my vehicle, and have already killed a number of people, including an innocent young woman. There could be more, if we don't stop them."

"We," she said. "Doesn't Frank know you're hurt? Or that you need to rest?"

"Frank doesn't even want me working. But he's coming to pick me up. And if I look okay to him, maybe I can get back to the office."

Lindsey didn't reply.

Charlie wrapped his arms around her and kissed her on the top of her head. "I'm sorry. You don't need me laying around your place all day either. Nobody wants that."

Charlie's problem with laying around—he couldn't remember the last time he took a nap. That was about the only thing he could remember of his father, back when he was a little kid, the only couch they had in their home seemed to be always occupied just about every minute of the day. He wasn't sure if his father ever worked—outside of his apparent criminal activity—and seemed to always be on the couch, either sleeping or with a dozen empty cans of beer in front of him on the coffee table.

Lindsey put her hand on Charlie's face, then reached up and kissed him on the lips. "Please be safe," she said, gazing at him.

He loved her big brown eyes. And she smelled good, even if it was just the soap she used to wash her face.

"Will you at least have some more of my tea before you go?" She made a quick throat clear and smiled. "You know, my *witch potion?*"

Chapter 31

Charlie had his sunglasses on, already outside the Coyote Grille in the parking lot, waiting. He watched Frank pull in, driving the pickup truck, and heading toward him. Charlie walked across the lot to where Frank had parked, and did all he could to look normal with each step, keeping as upright as possible, ignoring any sign of pain.

The fact was, he *did* feel a lot better than he had. Maybe not as good as he'd tell Frank or as he'd told Lindsey before he left. But he felt good, and had little doubt he was good enough to get back in the saddle.

He opened the truck's door on the passenger side and stepped up into the cab, pulling himself up by the grab bar along the edge of the open door. He actually felt a little more pain with the way he had to stretch and get up onto the seat when he climbed up, but he did all he could to ignore it enough so Frank wouldn't notice.

Charlie pulled the heavy door closed and said to Frank, "How's an old man like you climb up in this monster of a truck every morning?

Frank gave him a look like he didn't appreciate Charlie's attempt at a humorous dig. "Now, I know you don't mean that. But maybe you're not the only one with some witch potion." He hit the gas and took off across the empty parking lot, dust kicking up behind the truck, the gravel from the lot popping under the tires and pinging against the truck's undercarriage.

Charlie said, "You laugh, but I'm telling you... it worked. I feel good."

"From tea?" Frank laughed, shaking his head with his eyes on the road ahead.

Charlie stared back at him, a serious look on his face. "It wasn't just tea. It was a whole bunch of stuff she says cranks up your immune system. Why's that so hard to believe?"

Frank gave him a quick look. "She does kind of have a look about her; she could be a witch. That long, dark hair, big brown eyes... A pretty one, of course. But, you never know." He laughed again, having a good time at Charlie's expense.

Charlie looked out the passenger window at the water crossing over Reem's Creek. "Where are we going? I'm starving." He grinned. "All I had was the tea."

Frank said, "I was thinking, maybe the Waffle House? There's one over there, off Weaver Boulevard."

"I almost died, and you claim this meetup is so you can see if I'm healthy enough to come back to work. And you're going to treat me to the Waffle House?"

"What's wrong with the Waffle House?" Frank said.

"Nothing's wrong with it. I was just—"

"And when did I say it was my treat?" Frank cleared his throat, turning the truck onto North Main Street.

They continued through the historical downtown with the redbrick buildings on either side, the power lines running overhead, from pole to pole, the yellow awning with the spinning barber pole in the window... A place called Vickey's Ceramics... Blue Ridge Hardware...

Charlie spotted a sign for the Sunny Side Cafe. "What about Sunny Side?" he said.

"You ever been?"

Charlie said, "Yeah. And they've got good pancakes." He held his hands up, about a foot apart. "Omelets this big."

Frank said, "All right. I'll go to the Waffle House myself some other time." He hit the brakes just past a parking space on the street, two doors down from the Sunny Side Cafe. Shifting into reverse, he backed the truck into the tight space in one try, like he'd done it a thousand times.

• • • ● • ● • • • •

Charlie was at the table with what looked like half a dozen plates of food in front of him when Frank walked out of the bathroom and slid into the booth across from him.

Frank said, "Well, I guess you've got your appetite back, huh?" He turned the one plate in front of him with the oversized omelet, picking up his fork. "You sure you're going to eat all that?"

Charlie rearranged the plates in front of him: one with a stack of pancakes, three fried eggs over easy on another, a small plate of fried potatoes, a side of whole wheat toast, and a bowl of fruit. Steam rose up from his cup of tea he'd ordered.

"I figure, since you're paying, might as well get what I could."

"I told you, I don't remember saying it was my treat."

Charlie tapped the side of his head. "See? The memory starts to go, a man at your age." He stuck a piece of pancake into his mouth.

Charlie knew Frank wasn't exactly someone anyone in their right mind would call old. Frank was as strong as an ox, in better shape in most men half his age, and smart as a whip. But he was older than Charlie, with white hair he kept buzzed so short he almost looked bald.

Frank smirked and looked at Charlie's cup. "So, what, now you're a tea drinker? Is this what hanging around with Lindsey is doing to you?" He lifted his own cup and sipped his coffee.

Charlie didn't respond, pouring more syrup on his pancakes. He cut off a big wedge from the stack, slipping it into his mouth, chewing. He closed his eyes for a moment and savored the sweet taste. Even the maple syrup was the real thing: something he knew he wouldn't have gotten from the place Frank wanted to go to. He swallowed what he had in his mouth. "So you see me, right? You believe me now? That I'm healthy enough?"

Frank had just taken a bite of his omelet. He finished chewing and wiped his mouth with his napkin, using both hands. "Just because you can eat a big meal doesn't prove you're where you need to be. But I guess you know what it takes, so I don't think I need to be the one to tell you one way or the other."

Charlie dropped his fork on the plate and stared at Frank. "Are you serious? I thought you said it was up to you?"

Frank took another bite of his omelet and chewed for a few seconds, then sipped his coffee. A grin showed up on his face. "Part of me's just giving you shit," he said. "You took a big chance yesterday, not only putting your own life at risk, but everyone else around you. Christ, you weren't even armed, Charlie. But, like I said, it worked out, so I'd be a fool to fault you for taking a chance the way you did." He leaned forward on the table. "Even at fifty percent healthy, I'd be kidding myself to think we'd be better off without you right now."

"Well, I'm better than fifty percent," Charlie said.

Frank took out Charlie's Glock covered by his jacket on the booth, the gun still in the holster. He put it up on the table and slid it across the table to Charlie, as if it were a gift.

They both looked around the restaurant, but none of the handful of people in there seemed to pay them much attention.

Charlie pulled the gun close and rested it on the seat. "Does this mean you believe I'm good to go?"

Frank said, "Even though you don't always act like one, you're a grown man. You tell me you're ready, then I'm not going to bother trying to argue with you. But I just need you to understand your health and safety is not only my responsibility, but a priority."

Charlie appreciated what Frank was saying. He lifted his cup of green tea and took a sip, but the bitterness was hard to swallow. He made a face, like he'd licked the bottom of his shoe.

"No good?" Frank said, then waved for the waitress and said to her, "You mind getting my friend here a cup of coffee?"

Charlie pushed the cup of tea out of his way, then leaned forward on the table with his hands clasped. "So, are you going to tell me what you know so far?"

The waitress came over with a cup of coffee for Charlie, and a pot she used to top off Frank's cup. "You boys need anything else?"

"Not right now, thank you," Frank said, waiting, watching her walk away.

Frank took another bite of his breakfast, then pushed it aside. He said to Charlie, "Apparently Sanborn's started to talk. He's got this buddy of his—a husband and wife—apparently involved in the same business they were in, also working under Denny Caprio. There's little information about them, and for whatever reason, the bureau has nothing either. There's no way just yet to know if Sanborn's being straight or not, but he said the husband, whose name is Nathan Parker, was the one who Sanborn partnered up with and ripped off Caprio."

"They were both working for him?" Charlie said.

"Like I said, this is news to all of us. No record of Parker or his wife having anything to do with Caprio."

"What if he's lying?" Charlie said.

"Sanborn? He could be. But that's all I've got right now."

Charlie said, "Do we know where these people are?"

Frank said, "Tennessee." He pulled out his phone and looked at the screen. "I'm waiting to hear back from Stan, but he seemed somewhat hesitant, maybe afraid we'd jump the gun, and—"

"He made it pretty clear there are bigger fish to fry," Charlie said, cutting off a piece of his fried egg with his fork. He stuck a bite in his mouth, then sipped his black coffee.

Frank's phone vibrated and he grabbed it, looking at the screen. He answered, "Yeah?" He nodded, listening, squinting like he was laser-focused on whatever the caller was saying on the other end. He looked at his watch. "We can make it up there in forty minutes." He stood, tossed two twenties on the table and removed the phone from his ear. He said to Charlie, "It's Stan." He gestured with his thumb that it was time to go.

Charlie took another bite of his pancake, shoving a couple of forkfuls in before he wiped his mouth, took another sip of coffee, and stood, his holstered Glock in his hand.

Frank said to Stan, "Now, what makes you believe they're up there?" His eyes widened and he looked at Charlie, the two still standing at the table. "All right, we're leaving now." He listened again. "Yeah, me and Charlie." He paused. "Yeah, he's good," he said, looking Charlie over. "All right, we'll see you soon. Okay, yeah. Citizens Bank. The one downtown. Got it."

Frank tapped the screen, slipped his phone into his pocket, and started heading for the door. He said to Charlie, "We're going to Erwin."

"What's the story?" Charlie said, hurrying to catch up with Frank, then stepping past him to grab the door.

Frank said, "I'll explain on the way, but from what Sanborn's telling them, he shared his secret about his friends, the Parkers, with Kristen Salvatore. The belief now is there's a good chance she told Whitlock about them."

Charlie clenched his jaw, looking down at the holstered Glock in his hand. "She told them what they wanted. And they killed her anyway."

Chapter 32

Frank turned off Interstate 26 and took the exit for Erwin, continuing on the off-ramp to Main Street. Charlie was looking for the Citizens Bank, when he saw the buildings down on the right, where a black Chevy Tahoe was parked in the bank's parking lot, facing the road.

Frank spotted it too. "There they are," he said, turning into the lot.

Charlie watched Kim step out of the driver's side and Deputy Holden out the passenger side of what looked like a shiny, new vehicle.

"Kim's Tahoe got repaired already?" Charlie said.

Frank pulled up next to it, shaking his head. "Nope. That thing was destroyed beyond repair. We picked this one up at the auction, only has twenty two thousand miles on it."

Charlie stared at Frank, like he couldn't believe it. "But I thought you said there was a new policy that—"

"I said there *may* be a new policy. Nothing's gone into effect yet," Frank said.

"Then why haven't I gotten a replacement for the Suburban?"

"You did," Frank said, turning off the engine. "The Town Car. You should see how good she looks, after they cleaned it up." He stepped out of the truck and slammed the door behind him.

Charlie sat still in the passenger seat, had his window down, looking over the Tahoe for a moment before he finally climbed down. "I don't get it," he said, following Frank, past Kim. "Why's she get a new four-wheel drive and I get the granny car?" He turned to Kim. "Why's he playing games with me?"

"I'm not playing games with you," Frank answered. "But when you destroy multiple vehicles over a few months' time, I gotta grease a few more palms. It doesn't help, all the hoops I have to jump through, get you something you won't complain about."

Charlie just stared at Frank in disbelief, then looked at the time on his phone. "What time's Stan supposed to be here?"

"I just got off the phone with him," Kim said. "He was twenty minutes away, five minutes ago. But then he got a call, said he'd call me right back." She looked at her phone, then slipped it back in her pocket. She looked Charlie over. "How're you feeling?"

"I'm good," he said. "Like new."

Frank smiled. "Lindsey made him some concoction, got him back up on his feet."

Kim looked from Frank to Charlie, like she wasn't sure if Frank was being serious or not.

Deputy Ethan Holden leaned against the Tahoe, not saying a word.

Kim said, "The belief right now is the wife is at the house. But the husband is not."

Charlie said, "Just so I have this all straight, these two—the Parkers—were involved in the same kind of scheme with Denny Caprio, but nobody's ever heard their name? All this time the FBI's been after Caprio and his underlings, like the Sanborns, but these people somehow slipped under the radar?" He looked from Kim to Frank.

"Apparently so," Frank said.

Kim said, "But I don't think we can make any moves just yet to bring either one in. There's no warrant, at least as far as I know."

"So who said the husband's not there?" Frank said. "Stan?"

"The local police," Kim said. "We've been coordinating with them. They've had the house under surveillance since this morning."

Ethan Holden straightened up from the front of the Tahoe. "What are we waiting for?"

Kim, Charlie, and Frank all turned to him, but nobody responded.

Charlie said, "So how far is the house?"

"Two and a half miles from here," Kim said. "It's a two-story mountain home, a little more than one hundred yards off the road."

"How far out are the police," Frank said, "from the house?"

"I believe they've moved closer. The house is surrounded by woods."

Charlie was thinking, looking at the road when a monster-sized pickup truck with an excessively loud muffler drove by. He turned to the others. "So right now, we have no idea if Caprio or Whitlock have already been to this house?"

"Correct," Kim said.

Charlie pulled at his chin. "So there's a chance they've come and gone, right? But we're certain the Parkers are both alive?"

Kim said, "The wife left the house, was gone for an hour, then got back home about forty minutes ago. Like I said, the belief is Mr. Parker is not at the house."

"But the police haven't gone in, so how do they know for sure?"

Kim just shrugged.

Deputy Holden hung his thumbs from his belt. "Shouldn't we just go up there, see for ourselves? If all we're doing is letting the local cops do all the work, then—"

"We're waiting for Agent Cooper!" Frank snapped, giving Holden a look like he didn't want the kid asking any questions or even saying another word, for that matter.

Charlie looked Holden up and down. "You're going to need to show a little patience in this business, all right?" He stared into Holden's eyes until the kid finally appeared to understand.

But then Frank looked at Charlie, almost like he was holding back a grin, the look on his face a reminder he'd said the same thing to Charlie quite a few times over the years.

Frank turned to Kim. "Any word if any other vehicles have been at the house? Have they spoken to any neighbors? Or..."

"Not as far as we know," Kim said. "But there's a good chance, assuming Whitlock killed Kristen Sanborn, they would've come right up after they left her apartment. Maybe sometime this morning, or possibly the middle of the night."

Charlie slipped his sunglasses back on, the way the sun was up and rising overhead, its the warmth and glow on his face.

Ethan Holden said, "But if the wife's just hanging around the house... No calls to the local police or anything, then—"

Charlie looked at the kid, almost like he wanted to tell him to stop talking. But the kid had a point. "She's a reluctant witness, and likely knows she'll face consequences for whatever role she played in this scheme Caprio was behind, if the FBI determines the Parkers were indeed involved."

"But there's no proof, right?" Ethan said. "I mean, that they've done anything wrong? This is all based on what Sanborn told them?"

Charlie didn't respond, nor did anyone else. He said, "Maybe they've got the husband, threatened the wife that if she says a word... he'd be dead?"

Frank and Kim both looked at him as if hoping that wouldn't be the case.

"I'd say that's a very real possibility," Frank said.

"I hate to side with Ethan here," Charlie said. "But I'm not sure waiting for Stan much longer makes any sense. We're already behind the eight ball, as we seem to've been from the start."

Holden said, "That's what I've been trying to say."

Frank looked at the kid, gritting his teeth. "Will you just do me a favor, Deputy? Keep that mouth of yours shut until one of us tells you to open it?"

Ethan's face turned beet red.

Few seemed to have much patience for Ethan. Frank had gone out of his way several times to give the kid a chance, but it was hard to look past the fact he never seemed to be cut out for the Marshals Service.

Of course, becoming a marshal was a rigorous process. Ethan clearly must've had what it took, along with a brief background as a local police officer. But his sometimes smug attitude, and a tendency to be a bit lazy, rubbed everyone else the wrong way.

And the thing was, Frank had managed to keep Ethan out of his hair, pushing him off on to the other deputies or making sure he was kept out of the field.

Frank's phone lit up and when he checked the screen; he tapped it right away and said to the others, "It's Stan." He put the phone to his ear. "Are you on your way?" He paused, listening. He looked from Kim to Charlie and said into the phone, "Where?"

Frank was quiet, head nodding slightly as he listened. "Maybe a couple of us should come out that way?"

Charlie was standing close enough to Frank he could hear Stan's voice coming through the phone but couldn't make out what he was saying. It was as if he was yelling.

Frank ended the call. "Nathan Parker's vehicle's been located off Interstate 26, down in Unicoi County. Flag Pond."

"So what's the plan?" Charlie said.

"Stan wants us to go up, talk to Mrs. Parker."

"What else did he say?" Kim said. "About the vehicle? Any clues or evidence of—"

"It had some damage, was driven off the road and hit a tree by a creek. They've got footprints in the mud. Not just one person's either."

"Maybe he was on the run, someone caught up to him?" Charlie said, doing nothing but speculating. But it made sense.

"I don't know," Frank said. "Stan doesn't know either."

Charlie said, "Maybe we should split up, two of us go talk to Mrs. Parker, the other two head down to where Stan is?"

"If Whitlock or Caprio's got him," Frank said, "I can't imagine they're hanging around waiting for us to show up. It'd be a waste of time."

Kim said, "I can try talking to her, see if we can get her to tell us what's going on?"

Frank turned to Charlie. "You go with her. Ethan and I'll stay back with the local police, out by the road."

Chapter 33

Charlie and Kim parked in the dirt driveway behind a parked Jeep, with Eastern white pines at least a hundred feet tall throughout the yard and plenty of leafless sugar maples deeper in the woods.

Smoke rose from a chimney, into the blue sky, and through the rays of sun cutting through the trees. The smell of burning wood filled the cool air as Charlie turned north, seeing the peaks of the Blue Ridge Mountains in the distance. He removed his sunglasses and gazed around at the property. "Wouldn't mind a quiet place like this myself one day." He peered at the two-story home with a full deck in back, built high off the ground above the concrete foundation. They were parked on the side of the house, and he could see a porch that wrapped from the front and around the side.

"Don't you already have a quiet place?"

Charlie didn't respond. His hand rested on his Glock holstered on his waist, his gaze moving from one window on the house to the other until he stopped at one on the second floor, and saw someone looking down at them.

But whoever it was disappeared.

"You see that?" he said.

"See what?" Kim continued up the blue stone walkway through the brown grass toward the front of the house.

Charlie hadn't answered her, moving ahead as if he didn't hear her question, up the steps and onto the porch. He unclipped his badge from his belt. To the left and right of the door were four big rocking chairs—two on each side—and a few bottles of beer on the floor, some tipped over. He crouched down and checked a couple of the standing bottles, both empty.

He recognized the decking Charlie believed was Ipe: Brazilian walnut. He was far from an expert on decking materials but knew enough to realize most of the house was a quality build: whoever owned it had to have money.

Whether these people obtained this money legally or not was to be determined, but wasn't Charlie's concern. Not right then.

He had one thing on his mind.

Kim stopped behind him, standing in the grass, peering along the house from one window to the next, her hand resting on her gun the same way as Charlie.

Charlie knocked on the heavy wood door. He leaned in close and raised his voice. "Mrs. Parker? This is Deputy U.S. Marshal Charlie Harlow." Turning his good ear to listen, he couldn't hear much of anything inside.

With his ear practically against it, the door opened.

A middle-aged woman stood on the other side looking out at him. She looked him over, then shifted her gaze to Kim at the bottom of the steps. "Can I help you?"

"Sonya Parker?" he said.

She paused, as if she wasn't sure she wanted to answer. "Can I help you?" She appeared nervous, almost shaking, her eyes puffy like she'd been crying.

But Charlie got a strong whiff of booze from her breath and thought maybe there was more to it. He repeated himself, "We're with the U.S. Marshals Service. I'm Deputy Charlie Harlow. This is Deputy Kim Riggins. We'd like to ask you a few questions, if you don't mind?"

She said, "May I ask what this is about?"

Charlie said, "I'd like to think you know why we're here. Or at least have a pretty good idea." He looked past her through the open door and into the house. "Are you alone?"

She waited a moment to answer, then nodded.

"Would it be all right if we came in?" Charlie could feel the heat coming out from inside the house. "Hate to stand here with that door open, losing all that warmth from inside."

She wore slippers and had a long sweater she pulled closed in front and closed the door behind her. "We can talk right here," she said.

Charlie had stepped back to give her some room.

Kim came up the steps, and the two stood side by side. "Ma'am," she said. "We're going to need you to be straight with us."

Charlie said, "Where is Mr. Parker?"

Sonya Parker paused, then said, "I... I don't know."

"You don't know?" Kim said.

"He's... he's not here."

Charlie took a deep breath, knowing the woman wasn't going to make any of this easy. "Listen," he said. "We're actually not here for you or your husband. We're looking for two men who may have already been here."

Sonya Parker shifted her stance but didn't respond.

Kim said, "Ma'am. We're looking for Dennis Caprio and a man by the name of Jack Whitlock. Can you please tell us if they were here or not? And if your husband is with them?"

Mrs. Parker held her gaze on Kim, like she was in some kind of shock.She started to cry. "He didn't do anything wrong," she said. "I swear, he—"

"Your husband?" Charlie said. "The truth is, we're not concerned at all with whatever you and your husband have done. What we need to do is find Denny Caprio and Jack Whitlock." He looked at the empty bottles on the floor. "Will you tell us if they've been here?"

"I swear, we had nothing to do with any of it. We just—"

"Ma'am," Charlie said. "I just told you, what you and your husband have done is not our concern. Now, I can't speak for any other law enforcement agency or department. But, right now, Deputy Riggins and I need to know where these men have gone. That's all we're asking you."

The tears grew and were coming down her face. She was crying now, to a point she was almost hysterical, maybe where she wouldn't be able to get any words out.

Charlie wasn't sure what to do, if he should console the woman or not.

Kim took a step closer to her. "Would it be all right if we went inside?" she said, taking the woman and turning her for the door. She reached for the knob and led the woman inside, rather than waiting for an answer.

Charlie had his Glock out and stepped in after them and closed the door. There was a sweet smell, like something had been baked. Maybe it was more of a syrupy smell, mixed with the wood-burning odor from the fireplace.

Inside the house, it was wide open, as if it was one huge room with a handful of doors off in different directions.

The kitchen area was to the back, overlooking the deck with tall and wide windows and a sliding glass door. Adjacent to the open kitchen was a living room area with two black leather couches and two matching black chairs. That's also where the fireplace was, a TV over it, cut wood stacked on the stone hearth.

A coffee table that looked like it'd been cut from the middle of a tree and placed on top of four logs sat on top of the furry skin of a bear. Charlie wasn't fond of using an animal to decorate a home. For all the shooting he'd gotten in trouble for over the years, never once did he aim a gun at an animal.

The bottle of Grey Goose vodka and an empty rocks glass on top of the coffee table explained the booze coming off Mrs. Parker's breath.

"I'm sure you don't want to be incriminating yourself in any way, Mrs. Parker, but—"

"Please, call me Sonya," she said, wiping her nose with a tissue. She hadn't really stopped crying. "I told you, I haven't done anything."

"We heard that," Kim said, stepping around to the other side of the dividing island, to where Charlie was standing. They had their backs to the living room area.

Sonya Parker stood facing them from the kitchen. "Can I get either of ya'll a drink?" She pointed with her thumb over her shoulder. "I can make some coffee, if—"

"I'm sure you're aware of the situation here?" Charlie said. "Those two men, if they haven't already, are likely going to kill your husband. And maybe we can save him, if you tell us what they were after, and where they took him?"

Sonya Parker's eyes welled up, and she burst out in a sob: her cry, a squeal, was so loud it hurt Charlie's good ear. "He doesn't know where it is."

"Where what is?" Kim said.

"The guns. The money. All of it. He told them he didn't know. But they wouldn't believe him."

Charlie pulled out his phone to dial Stan.

"Who are you calling?" Mrs. Parker said.

Charlie ignored her, walking over to the sliding glass door. He turned to Kim. "Give me a minute." He walked out onto the deck, glancing toward Kim's Tahoe parked below.

Stan answered, "Charlie?"

Charlie looked through the glass at Sonya Parker watching him.

"We're here with Mrs. Parker right now. She just told me this is about guns. Does that sound about right?"

Stan said, "We don't know for sure what's been sold, what hasn't, or whether or not Parker's got the money Caprio and Whitlock are looking for, or—"

"I thought this was all just... These people were supposed to be a bunch of white-collar criminals, caught up in some bullshit scheme. Are you telling me now they're all involved in trafficking?"

"Our belief, initially, as you said, was fraud. Ripping off poor old folks who didn't know any better," Stan said. "But now, it appears this whole operation has gone far beyond what any of us knew. I'd hate to say we dropped the ball, but—"

"We?" Charlie said.

"The bureau," Stan said. "This business, the fraud scheme... It's starting to look like it was more a front to steer us away from Caprio's real deal."

"Hiding a crime with a crime?" Charlie said, thinking about it. "So, did Sanborn say he and Parker got wrapped up in the gun trafficking?"

"It looks that way, but once Sanborn's lawyer showed up, he stopped talking. We got half the story."

"But if they were after Sanborn and Parker, it looks to me these two must've ripped him off. Does that sound right?" He looked in at Kim and Mrs. Parker, both standing on either side of the island, across from each other, talking. "What about Sanborn's wife? Obviously, she was in some kind of relationship with Caprio?"

"She threw her own husband under the bus," Stan said.

"All because he was screwing around?" Charlie said.

Stan didn't answer. "Let me call you right back," he said. "I gotta take this call."

"All right." Charlie ended the call but held it in his hand. He wanted to call Frank, but thought he should wait, hoping Stan would call right back.

He went back into the house and said to Mrs. Parker, "Can you tell me why Caprio and Whitlock left you here, by yourself? They weren't worried something like this would happen? Cops show up, and you end up talking?"

"I don't think they care," she said. "They're not afraid of the cops. Besides, I didn't think anybody knew we were here. We've been here for the past month and didn't tell anyone where we were."

"Well, somebody knew," Charlie said.

She nodded and let out a sigh. "Nathan was the one, told a friend of his to come out. He was supposed to show up with his new girlfriend, but he never came."

"You mean Scott Sanborn?" Charlie watched her, waiting for her reaction.

She swallowed hard but didn't answer.

"You don't have to say if it was him or not. We already know. We've got Sanborn in custody. He and his wife. Again."

Sonya Parker's eyes widened. "But, he would've never told those men we were up here. There's no way."

"He told the police," Charlie said. "But he didn't tell Caprio or Whitlock himself. What the fool did was tell his girlfriend about it, apparently. I suppose trying to convince her to come up here with him."

Mrs. Parker said, "She was supposed to come with him. Kristen, I believe her name is. We never met, but..."

"Well, she's not coming," he said. "But the chances are pretty good she's the one told Whitlock. And then he killed her."

Sonya gasped, covering her mouth with both hands.

"Sonya?" Kim said, walking around to the other side of the counter. "You have to tell us where they've taken your husband. Or where your husband's taking them."

Charlie didn't mention the car had been found but looked at his phone when it vibrated in his hand. He saw it was Stan and tapped the screen to answer. "What've you got?" Charlie said, turning from Sonya Parker.

Stan said, "We just found Nathan Parker's body."

Chapter 34

By the time Frank and the police had made it up to the Parkers' house, Charlie and Kim had done all they could to console Mrs. Parker once they let her know her husband had been found dead. She was shocked and hysterical.

But the news only got worse when Agent Stan Cooper showed up with a warrant for Mrs. Parker, having enough evidence to bring her in.

It didn't matter that her husband had been killed by the men she had been working for. Sonya Parker had committed crimes, and somehow flown under the radar for a good while, at least until both Scott and Claudia Sanborn had finally started to talk, after all the chances they had to do so the first time they'd been put behind bars.

Charlie felt bad for the woman. Maybe he'd been fooled by her, but he couldn't help but think she'd just been along for the ride with her husband. On the other hand, he knew there was something she was holding back, and once they told her Nathan Parker was dead, getting her to talk in complete sentences was just about impossible.

The evidence Stan shared appeared to be fairly clear at that point. Sonya Parker's husband, along with Scott Sanborn, had somehow devised a scheme to pull one over on Caprio. They wanted in on the gun trafficking and the money that came with it. Apparently, they'd hijacked a truckful of weapons meant for Caprio and Whitlock.

From what Stan told the others, Vincent Avella, the man left for dead at Moss Lake, in Shelby, had played a role helping Parker and Sanborn pull it off.

It appeared Caprio wanted revenge and may have gotten it. But, more than that, he wanted what was his.

Charlie leaned against Kim's Tahoe and watched Sonya Parker being led out of the house in tears, hands cuffed behind her back. She was still pleading with Agent Cooper.

Charlie turned to Frank. "Any word on the owner of the house?"

"Apparently the owner has been living in Spain," Frank said. "Rents this one out. Stan said they were able to contact him, and he'd never even heard of the Parkers. Their descriptions matched the way he described his tenants, so apparently he never got their real names, or went through any kind of trouble to confirm they were who they said they were."

"Some people are too quick to trust," Charlie said, turning again to watch Stan ease Mrs. Parker into the back seat of his car. He turned to Frank. "I think she knows more than she's letting on."

Kim looked at the house. "I'm going to go see if they've come up with anything yet." She walked onto the porch and in through the open front door.

Frank let out a sigh, shaking his head. "Maybe once Stan gets her in he can get her to talk."

"We don't have time for that," Charlie said. "Caprio and Whitlock are out there. And they're not going to wait around for us to find them."

"You don't think I know that?" Frank said.

Deputy Holden stepped over to Frank and Charlie, but this time kept quiet.

Charlie glanced at Sonya Parker inside Stan's vehicle, tears coming down her face. "How about I go give it one more shot, see if I can get Mrs. Parker to talk?"

Stan was outside the vehicle now, on the driver's side, talking to another agent.

Frank said, "I'm not sure that's a good idea. You'd better talk to Stan, make sure he—"

"Just give me a minute." Charlie walked away from Frank and in the direction of the vehicle, then over to Stan. "Hey, you mind I get in there with Mrs. Parker, see if I can get something more out of her?"

Stan looked at Charlie like he didn't know what to say. "You want to get in the back seat with her? For what?"

"I feel like we were close, until she found out her husband was dead. If I can just talk to her for a few more minutes?"

Stan said, "We'd prefer to take her in at this point, Charlie. I'll let you know what we get out of her. How's that sound?"

Charlie took a step closer to Stan, keeping his voice almost in a whisper so no one else could hear. "Listen. I'm not trying to step on your toes, Stan. But I think I can get her to talk. Like I was just telling Frank, these two men are out there looking for something. Or it's likely there's someone else out there who knows where these weapons are, and whatever money there may be. I'm just saying, we wait any longer..."

Stan started to walk away. "You had your chance."

Charlie grabbed him by the arm. "Why are you acting like this with me lately? You don't trust I'm trying to do the right thing here?"

Stan yanked his arm away and straightened out his tie. He said, "You've got five minutes. And I want to know every word she says."

Charlie gave Stan a quick nod, then opened the back passenger door behind the driver's side, sliding into the seat next to Ms. Parker. He gave her a somber, straight-lipped grin. "You doing all right? I'm sorry about your husband. I know how hard these things can be."

What he really wanted to say was when you break the law, and you screw around with dangerous people, the chances somebody ends up dead are usually pretty good.

But telling her the truth wasn't something he would do to a woman who'd just lost her husband, no matter what the circumstances.

"Listen," he said, pausing a moment before he pulled the door closed. He flipped the latch on the inside panel on the edge of the door, so he wouldn't get himself locked in.

"What are you doing here?" she said through her tears.

"Well, I wanted to see if you were doing all right. I know this is a difficult situation, in more ways than one."

"I had nothing to do with any of this," she said. "I swear, I—"

"I understand," Charlie said. "That's why I want to help you."

"Help me?" she said. "What if I don't want your help?"

Charlie wasn't sure how to answer without getting her upset.

She said, "You told me you weren't here for me. You lied. My husband's dead, and I'm going to jail, all because—"

"I had nothing to do with your arrest," he said. "It's just not what we do. I mean, we do arrest criminals, of course. But we didn't show up here to investigate whether or not you were involved in whatever crimes have occurred. I assure you, your arrest was out of my hands."

She stared straight ahead.

Charlie said, "Now, I'm not going to lie to you, say I wouldn't have taken you into custody had I been asked to—with a warrant, of course. But, again, I told you the truth, and why I was here." He waited for her to respond, but she still hadn't. "Now, the fact is your husband was involved in some pretty heavy stuff. Whether you played a role or not isn't up to me to decide. And, here's the thing... You may've only seen it as a way to make some money. But, let me just make it clear that guns end up in the hands of some bad people." He thought for a moment. "Or, on the other hand, on the streets, in the hands of kids who don't know anything other than shooting each other. Or firing into someone's homes. Shit, some grandmother on the floor with her grandkids under her, doing all she can to protect—"

"I get it," Sonya Parker said, turning her gaze to Charlie. "You don't have to be so dramatic. But, I already told you I had nothing to do with any of it."

"And I told you myself what you did or didn't do isn't for me to decide. But, again, I believe I can make things easier on you. I mean, the thing here is you're looking at a good ten, twenty years behind bars, if—"

"Twenty years?" she said.

"I'm just saying, you get the wrong judge, well, now, I was taught not to ask a woman her age. But I'm going to guess ten to twenty would have you back out in your, uh, later years?"

Charlie, of course, knew exactly how old Sonya Parker was. And he barely knew the specific details of the charges she was facing. But he felt pretty good he'd gotten her attention.

"I didn't have a choice," She cried. Swallowing hard, then turning her gaze ahead toward the front of the car, looking out where Stan Cooper was talking with three local officers, up a ways in front of the car now, closer to the house.

Charlie said, "As I was starting to say a moment ago. I don't know how much you know about the United States Marshals Service, and what we do, but part of our duty is ensuring the personal safety of federal judges. Did you know that?"

Sonya Parker shook her head, watching him. Waiting.

"I've been personally responsible for the security of dozens of federal judges all over the southeast. I've provided security for federal judges in courtrooms, but also in their homes and outside the courtroom. I've escorted judges when they've had to travel, so"—he cleared his throat—I guess what I'm saying is I've done a lot of good for a lot of judges, and what ends up happening is sometimes, between you and me, I get little favors here and there. All I'm saying is, there's a chance I can pull some strings, see to it the judge who happens to be assigned to your case could maybe be a little lenient with you." He looked her in the eye. "You know what I'm trying to say?"

"Can you really do that?" she said.

Charlie wanted to choose his words wisely, not cross the line with any false promises. "I just need you to be straight with me. And, remember what I said earlier: I'm not here to take you down. Whether you spend time behind bars or not isn't my concern right now. But if I don't stop Denny Caprio and Jack Whitlock from getting to whatever, or whoever, they're looking to get at..." Charlie put his hand on her knee. "I don't want either of us to feel responsible for any of it. You know what I mean?"

She swallowed hard again, eyes dry now but still somewhat red. "What do I need to do?"

The car was starting to get a bit musty and warm inside now, her perfume seemingly stronger than he'd first noticed. But Charlie didn't want to open the door and lose the trust he felt he was trying to build with Mrs. Parker. "I need you to tell me who else was involved with your husband, and where he might've gone with them, before he was killed."

She turned from Charlie, like she was thinking it through.

Charlie said, "Are you trying to protect them? Caprio and Whitlock? It turned out Mrs. Sanborn was fooling around with Denny Caprio, so I can't imagine you were—"

"Claudia? She was fooling around with Denny Caprio? Are you sure?"

Charlie just held his gaze, waiting. Claudia Sanborn hadn't admitted to any kind of romantic relationship with him.

Sonya Parker sat still, like she was thinking for a bit. "Nathan wouldn't have told them what they wanted. That's why he's dead. He had to protect her."

"Her?"

"Amy Barrett."

"Is that who Caprio and Whitlock are looking for?" Charlie said.

Sonya said, "I doubt they know who she is. Nathan didn't even tell me about her. But I overheard one of his calls, and saw her number on his phone."

Charlie wondered if there was a chance Sonya had made some inaccurate assumptions. Perhaps the husband was simply messing around.

She said, "Amy Barrett helped them hide the van."

"What van?"

"The one that's loaded with guns."

"He told you this? That she has the van?"

"Unless he was lying to me." Sonya turned from Charlie and looked out the window. "It wouldn't be the first time."

Charlie said, "Do you know where she lives?"

Sonya Parker took a moment to answer. "At the foothills of the Smokies. She's got a house on Douglas Lake. That's in Dandridge."

"Does she live there alone?" Charlie said.

"Her husband's dead."

Charlie looked out the window and saw both Frank and Stan walking over to the vehicle he was in with Sonya Parker. He said to her, "Your husband could have told them about her?"

"I don't think he would. He's not like that." She looked at Charlie, then took a deep breath, slowly exhaling.

"Do you know Amy Barrett's address?" he said. "And, maybe even a phone number?"

The door opened from the outside and Frank stood there, looking in at Charlie, Stan standing right behind him. "All right, come on, Charlie. Stan's gotta get her out of here."

Charlie looked up at Frank, reached for the door's handle and said, "One more minute. All right?" He pulled the door closed before Frank could answer, then turned back to Sonya Parker. "You give me that address, and Amy Barrett's phone number, I'll make sure I do what I said I would: make sure the judge knows how helpful you've been."

She looked at Charlie, shaking her head. "I don't know the exact road. I think I told you, it's in Dandridge, in Jefferson County. It's a big house. That's all I know."

Chapter 35

With Kim behind the wheel, driving south on Route 81 from Erwin, Charlie turned in the passenger seat to look out the rear window at Frank's truck, a handful of car lengths behind them.

Kim said, "I appreciate you forcing your way to drive with me. I'm not sure how much longer I can handle having Ethan tagging along."

"That bad, huh?"

"I'm surprised you're even asking," she said.

"I don't know," he said. "He can be a real pain in the ass, but sometimes I wonder if maybe we've stunted his growth somewhat, the way none of us really give the kid much of a chance."

"Well, he's with Frank now," she said. "It's not up to us to decide if he's ready to do more or not. All I know is he asked a lot of questions, and I got the feeling half of them were to see if he could stump me. Or he'd ask a question and answer himself, before I'd have the chance."

"Yeah, he does that," Charlie said, smiling. "Can certainly be annoying." He eyed the side-view mirror. "I just hope Frank doesn't shoot him. I don't think he has the patience he used to."

Charlie looked at his phone when it vibrated.

It was a text from Jennie:

Haven't heard from you. Just making sure you're doing okay?

Charlie had meant to call, tell her he was fine and back to work like nothing had ever happened. But the truth was, up until the past twelve hours or so, he would've been lying if he'd told her he was good:

Back to work.

He didn't give her any other details, but after a couple of moments felt like he was being somewhat short with her.

He sent another text:

Thanks for checking. All's good. Meant to call you. Duty calls.

There was a long pause in her response. But then she finally replied:

Duty calls? LOL.

Charlie, in fact, wasn't sure why he even wrote that in a text. It wasn't something he'd ever said before. But it was just his way of telling her he was working. And a lot had happened since she'd dropped him off at the office.

I'll call you tomorrow. No need to worry anymore.

He sent the text, not even sure why he'd used the word *anymore* even though he meant it. He didn't love to text, especially when it always seemed to take time thinking of how to say something, instead of just picking up the phone and letting the words go without having to think about it.

The thing was, Jennie was always worried about him. But lately it felt worse than it was when they were married.

The big reason for the divorce, or at least what Jennie had claimed, was she couldn't handle the stress of always being scared that one night Charlie wasn't going to make it home alive. She could never relax, and rarely slept when he wasn't there. It got so bad she had to take medication for panic attacks, to help her sleep, something Charlie didn't agree with but knew the drugs were the only thing to keep her from losing her mind.

Until they both realized having him out of her life was the best thing she could do.

Jennie didn't respond back to his final text, and Charlie looked up from his phone to see Kim as if she'd been watching him, even though she was watching the road.

"Everything all right?" she said, the headlights cutting through the darkness.

Charlie wasn't sure what she was asking, other than she knew him well enough to realize when something *wasn't* all right.

His phone's screen lit up.

Jennie had replied back:

Be careful.

She included a heart emoji, which left Charlie wondering what was going on with her.

Kim said, "You know, I almost called Jennie last night, before you had me take you over to Lindsey's. I wasn't sure whose turn it was to watch you, between the two of them." She smiled and huffed out a small laugh.

"What's that supposed to mean?" he said.

Kim paused, like she wasn't sure she should speak up. "Clearly, you've got yourself caught between two women. I like Jennie. And I like Lindsey. But, I can't imagine what good it is for you and Jennie to hang around each other the way you do. Maybe I'm wrong. Maybe it's okay to have a relationship with your ex. But my thinking is you've got to make up your mind, maybe move forward?"

Charlie sat there without responding right away, thinking about it. "There's nothing between me and Jennie."

Kim laughed. "Well, like I just said, I almost called her when you refused to go to the ER."

"Maybe that would've been all right," he said. "But I just figured with Coyote Grille only ten minutes away, it made the most sense."

Kim had both hands on the wheel. "So you only chose to stay with Lindsey because she was closer?"

"That's not what I'm saying, but—"

"It may be none of my business. And, of course, I'm no relationship expert, by any means," Kim said. "But I'm starting to think it's time you rip the bandage off. You and Jennie have been divorced for…" She glanced at him. "How long's it been?"

"Almost a year," Charlie said.

"Well, I feel like you see her more now than you did when you were married."

"I'm not sure that's true," Charlie said. "But I get your point."

"Unless," Kim said, "you have it in the back of your mind it's not actually over between you and her?"

"Me and Jennie?" Charlie nodded. "Of course it's over. We both know that."

"Do you?"

"Without a doubt. But, I don't know. I guess…" He sat, thinking about it. "You could say it's kind of like the game's ended, but neither one of us knows how to leave the field."

"So you're saying this is all a game to you?" Kim said.

"What? No, not at all. I'm just saying maybe we weren't ready to see it end when it did, even though it was over long ago, even before it was final."

Kim's phone, clipped to the dashboard, lit up.

"It's Frank," she said, reaching out for it. She tapped the button without picking it up, leaving it connected to the car's audio. "Chief?"

Frank's voice came through the car speakers, "I just got off the phone with Sheriff Joe Arnold, with Jefferson County. He said there's somebody home at Amy Barrett's house on Douglas Lake. I told him to wait until we get there to do anything else, but to let us know if anyone comes or goes."

Charlie said, "Did he say if she's alone, at present?"

"No, he doesn't know. I asked him about vehicles, and he said there's a large barn on the property, but no cars or other vehicles in sight."

"Where are they? On the property?" Charlie said.

"Sheriff Arnold? He and his deputies are on Lake Front Drive. Like I just said, he's holding still, until we get there. Sounds like the property's dark, other than a couple of lights on inside the house."

Charlie said, "And we still have no idea if Caprio or Whitlock know this place exists."

"You mean, you're wondering if Nathan Parker wasn't as tight-lipped as his wife said he was?"

"I think there are quite a few things Sonya Parker had wrong about her husband," Charlie said. "But either way, the sooner we get there, the better." He leaned over and glanced at the dashboard, saw Kim was driving 85 miles an hour. "Can't you go any faster?"

"Ignore him," Frank said. "We're doing just fine. We're twenty minutes away."

"We're making the assumption they're not there," Charlie said. "But the last thing we need is to walk in on another victim."

"We want this to end as much as you do," Frank said. The line went quiet for a couple of moments until he continued, "I wonder if perhaps I should call Sheriff Arnold back, tell him to proceed to the house. I think you're right, Charlie. We need to know Mrs. Barrett's okay."

"No!" Charlie said. "He has no idea what he'd be walking into if they're there. But do you both have to drive like a couple of old ladies?"

Chapter 36

Kim drove the Tahoe straight up the driveway. The modest-sized ranch had a barn behind it almost twice the home's size. Charlie was almost certain Sonya Parker had said it was a big house, or maybe it was someone else. But it didn't appear to be, at least from the outside. The lake was in the distance beyond the trees, but it was hard to get a good look with the darkness taking over.

Charlie looked at one of the windows and was almost certain he saw curtains move. Somebody must've been watching. "Maybe we should have been a little more subtle," he said, pushing open the passenger door, but only being half-serious. He knew he was better off there were no surprises.

Frank pulled in after them in the truck and parked off to the side of the driveway in an area where no grass had grown. He stepped out of the truck and said to Charlie and Kim, "Ethan and I'll wait out here. Maybe have a look around." He shifted his gaze, looking at the big two-story barn with three doors large enough to drive vehicles through, set back from the house and partly tucked among the trees. "I think we should go see if I can get a look in there."

They all turned to look when the front door opened. A woman stood in the doorway peering out at them.

"Can I help you?" she said, her right hand held behind her back.

Charlie never liked it when he couldn't see someone's hands. He glanced at Frank and could see by his expression he appeared to have the same concern.

Frank gave a slight nod, slipping the hem of his jacket aside to show off both his badge and his holstered gun.

Charlie did the same, except also removed his badge from his belt and held it up to the woman. "We're with the United States Marshals Service. I'm Deputy Charlie Harlow." He stood close enough she had to have been able to see his badge, the way she was staring at it. "Are you Mrs. Amy Barrett?"

He had his hand on his Glock now, still holstered but the snap undone. There was never a need to take a chance. "We're here about a friend of yours we'd like to talk to you about."

"What friend?" she said. "I don't have any friends."

Charlie cracked a slight grin, as if he thought she wasn't being serious. Maybe she was. Maybe she wasn't.

"You mind explaining what this is all about?" she said, looking from Charlie to Kim, then shifting her gaze to Frank and Deputy Ethan Holden—the two still standing near Frank's truck.

Charlie said to her, "You know a man, name's Nathan Parker?"

It took her a moment, looking Charlie over as he continued carefully walking toward her.

She finally answered, "What about him?"

"When was the last time you spoke with him?"

"Nathan?" She shrugged, appearing to chew the inside of her cheek. "You mind telling me what you want, instead of beating around the bush?"

"Nathan Parker's dead," Charlie said, fulfilling her wish and not wanting to waste another second. "The reason we're here is there's a good chance the men who killed him will eventually be showing up here, looking for something we believe you may know about."

She didn't seem to show much emotion or concern, or ask anything else about what exactly happened to Parker. Maybe she already knew.

He finally said, "You mind showing me what you have there behind your back?" He put his hand on his Glock but didn't remove it.

She seemed to hesitate, her gaze going from Charlie to the others, then finally pulled her hand out from behind her back, Charlie with his finger on the Glock's trigger.

She was holding an old-model revolver with a long barrel.

"Ma'am," Kim said, her own gun already out and by her side, walking over to Amy Barrett. She reached out, palm up. "May I take that from you?"

Kim, always polite.

The woman seemed hesitant, but didn't appear to be foolish, either, turning the gun with the grip away from her so Kim could take it. She said, "That was my daddy's. Colt Single Action. Army revolver."

Kim didn't appear impressed. "You'll get it back when we're done here."

Charlie said, "You always come to the door, armed?"

"I live alone," she said. "You never know who's going to show up at your door these days."

Frank stepped forward. "That's actually why we're here," he said. I'm Chief Deputy Carter."

"Are you the boss?" the woman said.

"The boss?" Frank said, nodding. "You could say that. But I just want to make it clear why we're here, in case there's any kind of misunderstanding. As Deputy Harlow just mentioned, Nathan Parker was killed not too far from here, and the two men responsible may be coming around—if they haven't already. It's our job to capture these men, but first thing we need to be sure of is if you have what it is they're looking for."

"I'm sorry, but I don't know anything about two men, or, whatever it is they may be looking for."

Frank looked at the barn, toward the back of the property. "Mind if I go have a look over there? Inside your barn?"

"There's nothing in there, other than some yard tools and a couple of old cars. My husband—he passed away a few months back—used to like to work on the old cars. I'm not even sure either one of 'em's running right now, to be honest with you."

Frank said, "So you don't mind if we go over there, have a look?"

"Go right ahead."

Frank waved for Ethan to follow him. "Come on, now; let's go have a look." He took a few steps, then stopped, and turned. "Is it locked?"

Amy Barrett nodded.

Charlie said, "I'm sure you don't want him to force his way in. So if you have a key..."

She didn't seem to want to move, but Charlie stepped forward and pushed the door open behind her. "Go on, get him the key. We don't want to have any trouble."

"I don't want any trouble," she said, her gaze on Charlie, her lip slightly quavering, like she was about to cry. "I'll get the key."

Charlie could hear the TV inside. He stepped in after her, just inside the doorway. The kitchen was at the back of the house.

He looked into the room to his left where the TV was, the place decorated nicely with bright colors. The room was small but looked like something from a magazine. And he couldn't see the lake, but imagined the view out back must be pretty good.

"You have a dog?" he said, seeing a bed in the corner of the room. But he hadn't seen or heard it, which would be odd for any kind of canine when someone approached a home.

She came out with a key in her hand and walked over to him. "He died, not long after my husband. I swear, the poor dog died of a broken heart. Just dropped one morning, never got up. He was up there in years, but..." She stood in front of Charlie and handed him a key. "It's been a rough year for me."

"I'm sorry," Charlie said. "And what about Nathan Parker? You didn't seem to show much emotion when we mentioned he was dead. But as far as I understood, you knew him?"

"Not enough to shed a tear."

"But, you knew him?" Charlie said.

She nodded but didn't elaborate.

Kim stepped inside the house. "You have the key?"

Charlie turned and handed it to her, and she looked at him like she was wondering what he was up to.

Kim turned and went back outside.

Charlie turned back to Amy Barrett. "So, you knew Nathan Parker? But you have no idea why we're here? I've been told you'd recently been in touch with him."

She didn't respond.

There was a narrow console table by the front door with a silver bowl on top of it. Inside the bowl were a few unopened pieces of mail and another key with a big plastic tag on it.

Charlie said, "Did Nathan Parker leave a van here? On your property?"

"No."

He gazed into her eyes and held it there, as if expecting her to break the act and come clean. The look he gave her said he wasn't buying it.

But she held steady. "I'm telling you the truth."

"Does that mean you've never heard the name Denny Caprio? Or Jack Whitlock? Because they're looking for a van full of guns, and maybe some cash too. The best thing you can do is be straight with us, so we can help you. Before they come looking for it."

Kim walked back into the house and said to Charlie, "Nothing but two old cars in disrepair and yard tools. It's empty."

"No van?" Charlie said.

Kim shook her head.

Barrett said, "Do ya'll even have a warrant, to be going through my home like this?"

"Well, so far we only looked in the barn, which you gave us permission to do so."

"Well, then I'm revoking my consent. I'd like you all to leave my property."

"We can easily get a search warrant," Charlie said. "That won't be a problem."

Amy put her hand out, palm up. "Can I have my gun back, please? I'd like to at least be allowed to protect myself."

Charlie said, "These men we're looking for are dangerous, assuming you don't already know that. The best thing you can do is leave your property. Maybe go somewhere you'll be safe for a few days."

"I don't have whatever it is you claim these men are looking for. You've made a mistake." She crossed her arms. "And I'm not leaving my house. Give me my gun back, there'll be nothing to worry about."

The front door opened again, and Charlie had his hand on his holstered Glock when he turned to see who it was.

Frank walked in to where they stood. "No van," he said. "But it's clear something's been driven in and out of that barn recently."

Charlie gazed at Amy Barrett. "You said the cars in there don't run, didn't you?" He left the kitchen and went back to the bowl near the front door, where he saw the key with the plastic tag on it. He looked at both sides and saw it had U.S. Truck Storage printed on one side, with UNIT 1071 on the other. He shuffled around the other items in the bowl and found a set of keys with Ford engraved on each one. He dropped them in his pocket and went back to the kitchen, holding up the key with the plastic tag. He said to Amy Barrett, "You mind telling us what this key goes to?"

She tried to reach for it but Charlie pulled it back from her. "I already told you I want y'all to leave my property now. Unless you have a warrant, you have no right to be in here, going through my things."

"U.S Truck Storage?" Charlie looked the tag over again and said to Amy Barrett, "It's a simple question I've asked." He tossed the key to Frank. "How about we take a little ride over to this place." He turned to Amy. "Can't be too far from here, can it?"

"Give me that key," she demanded.

"Why don't you just tell us what it's for? Unless there's something there you don't want us to see?"

"You can't just come in here, take my things," she said.

Frank looked at his watch and said, "We'll have a warrant any moment. FBI should be on their way too."

Charlie knew Frank was bluffing but said what he needed to. They were running out of time.

Amy Barrett finally let out a sigh as her shoulders dropped. "My husband's trucks are kept there. His work trucks."

"That's it?" Charlie said, looking at the plastic tag again. "So, we drive over to this place, we're not going to find a van full of guns?"

She had a nervous look to her, and Charlie had little doubt she was only telling part of the story. He said, "Why don't you just come clean with us? We've already pieced most of it together. Parker might be dead, but I'm sure you know Scott and Claudia Sanborn? They're both behind bars, and have already started spilling the beans."

"I don't know them," she said.

Kim said, "You don't know Scott Sanborn? His wife, Claudia? Are you sure of that? Because, if we find out you're lying..."

Charlie wondered himself if maybe Parker had been the middle man, perhaps not letting his wife in on his secret. Maybe Amy Barrett was telling the truth, too, at least the part about not knowing Sanborn. Too much of what they had to go by was dependent on bad people being honest. He knew, at that point, whatever Sonya Parker had told him while in custody in the back of that car could've been nothing but lies.

It was only fair. He'd lied to her too.

Charlie turned to Amy Barrett. "Whether you want to believe it or not, or you want to continue lying, there's a good chance your life is in danger. I promise you, it'll be in your best interest to tell us what you know."

She went over to the window and stood facing it, her back to the others. "Nathan came to see my husband a few months before he'd died." She turned. "He had prostate cancer. Robert, my husband, did. Nathan knew his life was coming to the end, and Robert had wanted to do whatever he could to make sure I'd be taken care of when he was gone."

She stepped to a round table in the corner and sat down. "My husband owned a construction company, did road work for the state. Nathan asked him to help close down a road."

Charlie looked at Frank and Kim, then shifted his gaze to Amy Barrett. "To close down the road?"

Kim said, "To hijack the van?"

Frank and Charlie both looked at her, then turned to Amy Barrett.

Charlie said to her, "Is that true?"

Amy Barrett stayed seated at the table, watching them. "Something went wrong. I don't know what. I don't know the details. Robert ended up hiding the van in the barn." She paused, her gaze right on Charlie. "I'm telling you the truth. I wasn't involved in any of this. And Robert didn't expect to get as involved as he did. I didn't know a thing about it until the day before he died; he told me what he knew, and that I shouldn't trust Nathan Parker if he ever shows up."

"Did he show up?" Kim said.

"He called me, said he was coming for the van. I told him I didn't know anything about it, or what he was talking about. And when he came here, I'd already moved it out of here."

"So you knew about the guns?" Frank said.

Amy shook her head. "Not at all. In fact I'm not even sure Robert knew what was inside that van. At least not at first."

Charlie said, "So Nathan Parker didn't know you were lying?"

"I don't think he believed me. But there was nothing he could do."

"That means there's a chance he didn't say anything about you or your husband to Caprio or Whitlock before they killed him," Charlie said, rubbing the stubble on the side of his face. He turned to Kim. "We need to draw them out here somehow."

"What do you mean draw them out here?" Amy Barrett said, her voice filled with fear.

"Either you hope they never figure out you have anything to do with it, or we flush 'em out of the hole and get to them before they get to you." Charlie paused, thinking.

"What is it?" Frank said, apparently familiar with Charlie's look.

Charlie was quiet, still thinking. "I have an idea."

Chapter 37

C HARLIE AND K IM BOTH signed their names on the clipboard, handed over the Glocks, and continued down the vinyl-tiled hallway following the prison guard ahead of them. They passed two female prisoners, both with brooms in their hands. One, probably close to three hundred pounds with an inch or two on Charlie, looked him over.

Charlie smiled and gave her a nod, following the guard farther down the hall until they stopped at a door with a small square window on it.

The prison guard peeked through the window, then unlocked the door and opened it for Charlie and Kim. She said, "Go have yourselves a seat. I'll bring her right in."

The room was a good size, with a couch and a cafeteria-like table with built-in benches, brown laminate tops, and tubular steel holding it all together.

After a couple of minutes, the door opened with the female guard leading Claudia Sanborn into the room. Her eyes widened, mouth open, looking straight at Charlie. "Deputy Harlow? I thought you were dead?"

Charlie just stared back without a reply, then gestured toward the table. "Why don't you have a seat?"

Claudia smiled at Kim. "Nice to see you again."

Kim gave a straight-lipped grin and didn't reply.

Charlie pointed at the table. "Go ahead. Sit down."

"If you don't mind, I'd like to stand," Claudia said, turning her gaze back to Charlie. "I hope you know, I had nothing to do with what happened to you. Either time. It wasn't my fault you—"

"You and all your friends, it seems nobody had anything to do with anything," he said. "You're all full of shit. But the fact is, we're not here to discuss what's already happened." Charlie saw the back of the guard's head in the small window on the door. He turned back to Mrs. Sanborn. "What exactly was your relationship with Denny Caprio? I understand you've denied there was anything personal between you, but I'm having a hard time believing it. In fact, I have a pretty good feeling there's much more to it than you've let on."

"I don't know who told you that," she said. "But it's not true. We had a business deal. That's it."

"A deal to help find your husband?" Kim said.

Claudia paused, taking her time with a response. "My husband's a snake. A cheater. And I could give two shits about him. So it didn't take much convincing to get me to help Denny."

Charlie said, "I guess you knew he was sleeping with a woman half his age?"

"Yeah, of course I knew. He's too stupid to get away with something like that."

"Do you know she's dead because of him?" Charlie said. "And, it appears, now your boys Denny Caprio and Jack Whitlock are responsible."

Claudia made her way to the table and sat down like she was about to lose her balance. "They killed Kristen?" She stared straight ahead, as if trying to make sense of it, then started shaking her head. "I didn't know they were going to *kill* her." She looked up at Charlie and Kim. "Are you sure?"

"The only thing I'm not sure of is why you're so surprised," Charlie said. "What did you think they were going to do?"

Claudia was quiet for a couple of moments. "She was actually a nice kid. I knew her from the restaurant. Her boyfriend worked there too. So when I found out about Scott and her, I was upset, of course, but..."

"The boyfriend is the one who found her," Charlie said. "And shot your husband."

"Scott?" she said. "He shot Scott?"

"Not dead," Charlie said. "In case you're hopeful."

She looked him in the eye but didn't respond at first. "Is Scott in custody?"

"In state prison," Kim said.

"Wow. What a dummy. I thought he'd be long gone by now."

Kim sat opposite Claudia at the table. "You know why Denny and Mr. Whitlock want your husband, don't you?"

Claudia waited a moment, then nodded.

"You know your husband allegedly stole a van full of automatic weapons that were meant for Caprio and Whitlock?"

"I had nothing to do with it," Claudia said.

"But you had knowledge of what had gone down?" Charlie said. "And, at what point did you decide to turn on your own husband? Was it an affair? Or—"

"Our marriage wasn't worth shit," she said. "Scott and I were more business partners than anything. I mean, of course I was bothered by him screwing around behind my back like that. But Denny Caprio was good to us. He let us make our money. Left us alone. I'm not even sure how Scott got involved in everything else, or what made him think he could rip Denny off the way he did and get away with it. But Denny told me he'd take care of me, do what he could to keep me out of prison if I helped him."

"How'd that work out?" Charlie said, a crooked smile on his face.

Claudia looked at Kim, then Charlie. "So what is it you want from me?"

"We need your help finding him."

"Denny?"

"Yes."

She said, "What makes you think I'd help you do that?"

Charlie put his foot up on the bench a few feet from where Claudia sat, resting his arm on his thigh. "We've already spoken to prosecutors, and will petition the court for a reduced sentence, on account of you helping us. Now, if you decide not to help, well, that'll be right there for the board to see when you're finally up for parole in eight years."

"You can't do that," Claudia said.

"Do what?" Charlie said.

"Threaten me."

"That's not a threat," he said. "I'm just telling you the way things are gonna work. Your help can be rewarded. But if you decide you don't want to..."

Kim leaned on the table. "You're not a killer, Mrs. Sanborn. We know that. But Denny Caprio is. Jack Whitlock is. There are at least four victims so far, including that young woman. And likely, there's more to come until they find what they're looking for."

"Denny's not a killer," Claudia said. "He's not like that."

Charlie almost laughed. "I don't know what would lead you to believe he's not a cold-blooded murderer."

"It's Jack Whitlock," she said. "He's the crazy one. He's the one who... Denny wouldn't. I swear, Denny's not a killer."

"Well," Charlie said. "The truth is, it's not the job of the U.S. Marshals Service to determine guilt. We've got a job to do, and that's capture two men on the run. The goal is to stop them before there's another victim. If you think it's all right they keep killing people just so they can find some guns that'll, of course, be used by others to kill more people, then"—he cleared his throat and straightened up off the table—"it could get very complicated for you by the time your case makes it to court. I know you like to say you're not involved, but I'm just laying out the facts. Those eight-to-ten years you're already looking at could certainly stretch to another ten. You'd be old and gray by the time you get out. And if, by chance, there's another reason you're protecting Caprio, perhaps there is some kind of deeper personal relationship between the two, well..." He stood at the window and looked out at the parking lot. "Caprio likely won't be there waiting for you in twenty years. It's likely he won't even be alive." He turned to look at Claudia. "He'd be, what, eighty-something by the time you get out?" He grinned, as if he enjoyed the way he'd put it out there for her.

Kim said, "Even if you were to ignore the crimes Caprio's already committed, the fact is he killed an innocent girl whose only mistake was fooling around with your loser husband."

Claudia sat there at the table in silence, then quickly stood and rushed for the door, pounding on it with her open hand. "Guard! Get me out of here! I want to go back to my cell!"

The guard had opened the door, and Charlie held out his hand, index finger up. "Just give us two more minutes."

But the guard just stood there, like she was unsure of what to do, her hand on her holstered gun.

Charlie said to Claudia, "You're still fairly young. You get out of here in, who knows, maybe five, seven years if you help us out. You get a fresh start. Who knows, this all works out, maybe the judge would agree to cut even more off your sentence. I can't promise you that, but..."

"Less than five?" Claudia said, looking from Charlie to Kim.

The guard's gaze went from Charlie to Claudia Sanborn. "Is everything okay in here?"

Claudia looked at her, as if she wasn't sure how to answer. "Yes, we're fine. Thank you."

The guard looked at her with a touch of suspicion on her face, then walked out, and closed the door behind her. She stood outside in the hall with her back to the window on the door.

Claudia said to Charlie, "You really think you can get me out of here in less than five years?"

"I won't promise you," he said. "But I'll do everything I can, you help us out."

Claudia was still, like she was thinking it all through, then closed her eyes. She looked like she was going to cry. "All right," she said. "What do you need me to do?"

Chapter 38

It was dark outside, almost pitch black Charlie, Frank, and Kim were at the storage facility where Amy Barrett's husband allegedly stored his construction vehicles, along with the van loaded with ten crates, each filled with thirty automatic weapons. Of course there was always a chance they'd gotten it wrong or been fed bad information.

The risks were high.

They wore tactical gear, Kevlar vests, and night-vision goggles. The three spread out around the property, staying out of sight and separated from each other; the only thing between them and the building was a chain-link fence.

They waited.

It was Claudia Sanborn who had made the call to Denny Caprio, telling him she knew where the van had been hidden. He asked if she was crazy, calling him from the inmate phone, then abruptly hung up on her without another word.

But even with the seed planted, they had no proof anyone would show up. Of course, there was also a chance Caprio and Whitlock would send someone else in their place to retrieve what they felt was theirs. But Charlie didn't want someone else. He wanted Caprio and Whitlock, and he wouldn't rest until he had both men in custody. He thought about what Agent Stan Cooper had told him, how they needed Caprio and Whitlock alive to get the bigger fish.

But Charlie and the others had a job to do.

Headlights glowed on the street in the distance, and Charlie signaled, speaking in a hushed voice into his two-way radio, "Possible target approaching." He looked at the flat roof on the building and wished one of them had gone up there, but there was no access to it.

The fact was, they could've used more manpower. But having the sheriff's office or the local police at the site was too much of a risk. The last thing they wanted was to spook Caprio or Whitlock.

When they had Claudia Sanborn call Caprio on a cell phone few people had access to, they knew there was a chance Caprio would be suspicious. One of the concerns Charlie had was knowing there was a chance Caprio could somehow make a connection to Amy Barrett. He didn't know what Caprio knew, but there was that risk.

For that reason, Deputy Holden stayed at the Barretts' house by the lake, just to keep an eye on her. And the last thing Frank had said to Ethan was to not screw it up, and left it at that.

Charlie hoped Ethan could at least handle what seemed to be a simple job.

The vehicle with the headlights Charlie had spotted on the street continued past the facility until it slowed down. He could see it through the trees, the red taillights glowing around the back of the vehicle until it finally took off and disappeared.

Charlie lifted his goggles from his face and spoke into his two-way. "Standby." He paused, making sure he had it right that the car was gone. "Negative. False alarm."

· · · ● · ● · ● · · ·

At least a couple of hours had gone by when Charlie thought they might need to regroup. It was no surprise Caprio or anyone else had still not shown up, and the three had already prepared for a long night that could easily lead into morning. He had his goggles resting on his head and walked along the fence through the darkness until he got to the area of the woods, in the far corner of the property, to where Frank was seated on a downed tree, sipping from a metal cup, his rifle leaning next to him.

Frank looked up, shaking his head. "I don't know, Charlie. I'm starting to think these fools aren't as foolish as we'd hoped. They would've been here by now."

Charlie said, "They've been after this van for how long now? You think they'd just let it go? Or change their minds?"

"That's not what I'm saying," Frank said. "But you have to admit, something's not right." He reached for the two-way's mic clipped to his vest. "Deputy Riggins. It's a no-go. We're moving out."

"What the hell do you mean we're moving out?" Charlie said. "Are you serious?"

"I didn't like this from the start," Frank said. "We're undermanned as it is. I feel like we're sitting ducks out here." He looked around the wooded area, then at the building. "I'm sorry. But I'm calling it off. We'll get the van removed in the morning." He looked at his watch, pressing the button on the side of it, dim light from it glowing against his face. "It's two a.m."

"Chief," Charlie pleaded. "I understand where you're coming from. But what's a few more hours? We don't even know if they were in the area when Mrs. Sanborn called them."

Frank's phone vibrated, and Charlie took a step so he could get a look at the screen. Deputy Ethan Holden's name popped up. "What's he calling for?" Charlie said. "Probably wants to go home too."

Frank answered the phone. "Everything all right, Deputy?"

Charlie watched the expression on Frank's face drop and his gaze shift to Charlie.

"Don't hurt him. He's just a kid."

Kim showed up and stood behind Charlie. "Who's he talking to?"

Charlie held up a finger, watching Frank with his mouth hung open like he had something to say, but whoever was on the other end wasn't done talking.

Frank nodded into the phone, running his hand down his face and shaking his head. "You son of a bitch," he said. "Anything happens to either of them..." He pulled his phone from his ear and glanced at the screen, then put it back so he could listen. "Hello?" He lowered the phone. "They have Ethan and Amy Barrett."

"Who does?" Charlie said. "Caprio?"

"Caprio. Whitlock. They're both there." He gazed at Charlie. "They want you to drive the van over to them, deliver it wherever they tell you. If you don't, they're going to kill them both."

The three stood in silence, a look of shock on each of their faces.

Charlie held his hand out to Frank. "Give me the keys."

"Now wait a minute," Frank said. "We need to think this through before you go driving off with that thing."

"Who called?" Kim said. "Which one?"

"Caprio. He's said he doesn't want anyone else to die, but he said his partner—I assume he meant Whitlock—is licking his lips, would love to kill a U.S. marshal."

Charlie's phone buzzed and Frank said, "That's him. He wants to talk to you."

Charlie looked at what said *private number* on the screen, then answered. He tapped the button to put the call on speaker. "Deputy Harlow."

"Take me off speaker," the man on the other end said.

Charlie did as the man said and raised the phone to his ear. "All right. I understand you want me to be your delivery driver?"

"You people think we're fools?" he said.

Charlie thought about it. "Who is this? Caprio? I like to know which fool I'm talking to."

"What's with the language?" the voice said. "Is that really necessary?"

"Is it necessary you keep killing everyone who steps in your way? Just to get your hands on some guns?"

"What's mine is mine," Caprio said. "It's been going on for way too long now. I'm happy to say we're almost at the finish line."

"Is that what you think?" Charlie said. He laughed into the phone. "This race has only just begun. You think you're going to ride off into the sunset, then—"

"There's a lot of money in that van," Caprio said. "So all I'm asking is you drive that van where I tell you to. You do exactly as I say, you don't have to worry about your deputy friend here. Or the beautiful Mrs. Barrett. I'd hate to see anything happen to that pretty face of hers."

Charlie said, "You're going to pay for what you did to that poor girl."

"Jack's a little crazy like that. He doesn't trust anyone to keep their mouths shut. So he might go to extremes to ensure they do, but..."

"You say it like you had nothing to do with it," Charlie said. He had his back to Frank and Kim now.

"I didn't kill anyone. Killing's not my thing," Caprio said. "Jack? Well, he's a different story."

"You're certainly far from innocent in any of it," Charlie said. "And I'm going to personally see to it you pay the price."

Caprio laughed into the phone. "I guess it's true what they say... You are a bit of a hothead."

"Charlie," Frank said. He didn't seem to like the way Charlie was pushing Caprio.

Charlie gave a nod and said to Caprio, "So what do you want me to do? Drive it to the Barretts' home?"

Caprio said, "What I'm going to do is give you the first location, then I'll call you again and tell you where to go from there."

"Do we really have to play these games?" Charlie said.

"I was under the assumption you like to play games," Caprio said.

"I don't know what gave you that impression. But I prefer to shoot straight. And I mean that literally."

"Is that a threat?" Caprio said.

Charlie paused. "More of a fact."

"Are you forgetting there are two people here whose lives are in your hands? All I have to do is give Jack the word."

The line went quiet, Charlie listening for what was to come next.

Caprio said, "I want you to drive the van to a school. Douglas Elementary. Someone will be there, watching you. Once I know there are no other vehicles in the area, and I know for certain you've come alone, then I'll let you know where to go next. But mark my word, I see anyone else—any vehicle at all—and one of these two are going to have to die."

"You don't sound like someone who claims to not be a killer," Charlie said.

"Well, I'm not the one who pulls the trigger."

Charlie again reached out his hand, waiting to get the keys from Frank, who finally reached into his pocket and handed them over.

Charlie said to Caprio, "I'm leaving now."

"Remember what I said," Caprio said. "We see a single vehicle, and—"

"How am I supposed to prevent someone from driving in the area? What if a cop sees me pulling in, wants to know what I'm doing this time of night, driving around an elementary school?"

"Let's just hope that's not the case."

Charlie could tell by the sound that Caprio had hung up. He looked at the screen and confirmed the call had ended.

Frank said, "I can't let you go out there alone."

"I don't think it's your choice," Charlie said.

Chapter 39

CHARLIE HAD THE WINDOW open on the van, letting the cold air from outside the vehicle come in. There was a foul odor inside, like old wood and mold or mildew. He didn't know the last time the van had been driven, or how long the crates in the cargo area had been back there.

The fact was, there wasn't a clear understanding of how the alleged hijacking went down in the first place. All they knew was there were a number of people involved, from Nathan Parker and Scott Sanborn to Amy Barrett's husband, together, pulling one over on Caprio and Jack Whitlock, a man who, some found out the hard way, was Caprio's partner.

According to Agent Stan Cooper, Sanborn claimed to have never heard the name Jack Whitlock. The plan seemed easy at first, to rip off the old man, Denny Caprio. Maybe if they'd known he had a psychotic partner they would've thought twice about stealing the van.

But the details didn't really matter to Charlie. Not at that point. It was up to him to somehow get Caprio and Whitlock, even though it seemed Charlie was walking—or driving—right into a trap he may not live through to regret.

He'd thought through Stan's request on the drive, and no matter how many ways he'd looked at it, his last priority would be to bring either one of the two in alive. But, more importantly, he had to do what he could to see to it that both Deputy Holden and Amy Barrett would be safe. He would do what he could to prevent Whitlock from adding two more to his growing list of victims.

Charlie slowed the van when he saw the sign for the elementary school, a one-story brick building with a circular driveway in front, and a wide driveway going to the side with BUS EN-TRANCE on a sign where it began.

He looked around, assuming Caprio was telling the truth when he said somebody would be there watching him. There was, of course, a chance Caprio was lying. But why bother?

Ideally, Charlie wouldn't have been alone. But there was no way having Kim or even Frank hide in the van would've made any sense. It wouldn't have worked. The only option Charlie had was to somehow talk his way out of getting shot, then do something—anything—to take one of the two down.

It wasn't much of a plan. In fact, it wasn't a plan at all.

In Charlie's eyes, that's the way he often preferred it.

The only other major concern was that being stopped in front of the entrance to the school, stopped with the van running in the circular driveway, Charlie was at risk of being ambushed. He thought about if he were in Caprio's or Whitlock's shoes, he'd see no reason to let him live. He was just being honest with himself, preparing for numerous scenarios and what could potentially happen.

He breathed in the cool air outside, his head leaning out the open window, looking left and right in the darkness surrounding the school, the lone light outside coming from a streetlamp over the sidewalk a few feet from where he was parked.

Charlie checked his phone, expecting a call.

Nothing.

He started to think about how it'd all started, a simple case to pick up a female criminal. A white-collar criminal, at that. Which, of course, turned out to be a small part of the story. He thought about the way he took the turn off the highway, and how they were there waiting for him, as if they already knew his moves. Or maybe they took a good guess, knowing the highway was backed up for miles, and that would be their best chance to grab Claudia Sanborn.

He wondered about the crooked agent. Perhaps he was somehow tied into USMS Communications. There'd even been a recent hack at the federal level, where cases the Marshals Service were working on had been exposed.

Nothing really seemed to add up. It never had. Even the fact he'd survived not only being shot at the first time, but being shot and almost killed. They got him good the second time, but he still survived. He had no plans to die at what he still considered a young age, even if the job meant he'd always have one foot at the edge of the grave...

The phone lit up the inside of the van, when it vibrated. He grabbed it and took a look at the text message that'd come through:

5781 Royal Mark Lane. Park the van in the driveway. Keep your hands where we can see them.

Charlie tapped the address and opened the map on his phone. He was ten minutes away. He put the address in Google to see what he was heading for. And it just so happened the house he was driving to was listed for sale by a local real estate company.

He wasn't sure it made much sense. Why would Caprio want him to drive a van full of guns to a home presently listed for sale?

Charlie took his foot off the brake and drove around the circular drive and back out onto the street, glancing at the direction on the phone, telling him to go left.

He made sure nobody was following him and dialed the phone, calling Frank, who picked it up on the first ring.

"Charlie?"

"Who'd you think it'd be?" Charlie said, making light of a sticky situation.

"It's good to know you're okay," Frank said.

"So far." Charlie looked in the rearview and could see tiny headlights far back in the distance. He wasn't even sure it was headlights at first. "I'm on my way to a house that's for sale."

"I thought you were going to a school."

"I already did. Not sure what the purpose of it was, other than to make sure I was alone."

Frank said, "Why don't you give me the address?"

"I don't think that's a good idea."

"What? You can't go there alone," Frank said.

"And you can't join me. Not unless you want the blood of Holden and Amy Barrett on your hands?"

"I demand you give me the address, Charlie. We need to know where you're going."

"And I need to do what I told them I'd do, and show up alone. No sense putting anyone else's life in jeopardy."

"We're not going to do that," Frank said. "But I need to know where you're going. Consider it protocol."

"Consider it a risk. Just hang tight, all right? I'll be fine."

"I don't like this, Charlie. Not one bit."

Charlie looked at the phone, and took the next right turn.

Frank said, "If something happens to you, and I have to explain I didn't know where you were, because you didn't tell me…"

"Well, it sounds like that'd be the point I'd be dead." Charlie peered into the rearview. But it was too far in the distance to know if there was someone following or not.

Neither of the two spoke for a moment.

The headlights behind him appeared to be getting closer. "Let me call you back," he said, and hung up before Frank could say another word.

The phone buzzed with Frank's name on the screen. But Charlie chose to ignore it.

The area was foreign to Charlie. All he could do was follow the GPS and turn when it told him to. And with every turn he made, the vehicle behind him did the same.

He was on a main street now, cruising past a 7-Eleven where a car with its headlights off, turned them on as soon as Charlie drove past. He looked in the rearview and watched the vehicle—a newer SUV he thought was a Cadillac Escalade—pull out behind him in front of the other vehicle he was sure had been following.

Charlie held the steering wheel with his knees and checked the magazine in his Glock with fifteen in the clip and one in the chamber. He reached down and felt for the .38 he had holstered on his calf under his pant leg, and unclipped the strap.

But he was well aware these men wouldn't be foolish enough to let him make a move without patting him down. He wondered if he should hide either the Glock or the .38 somewhere else in the van, but now that he was being followed, he realized he'd dropped the ball and should've done it sooner.

All he'd been through up to that point, and going on a lot of hours without much sleep at all, he needed to make sure he'd keep his head on straight. Right then, he felt like he hadn't.

His phone vibrated, and the private number popped up again. He answered, "That you behind me?"

"Just making sure you're going where you said you would. I told you, we don't need any games."

"Actually," Charlie said, "I think I was the one who said we didn't need any games. But I'm trying to figure out what you'd call this, making me drive in circles just to—"

"Just keep driving," Caprio said. "And whatever you think you're going to try and pull off... Think twice about it."

"I'm doing what you told me to do," Charlie said. He wanted to ask about the house, and who it belonged to, but it wasn't the time or place for any kind of in-depth conversation. "But I also hope you're going to keep up your end of the bargain, and release the hostages."

"Hostages?" Caprio said. "I don't like the sound of that. They're not hostages. I like to think of them as chip pieces."

Charlie didn't respond. He said, "Where are they now? At the house?"

"You'll know soon enough. As soon as I get what we're expecting, this'll all be over."

Charlie could only imagine what Caprio meant. It was hard to believe he or Whitlock would just let him deliver the van and they'd all go their separate ways. "I'm not pulling into that house until I see them."

"You act like you're the one in charge," Caprio said. "But let me just assure you, you are not. I'll be the one to tell you how this is going to work. I call the shots. You got it?"

Charlie thought about it before he replied. "Anything happens to either of them—"

"Just keep driving," Caprio said, then ended the call.

Chapter 40

CHARLIE STOPPED AT THE mailbox with the house number on it, then looked down the long driveway. He couldn't even see a house, surrounded by total darkness. Tall trees hovered over him on both sides of the road and blocked a good portion of the night sky. The FOR SALE sign out on the edge of the property was barely upright, the sign itself so faded now it was hard to read the number even with the van's headlights shining. He looked in the rearview and saw the two vehicles stopped behind him with the lights still on but parked far enough back, Charlie couldn't confirm the identity of either driver.

He gripped the wheel and leaned his head out the window to get a good look around before he drove in. He expected to at least see lights coming from the home, but there was nothing. He turned off the engine and listened. But he heard nothing. The silence was deafening.

His phone lit up with a text from the same private number: *What are you waiting for?*

Charlie didn't respond, but started the engine and turned down the driveway. He knew he didn't have the upper hand. He continued ahead. Beyond the trees, his headlights shone on what looked to be an old farmhouse, but there were no other lights on anywhere.

He drove until he was close enough to the house, but also leaving room to turn the van around, if needed. With the van still running, he kept the high beams shining.

Someone yelled out, "Turn them off!" He looked in his rearview and saw the headlights turn in, heading his way. A second vehicle followed. And as they both got closer, they killed the lights.

Charlie still hadn't turned off the van's engine or the headlights.

The man yelled again, sounding as if he was somewhere nearby, "Shut off the lights! You want one of them to die?"

This time, Charlie listened. He killed the engine and turned off the headlights, staring at the house, hoping his eyes would adjust. He looked at the upstairs windows, one at a time, then the lower level, where to the left was a two-car garage with a front door in the middle and three windows to the right.

He expected someone to be in one of the windows, but there was nothing. He saw nobody anywhere.

He stepped out of the van, his Glock tucked in the back of his pants, and started toward the house. "Where are they?" he yelled, glancing over his shoulder at the cars parked in the driveway and still a ways back. When he turned his gaze back to the house, a figure stepped through the darkness from the left side.

"Don't take another step," a man yelled.

Charlie raised his hands to show he wasn't armed. Or at least wasn't holding a gun. He said, "You have the van. Now give me what's been promised." But as his eyes continued to adjust to the darkness, he realized the figure coming from around the side of the house wasn't alone. It was a man with a gun pointed at the head of Deputy Ethan Holden.

"Ethan!" Charlie yelled. "You all right?"

"Yeah, I think so," Holden said. "You want to go ahead and take a shot at him, Charlie. I'm all right with it. I trust you."

Charlie almost smiled. Kyle had never been one to act tough. He had a mouth that made Charlie want to knock him out, but tough was never part of Ethan's act.

Or maybe it was, and nobody had given him a chance to show it.

A bright light came on from the other side of the house, and when Charlie turned to look at it, the light almost blinded him. He held up the crux of his arm and squinted, trying to get a look at who it was. It didn't take long to see another man was there with Amy Barrett, a gun to her head.

He yelled to her, "Are you all right?"

She didn't answer.

A man laughed. "Sorry, we had to put a little tape over her mouth. Had a hard time shuttin' up."

Charlie said to her, "Don't worry. You're going to be okay."

He wasn't sure he believed it himself, but he said what he knew he had to.

"Let them go," he said. "That's the deal." He nodded toward the van. "It's all there. We didn't take a thing from it."

He heard a cough behind him, from somewhere in the driveway. He turned to look and saw two men walking in his direction through the darkness. He couldn't quite make out what they looked like, but could see one man's white hair almost glowing under what little light came off the moon still hidden behind the trees.

As the two men continued their approach, Charlie could get a better look and saw the second man was rail-thin and hunched over. The man coughed.

One of them said, "Is it all in there?"

"Far as I know," Charlie said. "We didn't touch any of it."

"What about the money?" the other man said, followed by a cough.

They had stopped moving now, but were still far enough away, Charlie couldn't get a good enough look at either one.

"I don't know if there's money in there or not. But I assure you we didn't touch anything."

The light from the side of the house was still on Charlie, but it didn't reach the two men. But when he glanced back at who he knew by that point was Whitlock and Caprio, he could see they both had rifles in their hands.

He still hadn't reached for his Glock.

Whitlock was the skinny of the two and coughed again into what looked to be a handkerchief, then wiped his mouth.

"If I put my gun down on the ground, maybe you two can all lower your weapons? How's that sound?" Charlie said.

"You're going to put yours down, no matter what," Whitlock said. He coughed again, in a way that didn't sound like some kind of allergy. It was more along the lines of a lung falling apart inside the man's chest.

"We had an agreement," Charlie said.

"Just put your gun down on the ground, Charlie," Caprio said.

Charlie removed the Glock from the back of his pants and held it by the trigger guard, letting it almost dangle in front of him. "Are we on a first-name basis now?"

"I knew your father, you know," Caprio said.

Charlie almost wasn't sure he heard him right. "Come again?"

"Your father and I. I knew him, back in our younger days. That's part of why you're still alive."

Whitlock laughed, then coughed. "Yeah, and because you've got a shitty shot," he said, clearly talking to Caprio.

Charlie crouched down and placed the Glock on the ground, then came up with both hands raised so they could see them. "You've got the van. Now let them go. You want to take something out on me, then go ahead. These two have nothing to do with any of this."

"I'm not so sure that's the case," Whitlock said, his voice raspy and weak.

Charlie wasn't sure what the man meant. Maybe it was that Amy Barrett was more involved than she'd let on. Somehow, they knew to go to her house. But it didn't really matter at that point. Charlie was there for a reason, and would do whatever he could to ensure the hostages would not be harmed.

Whitlock went over to the van, holding the gun with both hands and pointed at Charlie. "Keys inside?"

"Actually, no," Charlie said. "They're here in my pocket."

Whitlock held the shotgun on Charlie. "Let's have 'em."

"Maybe they're not in my pocket?" Charlie said, looking around the ground and slowly turning as his gaze covered the full area surrounding him. He moved his hand to his face and pulled at his chin. "You know? I'm always losing my damn keys. I hope I didn't drop 'em somewhere on the ground, with it being so dark and all."

Caprio said, "What do we need the keys for? He wants to play games, we'll just load up my Escalade."

"You think I'm in any kind of condition to have to load these crates? And don't you think we've made them wait long enough? We gotta get this show on the road." Whitlock racked the shotgun and took another step toward Charlie. "Give me the goddamn keys, before I kill all three of you!"

Whitlock stood close enough now Charlie could see a face so white it almost glowed. He had little doubt the man was not well. "Now, hang on a minute," Charlie said. "You release those two, let them get far enough away from here, and I'll give you the keys."

Whitlock yelled, "Take them both in the woods and kill them!"

Denny Caprio had stepped closer and stood behind the van and also had a shotgun, but held it casually with a strap hung over his shoulder, the muzzle pointed at the ground. "Hold on a minute now, Jack," Caprio said. "You gotta learn to relax a little, you know what I mean? How many times I gotta tell you?"

"It's a little late for that," Whitlock said. "Let's just kill them all, get this over with."

"No!" Caprio snapped.

Charlie and Whitlock both turned to Caprio.

"You don't want to shoot me?" Charlie said. "Because you knew my father?"

Caprio seemed to pause, like he was thinking about it. "Your father helped me out once," he said. "It was a long time ago. But I never forgot it. And, well, I just don't think it'd be right of me to kill his only boy."

"Give me a break," Whitlock said, the shotgun up in front of him and pointed at Charlie's chest.

Charlie eyed the Glock on the ground.

"Go ahead," Whitlock said. "Pick it up. I dare you." He coughed from somewhere deep in his lungs, his cheeks puffed out, his lips tight as he tried to hold it in.

Caprio said, "Don't mind my friend. He can be a little aggressive with his guns."

"Is that what you call it?" Charlie said. "Aggressive? One of you shot me. Twice. Also killed an innocent woman for no reason, on top of the numerous bodies you've left in your wake."

Caprio nodded, blowing into his one free hand, trying to warm it up. "That wasn't supposed to happen," he said.

"Which?"

Caprio seemed to ignore Charlie's question, and instead went over to the van. He first tried to open the rear doors, but they were locked.

"They're not in there," Charlie said.

"What's not?" Whitlock said. "The guns?"

Charlie kept his eyes on Caprio near the front of the van. "They're not in there. The crates are empty. Once you release the deputy and Mrs. Barrett, I'll tell you where they are."

Now, of course, Charlie was lying. But he was doing whatever he could to stall for as long as he could. What would come of it, he wasn't sure. But he thought it'd be worth a try, knowing it was only a matter of time one of the two men would get into the van, whether he handed over the key or not.

He looked at either side, outside the house, but the two men holding Deputy Holden and Amy Barrett were gone.

Caprio tried the other doors on the van, including the driver-side door, the passenger door, and the sliding door to the cargo area. The only windows, besides the windshield, were the driver and passenger doors. Once he realized they were all locked, he walked over to Charlie with his hand out. "Give me the goddamn keys, Deputy."

Charlie had little doubt he was putting himself in danger. But he just stared back at Caprio without a response. Then he shifted his gaze to Whitlock, and watched him walk to the passenger window.

With the butt of his shotgun, Whitlock smashed the window.

Caprio said, "We still need the key to drive it out of here, Jack."

Charlie kept his eye on Whitlock, knowing once they saw the crates were actually filled with the guns he was going to have to make some kind of a decision. The chances they were going to let him or the others go were slim.

He couldn't imagine Caprio's connection to his father, whatever the details were behind it, was enough to keep him alive a third time.

He swallowed hard, knowing his luck was about to run out. But then he turned to the darkness surrounding the house. He didn't see Deputy Holden or the man holding a gun to his head. The other man with the bright light was still there, along with Amy Barrett.

Charlie watched Denny Caprio move closer to the van as Whitlock crawled over the passenger seat and into the cargo area.

It was almost as if the two had forgotten about Charlie.

Then he heard Whitlock's muffled voice say to Caprio, "These crates are loaded. The son of a bitch was lying." Then the side door slid open, and Whitlock poked his head out, one of the crates already open from the top. He reached in and pulled out one of the AK-47s, holding it out for Caprio to see. "Look at this beauty."

Caprio turned to Charlie. "What's the sense in bullshitting us about them being empty?"

Charlie didn't answer him, but the two men at that point were paying him little attention. He started to wonder if either one was as much on the ball as he'd once assumed. Caprio was an old man. Whitlock, maybe a little younger, but looking like he had something going on, perhaps one foot in the grave, Charlie started thinking maybe he'd have a chance after all. With his Glock still on the ground not far from where he stood, he felt maybe this time luck was on his side.

But he worried about Deputy Holden. He also hoped to not draw attention to the fact Holden and the man with him were no longer where they'd been up until a few moments earlier, or at some point during the commotion inside the van.

With the light now on inside the cargo area of the van, Charlie watched the two men pry open the crates. Like two kids under a Christmas tree, Caprio and Whitlock tossed newspaper print into the air and removed various weapons, inspecting each with a look of excitement on their faces.

The rear doors on the van blew open, lighting up the area behind it. Caprio crawled down like the old man he was, almost having trouble getting his feet down on the ground. But once he did, he went over to Charlie. "Where's the money?"

"I told you; I don't know what was back there. Whatever it was when we found it, is no different than it is now."

The flashlight that was shining from the right side of the house had gone off without notice, and Caprio stood facing the house with his back to Charlie. "Pablo?" he yelled, looking right, then left, then mumbled to himself, "Where the hell'd they go?"

All four were gone.

Caprio started to walk past Charlie, but stopped and gave Charlie a look that held some kind of warning. But then he must've realized his foolishness, bending down to pick up the Glock from the ground. He looked it over, then pointed it at Charlie. "Don't go anywhere." He continued toward the house and around the side until he, too, disappeared into the darkness.

Whitlock stepped out of the van with one of the AK-47s in his hands, almost giddy, with a smile on his face, running his hand over it, petting it as if it were alive. But then his expression changed to a frown when he raised his gaze with a dumbfound-ed look on his face. "Denny?" He glanced at Charlie. "Where the hell'd he go?"

Charlie had to assume the gun in Whitlock's hand was loaded, even though it'd come straight out of the crate and likely was not. But Whitlock had another automatic he'd been holding earlier, and Charlie had no idea where it was. He moved his gaze around the van and spotted what he believed was the same gun, leaning near the open back doors.

The more he watched these two clowns, the more he realized neither was the formidable foe he once suspected. Maybe they had money, knew how to get people to do things, and for what-ever reason liked to play with guns. Or maybe they were both simply past their prime.

They hadn't even patted him down.

The fools.

Whitlock strolled past Charlie without a word, heading for the side of the house. "Denny? You back there?" He continued until he stopped and turned ten feet from Charlie, with the weapon raised. "Let's go," he said, gesturing with the barrel of the gun. "You can go ahead of me, see what the hell's going on back there." He covered his mouth with the back of his hand when another deep cough came up from somewhere inside him.

Charlie stared at the muzzle pointed at him, his gaze going up the barrel and down at the steel-curved magazine on that AK-47. The chance it contained thirty rounds was just as good as the fact it could be empty.

A gunshot echoed through the woods and bounced off the trees until dead silence fell on the night.

Whitlock turned toward the house and started to move, gun raised ahead of him. "Denny!" he yelled. He didn't look back at Charlie.

Charlie reached for the .38 tucked in the holster on his lower leg, had it out and pointed at Whitlock in what seemed like a split second. He raised it and yelled, "Hold it right there! Drop your weapon!"

A shot rang out. But Charlie knew it didn't come from his gun. Looking down, he examined his own upper body with his eyes and hands to make sure he wasn't hit, as if he wouldn't have known. But there was no blood. No sign he'd been shot.

Whitlock had already let go of his gun, dropping it to the ground. He then let out another deep cough as he dropped to his knees, falling forward. His face slammed into the ground.

Charlie looked past Whitlock's body at the area around the side of the house, the .38 still in his hand but by his side now. He waited, watching...

Deputy Ethan Holden walked out from the darkness with his arm at his side and a gun in his hand, his other arm around Amy Barrett, shaking and crying next to him.

Chapter 41

By the time Frank and Kim showed up, Whitlock and Caprio were both bloodied and in custody. Charlie had handcuffed Whitlock. Deputy Ethan Holden had used the rope he cut from Amy Barrett's wrists to tie Caprio to the van's bumper.

The entire area around the house was well lit, spotlights shining on the scene from police and sheriffs' vehicles. Blue lights filled the night sky, mixed with red lights from the two rescues and a fire truck. There were at least a dozen law enforcement officials from multiple departments, both local and federal.

Charlie looked past all the commotion and saw Agent Stan Cooper step from his car and rush in his direction, looking right at the two bloody men being tended to now by the paramedics.

"They're alive?" Cooper said, looking from Charlie to Frank and Kim.

"For now," Frank said.

Stan breathed a sigh of relief. He said to Charlie, "This is a first, huh?"

Charlie said, "I can't promise they won't end up in body bags once all's said and done. But I had nothing to do with it. I never fired a shot." He gave a nod in Deputy Holden's direction, over near the side of the house, well lit now with spotlights. Holden was talking to a couple of deputies from the sheriff's office. "Go thank Deputy Holden. It was all him." He grinned, as did Frank and Kim.

Stan was still, a confused look on his face. "Holden? Are you for real?"

Charlie nodded. "He saved my life. All of our lives."

Stan looked from Charlie to Frank, like he wasn't sure what to believe.

"We're all just as surprised as you are," Frank said. "Goes to show you, give a man a chance to prove his worth, he may surprise you."

Kim said, "I'd like to think we all might get a chance without having to wait until we're tied up and held at gunpoint, before having to prove anything to anyone."

The others laughed.

Deputy Ethan Holden looked over at the others, as if he could hear what they were saying. He grinned and gave a nod back.

"Let's not let the kid's head get any bigger than it already is," Frank said. "Might have to put him on court duty for a couple weeks, keep him humble."

Charlie said, "Well, whether it's a connection or not that got him a chance with the Marshals Service, he still had to've had something in him to get to a point he'd have the honor to wear the badge in the first place. I feel like I never gave him enough credit for that."

Stan slapped Charlie on the arm. "Maybe he can show you a thing or two about taking someone down without having to shoot to kill."

"Easy for you to say," Charlie said, a grin on his face. "You smart guys are the ones, always showin' up when the bullets are done flying."

Frank said, "Well, hopefully these two clowns—assuming they're both going to live—can give you the information you need, so you can finally go fishing for the bigger ones."

· · · ● · ● · ● · · · ·

Charlie drove the Cadillac Escalade into the parking lot at the St. Morrison's Animal Shelter in Asheville. His phone buzzed as soon as he turned into a parking space and turned off the engine. When he saw it was Jennie calling, he almost didn't answer. Especially since he'd just left Lindsey's and made her a promise he was going to keep.

He stared at Jennie's face on the screen of his phone and wasn't quite sure he was ready to give her the news. At least not right then.

But he went ahead and answered. "Hey. I was going to call you in a little bit. But I'm in the middle of something kind of important. Are you all right if I call you later?"

"Later?" Jennie said.

The line went quiet.

Charlie stepped out of the Escalade and headed for the shelter's entrance. He kept the phone to his ear, and the glass doors slid open. But he backed away, turned, and let a younger man and woman go past him and inside. He walked back into the parking lot, determined to say what he knew he needed to, but more hesitant than he hoped he'd be.

"Listen, Jennie. I just... I've been thinking a lot. And, well, I think I need to... I think *we* need to, uh..." He was standing at the edge of the lot, looking into a trail going through the woods. A woman with a St. Morrison's Animal Shelter T-shirt came off the path with a leashed dog—one the size of a horse—and smiled at Charlie.

"Hello," she said.

He gave her a nod, and smiled at the dog. "Morning."

It was still chilly outside, but the sun had warmed up quite a bit. More than it had at any point over the last few weeks.

Once the woman and the dog were far enough away, Charlie continued, "Jennie, I think it's time you and I stop straddling the fence with whatever we've got going on between us." He paused, listening, expecting Jennie to come back with something.

But she said nothing.

"You there?" he said.

"Will you just say whatever it is you're trying to say," she said, "Stop the damn stuttering?"

He almost laughed. Jennie was sweet as could be but always had an edge to her. Especially when something was going on she may not like.

"I like Lindsey," he said. "And the truth is, it's not fair to her I keep hanging around with my ex-wife, acting as if one day things will be different between us. I mean, different from the way it is now."

"I'm not sure what you just said makes sense," Jennie said.

Charlie said, "I just mean, for a long while now, I guess I always had it in the back of my mind one day you and I would get back together."

"Did I ever give you that impression?" Jennie said.

Charlie knew she'd come back with something like that, making it look like he was a fool for thinking that way.

"I'm sorry if I misled you," she said.

"No, no. I don't think you did. All I'm trying to say is, well, I guess maybe I just wanted you to know how I feel about Lindsey." He thought about what he was saying and already wished he'd planned it out a little better before he opened his mouth.

"So, just so I understand..." Jennie said. "Would you rather us not have any kind of relationship at all? Because, if that's what you want..."

Charlie could hear anger in her voice.

"No, that's not what I'm saying. I guess I'm just afraid we've been hanging on to a thread of some sort, thinking maybe if we let go, it's more final than either of us will want to accept."

The line went quiet, and for a second, Charlie wondered if maybe Jennie had hung up.

But she hadn't.

"You're not wrong," she said. "I've been thinking the same thing, I guess."

Again, there were a couple of moments of silence on the phone.

Charlie felt it in his heart and in his gut, right then, more than he had when he signed the divorce papers and dropped them off for Jennie, after he held out for as long as he could.

•••••••••••

The doors slid open, and Charlie walked into the lobby of the shelter, where a banner that read "Half-Price Adoptions" was hung just inside the entrance. The dog barks and cries were unsettling to Charlie, as was the scene on the other side of a large glass wall where full-sized cats lay on carpeted platforms, sleeping or looking out as if they were gazing right at him.

The appearance was more how a daycare center might look than a shelter, with blue walls and cartoonlike paintings of dogs and cats, along with framed photos. There was a large, framed painting almost centered on the wall of an older woman posing, dressed in a brown suit with a white, silklike bow at her neck.

Charlie stepped closer and read the wood-and-brass placard under the woman's painting. It read *Anne Morrison, Founder. Morrison Animal Rescue.*

There was a woman with two children at the counter, talking to the woman on the other side. Charlie could overhear the conversation, where the woman with the children asked about puppies. The shelter employee told her all the puppies were adopted at a special event they'd just had, and why adopting an older dog was a good option for her.

But the woman with the two kids didn't seem to want to listen. And one of the two kids—a little boy—cried that he wanted a puppy.

Charlie watched two cats on the other side of the glass playing with each other, or maybe fighting, and turned back when the woman with the two kids headed for the exit.

"May I help you?" the younger woman behind the counter said. She looked at Charlie's USMS hat.

He leaned with his hands on the counter. "I'm actually here about a dog. She's not a puppy, but, well... I think when I brought her here they said she looked to be about two or three..."

"You brought her here?" the woman said.

"Oh, no. She wasn't my dog. I dropped her off a couple of Tuesdays ago. She showed up where I live, out on the Swannanoa River.

The woman had a look on her face like she wasn't understanding the story.

"She wasn't mine," Charlie said. "She was, I don't know, maybe forty pounds. Real skinny. Scared. Mix of black and white. Not sure what breed of dog, but not a purebred or anything. I thought at the time her rightful owner might've been looking for her, so I brought her here."

The woman pulled at her chin, like she was thinking. But then her eyes lit up and she smiled. "Chance," she said. "That's her name. Black and white, you said? A terrier mix?"

Charlie shrugged, then nodded. "Black and white, yes. I don't know what she was. But you think you know the one I'm talking about?"

The smile left the woman's face. "Well, the thing is"—she cleared her throat"—someone came in and claimed her."

"Oh," Charlie said. He felt immediate dejection. "That's good for her, right?"

The woman paused. "Well, not exactly. We did a house check a few days later, and apparently she'd run off again." She leaned closer over the counter, as if she was about to reveal a secret. "We don't always do house checks on dogs who're claimed by their present owners. But we were all somewhat suspicious. There were signs we feel may've shown abuse. But there's only so much we could do."

"Only so much you could do?" Charlie said, feeling the pressure build in the veins in his neck. "Why would you let this person take her?"

"When a person comes in and is the legal owner..."

"And nobody knows where she's gone?"

The woman just stared back at Charlie. "The truth is, sometimes dogs like... We often have a hard time finding their forever homes."

"Dogs like *what*?"

"Well, she was somewhat aggressive, so..."

Charlie wasn't mad at the woman, and had no reason to be. But he wasn't willing to believe Chance, if that was even the dog's name, wasn't good enough to have a real home. And the more he thought about whoever it was—this alleged owner—he thought about asking the woman for this person's name, maybe go teach a lesson or two.

But instead, Charlie pulled out his US Marshal business card and placed it on the counter. He grabbed a pen from the coffee mug on the counter and wrote his cell phone number on the card. "If by chance she happens to show up, or you hear anything about her, would you do me a favor and give me a call?"

Chapter 42

It was nighttime, and Charlie sat outside the Winnebago in the Adirondack chair, a bottle of Jack Daniels and an empty glass, with his Glock next to him on the cut stump he used as a side table. He rested his feet, boots up on another stump in front of him, feeling the heat from the firepit on the bottom of his soles.

The smell from the burning wood filled the air all around him, as did the light-gray smoke. A cold front was coming through, and as much as Charlie had sometimes wished for warmer days, he didn't mind the cold. The firepit was all he needed.

The way the glow from the moon glistened off the Swannanoa River... the way the trees surrounding him stood still, he couldn't help but think everything felt right. He sipped his whiskey and felt the warm, burning sensation on his tongue, holding it there for a brief moment until he swallowed, and felt the same going down his throat and into his chest.

For the first time, in a long time, Charlie felt a sense of peace.

He straightened up when he heard the crackle of dry leaves from somewhere in the woods. Reaching for his Glock, he turned, staring into the darkness. He listened and heard another snap, as if a stick had broken. Standing up from the Adirondack, he threw back what was left in his glass and took a step closer to whatever it was he'd heard. Even with the glow from the moon, he could only see as far as maybe ten feet or so through the trees, where the darkness went from blue... to gray... to black.

It was as if he was staring at a painted canvas. It was all so still.

He wasn't scared, but there were plenty of wild animals living along the river, from black bears and mountain lions to raccoons, foxes, and coyotes.

Holding the Glock by his side, he took another step closer to the woods.

Other than the bubbling river, it was nearly silent. But he still couldn't shake the feeling he was being watched.

"Why don't you get out here and join me," he said, his words somewhat more slurred than he'd expected. Other than sipping his whiskey, he hadn't even moved his lips since the sun had gone down.

Charlie turned to look in the other direction when he heard the distant growl of an engine, watching until he saw the headlights shine through the trees, the beam of light bouncing through the air. He looked into the dark woods, placed the Glock back down on the stump, and poured himself another glass of Jack.

He knew the sound of Lindsey's truck, and almost had a childlike grin on his face as the lights from it grew, then turned to where he'd parked the Escalade and stopped.

The lights turned off, and the truck went silent. "Sorry I'm late," Lindsey said, stepping down from the truck with a paper grocery bag in her hand. "Are you hungry?"

"Not really," Charlie said.

She placed the bag down on the picnic table and went right over to him, wrapping her arms around his midsection and pulling him close. They kissed and she laughed. "Whoa, I could get drunk off your lips."

Charlie grabbed the empty glass from the stump and poured Lindsey a shot, handing it to her as he kissed her again. "I'm happy you're here," he said, then raised his glass to her.

They both took a drink.

"I can't believe you actually have a day off," Lindsey said. "And you didn't have to get shot for it."

Charlie grinned, once again filling up both their glasses from the bottle. "Two days," he said. "Should be enough to get rid of whatever I'm feeling, tomorrow, after we finish this bottle."

The fact was, now that Deputy Ethan Holden was more than just a body in the office, it made it possible for both Charlie and Kim to get more time off than they had in the past few months. Sure, with all the retirements, they were still short by three or four deputies. But working normal hours, at least for a while, was good for everyone.

Lindsey stepped away and stood close to the edge of the river. "I guess I understand why you always want to get home," she said, her back to Charlie. "It's so peaceful out here."

"That it is," he said, peeking into the grocery bag. "You want me to fire up the grill?"

"I thought you weren't hungry?"

"I'm not. But"—he reached in and pulled out a package of hamburger—"I can always eat." He turned toward the woods to his right when he heard more crackling.

"You hear that?" he said.

Lindsey walked back to where he was standing. "What is it?"

"I don't know," he said. "Maybe a raccoon. Or a fox."

But then he heard it again.

"I heard it that time," Lindsey said, grabbing on to Charlie's arm.

He grabbed his Glock and again held it by his side, narrowing his eyes to see if he could see a little better through the darkness. But even if it were daylight, he'd had enough to drink at that point, there was little chance he could get his eyes to focus.

"Where are you going with that?" she said.

"Well, I'm not going to shoot it, if that's what you're asking. But a shot in the air'd make it think twice." He took a step forward. "Flashlight's inside," he said. But then something caught his eye. "You see it?"

"No." Lindsey was right by his side. "There's a wolf out here," she said.

Charlie kept his eyes peeled. "Ain't a wolf," he said. "Maybe a coyote." He took another step, and by then could almost make out the shape of whatever it was. He could see the glow from the moon reflecting off its eyes.

His mind started to get the better of him, and he continued taking one small step at a time, slowly. "Hey," he said, his voice almost in a whisper. He was crouched over now, looking over his shoulder at Lindsey. "Well, I'll be..."

"Be careful," she said.

Charlie got down on one knee. "It's her."

"Who?"

He didn't answer, instead turning to point at the picnic table. "Get me that meat."

"Our dinner?" Lindsey said.

"Hurry."

Lindsey grabbed the meat and handed Charlie the whole package. He tore the plastic off the top and placed it down on the ground, at the edge of the woods. "Come on, girl. We're not gonna hurt you."

"How do you know it's a girl?" Lindsey said, standing right behind Charlie, still down on his one knee.

Under his breath, he said. "I don't believe it." He turned and looked up at Lindsey. "It's her. The dog I told you about. Her name's Chance."

The smile on his face was so wide it looked like it could crack from the cold. He watched the dog moving out of the woods in a slow crouch, as if trying to make herself small.

Her eyes darted around, wide and fearful.

"Come on, girl," Charlie said, pushing the package of meat closer. He broke off a piece of raw meat, then held it out in his hand. Waiting for her, his heart raced. He was worried she might turn and run.

He hoped she'd stay.

Getting as low as he could to the ground, Charlie was at eye level with the dog. The two stared at each other, Chance giving a quick glance at Lindsey, making sure it was all right, then slowly approached Charlie.

It felt like ten minutes, but Charlie waited until she was ready.

Chance looked up at Charlie as he backed away from her. "Go ahead," he said.

The dog finally made it to the tray, sniffed it, then ate like she hadn't had a thing to eat in weeks. The meat was gone, and she licked the tray, holding it still with her paw.

Her tail wagged when Charlie asked if she wanted more.

"Here," he said, crouching down with his hand out, a ball of raw burger in his hand. "I'm not going to hurt you, girl. You know that, don't you?"

Chance hesitated and turned as if she was getting ready to run. But her tail continued to wag.

Charlie threw the meat on the ground in front of her, and it was gone in three seconds. He gave her more, and when she was finished, she lay down right there, close to him but far enough away.

She lowered her chin onto her paws, eyes up on Charlie.

"I guess I was wrong when I thought I was done having to share your heart," Lindsey said, wrapping her arms around Charlie from behind.

Also by Gregory Payette
Visit GregoryPayette.com for the complete catalog:

HENRY WALSH MYSTERIES
Dead at Third
The Last Ride
The Crystal Pelican
The Night the Music Died
Dead Men Don't Smile
Dead in the Creek
Dropped Dead
Dead Luck
A Shot in the Dark
Dead or a Lie

JOE SHELDON SERIES
Play It Cool
Play It Again
Play It Down

U.S. MARSHAL CHARLIE HARLOW
Shake the Trees
Trackdown
Half Moon Rising

JAKE HORN MYSTERIES
Murder at Morrissey Motel
Body on the Beach

CRIME FICTION/STANDALONES
Biscayne Boogie
Tell Them I'm Dead
Drag the Man Down
Half Cocked
Danny Womack's .38

Join My Readers' List

I'd like to invite you to join my reader list to receive free stories, giveaways, and VIP announcements when my new books
are released.

To sign-up, visit: GregoryPayette.com